THE
HEADMASTER'S
WIFE

THE HEADMASTER'S WIFE

A NOVEL

STEPHEN BIRMINGHAM

OPEN ROAD
INTEGRATED MEDIA
NEW YORK

Copyright © 2024 by Carey G. Birmingham

ISBN: 978-1-5040-8112-2

Published in 2024 by Open Road Integrated Media, Inc.
180 Maiden Lane
New York, NY 10038
www.openroadmedia.com

For Carroll Edward Lahniers, Ph.D.
Sine quo nihil

THE
HEADMASTER'S
WIFE

"O, Crittenden"
(The Crittenden School Song, sung to the tune of
"The Church's True Foundation")

O, Crittenden triumphant, Over land and sea!
O, Crittenden triumphant, Thy loyal youth are we!*
O, Crittenden triumphant, Proud and strong and free,
O, Crittenden triumphant, Our song shall rise to thee. . . ."

---

* Prior to the Crittenden School becoming coeducational, it was an all-boys' school, and the lyric was "Thy loyal sons." When girls arrived, it was changed to "Thy loyal youth." Some people, notably curmudgeonly old male alumni, feel that this one-word change robbed the anthem of much of its former vigor.

PART ONE

SPRING TERM

From Clarissa Spotswood's Journal:

This afternoon, when I was rummaging in my jewelry case, looking for the mate to one of my earrings, I noticed a small key tucked in one of the ring cushions and wondered whether that just might be the key to the center drawer of the small lowboy that stands in the front hall, just inside the front door. That little drawer has been locked, and its key has been missing, for years. I tried the key, and it worked. That's where I found the photograph that I am looking at now.

You know how we old WASP families are. We never throw anything away. And there it was, the photograph of us, taken twenty-five years ago in September of 1974. There is Hobie, looking serious and forceful as ever, with the same strong jawline, straight nose, and piercing eyes that I first fell in love with years ago. There am I, looking prettier than I can remember feeling at the time, or, rather, prettier than I ever thought I looked. And there is Johnny, age five, in a white sailor suit, short pants, and a middy blouse with blue piping. I'm wearing a dark blue dress. I remember that blue dress well because Hobie picked it out for me, just for that photograph. Its skirt hung a proper two inches below the knee, it had push-up sleeves and a shawl collar with a modest V neckline, and I'm wearing my double strand of pearls. Those pearls were my aunt Minnie's gift to me when I graduated from Smith. There were originally three strands of pearls, but Hobie thought three strands of pearls were too showy, and so I had the jeweler remove one of them.

I am sitting, with my ankles crossed, in the wing chair—the one that is now covered with burgundy leather in the library. At the time, it was covered in a diamond-patterned fabric. Little Johnny, standing beside me, has his upper body leaning somewhat artfully across my lap. This pose was the photographer's suggestion, designed to conceal the fact that I was pregnant with Sally.

Oh, how Hobie fretted about that pregnancy! This, you see, was to be the "official" Spotswood family photograph, the one that was to appear on the cover of the *Crittenden School Alumni Magazine* when the school announced its appointment of Hobie as the new headmaster. The school's trustees had not been told about the pregnancy, and, since his contract had yet to be signed, Hobie worried that my pregnancy might jeopardize his job. Hobie and I had of course been interviewed by the trustees (all of whom were men, at the time), and had several dinners with the trustees and their wives (who were also expected to pass judgment on me). But, while all that was going on, I hadn't begun to "show." Now, all at once, I was beginning to show a bit. What would the effect be, Hobie wondered, on the students at an all-boys' (as it was then) boarding school, if the new headmaster arrived with an obviously pregnant wife? Would it set their young and impressionable minds to thinking of the very human act from which all pregnancies derive? Hobie worried about this, and he worried that the trustees might also worry and withdraw their offer. And so it was agreed that, during the first months of his tenure, I should keep myself out of sight as much as possible until the new baby was born. He also insisted that I must not nurse the new baby, as I'd done with Johnny. All this explains Johnny's somewhat artificial pose in the picture, with his elbows on my knees and his head on my right shoulder, a pose intended to disguise the pending arrival of his little sister.

If you children read this journal, as I hope you will someday, I thought this small detail might amuse you.

If you study this photograph, I think you'll notice a strong resemblance in your father's face as to the portrait of his ancestor, General William Spotswood, who fought under General Washington in the Revolution, at both Bennington and Saratoga. You've probably noticed in the plaque under the portrait that he is identified as "Gen. Wm. Spottiswoode." It was his grandson, another William, who simplified the spelling of the name. For many generations, the eldest son in the family was named either William or John, alternating the names with each generation. This means, Johnny, that you could style yourself John Spotswood VI if you wished, though your father always disapproved of this sort of thing.

The practice continued until your father was born and his grandmother Hobart prevailed on his parents to name him after her husband's family. The Hobarts had helped found Hobart College in Upstate New York, and Granny Hobart was very proud of her Hobart in-laws. Granny Hobart, whom, of course, you never knew, was a very forceful character and always got her way. She managed to convince my husband's parents that she was very rich, and that if their son was not named Hobart, she would not leave them anything in her will. When she died in 1957, a very old lady of ninety-eight, it turned out she had hardly any money at all—just a few old and worthless railroad bonds—and there was not even any will. She had recently repapered her living room, and someone suggested that she might have covered her great wealth—stock certificates, bonds, even cash—under the wallpaper. The new wallpaper was steamed off, and all that was found under that was another layer of wallpaper, and another under that, and on and on, down to the bare plaster. Your father, of course, was expected to pay for his share of this rather expensive undertaking.

You children may have heard your father speak sarcastically, even caustically, of his granny Hobart. But don't judge her too harshly; I have always admired the kind of woman who knows how to get exactly what she wants, and Granny was that kind of woman.

Granny Hobart, meanwhile, was the only person I can recall who ever called your father Hobart. To me, he has always been Hobe or Hobie, and his parents—at least when Granny was not within earshot—always called him Billy, which would have been his name if they had got their way, since his father was a John. Here at Crittenden, of course, your father has always been called Spots or Spotty. It is a nickname that can be used as a noun, adjective, verb, or even as an adverb. I've heard a student say, "I've been Spotsed." (Translation: I've been reprimanded.) Or "he did a really Spotsy thing to me." Or "Spots Spotsed me really Spotsily when I tried to Spots him back." Your father doesn't find this particularly amusing, but I do.

I mentioned all this about names, Johnny, because, when you marry and have children (as I hope you will), and if you choose to follow the Spotswood family tradition (or, rather, pick it up again) you might consider naming your first son William. It will be a William's turn. And traditions are not a bad thing, it seems to me.

Your father always wanted to be a boarding school headmaster. He confessed that to me when I first met him in his junior year at Harvard. It is not the sort of job that just any man could do, or that just any man would want to do. There are a lot of pressures—from the trustees, from faculty, from parents, from alumni, and of course from the students themselves. Yet this is what he always wanted to do, and it was a very difficult time in our marriage when Crittenden was considering him for its new head, and he knew that there were at least five other candidates whom the Search Committee was considering just as seriously. Something as natural as my pregnancy with Sally could, I suppose, have made a difference.

He may have been disappointed that the better and more famous New England Schools—Groton, Millbrook, or St. Mark's—had passed him over, and I know that he considered Exeter and Andover both to be too big for him to handle. But Crittenden was—and is—a fine middle-size school, and so he set his sights on Crittenden and, in the end, Crittenden picked him.

To my everlasting relief.

It is not a job that pays a lot of money. To be sure, every three years, when our contract is renewed, there is a small salary increase. It's due for renewal in September. And there are nice perks. The school pays for Rose, our cook-housekeeper. We are each provided with an automobile, and the school pays for our gasoline. We pay no property taxes or utility bills and can eat in the school dining room whenever we want. You children could, if you'd wanted, have attended Crittenden for free, and, since you didn't, most other New England schools extend generous scholarships to the children of other headmasters. Crittenden offers a good medical and retirement plan and, after age sixty-five, a comfortable pension. We can all use the school tennis courts, golf course, gym facilities, and pool for free, though I've never swum in the pool since Hobie never wanted me to appear in a swimsuit on campus. For the most part, our summers are free when the acting head takes over the summer school.

But one of the drawbacks of the job is that it is considered a job-for-life. The job is an end unto itself. You hardly ever hear of a prep school head who has gone on to become a college president or a corporate executive or a captain of industry. Once a man has committed himself to a job like this one, he is expected to remain committed to it until he retires. It is a job that leads to nowhere else. It is not a stepping stone. Being a prep school head is a man's career, and it is final.

I knew all this when I married Hobe. I went into my marriage with my eyes wide open. But perhaps the worst part is—

Hobe has just buzzed me from his study downstairs, and I see that it's six o'clock already, time for me to fix his evening dry martini. He says no one can mix them the way I do.

ONE

And now Clarissa Spotswood is being interviewed by a reporter from the *Litchfield Times*, a woman named Alexa Woodin, whose title is Women's Feature Editor. Clarissa pours tea.

"Mrs. Spotswood," Miss Woodin says, "what, from your point of view, have been the greatest changes in the Crittenden School since your husband took over the headmastership twenty-five years ago?"

"Well," Clarissa says, "the answer to that is simple. Coeducation. When I first came here in the late 1970s, this was an all-boys' school. The addition of girls has changed absolutely everything."

Miss Woodin gives her a sideways look, her pencil poised. "I assume you mean to say, 'young women,' and not 'girls,'" she says.

"No," Clarissa says a little sharply. "To me, a female person between the ages of fourteen and eighteen is still a girl. After that, she may be called a young woman. What we have at this school are boys *and* girls."

Alexa Woodin shrugs and scribbles something on her pad. "Are you saying that the presence of *girls* has had a negative impact on the school?" she says.

"No, I did not say that," Clarissa replies. "I said nothing of the sort. The impact of girls on this school has been the same as it's been on other schools our size, ever since, back in the sixties, coeducation was touted as the wave of the future. Crittenden turned to coeducation a little later than most other private secondary schools. We were a little more conservative at the time. We were a holdout, and moved more slowly, because my husband wanted to observe what kind of impact the move was having on other schools. That's the only difference between us and the others."

"Describe the impact, would you please, Mrs. Spotswood?"

"Well, for one thing, when I came here there was a strict dress code. Boys wore jackets and ties in the dining room and in the classrooms. Trousers could be chinos or corduroys, but no blue jeans. Collars had to be buttoned—no loosened neckties. Shoes could be Oxfords or loafers, no sneakers. Casual clothing was restricted to sports and in the dormitories. On hot days, boys could remove their jackets in the classroom, but only if their teacher gave them permission to do so. In those days, the teachers were called masters. Masters were addressed as 'sir,' and their wives as 'ma'am.' When a woman or an older person entered the room, the boys were taught to rise. In the dining room, proper table manners were stressed. There was a nonde-nominational chapel service—compulsory—every morning, and twice on Sundays. Clergymen, rabbis, and lay speakers came to speak. All that's gone now. No more dress code. The kids wear what they want. The teachers are called by their first name. There's no more dining room, just a cafeteria. With more students, the chapel is obsolete. The kids won't all fit into it. But the pews still have nice soft cushions, and so the boys and girls use the pews for what they call 'making out,' which means whatever they decide to make it mean. And free condoms are dispensed at the infirmary. Do you call this *progress*?"

Miss Alexa Woodin is scribbling, scribbling furiously in her steno notepad. "It seems to me that what you're describing is a negative impact on the school," she says.

"No, not negative," Clarissa says. "Just different. You were asking me about differences. We live in a very different world in the 1990s from what it was in the sixties and seventies, which sometimes makes me wonder how long this whole new world will last—what it will be like twenty-five years from now. But coeducation has changed this school completely—the feel of it, the personality of it, the *look* of it. It's also made it a much more expensive school to run. Tuition costs have risen more than two hundred percent since my husband came here, but the same's true for other schools like ours. Even comparatively wealthy families are applying for financial aid to send their children here. But we have the cost of maintaining separate boys' and girls' dormitories—we haven't come to coed dormitories yet, but perhaps that's coming—and you'll hear an unholy outcry from parents if that happens! Then there's the cost of policing the hours when boys and girls are permitted to visit each other in their rooms—and the kids squawk about that because they think they should have complete freedom. It's all made my husband's job much harder for him. Now, twice a year he has to go around the country, hat in hand, asking for money from parents and alumni. He's about as welcome in their homes as an insurance salesman! When alumni come back to school to visit, they're often unhappy with the cosmetic appearance of the place—the boys in their baggy jeans, worn down around their hips, the T-shirts, the running shoes, the backpacks strewn all over the floor in the main entrance hall. 'It looks more like a youth hostel than a school,' I heard one alumnus say. And what's the first thing an alumnus wants to do when he comes back to school? He wants to visit his old room. But now he finds it double-locked. That never used to be permitted. We had regular room inspections."

"For drugs?"

"Oh, I was sure you'd come to that," Clarissa says with a sigh. "Yes, we've had some problems with drugs here, just like the other schools, but that seems to be on the decline right now. More important seems to be alcohol—beer—and cigarettes. Cigarettes are a fire hazard, and the school's fire insurance rates have gone up. And thievery! We always used to have a certain amount of that. Teenagers will try anything once, even stealing, but it was usually just small amounts of cash, a few dollars, and the culprit was generally easy to catch. But today, despite the locks on the doors, it's whole expensive sound systems, computers, television sets! Lord knows what they do with them, but somehow, it's harder to catch a thief who's stolen a large object than a little one. We've had parents threaten to sue the school for their child's equipment that's been stolen, and now we have to carry insurance for that."

"You're listing a lot of negatives, Mrs. Spotswood."

"Am I? Well, perhaps I'm old-fashioned. I won't say I don't miss the good old days. It seems to me that we all had better manners then. We were more polite then. It seems to me that good manners keep the peace. I used to be a prison visitor, you know. I used to drive over to Ossining and visit the inmates there. I'd read to them, or just talk with them. I had a convict say to me, 'The three most important phrases to learn to say in prison are, 'please,' 'thank you,' and 'I'm sorry.'"

"You'll pardon me, but you seem to be saying that Crittenden is turning out a bunch of ill-bred ruffians," Miss Woodin says with a condescending little laugh.

"Please! I did not say that. Our college acceptance rate is as high as any school in New England, and at the top colleges, led by Harvard, Yale, Stanford, and Brown. And that's what a prep school is all about, isn't it? Preparing a child for college? Of course, there are some educators who claim that the colleges' standards have gone down in recent years, though I can't speak on that subject. But perhaps the saddest thing is—"

Alexa Woodin flips a page of her notepad. "Yes? What is the saddest thing?" she asks.

"At least once a year, sometimes more often, we have to send a girl home to her parents because she's pregnant. I often wonder what happens to those girls, and to their babies. Because we usually never hear from them again. But don't put that in your story. Please, that's off the record. These are thirteen- or fourteen-year-olds we're talking about. We need to respect their privacy."

Miss Woodin nods. "Did you attend an all-girls' school, Mrs. Spotswood?"

"I did. Shipley, in Pennsylvania. And then Smith College."

"And didn't you miss the companionship, the competition— the interaction—from the male sex?"

"Absolutely not! We felt we were very special creatures in this elite all-girls' school, that we had the best of everything, better even than what the boys had. And there were always plenty of boys around. There were interschool dances with boys' schools in the area that we looked forward to with great excitement! We planned our wardrobes very carefully, we really dressed up for these boy-girl events. The boys, also, in black tie and dinner jackets. We saw as much of boys as we wanted to or needed to. In a way, without the boys underfoot day after day, it was all so much more—well, more romantic!"

Alexa Woodin uncrosses her legs, leaning forward slightly in her chair. "One last question," she says. "As your husband approaches his twenty-fifth anniversary as headmaster of

Crittenden, do you have any regrets, or is there anything you, personally, wish you had done differently?"

Clarissa hesitates. "Well," she says, "when the girls first started coming to the school, it was a very exciting time for both of us. The school was turning over a whole new leaf. We felt the school was on the cutting edge at last, and that was thrilling, and also a little scary. What I hoped was that I could become a sort of surrogate mother to these girls, that these girls would come to me with their problems, and we could talk them out, the way my own daughter always did. My daughter, Sally, and I have always been very close and, at the time, Sally was close to the age of these girls. However, in most cases, I don't think I succeeded with that surrogate mother ambition. I don't know why. Maybe it was a foolish ambition. The girls at school and I have always gotten along well, but on a somewhat superficial level. Never more than that. And I suppose I regret that."

Miss Woodin closes her notebook. "Well, thank you, Mrs. Spotswood," she says. "You've given me a wonderful interview. I think it'll be a great story."

"Well, I hope so. More tea?"

"No, thank you." She stands up, smoothing the front of her skirt. "Thank you again for giving me so much of your time."

"You're most welcome." Clarissa follows her visitor out of the library, down the wide front hall to the door.

At the door, she smiles and waves good-bye to Alexa Woodin. But as she watches Miss Woodin walk briskly down the gravel walk to her car, slapping her notebook against her thigh, a worried look crosses Clarissa's face.

The Crittenden School. Founded in 1894 by Eliza Crittenden, the widow of Asa Crittenden, who made a post–Civil War fortune in fertilizers.

Asa Crittenden went down to the high desert of northern Chile in 1867 and mined for nitrates he had heard were there and found them. There, in the blazing sun of the subequatorial summer, he wore boots and jodhpurs, a safari jacket and a pith helmet, and he brandished a riding crop to exert his authority over his native workers who worked, nearly naked, to strip his mines. Whole hillsides were gouged out and mountaintops were leveled by Asa's crews. There in the Atacama, one of the driest regions of the world, where it almost never rains, Asa's crews dug wells that produced only brackish water from the salt lake in the central plateau, and so Asa's crews dug narrow ditches to carry water that was barely potable from the melting snows in the Chilean Andes. Yellow fever and malaria were endemic, and there was much mortality among his workers, but the mines brought a new prosperity to the region, and what had once been sleepy Indian encampments became small boom towns. One of these towns he named Crittenden. Saloons and brothels proliferated, and, since Asa owned these, too, these businesses fattened his wallet as well. Every night at sundown the natives gathered in the bars to drink themselves silly on Asa's *pisco*.

Asa's mining operations flourished for nearly thirty years until the late nineteenth century, as the mule teams drove the raw nitrates to the coast, where they were loaded aboard Asa's ships to be shipped northward to the States to be refined. In the meantime, however, man-made fertilizers were being developed that were much better, and cheaper to produce, than Asa's imports. The Chilean nitrate industry failed. The settlements and work camps were abandoned. Slowly, the winds of the Atacama smoothed and rounded off the hillsides and mountaintops that Asa's laborers had slashed and defaced. The irrigation ditches silted in; the native Indians returned to the lives they had been living for hundreds of years before. The town of Crittenden disappeared altogether.

In 1890, thinking himself a failure, and after writing a short note of apology to his wife, Asa placed the barrel of a long rifle in his mouth and, using his big toes, stepped down on the trigger. But though his mines had failed, he had died rich. His estate was valued at more than five million dollars—not a great deal by today's standards, but worth a great deal more than that in terms of the buying power of the times. His widow, Eliza, found herself the richest woman in the state of Connecticut. She had her husband's remains sent home and had them placed beneath a marble monument of extravagant design.

With that out of the way, Eliza turned to other matters or, more accurately, other matters turned to her. The Crittendens' marriage had been a childless one. To be sure, over the years, a number of pretty Indian girls had been seen slipping in and out of Asa's mining tent, and so there was no way of telling how many dusky-skinned children he had fathered in the Atacama. But Eliza was his only legal heir, and, with her new wealth, she found all sorts of people coming to her with helpful suggestions as to how she might usefully dispose of some of her money. In Hartford, it was suggested that the addition of an Asa Crittenden Memorial Wing to its hospital would be very nice. In New Haven, the offer was made to build an Asa Crittenden Memorial Library. Middletown had never had an opera house and proposed to build the Asa Crittenden Memorial Hall of Music.

But, having entombed her late husband in marble, Eliza decided that she had memorialized him sufficiently. By then in her late sixties, with little interest in marrying again, she decided that the time had come to memorialize herself. Before marrying Asa, she had been a schoolteacher, and so she came to the conclusion that building a school might be just the thing. College preparatory schools for boys had been cropping up all through New England. Higher education for women was still not a popular notion in America, and so it seemed quite natural that it would be a school for boys. And so was born what was originally called the Eliza Wells Crittenden College Preparatory School for Young Men.

Eliza's initial gift was $200,000 in cash, plus forty-seven acres of choice real estate she owned—which included a large barn—high on a hilltop in the northwest corner of the state, overlooking a small stream, which meandered down from the foothills, and a blue, pure lake called Kinishawah which, according to locals, means "bottomless water." Though Lake Kinishawah does indeed have a bottom, it is exceptionally deep—nearly two hundred feet at its deepest point—for a small lake in the Berkshire foothills, and its waters are exceptionally clear. Eliza turned out to be unusually environmentally minded for her time. With her gift, she specified that, when built, her school must have its own sewage-disposal system, with holding tanks and leaching fields, so that no effluents from the school could ever be permitted to poison the stream.

A board of trustees (all male, of course) was appointed, a headmaster hired, ground was broken in 1894, and two years later, the school opened its doors to a small freshman class of fifteen boys.

From the outset, to Eliza's displeasure, the trustees of the school made it clear that they, and not she, were running the school. Though she had had her brother placed on the board, he was routinely outvoted. One of the first things to be changed was the school's name. It was felt that having a woman's name attached to a boys' school was sissified. Crittenden boys, it seems, were being teased for attending "Miss Crittenden's." Within a year, new stationery was printed, simply headed:

THE CRITTENDEN SCHOOL

Eliza considered this a personal slight. Though the trustees came back to her year after year to contribute more money, she stoutly refused. When she died in 1901, her estate was distributed among various nieces and nephews, with not a penny to the school.

With a graduating class of six in 1900, the school set its sights on growth and the preparation of male students to strive for, and achieve, academic excellence toward future education at New England's finest colleges and universities, including Harvard, Williams, and Yale, to name only a few. Crittenden's curriculum included the classics such as Greek, Latin, mathematics, English and English literature, the sciences, and of course physical exercise (although no formal gymnasium would exist for another twenty-five years). The difficult curriculum was evidenced by the fact that, even to this day, only an average of twenty-five percent of the students completed all four years at Crittenden. In and out of the classroom, respect for the faculty was paramount. Students were required to address male (and they were entirely male) faculty and staff as "sir," "mister," or "master." (This led to some amusing conjugations later in the school's history. In the 1950s, a particularly stern and demanding math teacher, Joshua Bates, joined the faculty, allowing the students to give him the unfortunate sobriquet "Master Bates." Legend had it that one bold student even broached the name during Algebra II, asking, amid much sniggering, "Master Bates, could you give me a better idea on how to *handle* that problem?" After a quick and withering glance at the student, the teacher didn't miss a beat and explained in concise mathematical language the algebraic solution; the student spent every evening of the next week in mandatory study hall.)

As it expanded, the school grew a respectable faculty in all the scholastic trades, and, by the time of the Great War, it boasted professors with master's degrees and PhDs. However, with the advent of WWI, student enrollment waned, and the graduating class of 1916 (composed of seven) would lose two in the Battle of the Argonne Forest in 1918. Arthur Buhl and Charles Colby would be memorialized on the walls of the school study hall during Crittenden's expansion in the 1920s. Eventually, Crittenden administrators named two new dormitories after the fallen alumni during construction in the late 1940s.

At inception, the school's student body was modeled after the preparatory schools of Great Britain in the nineteenth century, with freshmen referred to as Third Formers, sophomores as Fourth Formers, and so on, with seniors as all-powerful Sixth Formers. Sixth Formers were considered, as a result of their chronological age and presumed experience, to be the "middle management" of a prep school's organizational hierarchy, reporting to faculty members on the most significant matters of discipline and morale. In the obverse, Third Formers were thought of as at the bottom, with only servitude and obeyance the required factors. Seniors served in positions of authority and, later, when the student body grew and new dormitories were constructed, they would serve as "prefects" in charge of the dorms' discipline and order, as well as communication with the faculty and administrators. The de facto president of the student body was referred to as the "head prefect" and he (there were no women) reported directly to the headmaster of the school, much in the way a colonel would report to a general.

Also, designed in the tradition of old English prep schools, the Crittenden campus comprised a small dormitory, with the original barn initially acting as its centerpiece. In its early years, the number of students and faculty was small, and there were regular assemblies in the barn for general school announcements and theatrical performances put on by students. Acknowledging that no student's education is complete without a respect (if not fear) of the Almighty, regular, daily nondenominational church services were also held in the barn until the construction of a formal chapel in 1947.

During the 1920s, Crittenden would expand its student body exponentially, if not numerically. Whereas the first graduation class after WWI numbered ten, by 1929, the graduating class grew to twenty-one, with an entire student body of seventy. The school survived the period of the Great Depression quite well actually, insulated (like so many other prestigious prep schools in New England) by wealthy and powerful parents in finance and government and a growing endowment from alumni and alumni parents who made fortunes in the postwar years. This required construction of new dormitories, a gymnasium, a formal dining hall, and the expansion of the Barn (as it unimaginably became known), all to accommodate a growing student body and new faculty.

By 1939, the entrance road to the campus, previously a dirt track that ran alongside a stream and was suitable for carts, was paved and improved to connect the main campus to Route 103, which in turn connected outlying small Connecticut towns nearby. Unfortunately, during periods of intense rain, the stream would occasionally flood, restricting access to the campus to other ancillary and lengthy back roads. Engineers were engaged and a dam was built to control the flooding, creating a small pond on the south side of the access road. Along with the access road, new facilities included additional faculty housing, an ice hockey arena, and a four-hundred-meter-high ski hill complete with rope tow.

During WWII, growth continued unabated, as students were too young for service overseas and graduates were exempted by nature of their wealthy and powerful parents or the requirements of a university education. Nevertheless, Crittenden graduates served honorably in the US military during WWII, with one graduate of the class of 1936 surviving the sinking of the USS *Arizona* during the Pearl Harbor attack of 1941, for which he received a Purple Heart and later the Bronze Star. During the war, students and faculty alike combined efforts to support the US's overseas efforts by collecting and recycling metal, rubber, and other materials. This was the beginning of the idea of "community service."

Completion of new buildings in the 1950s saw five dorms and the administration building surrounded by a large quadrangle (the "Quad") and a new chapel (named for the first headmaster, Aldous Callard) prominently at the Quad's north end. The administration building, named Main Building, had classrooms on the basement level; faculty offices and break rooms were on the first level; and a study hall and library were situated on the top floor, accessed by a grand winding staircase. Dormitories included student and faculty living accommodations and classrooms on the lower levels. Dorm rooms were also added above the Dining Hall.

Crisscrossing between the buildings and across the Quad were asphalt paths guiding future leaders of industry and politics to and from their classes and daily activities.

Days and evenings were strictly regimented for the young men of Crittenden, with period changes announced by the ringing of a ship's bell attached to the Barn (rumored to have come from a WWI destroyer) calling students and faculty to classes, meals, and assemblies. For students and faculty, apart from an adherence to scholarly excellence, the early years of Crittenden were more akin to a country club setting than a normal "public" school. All were expected to be well groomed and in jacket and tie at all times during the day. Meals, in a formal, sit-down setting (including breakfast promptly at 6:15 a.m.) were served in the Dining Hall by white-coated kitchen staff.

In the 1950s, the school would also expand "community service" and formalize the program and policy, whereby a multitude of functions and services previously performed by outside contractors and laborers would now be performed by the students with, of course, a Sixth Former in charge and a faculty member available for oversight. Eventually the CS program proved enormously successful, not only for the bottom line of the (tax-exempt) institution, but also for instilling a work ethic into young men used to having servants, cooks, and occasionally chauffeurs at their behest.

In CS, students performed virtually all normal day-to-day chores of the school, which were to be completed in between classes and on weekends, the theory being "idle hands are the devil's workshop." Third and Fourth Formers served meals as waiters; Fifth Formers operated as dishwashers in the dining hall (dishwashing being a widely desired function, as it did not require coats and ties), operated a bank, school store, post office, fire brigade (complete with four WWI-era two-man pull carts each containing a hundred yards of fire hose), trash collection (another sought-after function, allowing the student driver to leave campus and drive the garbage truck to the local dump, perhaps stopping along the way for breakfast). Theatrical functions in the Barn (lighting, stage design, and construction) as well as a myriad of other services around campus were all performed by the students. When fully implemented, the only outside services required from professionals were landscaping, housekeeping and laundry, meal preparation, maintenance of the physical plant, and a barber (or, as one erudite faculty member referred to the latter, a "tonsorial artist"). With almost everything else run by students, the result was a completely self-sufficient and insular community.

With the advent of the Cold War, the school was put on edge, fearing, as so many did during that time, an imminent nuclear attack. With safety in mind, the administration purchased and installed a WWII–era air-raid Klaxon, which, in the event of an emergency, would emit an earsplitting wail reminiscent of sirens during the Blitz.

It was also during this period that the school welcomed its first nonwhite, non-WASP student, Arturo de Toro de Sangre, nicknamed "Tor" by his fellow freshmen. Arturo was the progeny of a successful banker in Mexico City who later served as Mexico's ambassador to the UN, so Tor had the heritage and upbringing well-suited for an exclusive school like Crittenden and fit in fine, graduating in 1959 and eventually serving in the army as a lieutenant in Vietnam.

As the school entered the turbulent 1960s, it expanded upon its diverse student body in terms of ethnicity, if not sex—women would not be admitted until the end of the 1970s. The broadening of admission policy to include those other than New England prominents came about not only from a sense of liberalism and social diversity but also as a result of expanded competition from other, growing preparatory schools. This necessitated Crittenden recruiting students from the Midwest and as far south and west as Texas and California.

Reflecting a commitment to social responsibility, the school also joined "Project Broad Jump," which solicited economically disadvantaged students from inner cities (in Crittenden's case, New York City), offering a summer school academic program and, based on an individual candidate's performance, a full scholarship to the school. The program, which shared duties with other prep schools, was a success, producing numerous young men of varying ethnicities and backgrounds who would wind up contributing to industry and their communities.

Also with the '60s came a new awareness of environmentalism and conservation. In light of this new awareness, Crittenden constructed (with student labor) a bridge across the dam and created a zoo, operated and maintained by students as part of their community service. A program unique to Crittenden, the zoo eventually housed a myriad of animals, including a facility for students of falconry, various monkeys and apes, an aquarium, and an ornithological house that contained an impressive array of mounted and stuffed species of birds. The zoo would become the school's signature appeal to new students' recruitment in the coming decades of its growth.

During this period, the student body grew to over 225, and by the end of the decade had a new headmaster.

Hobart Spotswood is the seventh headmaster of Crittenden. Two of his predecessors turned out to be not up to the job and lasted only a year or so. But one served a full twenty-six years before retiring.

It is this record that "Spotty" hopes to achieve, or even better. He's told Clarissa this, privately of course.

And now, outside the heavy walnut door with the word HEADMASTER stenciled on it in simple gold lettering, sits young Mr. Avery S. Broadbent III, senior, age almost seventeen, on a leather bench. A buzzer sounds, and Mary, Hobart Spotswood's secretary, rises and opens the door. "Mr. Spotswood will see you now," she says and offers the boy a small, sympathetic smile. Young Broadbent also rises and steps into the headmaster's office. The door quietly closes behind him.

Seated behind his desk, an unlighted pipe clenched between his teeth, Hobart Spotswood does not immediately look up. Instead, he riffles through a small stack of papers on his desk, lifting a page with his fingertips, glancing at it, then setting it to one side. Sitting prominently in the center of the headmaster's desk is a six-pack of Colt 45 beer bottles, two of which have had their caps removed and appear to be empty. Presently, without looking up, the headmaster says, "What time is it?"

Young Broadbent glances nervously at his watch. "Three fifteen, sir," he says.

"Ah," the headmaster says, still leafing through his papers.

Avery Broadbent sits down in one of the two leather chairs opposite the desk.

Now the headmaster looks up. Removing his pipe, he says, "Did I ask you to sit down, Mr. Broadbent?"

Quickly the boy jumps to his feet again. "No, sir!" he says.

"Did I ask you to stand up?"

"No, sir!" He starts to sit down.

"When should you sit down?"

"When asked, sir!"

"Please sit down," the headmaster says. The boy quickly sits again.

"Now, Broadbent," the headmaster says, "do you have any idea why I asked you here this afternoon?"

"No, sir."

"None whatsoever?"

"No, sir."

He gestures toward the six-pack of beer. "This was found in your room this morning by a member of the school's housekeeping staff when she was running the vacuum cleaner. It was under your bed, behind your laundry bag."

"Someone must have put it there, sir."

"I see. Do you have any idea who might have put it there?"

"No, sir."

"Or why?"

"No, sir." A small trickle of perspiration is starting from the boy's hairline and moving down across his left cheek.

"Curious," the headmaster says. "I suppose we could have these bottles checked by Campus Security for fingerprints. That would tell us who the culprit was. Shall we do that?"

"No, sir. I mean, I said somebody must have put it there. I didn't say the somebody wasn't me."

"But when I asked you who that person was, you said you had no idea."

"Yes, sir. But what I meant, sir, was—"

"And so that was a lie."

"Yes, sir, I guess so. But I meant—"

"Do you know, Broadbent, that possession of or consumption of alcoholic beverages by students on the Crittenden campus is strictly forbidden by the school's rules? Rules that you received a copy of when you entered school last fall? Rules that you were given and asked to commit to memory? Did you know that?"

"Yes, sir, but—"

"Did you know that a violation of any of these rules is punishable by expulsion?"

"I guess so, but—"

"Do you not consider beer to be an alcoholic beverage?"

"Well, not really, sir."

"Oh? What do you mean by that?"

"I mean it's not *vodka*, or *whiskey*, or—"

Mr. Spotswood lifts one of the bottles from its carton. "If beer isn't alcohol," he says, "then why has the manufacturer printed this warning on the label: 'Consumption of alcoholic beverages impairs your ability to drive a car or operate machinery, and may cause health problems'?"

"Well, I guess it's sort of alcohol," he says, looking down at his hands.

"This warning is a US government warning, Broadbent. If the United States government says beer is an alcoholic beverage, then I guess we can assume it is one, can't we?"

The boy spreads his fingers, the nails of which are bitten down to the quick. "Yeah, I guess so," he whispers.

"Broadbent, what is the legal drinking age in Connecticut?"

"I think it's—twenty-one, sir."

"I think so, too. And how old are you?"

"Sixteen. Almost seventeen."

"So you have broken two sets of rules. The school's rules and Connecticut's state law. And, on top of that, you tried to lie to me about it. That makes the offense somewhat more serious, don't you agree?"

"I guess so—but lots of guys do it."

"Do what—lie?"

"No, I meant buy beer."

"*Lots* do it? That's rather vague. Be more precise. How many do it?"

"Well, some do it."

"You're saying some people break the law. I'm quite willing to agree with you on that. All you have to do is read the daily headlines to know that. But you may have also noticed that, in our society, people who break the law quite often get caught. This is what has happened to you. People who break the law often get caught and get punished for it. Broadbent, what are laws *for*?"

He shrugs. "I dunno," he says.

"You don't *know* what laws are for?"

"Well, what I mean is—"

"If you honestly don't know what laws are for, you're in even worse trouble than I thought you were, young man."

"Well, I mean, I guess they're to protect—"

"Exactly. Laws are to protect people from other people, to protect people from themselves. Laws are to protect people from harm, to try to maintain a safe and civilized society where people don't hurt other people. Now, have you stopped to consider how many people you have threatened to hurt with this little caper of yours?"

"Nobody, not really."

"Oh? Where did you buy this beer?"

"The A&P."

"Then consider the salesperson who sold you this beer. He or she was breaking the law by selling it to you. That person could be penalized with a stiff fine and would probably lose his job. Consider the manager of the A&P. He could also be fined and fired from his job. A young man like you, who's never held a steady job, probably has no idea what the loss of a job can mean to a person. Let's assume that the clerk who sold you the beer and the store manager, both have families, wives and children, who depend on their income to feed and support them. Your little illegal purchase had the potential to damage their lives also. Our little list of lives you've put in jeopardy is getting longer, isn't it? Can you think of any other people you might have hurt by your action?"

Broadbent shakes his head mutely.

"Beer on this campus is grounds for expulsion. How will your parents feel when you are sent home from Crittenden? Will they feel good about that?"

"No," he mutters. He is sweating profusely now, though the day is not warm.

"Or your grandparents, aunts and uncles, and other relatives? I imagine that they, too, will feel disappointed in you, let down, hurt—don't you?"

He nods, blinking his eyes rapidly.

"Can you think of anyone else you could have hurt?" Once again, he shakes his head.

"What about your friends and schoolmates here? Since you have had the poor luck to get caught, won't all the others who have broken school rules, or who have considered breaking them, feel threatened, angry, and endangered? So, you see our list keeps getting longer and longer. There are literally hundreds of people who could have been hurt when you bought that beer and brought it onto the campus. But you've also hurt two other people by your disobedience. Can you tell me who those people are?"

"No . . ." His chin is resting on his chest now as he slumps in his chair, his long legs stretched out on the carpet in front of him.

"One is myself," the headmaster says. "I am deeply disappointed and hurt by what you have done. You have flouted the rules, one of the most important rules of my school, and in so doing you have shown that you have no respect for me or for my position here. The other person you've managed to hurt, perhaps irreparably, is named Avery S. Broadbent the third, the young man sitting right there in your chair. By trying to tell a lie and trying to place the blame for what you did on someone else, you have shown yourself to be a person who cannot be trusted, a person of low moral character. If this flaw in your character is not corrected, and soon, you will find yourself quite alone and friendless in this world, I'm afraid. Now, tell me this—is there anything you have learned from this little talk today?"

Broadbent's silent for a moment, still looking at his hands. Then he says, "I guess it's—don't bring beer on campus."

Hobart Spotswood shakes his head slowly back and forth. "Your answer disappoints me, Broadbent," he says. "I was hoping you'd say something about the importance of considerateness to others."

Broadbent nods his head vigorously. "I did think about that, sir—considerateness to others."

"Even more important, I hoped you might say something about the need for learning to weigh the consequences of your actions. Every human deed has consequences in one form or another, and illegal or antisocial deeds usually have unfortunate consequences. Had that thought also occurred to you?"

"Yes, sir, it did, sir."

The headmaster paused. "So," he says at last, "what would you suggest I do with you, Broadbent?"

His answer is a despondent shrug.

"First, I am going to ask you to stop biting your fingernails," the headmaster says. "It is an unattractive and unsanitary habit. I am not going to graduate you from Crittenden unless you can show me a set of clean, neatly trimmed, well-manicured fingernails."

There is a stifled, but still audible, sob of relief when Broadbent hears the word *graduate*.

Is there a twinkle in the headmaster's eye when he says this? It is hard to say. His face is a solemn, frozen mask.

Changing the subject, Hobart asks, "How are the rest of your studies and community service going?"

"Fine, sir."

Opening a small manila folder, the headmaster refers to some notes.

"Your grades appear excellent. You serve as captain of the fire brigade as well as captain of the baseball team, is that correct?"

"Yes, sir!"

"How about family life? I understand you have a brother over at Millbrook."

"Yes, sir, my identical twin brother, in fact. He's doing well, with a bunch of athletic trophies, and he's on the honor roll. He and I are very close."

"I'm glad to hear that, but I'm also glad that you chose Crittenden."

Switching back to the subject at hand, the headmaster continues, "Here at Crittenden, we teach a course that is not in the academic curriculum and is not listed in the school catalog. I call this Lessons in Living. Perhaps you have heard me speak of this before. Colleges and universities do not offer it, but we do. Honesty, considerateness of others, and learning to weigh the consequences of one's actions are part of it. But I'd like to offer you one more lesson in living today, and it is this—" He gestures to the six-pack on his desk. "Never buy, or serve to your friends, beer in long-necked bottles, Broadbent! Long-necked bottles do not meet Crittenden's high standards of taste and refinement. Long-necked bottles are for blue-collar workers, not educated ladies and gentlemen. A Crittenden alum would certainly never offer a beer that calls itself 'Colt 45 Malt Liquor.' Similarly, a Crittenden alum would never buy or serve wine from bottles with screw-on tops. Good wines are always sealed with corks. Is that clear?"

"Yes, sir!" Broadbent says. "I'll remember that!" And he starts to rise.

The headmaster holds up his hand. "Just a minute, Broadbent," he says. "I am not finished. Your punishment for your infraction of the school rules will be four weeks' probation and confinement to the school campus."

"But, *sir*—!"

"I realize this means you will have to miss the important game up at Andover next Saturday," he says. "And I'm sure your teammates will also miss that good pitching arm of yours. And if Crittenden ends up losing this big game as a result of your inability to go up against Andover with the team—well, that will be just another unfortunate consequence of your poorly thought-out actions, won't it? Those consequences we spoke of. You may go now, Mr. Broadbent."

Picking up his unlighted pipe, Hobart Spotswood returns his attention to the papers on his desk, and the young man rises and staggers almost blindly to the door.

Suffice to say that Avery S. Broadbent III has just experienced what it is like to be "Spotsed"—stretched out across the rack, the screws tightened, then tightened a bit more, and then eased slightly before the final whammy.

TWO

About once a month, though on no particular schedule, John Spotswood and his sister, Sally, have lunch together in New York. They usually meet at the Union Square Cafe on East Nineteenth Street near Park Avenue, where they've met today, because it's close to John's downtown office and, by mutual agreement, Sally always picks up the tab. This is because, as John cheerfully puts it, he is "just a struggling young architect." He specializes in residential designs and, as he explains, "There's no money in residential stuff. If I wanted to design churches and hospitals and office buildings, I could probably make a bundle. But I just don't like doing that sort of stuff. I like designing houses, places where people live. Guess I get that from my dad. Dad was always more interested in educating young people than in making a pisspot full of money."

Sally, on the other hand, though five years younger than her brother, seems always to have had—without ever having seemed to want it—a sort of Midas touch. She works as an account executive for a small boutique-type advertising agency on Madison Avenue that specializes in travel accounts. Their clients include several foreign airlines, a luxury cruise line, and a number of exclusive hotels around the world. Sally's is definitely a New

York glamor job, but one that has the distinction of paying her a comely salary of $95,000 a year. Quite a bit of client-paid first-class travel is thrown into the deal for good measure. John often refers to Sally as "my rich baby sister." Sally herself says she got the job "only because the woman who interviewed me liked the way I tied my Hermès scarf."

Sally Spotswood's relative affluence allows her to afford her own one-bedroom apartment, with a terrace, on the Upper East Side, in a building that has a doorman. Her brother shares a walk-up in the Village with two friends—for $450 a month apiece.

They are a study in contrasts, these two. Sally is dark, like her mother, with large, thoughtful eyes and an oval face, which, when she wears her hair pulled back in a simple ponytail, as she has done today, give her a Mediterranean look. In Madrid, where the Ritz Hotel is one of her accounts, she is often mistaken for a native. Of course, the fact that she speaks flawless Castilian Spanish (as well as French, Italian, and a bit of Japanese) adds to the illusion and was certainly one of the qualifications that helped her get this job. Her brother is fair, with sand-colored hair like his father used to have before the gray took over, which always looks a little windblown. At six foot one, he is an inch taller than his father, and, like his flat-bellied and ramrod-straight father, Hobart Spotswood's son keeps himself a fit 175 pounds and runs two miles every morning along the roadbed of the old West Side Highway.

In Sally's job, it is important to dress well, and that is fine with her. She loves good clothes, and wears them well, and is glad that she can afford them. Her brother, on the other hand, usually looks a bit rumpled—as he looks now, shirt collar unbuttoned, tie askew. As he vigorously attacks his lamb chop, a lock of fair hair falls across his forehead. He pushes it aside with one hand, his fingers ink-stained from his drafting board.

Sally, who is having a Caesar salad, pauses and takes a sip of her wine. "I've been wanting to talk to you, Johnny," she says. "I'm worried about Mother."

"Oh," he says. "What's the matter with Mom? I talked to her a few days ago. She sounded fine."

"Oh, she sounds fine and insists she feels fine. But how long has it been since you went up to see her up at the school?"

"Maybe . . . six months? Eight months. It's a two-and-a-half-hour drive. I've been pretty busy."

"I drove up to Crittenden last week, after I got back from Bangkok. She's gotten so terribly *thin*, Johnny. Her clothes just hang on her. I mentioned this, and she just said something about avoiding Rose's rich desserts, and that maybe she'd lost a little weight. A *little* weight. She looks as though she's lost at least twenty pounds. Suddenly she looks *old*, Johnny."

"Hmm," he says, taking another bite of his chop. "How old is Mom now, anyway?" he says, speaking with his mouth full.

"Fifty-seven. That's not old for a woman nowadays. It's too young for a woman to start looking old. And that's not all. Something seems to have happened to her spirit."

"Her spirit? What do you mean?"

"I can't quite put my finger on it. But here's an example. I brought her back a few yards of Thai silk—iridescent reds, purple, and black, with gold and silver threads running through it. I suggested that she could take it to her dressmaker and have a cocktail dress made out of it. She just sat there with the fabric spread out on her lap, just stroking it and saying nothing. Then she said, with sort of a sigh, 'It's very pretty, darling. But I could never wear these colors here. Why don't you keep it, dear?' And she handed it back to me. It just didn't seem like her, Johnny. And then there are her headaches."

"Mom's always had her headaches."

"Yes, but the difference is she doesn't complain about them anymore. But she still has them. I walked into a room where she was sitting, and she didn't see me. She was sitting in the wing chair with her fingertips pressed against her temples and the most awful look of pain on her face. Then she saw me, and she smiled, pretending nothing was the matter."

"Well, I guess thirty-plus years of living with our old man could do that to you," he says.

"Don't make jokes, Johnny. I'm really very worried."

"Did you speak to Dad about it?"

"Yes, and he told me he's asked her again and again to see a doctor, but she won't go. He said to me, 'I can't *force* your mother to see a doctor.' But the school has its own doctor. Surely the headmaster could get the school doctor to come and see his wife."

"Old Doc Jethro? Death Row Jethro, the kids used to call him. He's never prescribed anything more potent than Sucrets."

"Yes, but he might be able to get her to go to someone who could help her—some sort of specialist. Did you know that Mother had a mastectomy years ago?"

He puts down his fork. "No. I never knew that."

"You're not supposed to know. No one's supposed to know. It's a big secret. I'm not even supposed to know, but one morning, years ago, I walked into her dressing room when she was slipping out of her nightie, and I saw the scars—terrible scars. Mentioned all this to Daddy, and he was furious that I knew about that. I think it happened not long after I was born. It may have been something they discovered when she was in the hospital, having me."

"But . . . a cancer. That operation must have cleared it up. It wouldn't come back after all these years—would it?"

"I don't know. But it might. It's one of the things that worries me."

John stares at his plate. "I've lost my appetite," he says.

"Anyway, I wish you'd make it a point to go up to the Castle to see her." The Castle is what the headmaster's house is called.

"I will. I'll make it a point. Maybe this weekend."

"Good." She covers his hand with hers. "And talk to Daddy. You know how Daddy always is with me."

"What do you mean?"

"Always—just sort of dismissive. Doesn't pay much attention to a lot of what I have to say. Thinks I'm sort of frivolous, work at a frivolous job. Sometimes I wonder if Daddy even likes me."

"Nonsense."

"I'm serious. Even when I was a little girl, I used to feel that where Daddy was concerned, I was sort of in the way. It was as though I was just this little female creature who was always underfoot, always tugging at his trouser leg, wanting attention that he never had the time to give me. But he's always listened to you. You were always his fair-haired boy."

He winks at her. "Still a little bit of sibling rivalry, Sal? After all these years? Hell, you're just talking about the Spotswood family thing. The oldest son—William, John, William, John, down through the corridors of recorded time. Why, I could be John the Twenty-Third if I wanted to be!" He strikes his forehead with the palm of his hand. "I could be like the pope! God, why did I have to be born into a family with an illustrious pedigree and no money?"

She laughs and changes the subject. "So—how's your love life?" she asks him.

"Funny you should ask. It's lousy."

"Blair?"

"No more. Over. Kaput. Finished. History."

"Aw. I liked Blair," says Sally.

"Oh, I like her too. Blair's okay. We're still friends. We still talk. I take her out now and then. But I had to tell her to cool her jets."

"Why? What happened?"

"She kept wanting me to commit. Commit what? 'Why won't you make a commitment?' she kept asking me. Commit, dammit, commit! Of course, I know what she means by commitment."

With his right index finger, John touches the ring finger of his left hand. "But I'm not ready to get married."

"You could do a lot worse than with a girl like Blair."

"I can't *afford* to get married, for Chrissake! I can't even afford to take you to lunch. I can't afford my bill at the liquor store, much less my rent. I certainly can't afford to produce a son and heir for dear old Dad, that next William he expects from me." He lowers his eyes. "Besides," he says, "I think perhaps I'm gay."

Sally is unflappable. She knows her older brother well, but not always well enough to know whether he is being deadly serious or just pulling her leg. She says nothing and merely stares at him, her hands folded in her napkin.

He flashes her a quick smile. "But of course, the only trouble with that is—"

"That Daddy would never stand for it," she says. And they both laugh.

The Castle at the Crittenden School was built in 1900 and would eventually serve as the headmaster's house. An example of the late Victorian shingle style, its roof is punctuated with many gables facing in all directions, and on the two principal floors, the large single-pane windows are bordered with stained-glass panels in pastoral motifs. Its front door, approached by a wide flight of stone steps, is topped by a stained-glass fanlight, and over the fanlight is a carved pineapple, the symbol of welcome. It was an era when interiors of dark walnut paneling were favored, and most of the public rooms are done in this. From the entrance hall, a double staircase with carved walnut railings, spindles, and treads rises to the floor above. It is a house designed to impress, and perhaps intimidate, the young with the importance of its occupant.

To the right of the entrance hall is a large reception room, designed, as its name suggests, for formal gatherings as well as for faculty meetings. To the left is the library, and from there a door leads to the family living room and the family dining room. The rear of the house is taken up with a butler's pantry, a maids' dining room, and a capacious kitchen equipped with deep copper sinks, a huge gas range and ovens, and a walk-in refrigerator. The most modern appliance in the kitchen is an electric dishwasher, which the school purchased in 1969 and has shown no signs of failing.

Upstairs are what are considered private quarters, the headmaster's study and small sitting room, six large bedrooms with baths, and a room that was originally designated as a sewing room, but which Clarissa has converted into a little study of her own upon moving in, with a desk where she works on her journal. The bathrooms on this floor are large and old-fashioned, featuring pedestal sinks of heavy porcelain and massive bathtubs standing on ball-in-claw feet. In 1952, a stall shower was installed, somewhat reluctantly, in one of the master baths to suit a headmaster who insisted he could not tolerate tub baths. As it turned out, the school could not tolerate him, either, so two years after the shower was put in, he was out looking for another job.

The Castle dates from an era when it was assumed that no proper family could live without a complement of servants and, on the third floor, under the gables, and reached by a narrow back staircase, were placed the servants' rooms. These tiny cells, some of them windowless, are barely six feet by six feet in size—room enough for a narrow bed, a dresser, and a chair; they were served by a common, rather primitive, bathroom. This warren of attic rooms is now used only for storage.

It was also an era that was fond of wide, covered verandahs, and wrapped around the south and west sides of the house, just off the reception room, there is an L-shaped one of these. It provides a pleasant setting for warm-weather cocktail parties, with views of sunsets over the Berkshire hills and the lake below.

The school, naturally, maintains the Castle and its grounds; staff tend to the lawn and gardens. Over the years, various head-masters and their wives have attempted to add personal touches to the house, but, since any major renovation or refurbishing requires the approval of the school's trustees, these attempts have, for the most part, been half-hearted. At least one head-master's wife was independently quite wealthy. She wanted to bring her decorator up from New York and had plans to redo the entire interior—a project that involved tearing down walls, replacing windows, altering the staircase, painting the wood-work, replacing the plumbing, and installing an entire new modern kitchen. She even wanted a Jacuzzi whirlpool bath in her bathroom. She would gladly pay for the whole thing herself, she said; it would be her gift to the school.

It was probably the whirlpool bath that did her in. The trustees nixed the entire project. They would not even let her bring in her waterbed. The walls of the house would not support its weight, they said.

Clarissa's main contribution to the house—since she is not rich—has been to take down, and store, the heavy velvet portieres that separated the rooms on the ground floor and, to relieve the gloom of the dark paneling, to fill the rooms with as many bowls and vases of fresh flowers as she can gather from the cutting garden behind the house.

And so, the house maintains its somewhat dated look and musty, waxy smell. A small, fading sign in the driveway with an arrow still points to the "Trade Entrance" in the rear, where the kitchen is located.

Now Clarissa and her husband are sitting in the library, where Clarissa has placed a bowl of fresh white tulips on the table between their chairs. Though it is May, and still light outside, the curtains to the library windows are drawn closed. Hobe does not think it is quite right for the students, who might be passing by, to look in and see the headmaster and his wife enjoying a cocktail. He sips his drink. "I think you've put just a tad too much vermouth in this, Cissie," he says.

"Then let me fix you another, kind sir!" she says, jumping to her feet and reaching for his glass.

"No, no," he says. "It's all right. It'll do."

"I try to put in just a whisper," she says. "Just pass the cork of the vermouth bottle over the gin."

"It's fine," Hobe says.

She seats herself again and reaches for her own glass. "À la tienne."

"À la tienne." It is the same little toast they have been giving each other for years.

"Well, darling, how was your day?" she asks him. It is the question with which Clarissa always starts off their cocktail hour, her favorite time of the day.

"Complicated," he says. "Mike Rubin came by to see me."

"Oh?" Her eyes flicker with interest. "How nice!" Michael Rubin is considered Crittenden's richest living alumnus, from the class of 1964.

"Nice? Well, it depends on how you look at it. As usual, he wants something. People like Rubin always do."

"What does he want?"

"He wants to go on the board of trustees."

"But of course, that's not something you can decide, darling, is it?"

"No, but Rubin knows it's where to start. He just wants it for the prestige, of course. Another feather in his cap, another notch in his belt. And of course, there's a condition attached. There always is with men like that."

"What's the condition?"

"He's offering to give the school ten million dollars."

She claps her hands. "Ten million! How fabulous, Hobe!"

"To build an arts center. To be called the Michael J. Rubin Center for the Arts. Naturally."

"How wonderful!"

He frowns. "There are a lot of things the school needs more than an arts center. We're planning to convert Van Degan Hall from a boys' dorm to a girls' dorm. It's going to cost nearly a million just to tear out the urinals. But of course, someone like Rubin wouldn't be interested in contributing for anything as prosaic as toilets."

"But he has a fantastic art collection."

"Yes, and that's another thing. He's offered to throw in a couple of Picassos as a part of his gift. And he offers to loan the school various pieces from his collection, on a sort of rotating basis, until the school builds up its own permanent collection."

"It sounds terribly generous to me."

Hobe is still frowning into his glass. "Yes, but he's going at it all backward. Usually, a donor makes a gift, and then waits to see if he'll be invited to join the board. But Rubin's saying that he won't make the gift unless he's put on the board *first*."

"Well, maybe that's why he's considered a brilliant businessman—all those mergers he negotiates on Wall Street."

"No board membership, no gift. Doesn't that smack a little bit of bribery?"

"I see what you mean. How will that strike the trustees?"

"Not very well, I should think. But of course, I have to pass this . . . this rather peculiar proposal along to the board."

"But wouldn't it be wonderful for the school to have its own arts center? I mean, what other secondary school in the country—"

"Yes, but then there's the problem with the name."

"Name? What name?"

"He insists that it be called the Michael J. Rubin Center for the Arts. Doesn't that sound—well, a bit out of character for our school?"

"You mean because it's—Jewish?"

"Now, Cissie, that's not fair. Don't forget that I'm the one who got rid of the quota system for Jewish students at Crittenden. I'm the one who got the school to take in more Blacks. I have nothing against Jews."

"Then what's the problem, Hobe?"

"Michael Rubin is known as a Wall Street wheeler-dealer. Do we want his name attached to one of our buildings? He somehow doesn't fit in with the Crittenden image. You see what I mean, I hope."

She sips her drink thoughtfully. "But if the school rebuffs his proposal—"

"Exactly. This Rubin is a tough customer. If he's turned down, he could threaten to cut off any further giving to the school."

"You really think he might do that, Hobe?"

"He might. That's a risk we're going to have to take."

47

"I'm sure the board will take that into consideration, too."

"Sure, they will."

"Perhaps some sort of—compromise?"

"This Rubin doesn't strike me as a compromising sort," he says. "Anyway, that's not my problem. That's the board's problem. All I have to do is present them with it—which is not something I'm particularly looking forward to."

"Ten million dollars," Clarissa says softly. "Would that be the largest gift the school has ever received?"

"From an individual, yes. Of course, he's probably got some sort of shifty tax dodge worked out for it. Those types always do."

They sit in silence for a moment, sipping their drinks. Clarissa is thinking: the school's trustees are scattered across the country. One is in Detroit, another in Cleveland. Two live in Los Angeles, one in San Diego, one in Dallas, one in Fort Lauderdale, and so on. They meet at Crittenden twice a year, in the spring and in the fall, and their next meeting will be at the end of the month. These meetings are usually disputations, and everything is put to a vote. The majority wins. The majority is smug, the minority is sore. Michael Rubin lives just down the pike, in a well-guarded apartment at the Hotel Pierre in Manhattan. His private telephone number is in the Crittenden School Alumni Directory. Clarissa sits forward in her chair.

"Do you think, Hobe," she says, "that it might be helpful if I called Mike? He and I have always gotten along well. Maybe I could persuade him to be a little more reasonable in his demands."

He shakes his head. "No, no. You stay out of it, Cissie. I'll handle it." They fall silent again.

Clarissa rises and moves to one of her pair of lamps that sit on the library table. With the tip of one finger, she whisks away a tiny cobweb that has spun itself across the top of the shade and adjusts it. "This shade will not stay straight," she says. "It's missing its finial, and so it keeps wobbling."

He sips his drink.

"I've spoken to Rose about it," she says. "She says she's filled out a requisition form and given it to Housekeeping. But that was weeks ago. What takes these things so long, I wonder?"

Her husband still says nothing.

"What it needs is a little egg-shaped crystal finial, like the ones on the other lamps in this room. I'd go out and buy one myself if I had any idea where to find one, but I don't. The finials should all match, don't you think?"

"Yes, I guess so."

"And I think the others are rather pretty, don't you?"

"Mm-hmm."

"Until we find one to match, we have that ugly little bare screw sticking up. And the lampshade won't stay straight. The slightest little breeze . . . Well, I'd just like to get everything in this house as shipshape as possible before the trustees descend upon us. They notice every little thing, particularly the women."

The trustees take a peculiarly proprietary interest in the Castle, Clarissa has noticed, and tend to regard it as though they own it, which, in a sense, they do, since it is school property. The slightest thing amiss will draw comment, and there is always the implication that she herself has somehow been lax in her stewardship of the place.

"Well, remind me in the morning to speak to Miss Stimpson about it," he says. Clarissa reaches for the silver cocktail shaker. "Here's your little dividend," she says, and fills his glass, then fills her own.

"So," he says, "how was your day?"

"Nothing out of the ordinary. I answered a few letters, paid bills, did birthday cards." All Crittenden alumni get birthday cards from the headmaster and his wife. "Oh, and Alexa Woodin from the *Times* came by to interview me."

His eyebrows go up. "From the *New York Times*?"

She laughs. "No, darling. The *Litchfield Times*. She's the women's page features editor. She's doing a story on our twenty-fifth anniversary with the school."

"You never mentioned this to me, Cissie!"

"Didn't I? I guess I forgot. It didn't seem that important."

"Why didn't she want to interview me?"

"She's doing this story from a woman's angle, Hobe."

"Well, I just hope that you insisted that she let you review any quotes before she runs her story."

"Actually, I didn't insist on that—no. I've read her column. She's a good writer."

"Dammit, Cissie, you've *always* got to insist on that! One always does. You know how these journalists are. They put words in people's mouths. They can make you look like a fool!"

"Don't worry. I trust Alexa."

"You *cannot* trust these people. You *cannot* trust this whoever-she-is. All these people are looking for is something sensational, something that will make headlines, something that will sell newspapers. She could take the most innocent little comment of yours and twist it around into something that could discredit the school! What sort of questions did she ask you?"

"We talked a bit about coeducation—its impact."

"Sex?"

"I mentioned that we'd had some problems—"

"Drugs?"

"I said we'd had some problems in that area, too. Which we have had."

His voice is rising. "Goddammit, Cissie! Don't you see what you may have done? I can see the headlines now: 'Sex, Drugs

Plague Crittenden School.' Is that the kind of publicity you want for my school?"

"Don't yell at me, Hobe."

"But, dammit, don't you know how journalists operate? Didn't it ever enter your stupid head to insist that you be allowed to check your quotes before publication? That should have been a *condition* before you granted the interview, before you even opened your trap to this woman. Now, of course, it's too late. You can't attach that condition now. They'll start screaming about the First Amendment and freedom of the press!"

"Please, Hobe—"

"I see I can't trust you out of my sight for a minute. I turn my back on you, and you go babbling on to some reporter about sex and drugs at my school. I'm really very angry about this, Clarissa!"

She presses her fingertips to her temples and says, "I'm sorry, Hobe. I feel one of my headaches coming on. I'm going upstairs. I don't feel like having dinner. Do you mind having dinner alone? Rose has fixed a nice chicken and noodle casserole, your favorite—"

"You and your damn headaches! I mentioned your headaches to Simon Jethro, and he says they're probably psychosomatic."

"Yes. I'm sure he's right. Excuse me." She stands up, her drink in her hand.

"That's right—run off to your room. All I said was that you should have insisted on your right to check the way you're being quoted."

She starts across the room. "I'm sorry," she says.

"And if this is a story about my twenty-five years as head-master here, I should have been present during the interview."

She pauses at the door. "But her story is about a headmaster's wife," she says. "After all, that's all I am, isn't it? A headmaster's wife?" Is there a sob in her voice when she says this? She leaves too quickly for her husband to say, carrying her half-filled glass.

"*Cissie!*" he calls after her. But there is no reply.

———

From Clarissa Spotswood's Journal:

I'm afraid I may have hurt Sally's feelings the other day. She was just back from a business trip to Bangkok, and she brought me back several yards of Thai silk. I took the fabric out of its tissue paper and spread it across my lap, and it was the most beautiful piece of silk I think I've ever seen—various shades of red, with tiny gold and silver threads running through. But that wasn't all I saw.

It was a kind of déjà vu. It wasn't identical, of course, but it was almost startlingly similar to the fabric in a dress I'd seen in Bergdorf's window years ago and dreamed of wearing to the Yale prom. Sally suggested a cocktail dress, but the dress on the skinny mannequin at Bergdorf's was a full-length evening gown. In front, it was slit open to the knee, and it had a flouncy ruffled train in back, the kind that would have to be lifted and carried over one arm if you were going to dance. With the train draped over an arm, that dress would show off quite a bit of leg. I went home that night and stood in front of my mirror, practicing how I would toss that saucy little train first over my left arm, then over my right, wishing I was as skinny as that pencil-thin wax model in Bergdorf's window. I'd fallen in love with that dress. It was designed by Elsa Schiaparelli.

I was sure the dress was very expensive, and that there was very little chance that my mother, a clergyman's wife, would offer to buy it for me for the prom. But I took her past Bergdorf's to show it to her in the window anyway.

Mother never really trusted Bergdorf Goodman. She felt it was a store for kept women. I think she felt this way because she had once seen a disproportionate number of businessmen shopping at the lingerie counter. And when I pointed out the dress she said, "Oh, but that's much, *much* too old a style for you, dear. You'll have plenty of time to wear a dress like that— puh-*lenty* of time. Besides, reds and purples aren't a young girl's colors. They're a harlot's colors!"

But the dress didn't seem that hoydenish to me. It seemed to me that Schiaparelli had designed that dress knowing what every girl dreams of being: infinitely desirable and infinitely unattainable. That dress whispered Grace Kelly. In it, I would become Audrey Hepburn.

In the end, Mother altered one of her old gowns from her own debutante days for me to wear to the Yale prom. It was a beigey yellow, with thin spaghetti straps, and the bodice was sewn with hundreds and hundreds of tiny seed pearls. There was a matching pair of opera-length gloves. She let me buy new shoes to match.

I don't remember who the boy was who'd invited me to the Yale dance. He was nobody I particularly cared about. In those days, it didn't matter who asked you to that party. The important thing was just to be asked! And I don't remember the name of the boy I was dancing with, but I remember the room was warm, and I was perspiring—perspiring out of nervousness, probably, as much as from the heat, and he was perspiring, too, in his dinner jacket. I remember, though, that Lester Lanin's band was playing "I Get a Kick Out of You," a fairly lively number, but we were dancing pretty close, and I could feel him getting an erection, and that tickled me no end. Funny how selective memory is. And all those memories came flooding back as I stared down at that fabric in my lap.

When the music ended, the boy led me back to my seat, his arm around my waist. I thanked him for the dance, and he released me, and then looked down at his right hand. His poor, damp young palm was literally covered with seed pearls, like white candy sprinkles on a pink cupcake. The threads that held the pearls had obviously weakened over the years. He gasped. "Look what I've done to your dress!" he said, and then he laughed, he was so embarrassed.

"It doesn't matter," I said. "It's an old dress." And I remember fervently praying that I'd never set eyes on this boy again. And I never did.

"Reds and purples are a harlot's colors," my mother had said. "Well-brought-up young ladies don't wear colors like that, certainly not at your age. You don't want to be mistaken for a hussy, dear." But what she couldn't have understood, and what I never could have explained to her, was that I wanted to be a hussy that night at the Yale prom. I wanted to be a harlot, and a hoyden, and that other word that sounds as though it begins with "h," but actually begins with "w." A well-turned-out whore doesn't go to a party in hand-me-downs. She wants to be—iridescent!

THREE

Now it is the afternoon of the annual faculty women's tea. Throughout the school year, Clarissa must preside as hostess at the Castle for over nine regular functions. The two most important, of course, are the two trustees' dinners, one in the spring and one in the fall, which precede the trustees' meetings, and where everyone pretends that the needs of the Crittenden School have been well served by the deliberations of these high-minded and well-placed men and women. Then there are a pair of faculty cocktail parties, one just before the opening of school in September, and another just after the students depart in early June. The faculty women's tea takes place in early May, when the dogwoods are in bloom, and is the only all-female event of the year. Then, spaced throughout the winter months, there are four more teas for the students, one for each class. This schedule has been more or less kept since the school's founding, except for the Prohibition years, when the cocktail parties were also called teas, though plenty of hip flasks were always in evidence.

In addition to these traditional gatherings, the headmaster and his wife are also expected to host small dinners, for six or eight in the family dining room, for faculty members, visiting alumni, parents, townspeople, or other friends of the school.

In the Castle's kitchen, Rose Finney is busily arranging ladyfingers, deviled eggs, and little tea sandwiches on silver trays. Rose's specialty is her teeny-weeny bite-size hamburgers. Today, she has made a hundred and thirty of these. It doesn't matter how many she makes. They'll all be gobbled up first thing.

The faculty women's tea is not Rose's favorite event of the year, and she is not in a good mood. She can remember when this was called the faculty wives' tea, and that was quite a different sort of affair. That was when the faculty was composed entirely of gentlemen, and their wives, for the most part, were *ladies*. Now it is all a hodgepodge. Now there are single faculty women and single faculty men, and there is a lot of sleeping around. Everybody knows it. There are wives of faculty husbands and husbands of faculty wives, and there is a lot of sleeping around in this group, too—wives with the husbands of other wives, and husbands with the wives of other husbands, and God knows what all. To Rose, it is a disgrace, and she dislikes the thought of her famous bite-size burgers going down the gullets of this pack of adulterers. What kind of an example do they think they're setting for the students at this so-called elite school? Not much, Rose thinks.

Not that the students are all that elite nowadays, she might add. When the school was only boys, you got boys who'd been brought up by governesses and nannies, and they'd been taught their manners. Not that they didn't know how to raise all particular hell, but at least they knew how to say they were sorry for what they'd done. The boys even used to *cry*. Now, with girls around, they won't cry. They just strut and swagger and stick their chins out. And the girls aren't much better. Why, there's one girl in particular—Rose won't mention her name— who's supposed to come from this fine old family. This family even has a dormitory named after it! But this girl's no better than she should be. She's worse, in fact. Rose has heard that this girl's problem is that she's a nymphomaniac. That makes it sound as though she has some sort of disease. Well, to Rose Finney's way of thinking, nymphomaniac is just a twenty-five-cent word for slut.

Boys have been seen sneaking in and out of this girl's dormitory room at all hours of the night. And not just boys. Some say that some of the male teachers, both the married and unmarried kind, have been seen doing the same thing. Of course, Rose knows none of this firsthand. But it's been the talk of Buhl Hall. Buhl Hall is the building at the east end of campus where some unmarried members of the school's housekeeping and groundskeeping staff have their quarters, along with dormitory rooms for students, and, if you were to ask Rose, the people in Buhl Hall have a better idea of what goes on at this school than anybody else, including the headmaster. The housekeeping people, who change the linen and the towels once a week, and who clean the classrooms and the labs and offices after hours, have their eyes open. And the groundskeepers, who do things like clip the hedges and trim the ivy around the windows—they're not blind or deaf, either. They see things and hear things, too.

Mr. S, as Rose calls him, is the third headmaster Rose has kept house for in the Castle and, in Rose's humble opinion, he is by far the best of the lot. The other two weren't worth a damn, in Rose's opinion, and had no idea how to deal with adolescent boys, which was all the school had in those days. Which was why those two didn't last long. And their wives were no help. Why, the wife of one of them was so snobby and la-di-da that she hardly spent any time at the school at all. Only came up to Crittenden when she absolutely had to. Spent most of her time gallivanting around New York City with her rich and social friends and getting her name in the society columns. And when she did appear, all she did was complain—about the food, about the house, about her lumpy mattress, even about the weather. Rose was more than happy to say good riddance to her.

The good thing about Mr. S is that he's always *fair*. He's just about the fairest man Rose has ever known or worked for. When something goes wrong, he doesn't try to blame it on somebody else. He takes the blame himself. Just to take one instance, there was the time that Rose was serving lunch for the headmaster and his wife and another couple—parents of a prospective student, Rose thinks they were. The headmaster was talking to the other lady, and Rose was serving the soup course, and just as Rose was to set down the soup bowl in front of the lady, Mr. S made a gesture with his hands and knocked the bowl out of Rose's hand. The soup spilled all over the front of the lady's dress, and the cup and saucer landed in her lap. Thank goodness it was a cold soup! Mr. S jumped to his feet and grabbed his napkin. "That was my fault," he said. "My mother used to tell me not to talk with my hands!" The poor lady's dress was a mess, and Mr. S began mopping her up with his napkin.

A smaller sort of person might have tried to blame the house-keeper, saying she was serving the soup from the wrong side. Rose knows which side to serve from—from the left, always.

Then, to take just one other instance, there was the time a couple of years ago when a boy and a girl disappeared from campus altogether. A police alarm was sent out through the tristate area! It turned out that the boy had gotten the girl pregnant, and he'd arranged for her to have an abortion down in the city, arranged to pay for it and everything. And he'd gone down to New York with her, to be with her while it was done.

Leaving campus without permission is an offense punishable by expulsion. The girl's parents withdrew her from the school voluntarily, but a special faculty meeting was called for what to do about the boy. A vote was taken. The faculty voted for expulsion. But the headmaster has a veto power in these matters, and he used it then. He argued that, after all, the boy was doing the right thing, the gentlemanly thing, by staying with the girl while she went through her ordeal, since he knew that he was the one responsible for getting her in a family way. Instead of expulsion, he got two weeks' probation, which meant he had to miss playing in an important soccer game with Choate. That was fair, Rose thinks.

Yes, it is Mr. S's sense of fairness that has kept him in this job so long.

And, no, the students do not exactly love Mr. S, whom they call Spots or Spotty. And, to Rose's way of thinking, this is the way it should be. A good headmaster should not be a lovable Mr. Chips type. Instead, a headmaster should have the students' *respect*. They should respect the man, and even be a little bit afraid of him. After all, he is sort of their substitute father during these teenage years, when they've been sent away from home to boarding school. And Mr. S disciplines these youngsters just the way a parent would, the way Rose's own father did when she was growing up.

And, as for Mrs. S, she is as close to perfect as a headmaster's wife could be, in Rose's opinion, always the perfect lady. It is not an easy job to be a headmaster's wife, or at least a *good* headmaster's wife—Rose knows that. A headmaster's wife is required to do a lot of boring things—hostessing this faculty women's tea, for instance. But Mrs. S tackles them all with a smile. A lot of these faculty women do not like each other much. There's a lot of jealousy here, mostly over how much who gets paid. And Rose is sure there are a lot of women in that group whom Mrs. S doesn't like, either, but she's always nice to all of them, treats them all alike. If Rose has one complaint about Mrs. S, it's that she doesn't eat enough. Lately, she hasn't had much appetite. She'll put her fork down in the middle of a meal, leaving her plate half full. She's getting too thin, in Rose's opinion, but that's her only complaint. Rose would like to fatten her up.

Rose puts the finishing touches on her trays, tucking a wedge of lemon here, a sprig of cilantro there. She glances up at the kitchen clock. It is nearly four o'clock, and she can hear the first guests beginning to arrive. It is time for her to set her trays of goodies out on the buffet table, to feed this bunch of bickering biddies. *No, make that bitches*, Rose thinks. She removes her kitchen apron, hangs it on a hook on the back of the pantry door, and smooths the front of her black uniform.

These teas are not the formal affairs they once were. That is, Clarissa does not pour. Instead, the food is set out on a long table in the reception room, buffet-style, and the guests help themselves. On a separate table are urns of coffee, regular and decaf, and tea, along with pitchers of iced tea and lemonade, cups, saucers, and glasses, and guests serve themselves this as well, while Clarissa is free to move about the room, mingling, trying to have a few words with each guest.

On the other hand, for her four annual teas for the student classes, Clarissa does believe in doing things the more formal, old-fashioned way—with the hostess seated in a chair, a tea table in front of her with the full gleaming silver tea service, teacups, and napkins, asking, "Cream or lemon? One lump or two?"

Clarissa knows that formal teas may seem a bit anachronistic. Lord knows, many of these young hoodlums may never be confronted with a tea table and service again in their lives. But Clarissa feels that it is important that Crittenden students at least be *exposed* to this sort of thing. It is the sort of ceremony, with its tradition and accompanying integrity, that should not be altogether lost to today's young people. They should know it exists. Naturally, for their class teas with the headmaster's wife at the Castle, the students are expected to put on their best bib and tucker. And Clarissa has noticed, when the students' appearance improves, so do their manners.

But, today, it is all very casual. Several women are in pants and sweater sets. One young French teacher is wearing jeans.

As she moves about the room, picking up empty plates, cups, and glasses, Rose Finney listens to the scattered conversations.

"Ooh, these yummy little burger things!" she hears one woman say. Rose decides she likes that woman, whoever it was who said it. She checks her tray of burgers. It is already two-thirds empty. She checks the coffee urns.

"And so, I said to him, 'Abdication is spelled *a*, *b*, *d*, and not *a*, *d*, *d*, like addition or addiction.' And he said, 'That is a *b*,' and I said, 'A *b* has a bulge to the right, and a *d* has a bulge to the left. You're bulging in the wrong direction.' 'But couldn't you indulge me a little?' he said. And I thought that was pretty clever, so I raised his grade two points, and passed him." This is Mrs. Smithfield speaking, who teaches American history. There is light laughter at this story.

In another part of the room, someone else is saying, "And so I told him, 'Well, if you waited all week to get drunk, you sure did a good job!'"

Rose is surprised to see Ms. Anne-Marie Chabot (French, all levels) chatting pleasantly with Mrs. Adelaide Schlachter from the Chemistry Department. It's surprising to see them on such friendly terms because Ms. Chabot is supposedly having an affair with Mrs. Schlachter's husband. At least this is what the Buhl Hall people say. The Buhl Hall people also clean faculty residences, and so they ought to know. Ms. Chabot (who pronounces her name *Shab*-oh) likes to be called *Mademoiselle* Chabot. Mrs. Schlachter's husband doesn't seem to do much of anything, just sits around the house all day. He's supposed to be a poet. Have you ever heard of a poet named Winston Schlachter? Rose never has.

Mr. and Mrs. Leonard Marek are new to the school this semester. Mr. Marek teaches Freshman English. This is obviously Mrs. Marek's first time inside the Castle, and she has been poking her nose into some of the other rooms, which is really against the rules. Now Mrs. Marek is speaking to Clarissa. "That portrait of the man in military uniform over the mantel in the library . . ." she says. "Is that one of the founders of the school?"

Clarissa laughs. "No, that's an ancestor of my husband's," she says. "He fought in the Revolution under George Washington. My husband's family is much more illustrious than mine, I'm afraid."

"And those pictures in the silver frames on the piano?"

"Those are our two children, John and Sally."

"Any grandchildren?"

"Not yet I'm sorry to say. Neither of them is married yet."

Smiling, Clarissa moves on to another group.

"They're calling it a gang rape," Mrs. Schlachter is saying to Mlle Chabot. "But from what I've heard, it sounds more like what we used to call a good old-fashioned swingers party!"

"What on *earth* are you two talking about?" Clarissa asks them.

"Why, about what happened in Colby Hall last Saturday night, of course!"

"Well, what *did* happen in Colby Hall?"

"You mean you haven't heard about it?"

"No, I haven't."

"A group of boys—some say as many as fifteen of them—were lined up outside a girl's room, taking turns having sex with her—that's what happened," Mrs. Schlachter says.

"Does my husband know about this?"

"Oh, I'm sure he does," Mrs. Schlachter says. "Everybody on campus is talking about it."

"Everybody?" Clarissa says. "Who is everybody?"

"Well, I mean—just everybody. First, the boys were all whispering about it among themselves, though no one will admit having taken part in it. Then the girls began talking about it because, supposedly, some of the girls were there in the dorm while it was all happening and knew what was going on."

"Who was the girl?" Clarissa asks.

"Well, of course that's part of the problem," Mrs. Schlachter says. "They say—well, what everybody's saying is that the girl was Linda Van Degan."

Clarissa laughs sharply. "The most unattractive girl in the school! She must weigh two hundred and fifty pounds!"

"But isn't that always the case? The fat, unattractive girl has only one way to get attention—sex. And of course, Linda Van Degan's father is on the board, which makes it a sticky wicket for the school, doesn't it?"

Mlle Chabot reaches out and touches Clarissa's arm. "Poor Clarissa," she says. "You look so shocked. But I suppose, when something like this happens at the school, you're the last one to hear about it!"

Clarissa's smile remains frozen on her face. "But what you're telling me is all hearsay, isn't it? It's nothing but rumor, nothing but gossip. You say, 'they say' the girl was Linda Van Degan. You say that supposedly other girls witnessed this. But nobody's admitted anything, nothing's been proven. Am I correct?"

"Well, you know what they say—where there's smoke there's fire."

"I don't agree with that at all. As often as not there's nothing but smoke. It seems to me that there's entirely too much of this malicious sort of gossip at Crittenden. There are too many nasty rumors circulating around this place. That's what shocks me—that people like you keep this sort of talk in circulation."

"But everybody says the girl's a nymphomaniac."

"There you go again—'everybody says.' Why, if I believed every ugly rumor I've heard, I'd think this school was a cesspool of vice!" She turns to Mlle Chabot. "For instance, Anne-Marie, I've heard it said that you and Win Schlachter are having a hot and heavy love affair. Neither of you women would like me to believe that nasty piece of gossip, would you?" She turns quickly away from them.

Bravo! thinks Rose Finney from the sidelines, over by the coffee urns. *Good for you, Mrs. S. That's tellin' 'em, the bitches!*

But of course, Rose has also heard the story about Linda Van Degan and Saturday night at Colby Hall.

Now she hears Clarissa say, "Darling! What a surprise! Why didn't you tell me you were coming?" Young John Spotswood, carrying an overnight case, has just walked into the room.

He looks around the room. "I can tell I've picked a bad time, Mom," he says.

She kisses him on the cheek. "It's a wonderful time, darling!" she says. "But I do have forty-five ladies here for tea. Why don't you run up to your room? This will all be over by six o'clock, and I'll be straight upstairs to see you."

And that's another thing about Mrs. S, Rose thinks. With all the things she's had to do as the headmaster's wife, she's also managed to raise two wonderful kids. Rose has known Mr. John since he was a little boy and Miss Sally since she was a newborn baby. Two nicer, more well-behaved, or better-looking kids a mother couldn't ask for!

She continues picking up empty cups and glasses.

* * *

Now Clarissa is sitting on the corner of her son's bed in his old room. "I'm so happy to see you, Johnny," she says. "I'm sorry about the damned tea party."

"I should've phoned you first, but it was a nice day, I was having a slow afternoon, and I thought, hell, why don't I drive up and see you guys?"

"Can you spend the weekend?"

"I really ought to get back to the city tomorrow afternoon."

"Well, at least we can have a nice evening together. Your father will be so pleased to see you."

"By the way," he says. "Your private line was ringing when I came upstairs, so I took the call. It was a Mr. Rubin. He wants you to call him."

She quickly touches the double strand of pearls at her throat. "Rubin?"

"Michael Rubin. What's wrong, Mom?"

"Nothing—but are you sure he wants to talk to me? Are you sure he wasn't calling for your father?"

"He asked for you, Mom." John studies her face. "Mom, are you sure you're all right?"

"Of course! I'm fine. It's just that I can't imagine why Michael Rubin would be calling *me*."

"Anyway, here's his number." He hands her a slip of paper. "Say, that's not *the* Michael Rubin, is it—the zillionaire?"

"Yes. In fact, it is."

"He went to school here, didn't he?"

"Yes. The class of 1964."

"You know, Mom, you're really amazing. You remember the names of all these kids—even the years they graduated. And 1964—that was before you and Dad even came to the school!"

She laughs nervously. "Well, that's part of my job," she says. "And don't forget I worked as your father's secretary for a while. And that particular *kid* is about my age by now."

He is still studying her intently. "Something's upset you, Mom," he says. "I can tell. What is it?"

"No, no. It's just that—nothing. It's just that I wasn't expecting a call from Michael Rubin. After all . . ." Her voice trails off.

They sit in silence for a moment. "You've lost weight, Mom," he says as last.

"Yes! Thank you. Thank you for noticing! I was eating far too many of Rose's rich desserts."

"Don't lose too much too fast, Mom."

"I'm at my perfect weight right now. Just about the weight I was in college." She glances at her wristwatch. "We'd better go downstairs," she says. "It's just six o'clock, and your father will be home and ready for his martini."

"Am I okay like this?" He gestures to his polo shirt and jeans.

"You're perfect. It'll be just the three of us for dinner. I told Rose to tell your father that we'd be having a mystery guest, so we'll surprise him."

They both stand up and move toward the door. With one hand on the doorknob, Clarissa reaches out and touches her son's arm. "Just do me one favor, darling," she says. "Don't mention to your father that Mr. Rubin called me. Okay? Primrose promise, as we used to say when you were children?"

"Primrose promise."

FOUR

The Old Forge Inn in the nearby town of James Falls is where the parents of Crittenden students prefer to stay when they come up to visit sons and daughters. It is a fairly typical New England inn, with lots of chintz and maple furniture, four-poster beds and braided throw rugs in the bedrooms. But it only has fourteen guest rooms, and so these rooms are always at a premium during the school year. Also, since the Old Forge offers the only decent lodging in the area—a Holiday Inn in Great Barrington is half an hour away—it charges exorbitant prices: $350 a night for a double room on weeknights, and twenty percent more on weekends.

Its candlelit dining room is cozy, with a big, old-fashioned fireplace decked out with many copper pots and cast-iron skillets, and the serving plates are pewter. Its menu offers what is called "American home cooking," which means your best bet would be roast chicken in giblet gravy, mashed potatoes, and green beans. That entree will run you twenty-six dollars.

It was here that Clarissa and Hobe had been put up in June 1974, for their first "official" visit to the Crittenden School. Little Johnny had been left behind to stay with Clarissa's mother in New York. Up to then, Hobe had been teaching math at Elder, a rather obscure boys' school outside Baltimore, but he had been tapped by Crittenden's Search Committee and became one of a field of six candidates for the school's new headmastership. He now faced a rather grueling gamut of evaluations with the trustees, a one-hour interview with each, and there were seventeen trustees in all. One day, Hobe would come back to the inn optimistic that the day's interviews had gone well. But the next, he would return to his wife discouraged because the conversations had gone less than well. It was a tense week for them both, to say the least.

Hobe's daily schedule of meetings had left Clarissa with very little to do during the day, besides worrying about how her husband's meetings were going. She had been offered a guest membership at the local country club, but she was not a golfer. She had, however, packed quite a few paperback books and planned to do a lot of reading. In the evenings, of course, there were a series of small dinners at the inn with various trustees and their wives, which Hobe and Clarissa were expected to attend together. She knew that she was being scrutinized as carefully as he was, and she had packed very carefully for this trip—with Hobe hovering over her shoulder as she laid out each outfit across the bed for his inspection.

And so that was how she happened to be sitting alone in the chintz-covered lobby of the Old Forge Inn that June day in 1974. She had been reading a new paperback by Kurt Vonnegut Jr. called *Breakfast of Champions* but was finding it rather heavy going and was thinking of going into the dining room for lunch. In fact, she had just turned down the corner of a page to mark her place when the most extraordinary-looking young man she had ever seen walked into the room, his hands thrust deep into the pockets of his chino pants. "You somebody's sister?" he asked her.

She put down her book. "Well, I do have a sister, if that's what you mean," she said.

He was tall and dark, with wet-looking black hair and what appeared to be double eyelashes. His looks reminded her of the young Tyrone Power in one of his wartime movies. He flopped down in one of the chairs opposite her and tossed one long leg over its arm. "You're pretty," he said.

Her impulse was to say, *And so are you*. But instead, her response was a prim, "Thank you."

"I meant were you a sister of one of the kids at school," he said.

"No," she said. "My husband is visiting the school for a series of job interviews." She tried to place a certain emphasis on the word *husband*.

He appeared not to notice and, instead, yawned loudly. Then he said, in a tone that was almost belligerent, "I'm a Jew. You got any problem with that?"

"Why, no," she said coolly. "I have a lot of Jewish friends."

"Sure. They all do. Their doctor. Their lawyer. Their dentist. Their stockbroker. The guy who does their taxes. What's your name?"

She hesitated. This young man seemed to be moving awfully fast. She glanced across the room and was reassured to see that the two of them were not alone. Behind the front desk, the female receptionist was reading a copy of *Cosmopolitan*. "Clarissa Spotswood," she said at last.

"Oh, wow!" he said. "What a name! That's a WASP name if I ever heard one. It's almost like you fuckin' made it up!"

She smiled a thin smile. "Do you live around here?" she asked him.

"Shit, no. New York. I came up here for my class's fuckin' tenth reunion."

She started to pick up her book again and terminate this conversation. But there was one rule of boarding schools that Hobe had drummed into her from the beginning: Always be nice to the alumni. So she kept her face frozen in the same thin smile.

"You don't believe I'm a Crittenden grad, do you?" he said. "Well, here's the fuckin' beanie they gave us all to wear." He reached in his trousers pocket and pulled out a crumpled red duckbill cap, with "C '64" emblazoned on it in white. He clapped it on his head. Then he crossed his eyes and stuck out his tongue. "Pretty fuckin' stupid, huh?"

She repressed a laugh. "Yes," she said, "but mostly I'm curious—do all Crittenden boys use language like yours?"

"Fuck, no! But I like to say it like it fuckin' is. You got a problem with that?"

"No," she said coolly, "I really have no problems with anything."

"Oh, I know what you mean," he said. "Us Crittenden boys're supposed to represent the *finest* fuckin' families in America. Shit, baby, we got Mellons here. We got Rockefellers. We got fuckin' *du Pants*. We're all veddy la-de-da. Well, I'll tell you something. They're all a bunch of assholes. Faggots. Cocksuckers."

She looked at him steadily. "If you're trying to shock me with this sort of talk, you're not succeeding," she said.

He grinned at her, showing remarkably white and even teeth. "I know," he said. "A lot of classy-looking broads like you like to listen to dirty talk."

"That's not the case, either," she said. "This particular broad is not impressed one way or another."

"Hey!" he said. "I like you. You can give as good as you take, can't you?" He leaned forward, his hands on his knees. "Well, let me tell you something else, baby," he said. "It's because I tell it like it fuckin' is is why I'm a fuckin' *success*. And all those other shitheads and assholes in my class are trying to sell life insurance. Or sitting on their rich, fat asses clipping coupons. Well, fuck 'em all, I say. Because now I'm *rich*—richer than all those motherfuckers put together!"

Why was she beginning to enjoy all this? It wasn't just the dirty talk. But there was something about his outrageousness that was just too outrageous to be believed. She was watching some sort of bravura stage performance—but for what reason? She decided to have some fun with him. "I'm sure I should know who you are," she said. "But I haven't a clue."

He winked at her. "That's because I haven't told you," he said. "If I told you, you'd shit."

"Would I, *really*? I noticed a tent set up in the school quadrangle for the class of 1964. It's none of my business, but isn't that where you should be right now? In the tent with your class? Showing off for them—not me?"

"Yeah, that's where I fuckin' *should* be. But that's where I'm fuckin' *not*. Let 'em wonder where I am, I say. They'll be having lunch right now—getting drunk and eating cold chicken from the Colonel. They'll be saying, 'Where is he? Where's our star?' Because that's what I turned out to be—the star of the class of 1964. Dots-a me, baby. Not two years out of Yale, and my picture's in the *New York Times*. Front page, business section. Above the fold. You know what the *New York Times* called me? 'The new wunderkind of Wall Street,' that's what the *New York Times* called me. You know what wunderkind means? It means 'miracle prodigy.' I looked it up."

"You'd think you'd have run across that word at Yale."

"I'm the miracle prodigy of the class of 1964. Now they all want to rub shoulders with me—maybe some of the miracle shit will rub off on them. Well, fuck 'em. Fuck 'em all. They didn't treat me that way when I was back in that school, baby. Boy, I hated that fuckin' school. Four years, and I hated every fuckin' minute of it, and I hated them also—the stuck-up snobs!"

"But I'm confused," she said. "If you hated the school and your classmates so much, why did you come back to this reunion?"

"Why? So I could rub the little fuckers' noses in the kind of shit they handed me! Know what they called me? I was the Jew-boy. I was the yid. I was the Hebe; I was the kike. I was Kikey-Mikey—Mike the Kike. Eighty guys in our class, and eight of us were Jews. Exactly eight. You don't need to be a rocket scientist to figure that one out, do you? That was the quota for us Jew-boys—ten percent. You know how it goes. 'Can't have too many Jew-boys in a school like Crittenden. We got to set a limit. You let one in, and they'll want to bring in all their friends and relatives. But don't call us prejudiced! Don't call us Jew-baiters. Just don't let in too many of the sheeny bastards.' Well, I say all the sons of bitches are fuckheads, assholes, shitheads, asswipes, motherfuckers, and cocksuckers. But now, I'm rich and famous! Back then, I was 'Rubin the Jew-bin.'"

"So, is that your name? Mike Rubin?"

"Dots-a me," he said. "Dots-a me."

"Forgive me," she said, "but would it upset you if I said I've never heard of you? I'm failing, as you'd put it, to shit now that I know your name."

"That's because you don't read the *Wall Street Journal. Business Week. Manhattan, Inc.*—profile of me last week."

"I'll plead guilty to that," she said.

He swung his right leg off the arm of the chair and planted both feet on the floor. He twisted his duckbill backward on his head so that the bill hung over the back of his neck, and a lock of black, wet-looking hair fell across his forehead. He eyed her carefully. "You really are pretty, Lucinda," he said.

"Clarissa. My mother had just read *Mrs. Dalloway*."

"Clarissa. I've got a room upstairs. Want to fuck?"

She stood up quickly, her book in her hand, her finger marking her place. The book would be good to swat him with. "Excuse me," she said. "I've got to go."

"You got a problem with that?" he said. "You look eminently fuckable to me. Noticed that the minute I walked in here."

"I'm bored with this nonsense," she said. "Goodbye." She turned and moved quickly toward the dining room, without looking back, leaving him sitting there.

Bugger off, asshole, she thought. She really should have slapped that shockingly handsome face with her paperback. And yet she hadn't. He probably wouldn't have even reacted if she had, the insolent, foulmouthed, arrogant, conceited young roughneck!

And yet, even as the hostess seated her at a small table in the far corner of the room, why had she experienced a small, guilty shudder of regret for having left him there? She had lied to him. She hadn't actually been bored. And, after all, she had nothing else to do that afternoon.

That evening, when Hobe returned to their room at the Old Forge Inn, Clarissa was lying on top of the quilted bedspread of one of the twin four-posters, still struggling with the Vonnegut. Young people were said to adore this author. Clarissa, at thirty-two, was hardly old, but why couldn't she get with this book? There was not even much sex in it. She laid the book aside. "Well," she asked, "how'd it go?"

"Better than yesterday, I think. Today, they seemed mostly interested in whether we had any pets."

"Did you mention Missy?"

"No, I didn't mention Missy." Missy was their Siamese.

"If you get the job, would we have to give up Missy?"

"I really don't know. I don't know if there's any school *policy* on pets. But just to be on the safe side, I said we didn't have any." He sighed. "Two more days of this," he said.

"And even then, you won't know for sure, will you?"

"It could be months. They still have two more candidates to put through this inquisition. I did learn one thing, though."

"What was that?"

"If I'm chosen, I'll be the youngest headmaster in Crittenden's history. What do you think of that?"

"Well, I suppose one way to think of it is that if you're *not* chosen, your age could have been a deciding factor—youthful inexperience, that sort of thing. After all, there's nothing you can do about your age."

"No, but I'd like to be the youngest."

"Of course you would!"

He started loosening his necktie. "Well, I guess it's time to get dressed for dinner," he said. "Tonight, it's the Tuttles and the Morses. It's Burton and Suzanne Tuttle, and Jim and Elsie Morse. Can you remember that?"

"Of course."

"Elsie Morse is a Vanderbilt. She's the one with the money."

From the bed she looked up at him as he unbuttoned his shirt. "Darling, do we have time . . ." she began.

"Time for what?"

She turned her face slightly toward the wall. "It seems like the longest time since we've made love," she said.

But he hadn't seemed to hear her. "Tonight, I think your blue ballerina, don't you?" he said.

The next morning, she had decided to take the car and drive north up Route 7 into Massachusetts, looking at antiques. This stretch of highway was sometimes called Antique Alley and was virtually lined with antique and secondhand shops on both sides of the road. She had spent the morning poking through shops and old barns, but she hadn't seen anything she particularly wanted, or that seemed to her particularly good. Now it was noon, and she was returning to the inn empty-handed. She pulled into the lot, parked, turned off the ignition, and was about to step out of the car when she saw him striding toward her.

Her first impulse was to stay in the car, slam the door, push down all the lock buttons, and raise the window. But then she decided that she had nothing to fear from this smart-ass. She stepped out of the car, closed the door, and stood there facing him. He was grinning.

"I shocked you yesterday, didn't I?" he said.

"No, as a matter of fact, you didn't," she said. "I just began to find your line of chatter boring."

"I don't always talk like that," he said. "But I got your attention, didn't I?"

"I suppose so. In a rather obvious way."

"I have two rules for success," he said. "The first rule is—just being there, in the right place at the right time. The second rule is getting them to notice you. It doesn't matter how you do it. Just as long as you grab their attention right away. I'm thinking of writing a book about it."

"Well, good luck," she said.

"So, you see, yesterday I was just putting my rule number two into practice. And it worked. It always does. You sat up and took notice. I made an impression. So, you see, you may not like me, Clarissa. But at least you'll never forget me—right?" He turned away from her, heading for the inn, taking the same long strides.

She held up her hand. "Wait!" she said.

* * *

And now Clarissa and her husband and their son, John, are having dinner in the family dining room at the Castle. Rose Finney is serving the asparagus. "And so, Pop," John is saying, "how're you doing after another school year dealing with adolescent truculence and rebelliousness?"

"Pretty much the same old seven and six, Johnny," his father says, securing three asparagus spears with the silver tongs. "Nothing much changes from year to year around here. Does it, Rose?"

"No, Mr. S," Rose says.

"Of course, I don't remember that I was ever truculent or rebellious at that age," John says. "It seems to me that I was always a pretty angelic kid."

"Angelic?" his mother says. "I wouldn't quite use that word, Johnny. What about the wallpaper incident? And what about your famous catsup caper?"

"Um," he says between mouthfuls. "Well, maybe I did act up a couple of times." He doesn't exactly remember the thing about the wallpaper, though he remembers it had something to do with crayons. But he does remember the catsup caper. He was twelve or thirteen, and his uncle Arthur Barnes had given him a toy cap pistol for his birthday. It was a stupid gift. He was much too old to play with cap pistols. But Uncle Art had no children and had no idea what kind of a gift a boy that age would want. And it was a very realistic-looking little weapon, the exact size and shape of a Colt .38, and so John had decided to have a little fun with it.

His mother had gone out on a short errand, and, in the kitchen, he had found a catsup bottle and rather lavishly slathered catsup across the front of his white shirt. Then he went out to the front hall, lay down on his back across the front stairs, the pistol in his right hand, and closed his eyes—he'd be the first thing she would see when she came through the front door.

He will never forget her scream when she saw him lying there. She dropped her bag of groceries on the floor and went running to him, flinging herself on her knees on the stairs, gathering him into her arms and sobbing, "Johnny! *Johnny!*" Then he giggled, opened his eyes, and winked at her. "Hi, Mom!"

He had never seen his mother so enraged before. She jumped to her feet and slapped him hard across the face, something she had never done before. "Oh, you are wretched, *wretched* child!" she had screamed at him. "You are horrid, wretched, evil little child! Get up to your room and clean yourself up! And don't come down for dinner! Don't come down until I say you can!"

"I guess it wasn't really very funny," he says now with a sheepish grin.

"It most certainly was not!" his mother says.

"What bugged me was how angry you were to find I wasn't dead," he says.

"No comment," she says. She turns to her husband. "By the way, Hobe," she says, "I heard a rather disturbing piece of gossip this afternoon. Something about Colby Hall on last Saturday night."

Her husband frowns and puts down his fork. "Who told you this?"

"Adelaide Schlachter and Anne-Marie were talking about it at the women's tea. I'm afraid I rather lost my temper with those two."

"So now it's gotten to the faculty," he says. "Did it involve the Van Degan girl?"

"Yes."

John Spotswood's eyebrows go up.

"Sex?" he says.

Hobe says, "I can assure you there's not a word of truth in any of it, Cissie."

"*Sex?*" John says again.

"How do these horrible rumors get started, Hobe?"

"I'll tell you exactly how. To begin with, the Van Degan girl is not exactly the most popular girl on campus."

"No, I wouldn't imagine she would be."

"Partly, it's all her family's money. She can be a little—"

"Snooty?"

"Yes."

"And then her looks."

"That's part of it, too."

"For God's sake," John protests. "You two are talking right over my head. Aren't you going to tell me what the ugly rumor *is*? Come on—the suspense is killing me!"

But his parents ignore him. "Anyway, there's this little clique that's developed over at Colby Hall. It's a very *cliquey* little clique of girls. They call themselves the Colby Club—just five or six juniors who've taken to hanging out together. Valerie Winston and Cecily Smith are the leaders of it—you see, I've looked into the whole thing very carefully, Cissie. This clique has decided to make Linda Van Degan their personal scapegoat, their whipping boy. They've made up this story of Saturday night out of whole cloth just to throw Linda Van Degan into a worse light than she's in already."

"Dad! Come *on!*"

"I understand that there are some boys who are now hinting that they took part in it—just dropping little sly hints, of course. They wouldn't dare admit to anything. But I assure you, Cissie, that what they're hinting amounts to nothing more than adolescent wishful thinking." He smiles a thin smile.

"The teens are such a cruel age for boys," she says. "*And* girls."

"Yes, I suppose so."

"One thing I'm definitely going to do," he says. "Next fall,

I'm going to see that the Colby Club is broken up. I'm going to scatter all those girls in different dorms. Cliques are never good for a school."

"Good idea. Well, I as much as told Adelaide and Anne-Marie that if there was any truth to the story, you'd have told me about it."

"Exactly. I didn't think that sort of garbage was worth repeating."

"Anne-Marie Chabot came to my tea in blue jeans."

John puts down his fork. "I give up," he says. "You tell me there's a nice bit of garbage going around the school, but you wouldn't even tell me what it is."

"I think," Clarissa says, "that what your father is implying is, that since this particular story is untrue, it should not be circulated any further than it already has."

"You think I'm going to go back to New York and repeat some story that's going around some dink-donk New England prep school?"

"Have you ever heard the expression, 'Father knows best'?"

"Shit," he says.

"Now, Johnny . . ." Clarissa places her napkin on the table. "I've had a busy day," she says, "and I'm a little tired. I think, if you'll both excuse me, I'll run upstairs to bed."

Johnny notices that his mother's dinner plate is still nearly half full.

"No dessert, Cissie?"

"It's cherry cobbler, Mrs. S," Rose says.

"Oh, *please*! Don't throw temptation in my path!" She rises from the table. John throws a quick look at Rose, who merely rolls her eyes.

"I'm going to let you men have a nice visit," Clarissa says. "Tomorrow, Johnny, if it's a pleasant day, let's you and I take a drive up into the mountains. The Berkshires are so lovely at this time of year. The dogwoods . . ."

"Let's have a nightcap in the library, son," his father says when they've finished their dessert. He rolls his napkin and slides it into the silver napkin ring.

In the library, his father selects a cigar from the small mahogany humidor. "Cigar, son?"

"No, thanks."

"I may be a little bit old-fashioned, but I still enjoy a good cigar after dinner." At the drinks cart, John fixes them each a scotch.

"You know, Johnny, I wasn't happy to hear you use the word 'shit' in front of your mother tonight."

"Oh, c'mon, Pop. It was just that 'Father knows best' bit. That's right out of Victorian England."

"Well, I may be a bit of a Victorian parent. To me, that kind of language does not belong at the dinner table. And I wasn't happy to hear you refer to Crittenden as a 'dink-donk prep school.'"

"That was just a figure of speech, Pop. I know you run a good school." They sit in chairs alongside the small table where Clarissa has placed a bowl of white tulips from the garden.

"We have one of the highest college acceptance rates of any secondary school in the country. And I'm talking about the top colleges—Yale, Harvard, Brown, Stanford. That's what a prep school is all about, isn't it? Preparing a young person for college?"

"Crittenden does a good job. I know that."

"You know," his father says, sipping his drink, "when I first came here, I was the youngest headmaster in the school's history."

"I knew that, Pop."

"And, if I last here just one more year, I'll have had the longest tenure in the job of any of them. I like to think our ancestor would be proud of me." He nods in the direction of the general's portrait above the mantel.

"Is there any reason why you wouldn't last another year, Pop?"

His father frowns. "Your mother doesn't know this," he says, "but my contract comes up for renewal in September. The trustees typically renew it for three years. But it could be for just two years, or only one year. Or not at all."

"Why wouldn't they renew it? You're in great shape. Your health is—"

His father waves his hand with the lighted cigar. "It has nothing to do with my health," he says. "Running a school is tricky. Little things go wrong. Sometimes it seems as though every day some little thing goes wrong. Like the unfortunate piece of gossip your mother alluded to tonight at the table. The trustees' philosophy is that headmasters can come and go, but Crittenden goes on forever. But this school is my whole life, Johnny. My whole *life*." He clears his throat with a small choking sound that sounds as though he might be about to weep. "It always has been," he says. "Always."

John sips his drink and then stares into his glass thoughtfully, trying not to look at his father. Finally, he says, "This is good scotch. Does the school still give you free booze?"

His father smiles thinly. "It's not that they give us free *booze*," he says. "They give us a budget for entertaining, and a certain amount of bills for liquor can be applied against that budget."

"When I was at school and college, I used to bring friends home, and sometimes we'd raid your liquor closet. I used to say, 'Drink up, guys! My old man gets free booze.' I bet you never knew we did that, did you? Raided your liquor closet?"

His father is still smiling. "I think your mother and I both noticed, after your friends were here, that the levels in the liquor bottles were often significantly lower," he says.

"Well, you always had good scotch."

"We sometimes entertain very important people, Johnny. We can't offer them cheap brands."

There is another short silence. Then John says, "Dad? How is Mom?"

"Your mother? Why, she's perfectly fine. Why do you ask?"

"I had lunch with Sally a few days ago. She's worried about Mom. She's gotten so thin."

"She's been on a diet, that's all. She's reached the weight she wants, and so she's eating a little less to try to maintain that weight. She's perfectly fine."

"Sally told me that she'd had a mastectomy years ago."

His father shifts uncomfortably in his chair. "Sally told you that? She shouldn't have. Your mother is extremely sensitive on that subject. It is something we never discuss. Besides, that was years and *years* ago. There's been no recurrence of—whatever the problem was. You're not supposed to know. She wears—padded bras."

"You mean the doctors got it all?"

"Yes. All."

John sits forward in his chair, cradling his glass. "Dad, can I ask you a kind of unusual question?" he says.

"What?"

"Do you still love Mom?"

"What a question! Why, of course—"

"I ask for a reason. I mean, you've been married now for more than thirty years. Did the love really last that long? You see, just a couple of months ago, I came dangerously close to asking a girl to marry me."

"Blair?"

"Uh-huh."

"Blair's a fine young woman, Johnny. And it's time you settled down."

"Well, anyway, we've split up. But it was close at the time."

"I'm sorry to hear that. The Gwinns are a fine old family."

"You mean a *rich* family. That was part of the problem."

"Why was that?"

"Her old man didn't think I was quite good enough for his only daughter."

"She could do a lot worse than to marry a Spotswood!"

"Yeah, I know all that. But he didn't think that the salary of a struggling young architect was good enough—"

"Money. But, Johnny, if you'd just try to get a commission to design an important building! Look at Philip Johnson! Look at that Jap fellow—I. M. Pei! He earns hundreds of thousands of dollars in commissions!"

"But I don't *want* to design important buildings, Dad. I want to design houses."

"You've always had this stubborn streak, Johnny. You don't set your goals high enough. I've told you that again and again."

"I didn't go into this for the money. I always thought I got that from you. You didn't become a schoolteacher for the money, did you? Maybe I'm an idealist. Like you. Don't you think you're sort of an idealist, Dad?"

"Well, yes, I suppose you could say that," his father says. "At least, I've always had high ideals, tried to set high standards, for this school."

"Anyway, that's only one of the reasons why Blair and I broke up. There were lots of other things wrong with Blair's and my relationship. Lots and *lots* of other things—I don't want to go into all of them."

"I always thought it was a mistake to let her move in with you. Her parents disapproved of that, too. I know it's done a lot these days, but I still disapprove."

"That had nothing to do with it, Dad."

"You already had two *male* roommates. It must have been damned awkward—four of you crammed into that little flat of yours! One bathroom!"

"Dad, it worked out *fine*. But can we get back to my original question? You still love Mom?"

"Of *course*!" His voice is growing angry now.

John rises and goes to the drinks cart. He splashes more whisky in his glass. "You ever cheat on her, Dad?"

"What a question! Never!"

"Not even once?"

"I said *never*, dammit!"

John takes a swallow of his drink. "It can't be an easy life for her here, Dad. Living like this."

"What do you mean? She has everything she could possibly want here—everything!"

"That's what I mean. Everything's supplied. Everything comes to her from somebody else. A budget for booze. Two cars, owned by the school. A budget for gas. A housekeeper, paid by the school. And what does Mom get? She gets to give teas for a bunch of gossipy old faculty biddies."

"My faculty is the highest caliber—"

"Nothing in this house is Mom's. Except—" He nods to the portrait over the fireplace. "But, no, that's not even hers. That's *your* ancestor. She can't even have a cat. Remember Missy?"

"Cats scratch furniture and draperies."

"But Missy had been declawed!"

"In life, we all must live by certain rules, John."

"Missy was my cat!"

"She most certainly was not. Your mother found her as a kitten, wandering along the highway, where somebody had—"

"And Mom gave her to me for my birthday!"

"In life, we all must make certain sacrifices, John," his father said.

John took another swallow of his drink, and now he felt tears welling in his eyes.

He knew he was a little drunk, but it was the stupidity of it all. Here they were, two grown men, a father and son, arguing over some long-ago perished kitten. He turns and faces his father. "I've just had an idea, Dad," he says. "Why don't you give Mom something she's never had before?"

"And what might that be, pray? A diamond necklace from Tiffany's?" His voice is heavy with sarcasm.

"I'm serious, Dad. I mean a house—a house of her own. Maybe just a little summer place. Maybe in Vermont."

"What's wrong with the house we live in now?"

"But it is not hers."

"It most certainly is. At least until I—"

"That's just it. When you retire, where will you both go?"

"I'm not planning to retire!"

"Let me design a house for you both, Dad. I won't even charge you a commission. You must have saved enough money by now to pay for a piece of land—"

"When I do retire, your mother and I will be comfortably provided for."

"By the fucking school? With some fucking pension?"

"Watch your language, young man!" His father shifts in his chair. "Nonsense!" he says. "You are talking utter nonsense. If your mother had ever been the least bit dissatisfied with the living arrangements Crittenden has provided for us, she certainly would have expressed her dissatisfaction to me. But

I assure you she has not. So, as usual, you are talking utter nonsense, son."

Now they are both staring angrily into their half-empty glasses. Johnny stiffens his own drink once more. He almost starts to say, *But if you really love her*—But he stops himself and says nothing.

"Your mother is a remarkable woman," he hears his father say. "And a remarkably *happy* woman."

Outside, the night is silent. All the lights on campus have gone out, except for the faculty residence, where a few lamps still glow. Inside the Castle, the only sound is the ticking of the mantel clock. From the bowl on the small table, a white tulip noiselessly drops a petal.

Upstairs, in the small study Clarissa has created for herself—the room which, in the original blueprints, was designated "Wife's Sewing Room"—Clarissa is saying, "I hope this isn't too late to call you, Michael. But I had the faculty women's tea this afternoon, and then Johnny arrived home unexpectedly, and this is the first chance I've had to get to the phone."

"No, this is fine," he says. "Clarissa, I need to see you."

"Well," she says. "I don't know quite how—"

"Any chance you could drive down to New York, and we could have lunch?"

"I just don't see how I could do that, Michael. Not right away, anyhow."

"Or I could drive up. We could meet at the inn?"

"No, certainly not at the inn."

"Then could we meet somewhere between here and there? What about that?"

"I just don't think it would look right, Michael. If someone should see us, I mean. It wouldn't look—quite appropriate. Why can't we talk on the phone?"

"No," he says. "No, I don't think that would be wise, under the present circumstances. Did Hobart mention my proposed gift?"

"He did. And I think ten mil—"

"Don't mention the figure on the phone, please!"

She laughs softly. "Goodness, you sound as though your phone might be tapped."

"It could be. I've been having a little trouble with the feds. You may have read about it in the papers. It's nothing serious. My lawyers have it under control. But I wouldn't put it past those bastards to have my lines bugged. Anyway, you know about my offer."

"Yes, and we both think it's very generous."

"Then is it a deal?"

"Well, of course it isn't my place to speak," she says. "But I think Hobe thinks that—well, that some of the powers that be may feel you're putting the cart before the horse, making one thing contingent upon the other." She is trying, now, to speak as guardedly as possible.

"Those are my terms," he says.

"So I understand."

"That's just one of the things I need to talk to you about. Couldn't you make some sort of excuse for coming to New York? To do some shopping? To see your kids? That's the only place we can really talk in private. Why don't you see what you can come up with, Clarissa? It's important."

"Well, let me think about it," she says.

"Don't think about it too long," he says. "I need to see you soon—as soon as possible. Understand?"

"Yes."

"Call me back at this number. Always use this number. If I'm not here, there'll always be someone who can reach me right away. Damn, I wish I could see you right now. I wish you'd married me when you had the chance."

She laughs again. "When?" she says. "Just tell me *when*. Tell me when I ever had the chance to marry you!"

FIVE

From Clarissa Spotswood's Journal:

Two more days at the Old Forge Inn turned out to be five more days. This was because several of the trustees, including the board's president, wanted further talks with Hobe. Hobe was very excited about this and took it as a good omen. "To be asked back for a second interview is always a good sign," he said. "It shows that they have more than just a routine interest in me." And as for myself, when I wasn't running back and forth between the inn and the local dry cleaners to have Hobe's suits pressed, I was enjoying my new friend.

He made me laugh. He had all these different voices. That tough, street-smart gutter language—in which he could combine, string together, and hyphenate four-letter words in more ways than I'd ever thought were possible—was only one of them. I told him that if he hadn't decided to become a Wall Street trader, he could have become a marvelous stand-up comic in Las Vegas. He did a hilarious imitation of President Nixon, for instance, in which he patched together bits and pieces of Nixon's speeches—the Checkers speech, the You-won't-have-Nixon-to-kick-around-anymore speech, and others—to make Nixon sound as though he was speaking utter gibberish. He could even make himself look like Nixon, with the hunched shoulders, the scowl, the twitching fingers.

Another of his imitations was of Dr. Renny, who had been Crittenden's headmaster when he was a student there. Dr. Renny, it turned out, was no kind of doctor at all—not a medical doctor, a PhD doctor, or even, as Dr. Renny let it be believed, a Doctor of Divinity. The uncovering of this bit of deception was largely responsible for his brief tenure at the school. Dr. Renny's principal crusade was against the smokestack from the school's power plant, which, he claimed, spoiled his view of the Berkshire foothills and the lake from his bedroom windows in the Castle. He wanted the trustees to plant full-grown spruce trees to block out the smokestack. In the end, he got a small grove of spruce saplings that, over the years, have grown almost tall enough to do the trick.

My friend would do an imitation of the spiel Dr. Renny liked to give parents of prospective Crittenden boys as he toured them around the campus. Speaking in a plummy, pseudo-English accent, Dr. Renny would pause whenever the offending smokestack appeared on the horizon. "Look!" he would say, pointing at the thing with one hand and clapping the other to his forehead. "Just look. The only feature of my school about which I am truly apologetic—that blasted smokestack. Too, too absurd, isn't it? Quite, quite uncalled-for. This beautiful rural landscape is utterly defiled by that monstrosity. Such a pity. Cannot something be done? I'm working on it, I assure you. But I take comfort in one fact." And at that point he would turn and point in the opposite direction. "It is that there—there stands the school's *true* powerhouse!" And he would point dramatically at the school chapel.

My new friend also told me some stories of his undergraduate days at Crittenden that were pretty disturbing. Each dormitory floor contained an apartment for one of the school's masters and, in most cases, these men were bachelors. Periodically, these corridor masters, as they were called, would do a bed check at lights-out to make sure all the boys were in their rooms and properly accounted for. Also, some boys had been known to bring flashlights out after lights-out, which was against the rules. In his junior year, my friend's corridor master was named Mr. Fish, who taught Latin I and II, and who also directed the school choir. One night, Mr. Fish stepped into his room for bed check. He found my friend safely tucked in bed and flashlight-less. But instead of simply closing the door and departing, Mr. Fish sat down on his bed, put his arms around his shoulders, said, "Goodnight, beautiful!" and kissed him on the lips.

I was astonished to learn that now, more than ten years later, Mr. Fish was not only still a member of the faculty, he had also attained what amounted to emeritus status, was much loved by the boys, and had become a powerful voice at faculty meetings and a force in school affairs.

The reason for Titus Fish's popularity with the boys was not hard to figure out, my friend said. It was said that he enjoyed a private income independent of his school salary. He was a natty dresser, favoring bespoke English tweeds and custom-made shoes from Lobb. Often, instead of a necktie, he wore one of a collection of sporty silk ascots. He drove a snappy red Buick convertible, in which he enjoyed taking boys for outings in the countryside. He also enjoyed inviting boys for trips to New York City, sometimes for overnight, to visit art galleries or museums, or to attend performances of opera, ballet, or the Broadway theater. It had been noted that he invariably chose the best-looking boys for these special invitations. On campus, he had earned the nickname of Tight-Ass Fish. Certain obvious sexual inferences could be drawn from this. On the other hand, with the name Titus, such a nickname might have been inevitable.

But it was this sort of thing that made me support Hobe's campaign for coeducation at Crittenden, though I have since changed my mind on that subject.

By now, of course, my friend's tenth class reunion was over, and his other classmates had scattered. But he had decided to stay on at the Old Forge Inn for a few more days. I like to think it was because he was enjoying my company as much as I was enjoying his.

Then, finally, it was over, and Hobe and I were driving back to Baltimore after the interviews. In New York, we would stop at my parents' house to collect five-year-old Johnny, and Missy, the cat.

At the wheel of our old Pontiac, driving down the Merritt Parkway, Hobe yawned audibly several times.

"Do you want me to drive for a while, darling," I asked him, "so you can take a nap?"

"No thanks," he said, smothering another yawn. "You know I like to do the driving."

I remember—isn't it funny how memory works?—Stevie Wonder was singing "You Are the Sunshine of My Life" on the car radio, and I was humming along with the song.

"You're in an awfully chipper mood," Hobe said to me.

"Well, why shouldn't I be?" I said. "You're the one who's been through this horrible ordeal of all these interviews. For me, it's just been a ten-day expense-paid holiday in New England. But you must be exhausted, darling."

"I'm not exhausted."

"And also, I'm happy because I just know you're going to get this job."

"Don't count your chickens," he said.

But of course, he did get the job.

Not long afterward, I read that my friend had married—to a nice Jewish girl from one of New York's fine old German-Jewish families. I wondered about the difference in their backgrounds. His father was a prosperous druggist in Queens, but a member of the Polish-Jewish *lumpen* proletariat, as he often put it. Unfortunately, this marriage did not last, though it produced a son whom they named Jesse, after his wife's maternal grandfather, who was a Seligman. And it was this first wife who got him seriously interested in collecting art. Since then there have been three other marriages, well publicized as he has become more and more well known in the financial community. And three more well-publicized divorces, alas.

Over the years, he and I have kept in touch. And I think I understand the motive behind this new, lavish gift offer to the school, and the reason why he has attached this particular string to it: First, he must be named to the Board of Trustees; then, he will write out that big check, not the other way around. Knowing him as I do, he will never budge from that position. The only surprising thing about this offer is that he is giving the school a little time to think about it. That's not like him. On Wall Street he is known as "Mr. Fifteen Minutes." He will bring a deal to the bargaining table and say, "Gentlemen, that's my offer. You have exactly fifteen minutes in which to accept it or reject it." Then he sets his stopwatch.

He has always been generous to Crittenden, never contributing less than five thousand dollars to the annual Alumni Fund campaign. But those gifts are tiny, compared to ten million. His motive is simple: revenge. Revenge for the way the school treated him when he was here.

And it has nothing to do with the anti-Semitic nicknames (Kikey Mikey, etc.) that he was given as an undergraduate. He took all that with good humor. He is still bitter, though, that when he was a senior, he was not made president of Cap & Bells.

Cap & Bells is the school's dramatic club. Back in those days, he toyed with the idea of becoming an actor. There were his good looks, for one thing. He really did look like a young Ty Power, and he most definitely knew it. And then there were his "voices," the imitations and parodies that he did so well. He once said to me, "I worked harder than anyone else in that organization. I worked on every single Cap & Bells production for four solid years. I did everything from painting flats to running the light boards and soundboards to performing in the shows we put on. I wrote blackout skits and raised and lowered the curtain. Nobody worked harder, or for more hours, than I did. When I went into my senior year, I was the logical person to be made president. Everybody said so. Everybody *assumed* I would be. But then, at the last minute, they gave the presidency to some other guy—some gonif with a Roman numeral after his name, who hadn't done half, not even a quarter, of the work I'd done for the club."

"Why?" I asked him.

"I think old Doc Renny was behind it—him, and some of the faculty, the so-called faculty advisers. The faggot Titus Fish was one of them. I heard that they said my attitude was wrong, that I lacked *leadership* potential. Hah! They should see me now, the bastards. It was a personal insult, a personal slap in the face."

Cap & Bells—even the name has a silly sound to it. Isn't it astonishing how a man's life can become polarized around a single trivial, seemingly insignificant incident? But that was it. Petty, wasn't it?

Now, at last, he sees a way to bring the Crittenden School to its knees. He wants the school to kneel, and then lift and kiss the hem of his garment, to utter a collective mea culpa, to murmur, "Forgive us! Please forgive us!" And then, when that has happened, to whisper, "Thank you! Oh, thank you! Thank you for forgiving us!"

He has told me that, if his gift of an arts center is accepted, he will stipulate that not a penny of the money is to be spent on the *performing* arts.

Revenge may not be the loftiest of motives. It was Hamlet's to be sure, but at least Hamlet was trying to avenge his father's murder. Still, from this and other things my friend has told me about the treatment he received here, I think I can understand his bitterness. I forgive him for it. Even in the most successful men, the ego is such a tiny, fragile thing. I am thinking of course of Hobe.

I want my friend to get what he wants. I have remained very fond of him over the years.

———

"Mrs. S, can I speak to you for a minute?"

Rose Finney is standing in the doorway of Clarissa's study, and Clarissa puts down her pen. "Certainly, Rose. What is it?"

There is a worried look on Rose's face. "Do you know Pauline Scanlon in Housekeeping, Mrs. S?"

"Pauline . . . let's see . . ."

"With the brown birthmark on her cheek."

"Oh, yes. Pauline."

"She cleans in Colby Hall, and a couple other dorms."

"Yes."

"Pauline's got a problem, Mrs. S."

"What is it, Rose?"

"This was in Colby Hall, Mrs. S. Pauline was changing the linens there on Monday, like she always does on Mondays.

Monday morning is always linen-changing day, you know. While the girls are in their classes."

"Yes, I know."

"Well, in this one girl's room everything was covered with blood, Mrs. S. Everything. Both sheets, top and bottom, and not just that—the bedspread, the mattress cover, the pillowcases, and even the pillow—everything covered with blood. Dried-up blood."

"Oh, dear. I suppose some poor girl got her period during the night."

"No, Mrs. S. Too much blood for that. I saw the mess. Pauline showed it to me. Would you like to see that bedding, Mrs. S? You'll see there's too much blood for that."

"Oh, no. No, I believe you, Rose."

Clarissa then asks, "You mentioned the mattress cover—what about the mattress itself?"

"All the girls' beds get rubber pads, Mrs. S, for situations such as you just mentioned, so the mattress is okay. I asked Pauline that self-same question. The boys get rubber pads, too, but for different reasons." She gives Clarissa a knowing look.

"Well, I suppose the best thing to do would be to send everything to the laundry and see what they can do with it," Clarissa says.

"Pauline's afraid to, Mrs. S. She's afraid the linen service would notice it and report it back to Miss Stimpson." Miss Stimpson is the school's Head of Housekeeping and is indeed much feared. She is famous for her strict inventory system, which is now entirely computerized. Her domain even extends into the school dining room (though not the kitchen, which is ruled by the chef and the school dietitian), where so much as a missing butter knife can be the cause of an investigation into pilferage by Miss Stimpson. Miss Stimpson has been with the school almost as long as Rose has, and she is also technically Rose's boss; she signs Rose's paycheck. But Rose's position in the headmaster's house is so secure that Miss Stimpson often overlooks certain accidents, like the time when one of the school's sterling silver teaspoons, engraved with the school's crest, fell into the garbage disposal. Rose simply reported the loss to Miss Stimpson, and that was the end of it.

"Where are the soiled bedclothes now?" Clarissa asks Rose.

"Pauline's put everything in a big garbage bag and hid it in her closet in Buhl Hall. Did I mention the blanket? The blanket's bad, too."

"Perhaps she'd better put everything out for trash collection," Clarissa says.

"It was a dumb thing for her to do, taking everything back to her room like that, and I told her so. But Pauline's not the smartest girl on God's green earth, I would have to admit. I told her what she should have done was report it to Stimpson right away. But she's afraid that Stimpson might report it to Campus Security, or even the police, and there'd be an investigation. Stimpson's done that before, you know. And, what with all the talk about what's been going on in Colby Hall, Pauline didn't want to get involved. So she panicked. Now she's going to be short on her linen count, which Stimpson does on Friday, when it comes back from the service. And if Pauline's linen count comes up short, Stimpson will take it out of her pay. And Pauline's got her eighty-eight-year-old mother that she has to support at Bright Oaks." Bright Oaks is a local nursing home. "And now it's too late to do anything about what's in that bag, since everything was supposed to go to the service on Monday afternoon. That's the rules."

Sometimes, Clarissa thinks, *this school seems to operate like a very well-run prison.*

"And the other thing is—well, even though everything's tied up real tight in a heavy-duty garbage bag, it's beginning to have—well, a bad smell, Mrs. S."

"Oh, dear. Well, there's an incinerator down at the power plant, you know."

"I mentioned that to her. But she's scared they'll make her open the bag to see what's in it. And when they see they'll report it back to Stimpson, and all hell will break loose. And, whatever she does with that bag, she's still going to be short on her linen count. And, considering the circumstances—I mean, considering that it was Colby Hall, and all this talk—well, Pauline is really scared, Mrs. S. I mean, she came to me in tears." She pauses significantly. "You haven't asked me whose room it was, Mrs. S," she says.

She looks up at Rose. "Do I really want to know?" she asks her.

"It was the Van Degan girl's," she says.

"Oh, dear," Clarissa says again, though she is afraid she knew that all along.

"And, you know, there's been all this talk—about what everybody is saying went on there, and with that girl, and all. I know you've heard the talk, Mrs. S. Everybody who lives in Buhl Hall is talking about it. And I know Mr. S is trying to put the hush-hush on that talk. It could look bad for the school and everything. And Pauline's scared that she's maybe hiding some kind of evidence or something. She's really scared, Mrs. S."

Clarissa hesitates. Then she says, "Does anyone else in Buhl Hall know about what you've just told me?"

"She's too scared to tell a soul. Only me."

"I wonder why she decided to tell you."

"Because she knows I work for you. She thought maybe you or Mr. S would know what she should do."

"Please," Clarissa says quickly, "please don't mention this to Mr. S."

"No, I didn't think that would be such a good idea," Rose says. "Poor man, he's got so much else on his mind. That's why I told you, not him."

Clarissa sits up straight in her chair. "I'll tell you what we're going to do," she says. "Bring that bag of bedclothes over to me. I'll take it to the incinerator myself. They won't ask me any questions."

"What about Pauline's linen count? Stimpson will dock her pay."

"Tell Pauline to make up some excuse. Tell her to act dumb. You say she's not that bright anyway. She just doesn't *know* what became of that bedding. If Stimpson docks her pay, tell her I'll give her a check for whatever it is."

"It could come to more than two hundred dollars, Mrs. S."

"That's all right. Whatever it is. Now go get that bag of bedclothes."

Rose shakes her head. "So much blood," she says. "You won't believe how much blood there is. Just too much for one girl. What I don't see is how she could have slept two nights in that bed with that mess."

Later, Clarissa lugs the heavy plastic bag down the back steps from the kitchen door and lifts it onto the open tailgate of her station wagon. The bag weighs more than she'd expected and, as she lifts it, she holds a hanky to her nose.

"Clarissa! What on earth are you *doing*?" It is Anne-Marie Chabot, in her customary blue jeans, taking the usual shortcut from Faculty Row to her French class through the Castle's backyard.

"Just taking some trash to the incinerator," she says.

"You mean to say you have to do that *too*? Poor Clarissa!"

"That's the second time in a week you've said that to me," she snaps back at her. "I don't appreciate being called 'poor Clarissa,' Anne-Marie!"

"Well, *pardonnez-moi!*" the teacher says with a sniff. "*A bientot,* Clarissa."

Clarissa slams the tailgate of the wagon closed, hops into the driver's seat, and drives off, sending gravel spitting from her wheels.

"Well, Mrs. S, what have we here?"

"Just some trash for the incinerator, George." George is the man in charge of the school's power plant and maintenance services.

"Here, let me carry that," he says, picking up the heavy bag. If he notices an odor, he is too polite to comment on it. "Didn't this get collected for you? You're on Big Tim's route. I think I'll have a word with him about this."

"No, it's my fault. I forgot to put it out."

He carries the bag to the incinerator, opens the door, heaves the bag inside, and closes the door with a clank. "All taken care of, Mrs. S," he says.

She follows him. "Aren't you going to burn it, George?"

"I like to wait until I get a full load," he says. "And I generally wait until after dark." He winks at her. "You know, some of the town folk have been known to complain when they see smoke coming from here."

"How does this thing work, anyway?" she says. "Is it this button here?" She touches a red button beside the incinerator door and immediately hears a deep rumble from somewhere in the ground beneath her feet. "Oh, dear!" she cries. "I've turned it on! I'm sorry! I didn't mean to do that, George!"

"Not to worry, Mrs. S," he says. "No harm done; I can assure you."

Back in the wagon, she turns her car toward home. But of course, it isn't really her home. And this 1997 Chrysler station wagon isn't really her car. A legend, painted in crimson on the outside panel of the door on the driver's side, reads "The Crittenden School." In her rearview mirror she sees smoke rising from the smokestack. It rises straight up into the cloudless, windless May sky. It is as though the smokestack, and all the green May hills around it, are being suspended from the heavens by a thin delicate ribbon of black.

SIX

A glance at the student schedules in the school secretary's office had been all Clarissa needed to station herself near the entrance to the Science Building the next morning to just happen to be there when Linda Van Degan emerged from her ten o'clock chemistry lab. Clarissa sees the girl heading in her direction now, with her backpack slung over her shoulders. She is wearing a long blue denim pleated skirt from the Gap, Nike sneakers without socks, and a boys' Brooks Brothers pink button-down, the shirttails untucked. "Well, hello, Linda," she says pleasantly. "How are you today?"

Linda at first seems uncertain about this encounter with the headmaster's wife. "Uh—hello, Mrs. Spotswood," she says, blinking.

"Which way are you walking?"

Linda points. "This way," she says.

"So am I. Mind if I join you?"

"Uh-uh."

Clarissa falls into step beside the girl. She notices, for the first time, that though Linda is definitely overweight, she really has a very pretty face, with long blond hair that falls straight down her back and lovely wide-set eyes, Wedgewood blue. If the girl could just shed at least twenty pounds of what appears to be baby fat, she could actually be considered gorgeous. "Have you had a good year at school?" she asks her. "Are you enjoying Crittenden?"

"Oh, yeah," she says. "Yeah, it's been a real good year."

"Any special summer plans?"

"Well—just—well, we go to Northeast Harbor for July and August," she says.

"Do you sail?"

"Some."

They pass Van Degan Hall, which was given to the school by Linda's grandfather in memory of a son—Linda's uncle—who was killed at Anzio, but Linda takes no particular notice of the building.

"Let's see—I forget which dorm you're in this year," Clarissa says.

"Colby," Linda says.

"Oh, yes. I heard the other day that some of the girls there have formed something called the Colby Club."

"Yeah."

"Valerie Winston and Cecily Smith I believe are in it."

"Yeah. And me and a couple of others."

"Really? You're a member, Linda?"

Suddenly she giggles. "I helped found it," she says.

"Really? What kind of club is it?"

"Just a club kind of club. All the other dorms have them. It's just—well, like it's just a real neat club, Mrs. Spotswood."

"What sort of activities do you do?"

"Activities? Well, we just mostly hang out together. Talk. Tell jokes. Not much. That's about all."

"So Valerie Winston and Cecily Smith are good friends of yours," she says.

"Uh-huh."

"They both seem like very nice girls."

"Uh-huh."

They are approaching the Main Building now, and Linda glances at her oversize watch and adjusts the straps of the backpack on her shoulders. "Well, I've got to go to French class now, Mrs. Spotswood," she says.

"You have Mademoiselle Chabot?"

"Uh-huh. Anne-Marie."

Clarissa laughs. "I can't get used to you students calling your teachers by their first names," she says.

"She wants us to, Mrs. Spotswood."

"You like her as a teacher, Linda?"

"Oh, yeah. She's really cool. I mean, like, she's a really cool teacher, Mrs. Spotswood."

Clarissa resists commenting that she cannot stand Anne-Marie Chabot. "Why don't you call me by *my* first name, Linda?" she says. "It's Clarissa. It's kind of an old-fashioned name, but a lot of my friends call me Cissie."

"Okay, Mrs. Spotswood," she says.

"Try it—please."

"Okay—Clarissa."

"Good. It was nice talking to you, Linda."

"And it was nice talking to you, too, Mrs. Spotswood."

"Goodbye, Linda . . ."

The girl half waves to her, then turns and walks hurriedly into the building.

In her French III classroom, Linda Van Degan slips off her backpack, drops it on the floor beneath her seat, and sits at her usual place at the U-shaped conference table next to Valerie Winston.

"We saw you," Valerie whispers.

"Saw me what?" Linda says.

"Just now. Sucking up to Mrs. Spotty."

"I wasn't sucking up to her. She was sucking up to *me*."

"What about?"

"Colby Club."

"What did you tell her?"

"Nothing! You're the one with the big mouth, Winston!"

At this point, Mlle Chabot comes swinging into the room with her usual French *elan*, her hands thrust deep into the pockets of her not-quite-too-tight jeans. "*Bonjour, chers amis!*" she calls out in her light soprano.

"*Bonjour,* Anne-Marie!" the dozen or so boys and girls respond in a chorus.

She takes her place at the center of the U. "*Et maintenant, pour commencer, un petit examen.*"

The dark-haired young woman on American's Flight 872 from New York to San Francisco has a laptop computer on the open tray table in front of her and is entering figures from a sheaf of notes in a folder that is also spread open on the table. The young man, who looks to be about her age, and who is also dark, seated in the aisle seat across from hers in first class, has been studying her. She has felt his eyes but has not looked up. "Excuse me," he says at last. "But you look so familiar. Haven't we met somewhere?"

"No, I don't think so," she says without looking up from her work.

"Funny," he says, "but I could swear we have. Was it—was it at Crittenden School? Did you go there?"

She looks across at him for the first time, and he does look vaguely familiar. "No," she says. "But my father is headmaster there."

He snaps his fingers. "That's it! I'm class of '92. I used to see you around the campus. When you came home for weekends at the Castle." He extends his hand across the aisle. "My name's Jess Rubin."

She takes his hand. "Sally Spotswood," she says.

"Sally—of course. Actually, we never did meet. But I remember we knew Spotty's daughter was named Sally. How're your mom and dad?"

"They're both fine."

"Old Spotty used to scare the bejesus out of me when I was there. But I got a damned good education at his school."

"That is the one thing Daddy would like to hear you say," she says.

"What takes you to San Francisco, Sally?"

"I'm an A.E. for an ad agency," she says, gesturing to the computer. "We're pitching for an account there. And you?"

"Some business for my old man. A little company he's thinking of buying out there."

"And your father would be—obviously—the famous Michael Rubin."

He grins at her. He has a nice grin, with nice teeth, and a nice wrinkle to his nose that goes nicely with the grin. "Or I suppose you could say the *in*famous Michael Rubin. The notorious Michael Rubin, some people might say."

"Also a Crittenden alumnus, right?"

"Class of sixtysomething. I forget the exact year."

"My father would be able to rattle that off instantly. And so, interestingly enough, would my mother."

"I remember your mother very well. I always thought she was a lovely lady. But, boy, we used to dread those annual class teas she had. Command performances. Best clothes, best manners. But at least I learned how to balance a teacup on my knee."

"Which is something you have to do quite often in your line of work, I imagine," she says.

Jess grins again. "The girls even wore little white gloves. How long's it been since you wore a pair of little white gloves?"

She laughs. "Years and years," she says. "But believe it or not, I still have a pair in a drawer somewhere."

In the aisle ahead of them, the flight attendant is lowering tray tables and squaring and smoothing small white tablecloths across them in preparation for lunch. Sally places her file folder and laptop on the empty seat to her left.

"Where are you staying in San Francisco?" he asks her.

"The Ritz-Carlton," she says. "That's the account we're pitching. We're hoping to get the entire chain. If we do, it would be a nice piece of business."

"I'm at the Stanford Court. Just up the street. How're you getting into the city?"

"I was planning to grab a cab."

"Well, look," he says, "I have a car and driver picking me up at the airport. Why don't you let me take you into town and drop you off? It wouldn't be any trouble."

"Well, that would be very nice," she says.

The flight attendant drapes the tablecloth across her tray table and smooths it with the palms of her hands. "White wine or red with your steak?" she asks.

"Red, please."

"Do you have any plans for dinner tonight?" he asks her.

She is about to say yes, she is sorry, but she does have plans but, in fact, she has none. Her presentation is not until tomorrow morning, and she is already well prepared for it. "Actually, I don't," she says. "I was thinking of just a sandwich from room service."

"Well, look—I'm free, too. Let me take you to Kuleto's, on Powell Street. Do you know Kuleto's? It's a favorite place of mine. Or wait—have you ever been to Chez Panisse?"

"In Berkeley? I've heard of Chez Panisse for years, but I've never been there."

"It's worth a trip to the East Bay, and I have the car. I'll take you there."

"That would be very nice," she says. "I'd like that."

"We've got a date. I'll pick you up at the Ritz. Seven thirty." He winks at her. "And, since I'm a Crittenden boy, you know I'm bound to be a gentleman."

She smiles. "I didn't realize that guarantee came with a Crittenden diploma," she says.

"Hobe, please lower your voice," Clarissa says to him. "This old house has thin walls."

But he is still shouting at her. "How could you do this sort of thing to me, Clarissa? How could you do this to my school?" He slaps the newspaper with the back of his hand. "Have you read this thing, Clarissa?" He shoves the newspaper in her face, with its front-page headline: "Crittenden, Coeds and Condoms; Headmaster's Wife Laments." By Alexa Woodin.

"Of course, I've read it. The headline is unfortunate, of course. And she told me it was for the women's page."

"Obviously, you gave her enough dirt to make it front-page material—which was what she wanted! Free condoms dispensed at the infirmary! For God's sake, Clarissa, are you some kind of fool?"

"Well, it's true," she says.

"But is this the sort of thing we want to publicize? Drugs? Alcohol? Sex in the chapel pews? Pregnancies? Abortions? Thievery? Is there any negative aspect of this school you could have possibly left out? Anything that would have embarrassed me—or the school—more than this?"

"It's only a little local newspaper," she says.

"But we have parents who live in Litchfield County! Trustees who live in Litchfield County! And this is just the kind of story that could be picked up—nationwide. And every rag that picks this up will pay this bitch more money! Oh, good job, Clarissa—you've shat all over the school, and all over me, and made Alexa Woodin rich."

"Nonsense," she says.

"It's not nonsense. What will the trustees think when they read this? What will the parents think—that I run some kind of whorehouse? What about parents of prospective students? You couldn't have done more damage to this school if you'd set out deliberately to destroy my reputation. And right now—of all times to try to do it!"

"What do you mean 'of all times'? Are you talking about the Van Degan girl?"

"I've told you there was nothing to that story."

"I'm not so sure."

"Are you calling me a liar? I tell you there's nothing to it! I'm talking about right now. The school commencement is coming up. And my contract comes up for renewal in September, in case you didn't know it."

"Of course, I knew it."

"How could you know that?"

"I know when your contract comes up!"

"Then that makes it even worse. I always knew you weren't very smart, Clarissa. But I always thought I could trust you to have a *minimum* of common sense. But now I see I can't even trust you not to meddle in my affairs. You're not just stupid. You're stupid, meddlesome, and untrustworthy. What am I going to do with you, Clarissa? I can't afford to let you out of my sight, or you'll go off blabbing garbage about my school to some reporter."

Now her voice is rising too. "Garbage?" she says. "Just tell me one thing, Hobart. Just tell me one thing. Is there one word in what I say in that story that isn't absolutely true?"

"The truth has nothing to do with your stupidity!"

"No, because you refuse to face the truth!"

He glares at her. "Do you know what I think the truth is?" he says. "The truth is that you're becoming senile. That's what's the matter with you. That's what these headaches are all about. You're losing your mind. You're a sick woman, Clarissa."

"*Sick?*" she screams. "Yes, I am sick! I'm sick of this school! I'm sick of this house and the life I live here! I'm sick of lying and covering up for you and trying to make you look good. And, yes, I'm sick of you—and all your goddamned pious hypocrisy!"

"Hypocrisy? You're calling me a hypocrite?" He raises his arm as if to strike her, then clenches his fist and brings his arm down again.

"Yes! Hypocrite! Hypocrite! A rich man offers your school a unique and precious gift, and you pretend to disapprove because you don't like the sound of his name. There's a troubled teenage girl who needs help, and you deny it. The school has serious problems, and you sweep them under the rug and pretend they don't exist. Yes, I'm sick! Sick of all that!"

"Are you saying you want a divorce, Clarissa? Is that it? Well, I suppose that would be typical of you—to divorce me, to humiliate me publicly right at this critical point in my career. Divorce—that would be your ultimate, typical form of female revenge. Have you ever stopped to consider what you would be, Clarissa, if it weren't for me?"

"Yes! I'd be a damn sight happier than I am right now!"

"Clarissa—" Suddenly his tone is softer, almost cajoling. "If only you'd stop meddling in school affairs, sticking your nose into matters that are no affairs of yours, and about which you have no knowledge or even a shred of understanding—then we'd have no problems, you and me. If only you'd let me handle things the way I know how to handle them, there wouldn't be any trouble. And yet you persist in tampering with business that isn't yours. I *told* you, you should have insisted that this journalist let you check over your quotes before she printed them. You should have let *me* check the quotes, since you were spouting off about my school! But no, you willfully ignore my advice, which is only for your own benefit, after all. And now, having created this mess, you want a divorce."

"I never said anything about divorce."

"You know what a divorce will mean, of course. The trustees won't renew my contract. You'll ruin my career."

"I said nothing about divorce!"

"Then what in God's name *do* you want?"

She turns away from him. "Just to get out of here. Just to get away from here for a few days. I want to go to New York for a few days to see my mother."

"That's right!" he says, his voice rising again. "That's quite typical of you, isn't it, Clarissa? Walk off. Walk out and leave me to try to clean up the mess you've made!" He slaps the newspaper again with the back of his hand. "I'm left to handle everything alone. What about the trustees' dinner? What about the faculty cocktail party? What about commencement, and the parents, and the class reunions? Leave me to handle all that by myself—is that it? And what about—?" But she has already run up the stairs to her room.

From the foot of the stairs, he shouts up at her. "Thanks, Clarissa! Thanks a lot!" He hears her door slam shut. "Bitch!"

Rose Finney, who has heard most of this exchange from behind the closed kitchen door, enters the hallway quietly. "Will you be having dinner alone tonight, Mr. S?" she asks him.

"Yes," he says. "Mrs. Spotswood is having one of her spells."

Silently, Rose moves away. In the family dining room, she removes one of the two place settings from the table.

———

From Clarissa Spotswood's Journal:

I am from a generation of Smith girls (we still call ourselves girls, you see) who, by the time they graduated, had to be engaged. It was virtually a requirement to get a diploma—that engagement ring. It had to be a diamond, of course, and, in Parsons Annex, we Smithies showed off our diamonds to one another, passed the rings around, tried each other's on, with appropriate expressions of delight and approval and congratulatory oohs and ahs. The diamonds had to be of a certain size to be truly acceptable. One carat in weight was considered the minimum. The girls who wound up with smaller stones were more to be pitied than anything else, and they knew it, and often offered excuses for their microscopic gems that nobody entirely believed ("He still has to get through Med School"; "I told him I just didn't want anything *too* big and flashy"). The girls who had the biggest diamonds obviously had landed the richest fiancés, and they weren't just envied, they were hated. I remember one girl, Mary Armour, had a cultured pearl solitaire set in a girdle of diamond chips so tiny they were almost invisible, but this, she insisted, was specifically what she had asked him for. But Mary Armour was always considered a little peculiar. My diamond from Hobe was midsize—1.24 carats— which put me in a competitive league with my classmates. For a girl to march into chapel for commencement with nothing at all on her ring finger—well, that was considered tragic. It was assumed that her life was doomed to spinsterhood and misery. Or it could be hinted that she was a lesbian. Patty Boswell was one. The class beauty.

Of course, very few of these marriages lasted long. In a recent survey of our class, it turned out that eighty-nine percent of my classmates have been divorced at least once. Forty-two percent have been divorced twice, and twenty-seven percent have had three or more husbands—that's almost a third of us! Hobe and I will have been married thirty-two years this October, and that fact definitely puts me in the minority among my classmates. I sometimes wonder whether I should count this as an achievement or not, or as something I should be proud of, or be given credit for. It is simply a fact.

I was very much in love with him when I married him. I admired his strength, his sense of purpose. He always knew exactly what he wanted to be—headmaster of a fine New England boarding school. He didn't have much humor, but I've always been a little suspicious—a little distrustful—of men who were *too* funny, too jokey, too cocky. Naturally, I'm thinking of a man like Michael Rubin, who always seems to be onstage, selling himself, putting himself across to others with his stories and imitations. I always saw Hobe as a very serious man, a very sober sort of man who had his eyes set on a goal, and who would work tirelessly until he achieved that goal. He seemed to me such a manly sort of man. And there were the physical attributes of Hobe that I found attractive. He was never technically handsome, in the Mike Rubin mode, but he was fine-looking: the square jawline, the thin, prominent Spotswood nose that Johnny has inherited, the firm physique that he still maintains. I felt when I first met Hobe much the way my father felt about him after first meeting him. "He's a fine figure of a man, Cissie," my father said. "A fine figure of a man."

So, of course, was my father. There was much of my father that I saw in Hobe, including the seriousness. To me, my father was a godlike figure.

My college classmates tended to agree with my father's appraisal of Hobe, though they were not above reminding me that a schoolteacher doesn't make much money.

At Smith, my major was art history. Sometimes friends would ask me, "But what are you going to *do* with that sort of degree? Are you going to teach?" No, I said, but as a schoolmaster's wife a little culture couldn't hurt. That was to be my career, you see— to be a schoolmaster's wife. I saw my role as three-pronged: I would be the supportive wife, I would be the careful keeper of his house, I would be the loving mother to his children. At the time, that seemed career enough to me.

Look at what's become of some of my classmates. Mousy little Mary Armour, she of the cultured pearl ring, is now a world-famous astronomer. An astronomer! Just the other day her picture was in the *New York Times*. From her observatory atop some Hawaiian mountain, she's discovered a new planet in a distant galaxy, and it will be named after her—Marianus! And the beauteous Patty Boswell, our lesbian, who was often mistaken for Gene Tierney, the movie star—well, she waited until age forty-three to marry a tall, skinny veterinarian and, against all odds, proceeded to produce four babies, all boys, bing-bing-bing-bing nine months apart, just like that. Now she's a plump little housewife living on a ranch in Montana with many animals. In the Class Notes of our alumnae magazine, she wrote of how she helped a mare to foal. She and her husband each grabbed a leg and yanked the baby out. And Susie Wilmarth, who was our class brain, has been through four husbands (one of them she married twice) and four divorces and is now a hopeless alcoholic, living on Social Security Disability. Am I worse off?

I used to think I was smarter than most of my classmates. At least I managed to hold on to the man I married. Our marriage has had its bumpy patches, it would be a lie to say it hasn't. But we've somehow managed to weather them. And it would be a lie to say that there haven't been times when I've wished for a different sort of life with a different sort of man in a different sort of world. And it would be still another lie to say that I've never thought about joining the majority of my classmates by getting a divorce. But, interestingly enough, whenever the word *divorce* has been mentioned, it has always been Hobe who's brought the subject up—not I. I've never used divorce as a threat, though I could have. Whenever he's used that word, I've seen the terror in his eyes. I saw it in his eyes tonight. You see, I know he needs me.

There's more to being a headmaster's wife than pouring tea, or diagramming the seating at a dinner table, or shaking hands and smiling and being polite to people I really don't give a tinker's damn about. (In twenty-five years, how many teacups have I filled, how many phony smiles and handshakes have I given? Hundreds of thousands, at least!) But my life here hasn't been just measured out in sugar cubes and Rose's paper-thin lemon slices. Just to pick a random instance out of my little hat of memories, there was Hobe's first crisis as the new head of Crittenden.

A parent, one Mr. Austin Beale by name, had written to complain that his fifteen-year-old son, Austin Beale Jr., had been the recipient of an "improper proposal" from Mr. Titus Fish, the beloved Latin master, choirmaster, and organizer of the school's glee club. "Improper proposal" had been as far as Mr. Beale was willing to go, but the implications were clear, and the incident had occurred during one of what Mr. Titus Fish called his "outings" with the boys, and which the boys themselves called Fishing Expeditions.

Hobe had had a word with Mr. Fish, who had indignantly denied any impropriety. Furthermore, he announced that if Mr. Beale or his son persisted with such a complaint, he would sue the Beales for defamation. And if Crittenden decided to dismiss him over this allegation, he would sue the school.

Hobe was simply paralyzed with fear over this situation. If Mr. Fish had made any improper overtures to the boy, Mr. Fish would have to go. On the other hand, Titus Fish was an extremely popular teacher. He had been with the school so long that he had what amounted to tenure. He was a chairman of the Classics Department, and who was there to replace him? He was adored by students and alumni alike, as well as by the trustees and most of the other members of the faculty. He'd had the senior yearbook dedicated to him twice. All Hobe could think of was that his first year as head of Crittenden was going to be befouled by a sordid academic scandal, an Oscar Wilde case with attendant publicity that could destroy everybody's reputations.

I decided to pay a visit to Mr. Fish in his rooms. Among other things, I said, "One of our alumni, Michael Rubin, class of '64, told me of an incident during bed check when you were his dormitory master. And if you're thinking of suing anybody, Titus, I can certainly assure you that Michael Rubin is not the sort of man who will be afraid or shy to testify about that incident in a court of law."

Mr. Titus Fish's face became very red. "That little Yid was just jealous because I never invited him on one of my outings," he said.

Nonetheless, a letter of resignation from Titus Fish was on Hobe's desk the following morning. I saw that sort of thing as part of my job, part of my career. There was no reason to tell Hobe about my meeting with Titus Fish. I was just doing something I felt needed doing, and I could do it. It was not a pleasant chore, but a part of doing any job well is just doing what you have to do, when you have to do it.

Once, when Hobe brought up the subject of divorce, as he did tonight, I said that if I divorced him I'd name the Crittenden School as correspondent. I was trying to be funny, though Hobe didn't think it was funny. But it's true. In addition to being married to each other, we've also both been married to the school. It's been a kind of ménage à trois. Awful. But wonderful.

The other day, when Johnny was here and we took a drive up into the Berkshires to see all the spring blossoms on Sunday morning, Johnny asked me if I still loved his father. Johnny seems to have love on his mind these days, and I suppose it has something to do with his breakup with Blair. But *breakup* is the wrong word. Young people don't break up nowadays the way they did in my generation. Johnny and Blair still see each other. They're still friends. They have dinner together every week or so. It's just that they don't live together anymore. In my day, that just didn't happen. A breakup was really a breakup, and one sobbed and cursed and kicked the stairs when it happened.

Anyway, I thought long and hard before I answered the question. Finally, I said, "Well, after thirtysome years of marriage, it's not just a question of love. It's more a question of need. I think your father and I need each other."

But if he asked me the same question tonight, after our argument about Woodin's article, what would I say? I might say that our need is based on fear. Hobe is afraid that he'll lose me, and I'm afraid that if I walk out on him now, something terrible might happen to him or could happen to us both.

And yet admitting that I need him tonight would be a little like saying I have cancer. I've had cancer, and I know the aftermath. It's terrifying, but there's not a hell of a lot anyone could do about it.

SEVEN

It is after lights-out, and in Fuller Hall, the junior boys' dorm, the three of them—Craig Hyzer, Jason Saunders, and Chad Wilkinson are in Wilkinson's room in their pajamas with their flashlights. "What I want to know is what you have to do to get laid by one of them," Saunders says.

"One of who?"

"The Colby Club girls, asshole."

"They do it for candy."

"Candy? I've got a whole box of Snickers bars in my room, if that's all it takes. My mom sent 'em."

"No, asshole, they don't do it for candy!"

There is the sound of slippered footsteps in the hall outside, and immediately the flashlights go out. Wilkinson hops into his bed and pulls the covers up around his neck. The other two quickly hide under the bed. The footsteps pass, and the Weasel, as Mr. Weisel, the dorm master is called—if in fact it was the Weasel, and not just another classmate going down the hall to take a leak—has not chosen Wilkinson's room for bed check. The two crawl out from under the bed, and the flashlights flip on again.

"Then what *do* they do it for? Whores don't do it for nothing. Money, you think? I want to get laid."

"No, it's not money. Van Degan is rich. Her old man owns the whole goddamn Rockefeller Center, or some goddamn thing."

"It's the Empire State Building, moron."

"Maybe it's Rockefeller Center and the Empire State Building. Who gives a shit? Anyway, he's loaded."

"Maybe she does it for kicks."

"Naw, girls want more than kicks to do the kind of stuff I've heard she does."

"They say Van Degan's a nympho."

"Van Degan has a fat ass. Can you picture pluggin' it into that fat ass of hers?"

"Well, you know what they say. The bigger the cushion, the better the pushin.'" The boys giggle at this as silently as possible.

"Winston and Smith are supposed to be in the club too. Winston's not bad looking. Where do they do it, anyway? I wanna get laid."

"In their rooms. Where else?'

"You ever get laid, Saunders?"

"No. Well, yes. Sort of."

"Whadaya mean, sort of?"

"Sometimes I let my sister jack me off."

"Your sister? That's really disgusting, Saunders. I mean that's, like, really gross, Saunders, you know!"

"What's wrong with that? I mean, she's five years older than me. She does that with lots of guys. It's not like I'm actually fucking her. I mean, she likes to do it."

"Still, that's really gross. That's really and truly, totally, grossly disgusting, Saunders. You know? I mean totally."

"But how do we get laid by those girls over in Colby? That's what I wanna know. I wanna get laid."

"Saunders, you don't have a chance. In fact, none of us do." This is Wilkinson speaking.

"Why not?"

"Yeah, why not?"

"Well, I've got this theory," Wilkinson says. "One of the guys who's been definitely fucking all those girls is old Sandy McFarland. What does that tell you?"

"First McFarland said he did, then he said he didn't. One way or the other, he's got to be lying."

"First he said he did because he *did*. Then he said he didn't because he was scared old Spotty would hear about it. I happen to believe he did, you know? And more than once. A whole bunch of times—with Smith and Winston and Van Degan, too. So what's old McFarland got that we haven't got? Think about it."

"McFarland's a jock."

"Nothing to do with it."

"He's good-looking."

"Nothing to do with it, either."

"He's got a big dick." More giggles at this.

"No, no. You're all way off. Think again. What else has he got?"

"McFarland's a senior."

"Now you're getting warmer. What else?"

"McFarland's a brain. Top of the senior honor roll."

"Bingo! You got it. That's my theory."

"Huh? I don't get it."

"Neither do I."

"Don't you see? Those broads in Colby are all juniors. They'll only do it with seniors. And only with smart seniors. And they'll only do it with guys who promise to help them with their final exams and help write their term papers. Why do you think they're all so busy right now? Exams coming up. Term papers coming due. That's what the broads in Colby are doing it for."

"But what about Simpy Raymond? He says he did it with them, too."

"Simpy Raymond's an asshole. He just says that so guys will think he's in a league with McFarland."

"Christ, I haven't even started my term paper!" Saunders says.

"See? So, what did I just tell you, idiot? That's why you won't be getting any invitation to spend an evening with the girls at Colby Hall. You won't be invited to get laid in return for a brilliant essay on Silas Fucking Marner."

"You really think that's what they do it for?"

"Well, it's only a theory. But it, like, makes sense, don't you think? Only smart seniors. Or teachers."

A shocked silence, then, almost in a paired voice, Hyzer and Saunders say, "Teachers, *too*?"

"That's what they say. I've heard old man Schlachter's made a few trips over there to dip his wick. Even our very own Weisel the Weasel."

Saunders rolls over on his side on the bed, pulls his pajama-clad knees up to his chest, and hugs them. "Oh, I wanna get laid!" he moans. "I've got a hard-on!"

"Yeah? Let's see it."

"Yeah? Prove it. Let's see it . . ."

And for several minutes the boys roll about on Wilkinson's bed, giggling and tickling and pinching and poking and throwing soft punches at one another, while their flashlights draw crazy patterns across the walls and ceiling of the small room. Then, once again, slippered footsteps are heard in the hall outside, and it is back under the covers and into their hiding places for the boys once more, and all is silence and darkness again.

He said to meet him by the seal pond at the Central Park and she is the first to arrive, a little early, and she stands at the railing watching the seals perform: lumbering up the slopes of their artificial rocks, then sliding down, diving under the water, disappearing, circling the pond, coming up for air, barking at their audience, then diving again, such awkward creatures on land, so graceful in the water. What must it be like, she wonders, to be designed to survive in two incompatible environments? As she used to as a child, she tries to count the seals, but this is impossible. There are at least five, perhaps six. She is so absorbed in watching the animals cavorting and playing their little games that she jumps slightly when she feels a man's hand take her elbow, and it is he, though at first she almost doesn't recognize him behind the oversized pair of aviator sunglasses. "We'll have lunch here at the cafeteria," he says, steering her toward the terrace and outdoor tables.

"I expected something a little more glamorous from the great Michael Rubin," she says. "Aureole, Le Cirque, even the Four Seasons—but not the local cafeteria."

"We don't want to be recognized, do we? Here, we're just a couple of New York tourists."

She sees that he has even slung a camera around his neck, to add to the disguise. Michael's sense of personal dreams always amused her. He would appear in a chauffeur-driven stretch limousine with tinted windows and vanity license plates. Or he would arrive elaborately camouflaged, as he has today. But the French cuffs of his bespoke shirts were always boldly monogrammed, and his much-photographed famous good looks— the wet-looking formerly jet-black hair now a wet-looking silver—usually gave him away. Even now, as they enter the cafeteria, a few heads turn, and there are whispers of recognition from several of the tables. "Who are you trying to hide from?" she asks him. "I'm the one who's supposed to be incognito."

"I told you I've been having a little trouble with the feds."

"Nothing serious, I hope."

"Naw. Effing IRS. I'm not worried. I've got the best lawyers in town working for me." He hands her a plastic tray. "They've got good hot dogs here. Footlongs. You like footlongs?"

"I adore footlongs," she says. "I don't think I've had one since I used to come here as a child."

"One or two?"

"One will be plenty for me."

"Two for me, with chili and onions," he says to the white-coated counterman. "And cheese. Lots of cheese." They move along the line. "Drink?"

"Iced tea."

He pays the cashier, ostentatiously, with a hundred-dollar bill so crisp that it must just have come off the government printing press. The cashier, unimpressed, counts out his change. "There's a table over there in the corner," Michael says, jerking his head in that direction. "We can talk." She follows him to the table.

When they are settled, and she has taken a first sip of her iced tea, he says, "Well, what did you think of my offer to the school?" He is smiling at her now and has removed the sunglasses.

"As I told you on the phone, I think it's very generous."

"And old Spotty? What does he think?"

"Spotty—Hobe—thinks it's generous, too. But—I think I told you this, too—Hobe is a little worried about how the trustees will react to the condition you've attached to the gift."

"He doesn't think my name is good enough to attach to a new arts center."

"Well, that's part of it. But it's mostly that you want to be appointed to the board first. He feels it smacks a little bit of—bribery."

He is grinning at her broadly now. "Say, that's real smart of old Spotty," he says. "Because that's exactly what it is. It's also called doing business. Quid pro quo. You scratch my back, I'll scratch yours."

"I figured as much, Michael."

"I've been called a wheeler-dealer, and I take that as a compliment." He takes a large bite of his overloaded footlong. "Of course, I can always up the offer," he says with his mouthful. "Christ, where are the napkins? Don't they put napkins on these tables?"

"I'll get some." She rises and returns to the counter and extracts a small handful of paper napkins from the dispenser. Returning, she hands him several. "Up the offer?" she says, sitting down again.

"Sure. I forget what I said I'd give the school. D'you remember?" He wipes mustard from his lips and fingers.

She is smiling now. She is sure he remembers what he offered to give the school, but she decides to play along with him. "I've forgotten, too," she says. "Was it—ten million?"

"Make it twenty million. It's all the same to me. It's only money."

"That's very, *very* generous, Michael."

"I suppose you're wondering why I want it so much," he says. "To be on the board, that is."

"Well, you always said how you hated the school when you were there. On the other hand, you sent your son to Crittenden, so there must have been something that you liked about the place."

"Crittenden's a tony school. I wanted my son to go to a tony school, like I did."

"So that's why you want to be on the board of a tony school. It will look good in your Who's Who paragraph. It'll get you *noticed*."

"Good guess," he says. "But it's not just that."

"What else?"

"It's the sort of thing a judge likes to hear, and that a grand jury likes to hear. You know—philanthropist. Friend of education. Concerned about the future of America's youth, and yadda-yadda-yadda. I mean, just in case they try to hand down some kind of indictment."

She frowns. "Indictment? That does sound rather serious, Michael, whatever it is."

"Nah, it's not gonna come to that. At least my lawyers don't think so. But when you're dealing with the feds, you never know. With the feds, you've got to think ahead. You've got to think of the possibilities—get ready for a worst-case scenario. So, I want this as a kind of insurance, against the unlikely possibilities, which you never know what they'll be when you're dealing with the effing feds."

"And so, I gather this is something you want to happen rather quickly."

"You got it. As soon as I get the trusteeship, you can start breaking ground for my arts center."

"And I also gather that this is something your lawyers have recommended that you do."

His gaze at her is steady. "You were always much smarter than you let on to be, Clarissa," he says and covers her hand with his left hand while, with his right, he takes a bite of his second footlong.

"So things are bad for you right now, Michael," she says quietly.

"Let's say they could be better," he says.

"And my role in this? Well, as I see it, I'm supposed to speak to Hobe and get him enthusiastic about your arts center. I was the art history major, after all. I'm supposed to be the little voice on the pillow. I'm to tell him that you're willing to up the offer. How high will you go? I don't know, but presumably even higher. I'm to try to get Hobe to present your offer to the board in as glowing terms as possible. Am I right?"

"And to the trustees themselves. And to their wives. The president of the board is a woman—Mrs. Curtis Lemosney, Alexandra Lemosney. She thinks highly of you, Clarissa, I happen to know. They'll all be meeting at the school in a couple of weeks. You'll be having them all at the Castle for dinner."

"I know."

"Help me, Clarissa."

"Dear Michael," she says. His left, noneating hand still covers her own, and, with her fingertips, she gives it a gentle squeeze. "There are only a couple of problems," she says.

"And these are?"

"For one thing, I don't intend to tell Hobe that you and I had this meeting today."

"No need to. He knows we're old friends. We could have had this conversation on the phone."

"For another, the little voice on Hobe's pillow won't be as effective right now as it might have been a few days ago. At the moment, I'm not in my husband's good graces, shall we say?"

"You mean that story in the *Litchfield Times* yesterday?"

She lowers her eyes. "You saw that?"

"Friend of mine who lives up there clipped it and faxed it to me. Knew I'd gone to Crittenden. I can see how old Spotty wouldn't be too happy about that."

"Unhappy? He's furious with me. We had a screaming fight last night. That's one reason I came to New York today."

"Just one reason?"

"Well, you said you wanted to see me," she says.

"Listen, I thought that story was *great*! I thought your quotes were great. You said things about the school that needed saying.

You know damn well that the problems at Crittenden are no different from the problems at any other coed boarding school. But you had the guts to come right out and tell it like it is. Old Spotty should be *grateful* to you. He'll realize this and simmer down right away, I guarantee you."

"I wish I could be so sure."

"I'm positive."

"And so I can be that little voice on the pillow again, you mean?"

"Will you try? I hate to ask favors of you, Clarissa. But this could be important to me."

"You know I'll do anything I can to help you, Michael," she says.

Now Michael lowers his eyes. "Thank you," he says, almost humbly. He finishes his hot dog and licks his fingers. "Where are you staying in New York?"

"I'm at Sally's apartment. She's in San Francisco for a few days."

"Yes, I know."

"How did you know that?"

He winks at her. "Oh, I have my spies," he says. "Shall we go there now?"

"All right."

"I didn't bring my car. We'll grab a cab." He stands up, and then looks down at Clarissa's plastic cafeteria tray. "Hey, you haven't touched your footlong!" he says.

"I really wasn't very hungry."

He offers her his hand, and she also rises.

As they enter the apartment on East Sixty-Seventh Street, Sally's telephone is ringing. "I'm not going to answer that," Clarissa says. "It could be Hobe. We'll let Sally's service pick it up."

He closes the door behind them, and presently the ringing stops. He takes her in his arms. "Mostly, I had to see you," he says. "It's so goddamn lonely without you, Clarissa."

"And for me too," she says and lifts her mouth to his.

Mary, Hobart Spotswood's secretary, opens his office door a crack and pokes her nose inside. "I know you don't want to be disturbed, Mr. Spotswood," she says. "But Mrs. Lemosney is on the phone." Her look is anxious. "Shall I tell her you're in a meeting?"

"Oh, Christ," he says. "The you-know-what has already begun to hit the fan." He bridges his left hand across his eyes. "No, I'll take it, Mary," he says and reaches for the receiver with the other hand. "Well, hullo, Alexandra!" he says in an entirely different voice. "How splendid to hear from you! How are things in Houston?"

"Bloody *hot*." Her richly diphthonged East Texas drawl makes "hot" come out almost as "ha-at." "But Curt and I are lookin' forward to our New England trip. And I'm wonderin', Hobart— did you happen to see a copy of yesterday's *Litchfield Times*?"

He clears his throat. "Yes, I did," he says. "And I think I can explain. There were a lot of mis—"

"A friend of mine called and read it to me over the phone. I think it's *terrific*. Tried to call Clarissa, but your maid at the Castle says she's out of town."

"Yes, she went down to the city to see her mother." And he adds, "Her mother's not been well," though this latter is a lie.

"Well, I must say it took gumption to say the things she said, and I really wanted to tell her so myself. I mean, we all know our little school has certain problems, Hobart, but Clarissa really laid them out for us. I've always said that a problem well stated is a problem half solved. Don't you agree?"

"Well, yes. Yes, of course, Alexandra."

"And these are the exact same problems that we must address at our meeting, Hobart! Clarissa's given us an agenda! You must be terrifically proud of her, Hobart dear."

"Well, yes. Yes, of course."

"So articulate. And so obviously caring—that's what comes through in the interview. She's obviously not the mousy little wife one might expect of a prep school head."

"No, no . . ."

"Anyway, it's given me an absolutely terrific idea, Hobart. Do you think we could get Clarissa to sit in on our meeting? It would be simply wonderful to have her input."

"Well, that's not exactly—"

"I know it's not exactly customary, sweetie. But she'd give our meeting a real shot in the arm. The board would adore it."

"Are you sure the others would—"

"Listen, those other old farts will adore it if I tell them to adore it. D'you think Clarissa would do it?"

"Well, I could ask her."

"Do ask her. Tell her how much it will mean to us all if she'd do it. Ask her and let me know right away what she says. If she has any questions, ask her to call me."

"All right," he says. "I'll ask her. But—"

"No buts, sweetie. *Beg* her to do this for me, and we'll have a helluva meeting." There is the sound of a telephone ringing on Alexandra's end of the connection. "Oops! I've got another call coming in. Gotta run, sweetie. Give Clarissa a big, sticky kiss for me. Cheerio!"

Slowly, Hobe replaces the receiver in its cradle, resting his hand on the instrument. With his free hand, he mops his brow with his pocket handkerchief. "Well, I'll be damned," he mutters to himself. "Well, I'll be goddamned . . ."

* * *

In the darkened bedroom in Sally's apartment, only a narrow wedge of afternoon sunlight from the street outside comes through the drawn curtains, and Clarissa wakes from a light sleep to realize that Michael is stroking the soft, smooth, yielding flesh of her chest that has replaced the harder scar tissue from where her left breast once was. Instinctively, she draws the sheet around herself.

"Don't," he whispers. "Please don't do that."

"That doesn't—turn you off a little? At the time, reconstructive surgery wasn't an option for me."

"Turn me off? Not a bit. It's kind of exciting, actually. My last wife was all silicone implants. This is you. This is real. I love what makes you, you."

She lets the sheet fall aside.

"Besides," he says, "I have a good memory." He continues stroking her there, gently kneading the flesh.

"My sacrifice for you," she says.

"I don't understand."

"The left half of me I gave up for you."

"I still don't understand."

In the darkness she is smiling. "Maybe sacrifice is the wrong word," she says. "Maybe the word is souvenir. Remember the old song, 'Among My Souvenirs'? Never mind. I'm not sure what I mean. Just don't stop. It does feel nice."

"Old Spotty ever do this?"

"Never! He can hardly bear to look at what's left of me there. He makes me undress in the dark. I shouldn't be telling you things like that. But I am."

"Old Spotty doesn't know what he's missing, does he? It's not too late for us, Clarissa. For you and me."

"Isn't it? I just don't know."

"It's not. Trust me." He raises himself on one elbow, tucking a pillow in his armpit. "By the way, do you know what Sally is doing in San Francisco?" he asks her.

"Not exactly. Some sort of business for her agency."

"I happen to know. She's making a pitch for the ad account of the Ritz-Carlton hotel chain."

"Hmm. How do you find out these things?"

"Spies. And, by a funny coincidence, I'm after the same chain. But I'm making an offer to buy them."

"All of them?"

"Controlling interest, with a group of other investors. Just the US franchises, but that's quite a few properties."

"To keep classing up your image, I suppose. A tony hotel chain."

"Exactly. And if Sally could land that account, it would be a nice piece of change for her agency. And a nice feather in her cap for her."

"Oh, I'm sure it would."

"And if I pull this deal off, I'll see to it that Sally gets that account."

She laughs softly. "Deals, deals," she says. "Always making deals, aren't you, Michael?"

"Dots-a me," he says. "Dots-a me. And your son, Johnny—he's an architect. Could commission him to design my arts center."

"Wouldn't that strike some people as nepotism? The headmaster's son?"

"I'd make it another condition for the gift."

She laughs again. "Bribery and more bribery. Everyone has his price."

"So what? I could make both your kids rich, is what I'm trying to say."

"Bribery's in your soul, Michael. But I don't care. I also like what makes you, you."

"Only like?"

"No, more than like. Much more than like."

"Dots-a better." He tosses aside the pillow, and leans across her, and covers her body with his own. "Dots-a more like it," he says.

In her mind are the words of the old song: *I count them all apart and as the teardrops start, I find a broken heart among my souvenirs.*

EIGHT

Rose Finney, for one, is glad Mrs. S didn't stay in New York for any longer than she did. And, though he obviously didn't say anything to Rose, she is sure that Mr. S missed his wife while she was gone. He spent much of his time in his study working on his commencement speech, or "address" as he prefers to call it. She could hear him in there, pacing back and forth and talking into his tape recorder and, from the expression on his face when he appeared at the dinner table at night, Rose could tell that the speech wasn't going well. Poor man. Rose knows that this is an important speech for him. It will be his twenty-fifth commencement address at the school, and she is sure that he wants it to be special and memorable. On the other hand, having listened to dozens of headmasters' speeches over the years, she can bet you dollars to doughnuts that this speech will contain plenty of the same old lines: "The future of America is in your capable young hands." "You face the challenge of assuming your country's social, business, and civic leadership." "In these troubled times, the world looks to you." And blah-blah-blah. Has there ever been a time when the times weren't troubled? Rose would like to know.

And Mrs. S has come home in such jolly good spirits, that's a relief, so different from the spirits she was in when she left.

She's even eating better. Of course, Rose can understand why she was in such a black mood when she left, after that dressing down Mr. S gave her that night. (Which, in Rose's opinion, she richly deserved, for shooting off her mouth like that to that woman reporter, talking about condoms in a family newspaper that children could read! Mrs. S should have known better. Mr. S was quite right, giving her hell about that, Rose thinks. It's a man's world.)

Anyway, now that she is back home and is settled in again, there are a few important matters that Rose needs to talk to her about. Woman-to-woman matters. She taps on the door to Mrs. S's little room where she works on those diaries that she keeps locked in her desk drawer.

"Come in, Rose."

"A couple of things, Mrs. S," Rose says. "First, I've drawn up a menu suggestion for the trustees' dinner. I know you like to have a different menu every year, and this year I've found a market in Canaan where I can get soft-shelled crabs, fresh. They fly them in from somewhere every day. Anyway, here's my suggestion for the rest of the meal." She hands her a five-by-eight card.

Clarissa glances at the card. "Sounds delicious," she says. "I'll look it over, and we'll go over the whole thing in a day or so."

"And then," Rose says hesitantly, "there's something else, Mrs. S."

"What's that?"

"It's about Pauline." Clearly, Clarissa has drawn a blank. "Pauline Scanlon—remember?"

"Oh, yes, the maid. What about her?"

"You did put that trash bag of stuff in the incinerator, didn't you, Mrs. S?"

"Absolutely. Saw it go in. Saw it burn. Why?"

"Pauline is still so nervous about the whole thing. She keeps asking me if I'm sure. And just like she said would happen, Stimpson caught her short on her linen count and docked her pay."

"And I said I'd reimburse her for that, didn't I? How much did it come to?"

"Two hundred and forty-seven dollars and thirteen cents. That's a lot of money for someone in Pauline's position, you know, with her mother and all."

"I realize that. I'll write her a check." She reaches in her desk drawer and takes out her checkbook and reaches for her pen. "Let's see, it's Pauline—"

"Scanlon. S-C-A-N-L-O-N."

Clarissa fills out the check, signs it, and hands it to Rose. "You can give this to Pauline when you see her," she says.

Rose folds the check carefully in half and puts it in her apron pocket. "Thanks, Mrs. S. Pauline will really appreciate this. And she's sorry she got you involved in this whole mess."

"Nothing to it. I was glad to help her out. And now it's all over, isn't it?

"Well, not quite, Mrs. S."

"What else?" Clarissa suddenly finds herself a little annoyed at Rose.

"Well, what I couldn't figure out was how that girl—that Van Degan girl—could have slept two nights in that bed of hers, with all that filth. I mean, there's no housekeeping services on weekends, you know, and if what happened happened on a Saturday night, the way they all say it did, and Pauline didn't find the mess until Monday morning, that would mean the girl slept two nights with the mess, if you receive my meaning."

"Well, I admit it's a rather unappetizing thought," Clarissa says. "But if she did, she did." She could add that she's known certain young women who have rather peculiar ways of dealing with their menstrual cycles. At Smith, Marylou Kearns, otherwise fastidious, had kept all her used Kotex pads stuffed in paper bags under her bed, kept them for months and months before disposing of them. But she decided not to go into that sort of thing with Rose. "Anyway, it's all over and done with," she says.

"But now Pauline's told me a little bit more about what happened than she told me at first," Rose says. "It seems that when she went into the girl's room that morning, she didn't find that mess in the bed. When she went into the room, she found the bed stripped completely bare, right down to the rubber sheet. Naturally, she thought: 'What's become of the linens I'm supposed to change?' She began to look around the room, and finally she found everything, all wadded into a ball in the back of the closet, like she was hiding it."

"Well, there's your explanation of how she slept in the bed," Clarissa says.

"But you don't understand, Mrs. S. The housekeeping staff is never supposed to look in the students' closets. Or in their dresser drawers, or in their desks. That's a real no-no, Mrs. S, to look around in their closets. That's the first rule they give the maids: Never go into a student's closet or dresser drawers. Those're private. With campus security, it's another matter, but if Stimpson found out that Pauline went into a closet she'd be fired on the spot!"

"Well, I don't see what any of this matters now," Clarissa says.

"It's the same with me, the same rules apply. I've never gone into one of yours or Mr. S's closets, or desks, or bureau drawers. Those areas are personal and private. Same with the students."

"Nonsense. You've helped me straighten out closets lots of times. You've put away laundry in my drawers."

Rose purses her lips. "Only when you were personally present," she says primly. "That's the rules."

"Well, I hardly see what difference any of this makes, or why you're bothering me with—"

"I told you, Mrs. S, that Pauline told me more about this since I last talked to you. It was a little more serious than that."

"What more?"

"Well, it seems, Mrs. S, that—well, there was a baby in it."

"What? What are you talking about?"

"There was a baby in it, wrapped in the blanket. Pauline saw a little hand and a little arm. All covered with blood, of course, but she saw it. That's what scared her so."

Clarissa nods, but then suddenly she is very angry. "And where does all this put me?" she says. "I've been made to incinerate someone's baby! Oh, thank you very much, Pauline— Pauline Whoever-you-are—someone I don't even know! Why did she have to get me involved in all this? Don't I have enough on my mind? And now, for thanks for all this, I get to pay this stupid woman two hundred and fifty dollars!" She slams her fist on her desktop. "Christ!"

"Don't be too hard on Pauline, Mrs. S. She's just a poor, simple country girl who never graduated from high school."

"And why did *you* get me involved in this? You're just as much to blame as she is—you and your effing rules!"

Rose's look is pious. "I thought you should know the truth, Mrs. S," she says. "As our Good Lord said, 'The truth shall make you free.' You just called on the help of our dear Lord yourself."

"The truth! Don't quote Scripture to me—my father was a clergyman! If you and that Pauline were so damned interested in the truth, why didn't you report the whole situation to the Housekeeping Department and let matters take their course, without dragging me into it? You're just as stupid as that goddamn Pauline!"

"Pauline has the school's best interests at heart, Mrs. S. As do I. If we'd reported it to Housekeeping, there'd have been a scandal. Police, newspapers. Would that have been so smart?"

"And so now you've made me some sort of accomplice in . . . in I don't know what! All I can say at this point is that I don't want to hear another word about this. And tell Pauline to keep her trap shut. If she's told you about all this, she might tell half a dozen other people."

"She won't. I can promise you that."

"And before we know it, the whole school, and the whole town will be talking. And you—you keep your damned trap shut, too!"

Rose gives her a narrow look. "You're the fine one to be telling someone to keep their trap shut," she says. "After that interview you gave to last week's paper. Maybe you should learn to keep your own trap shut, Mrs. S!"

Clarissa stares at her. "I could fire you for speaking to me like that," she says evenly.

"But you can't! You can't fire me! I don't work for you; I work for the Crittenden School! The only person who can fire me is Geraldine K. Stimpson!"

Clarissa sighs and turns her head away, and now there are tears welling in her eyes. "You have a point, of course," she says in a flat voice. Her gaze is fixed at the window. She refuses to let Rose see the two identical and unwilling tears that have just coursed across her cheeks. "Well, if we're stuck with each other, Rose," she says, "I suppose the least we can do is try to get along. Shall we try? Now please, I have things to do." Without turning her head, she reaches for Rose's menu card. "Give me a few private moments. I want to go over this menu of yours, for one thing." Rose turns on her heel and strides huffily out of the room, leaving the door open. "Shut the goddamn door!"

No response.

Clarissa rises slowly and closes the door. She is all at once terribly tired. She goes to the small sofa and lies back against the cushions, all in one motion, and sleep strikes her instantly like a dagger to the heart.

"Would you like me to fix your martini for you, darling?" she asks him. "Or would you rather fix it yourself? I don't seem to have been doing such a great job lately."

"No, you fix it, Cissie."

She goes to the drinks cart, fishes out ice cubes, and measures gin and vermouth into the shaker, and he goes to the windows and pulls the drapes closed. "Rose forgot to draw the curtains."

"Rose has been in an uppity mood since I got home," she says. "Don't ask me why." She hands him his drink. "Now, try that, kind sir," she says.

He takes a sip. "Very good," he says. "Excellent."

"Well!" They sit down in opposite chairs.

"How was your mother?" he asks her.

"Oh, she's just fine. We had a nice visit. We took in a couple of shows. Went to that new thing at the Whitney."

"That's nice."

"And how did you get along without me, darling?"

"Fine," he says. He clears his throat. "Alexandra Lemosney called while you were gone."

"Oh? How is Alexandra?"

"She's fine. But she had an unusual request."

"What was that?"

"She wants you to attend the board meeting on the twenty-ninth."

"Me?"

"You. Yes."

She stares at him. "Is it about that interview with Alexa Woodin?"

"Yes."

"Then no. I don't belong at their board meetings, and I won't go."

"She specifically asks that you be there, Clarissa. I don't need to remind you that Mrs. Lemosney is president of the board."

She shakes her head. "Sorry, but I won't do that," she says.

"But you must, Clarissa."

"Must I? But I shan't, and that's that."

"The board of trustees runs this school. They pay my salary."

"Sorry, Hobe. I'll do a lot of things for you, Hobe, but I won't do that. I'll have a lovely dinner for them. I'll shake their hands; I'll kiss their cheeks and hug their wives. I'll entertain them as nicely as I know how. But I will not sit down with all those rich people at that big boardroom table and let dozens of pairs of eyes glare at me reproachfully and remind me of the duties and responsibilities of a headmaster's wife and tell me that the First Amendment rights to freedom of speech do not apply to the wife of the headmaster of the Crittenden School. That, Hobe, I will not do."

"What shall I tell Alexandra Lemosney, then? That you're ill?"

"Tell her anything you want. Tell her what I've just told you. Tell her that attending trustees' meetings is not a part of my job description. Tell her that I refuse to sit in the prisoner's box and let a bunch of school trustees pass judgment on me. Tell her to put it in a letter. Or tell her, for me, that she can go to hell!"

"You're making me very angry, Clarissa," he says. "And I'm very sorry to hear that."

There is a long silence between them now. Clarissa sips her cocktail, crosses her legs at the knee, and lets the left heel of her Delman pump dangle from her toe, swinging her foot in a wide arc. Outside, on the manicured lawns of the school campus, the students' dinner hour is over. Daylight time has given them all an extra hour of sunshine after dinner, and the boys and girls are at play—shouting, tossing balls and Frisbees on the grass, twisting and hopping about on Rollerblades and skateboards on the sidewalks, sitting in pairs under the maples with books spread out in front of them, or in attitudes of half embrace. In hidden places, behind hedges, some joints are smoked. Dogs, joining the play, run and leap and bark. Everyone in the school community, it sometimes seems, with the exception of the headmaster, is permitted to own a dog. Some of these sounds penetrate the closed curtains of the library in the Castle. A boy's voice is heard to wail, "I wanna get laid!" Both Hobe and Clarissa elaborately ignore this. As any educator will tell you, the last couple of weeks of the spring term are known as the Silly Season, at any school or college, when nothing is to be taken very seriously.

In the icy silence of the library, Rose Finney appears at the door in her black evening uniform. "Dinner is served, Mr. Spotswood," she says.

Clarissa rises, smooths the front of her dress with one hand, and picks up her glass with the other. "Let's carry our drinks to the table, shall we, darling?" she says. She has not failed to notice that Rose omitted her name from her announcement.

In her New York apartment, Sally Spotswood says good night to her dinner guest at the door, closes the door, and leans back against it. Her look is expectant. "Well, what did you think of him?" she asks.

Her brother, John, is sitting in the white sofa, nursing his drink. "You want the truth?" he says.

"Of course!"

"What did I think of him? Not much."

She moves across the living room. "Oh, Johnny—why not?" She sits beside him on the sofa.

"I think he's a blowhard," he says.

"Oh, Johnny, you've only just met him. You don't know him at all. He can be so funny and charming, so witty, so nice and considerate and bright—"

"All that talk about all the *zillions* he and his old man are making on these deals of theirs, buying up this company, selling that, leveraging this and leveraging that, referring to the mayor as 'My friend Rudy'—"

"He was probably a little nervous tonight, Johnny. After all, it's the first time he's met you. He was just trying to make a good impression."

"He's got that Crittenden attitude."

"What's that?"

"They all get it at that damned school. It's an attitude of I'm superior. You know, condescending. Like saying, 'You wouldn't understand what I'm talking about because you didn't go to Crittenden.'"

"Actually, he's not like that at all. He's really very modest. He's almost apologetic about how much money their company makes. I think, tonight—well, I think it was just nervousness, because he's really rather shy."

"Shy? I think he's just a carbon copy of his old man. A fuzzy carbon copy."

"Johnny, that's not fair. We've never met his father."

"I have. Or at least I've talked to him on the phone."

"Really, Johnny? Why was that?"

"When I went up to the school to see Mom, there was a call for her on her private line. It was that Michael Rubin. It sounded like she and he were cooking something up together."

"I think Jess's father is considering a major gift to the school. That was probably it."

"Well, I didn't like the way his old man sounded—you know, tough, hard-edged, fast-talking, all business. I identified myself, told him I was her son, but he didn't even ask me how I was. Just said, 'Have your mother call me,' and hung up." He puts down his glass. "Do you really want to get mixed up with that lot, baby sister?" he asks her.

"What do you mean by 'that lot,' Johnny? Do you mean because he's Jewish?"

"Hell, no. I don't give a shit if he's a Jew, or a Buddhist, or a Shiite Muslim."

"Because he's not really Jewish. Jess isn't a practicing Jew, that is. He's what you call a secular Jew, which means he isn't much of anything."

"Jewish has nothing to do with it. I'm talking about that Wall Street gang. They're a bunch of man-eating sharks. Pete, my roommate, works on the Street, you know. He's told me some of the horror stories. He says Wall Street is motivated by just three things—cupidity, avarice, and greed. It's not the white-shoe, Joe College crowd anymore."

"So, Pete's one of the sharks."

He laughs. "He says he hasn't made enough money so far to be affected. But there's a definite Wall Street mentality. I mean, like tonight, when your friend Jesse was telling us about that deal he and his old man are trying to pull off to acquire Telecom. He said, 'By the time that meeting was over, man, there was blood all over the floor!' He acted like he was proud of that. He acted like he thought that was pretty funny. Well, I didn't think it was very funny."

"Oh, that was just a figure of speech," she says.

"He's just like his old man. And his old man doesn't have the greatest of reputations, you know."

"What's wrong with his reputation?"

"Pete was telling me something about Michael Rubin just the other day. Something about a rumor going around the Street about some government bonds that Rubin *père* is trying to put up as collateral for a loan—from Citibank, I think Pete said it was. The rumor is something about the fact that these bonds maybe aren't really Mr. Rubin's to put up. Stolen, maybe? Maybe borrowed from somebody else? Can you borrow money with collateral that you've borrowed from some third party? I don't remember all the details; I wasn't paying that close attention. But it all sounded a little fishy, a little shady, not quite kosher. Pete said the government is supposed to be looking into the whole deal."

"Well, I'm sure there's some explanation."

"Oh, sure. There always is, with those thugs on Wall Street."

She sits forward. "Johnny, Jesse is not a thug. If he sounded tonight a little, well, a little enthusiastic about his business, a little boastful, it was just because . . . because, as I said, he's just met you and was trying so hard to make a good impression on my big brother."

"Well, you asked for my opinion," he says. "And I, for one, was vastly—profoundly—unimpressed."

Sally sits back in the white sofa and tucks her legs underneath her, tailor-fashion. She looks upward at the ceiling and seems to be speaking to it. "Oh, I so wanted you to like him," she says. "And I think you will, once you get to know him. I really hope you will. Because the fact is—dammit, I never thought I'd hear myself say this, but—oh, goddammit, the fact is I'm in love, Johnny."

He takes a sip of his drink. "Hell, I knew that," he says.

NINE

From Clarissa Spotswood's Journal:

So Hobe lied to me. I lied to him, too, of course. I didn't go to New York to see my mother. I didn't even call my mother to let her know that I was in town. But mine was a different kind of lie, for a different reason, and I think there's an important difference there, between two kinds of lies.

I lied to spare his feelings. He would not have been happy to know that I went to New York to meet with Michael Rubin. And so, I lied because I was trying, as my mother would put it, "not to make heavy weather" between Hobe and myself. I lied because I wanted to keep things on an even keel between us.

Of course, it was also a self-serving lie. I admit that. All lies are also that.

But he lied to hurt me, to worry me, to scare me, to keep me flapping in the wind a little longer, uncertain about what was going to happen to me or to him. A kind of torture, Chinese water torture.

It's the motive behind the lie that counts. His was mean.

But, after Alexandra Lemosney called me this morning from Texas, I now know why the trustees want me at their meeting.

145

And I've decided that two can play at Hobe's little game. Tonight, when we meet for cocktails, I've rehearsed my little speech. I'm going to say:

"Guess what, my darling? I've changed my mind. It's a woman's prerogative, you know. I've decided to attend your trustees' meeting. Yes, I think it would be rather exciting and rather fun. Yes, I've thought about it, and I've changed my mind, and you can tell Mrs. Lemosney that I'll be there with bells on! If they want any input from me, I'll be happy to supply it. I'm really looking forward to the whole experience. Aren't you pleased, my darling?"

He won't be pleased. He won't be pleased when it will be I, not he, who will announce to the board that Michael Rubin is willing to double his offer of a gift to the school. He won't be pleased to discover that I, and not just he, can be a force at "his" school. He won't be pleased to hear me speak of it as "our," not his, school. And he won't be pleased when I speak my mind about some of the things that have been going on here. He's afraid, naturally, of what I might have to say because he's finally discovered that I am unpredictable!

For the next couple of weeks, I shall enjoy being the loose cannon. Now, let him do the fretting. Tit for tat.

———

That evening, as Clarissa stirs the vermouth and the gin in the silver pitcher—carefully, so as not to bruise the gin—she says, "Guess what, my darling?"

"I'm sorry to call you at the office, baby sister," her brother says, "but I have a few pieces of news that might interest you."

"Oh?"

"You know I mentioned that Pete, my roommate, works in Wall Street. And it seems that it's a rather small and gossipy world down there."

"Uh-huh . . ."

"I told Pete that I'd had the dubious pleasure of spending an evening with young Jesse Rubin, and it turns out that a girl Pete's been seeing works as a secretary for Rubin & Company. I asked Pete to see what he could find out about what's going on over there."

"And what did Pete come up with?"

"Several interesting things. First, there's the funny coincidence department. Remember a week or so ago there was a little item in the *Times*'s advertising column about yours being one of half a dozen agencies who'd been invited to make a pitch for the Ritz account?"

"Sure."

"Well, it seems the very next *day* Michael Rubin announced that he was preparing a bid to take over the Ritz chain. Doesn't that strike you as a funny coincidence?"

"No, not really, Johnny. The chain's been having problems. Occupancy rates are down. Several of the hotels have been accused of not being up to Ritz standards. That's why they're looking for a new ad agency. They'd be an obvious target for a takeover bid."

"Well, that's not all. This secretary friend of Pete's was given an assignment. She was to find out when you were flying to California, which airline—there's only American, TWA, and United—and even your seat and row number."

"You mean the airlines will give out that information?"

"If you're as good a customer as Rubin & Company, they'll tell you *any*thing. It took this girl about five minutes to find out everything she wanted. Then she was told to make a reservation for Jesse Rubin on the same flight, across the aisle from you, if possible."

"I see," she says thoughtfully.

"So it wasn't such a coincidence that you and he met on that plane. It begins to look, baby sister, as though Michael Rubin sent his good-looking son on that flight as bait, and as though you were the fish he was sent out to catch."

"I see," she says again.

"And which he seems to have succeeded in doing," he says.

"But why? If all this is true—"

"It's true. As Pete says, why would this girl make something like that up?"

"But why? Why me? If Jesse's father wants to take over a hotel chain, there's nothing that I, or our agency, could possibly do to help him—or to stop him, for that matter. We'd have no say in anything like that. We're just a small service business. It doesn't make any sense, Johnny."

"I was wondering the same thing, but there must be some reason why Mike Rubin wants little Sally Spotswood in his pocket. But he obviously does. And so, I put on my thinking cap. And I think—and this is just guesswork, mind you—that it all has something to do with Crittenden."

"Crittenden?"

"Yup. You said Mike Rubin has offered the school a pisspot full of money. Our dad doesn't have a vote in trustees' decisions, but they usually listen pretty carefully to what Pop recommends. I think Mike Rubin wants to make sure that his gift offer gets a favorable reception from the school. It would be pretty hard for Pop to recommend turning down a gift from a guy whose son is seriously dating his daughter, wouldn't it?"

"But why would the school turn down a big gift?"

"Bunch of reasons, the main one being Michael Rubin's

somewhat shady reputation. Crittenden is supposed to be an elite boarding school. Its benefactors have always been *Social Register* types, people like the Lemosneys and the Van Degans."

"Not Jews."

"Well, there's that, too, but you're not supposed to talk about that of course. But in Rubin's case, there seems to be a pattern developing. Pete's girlfriend told him a bunch of other stuff. It seems Crittenden isn't the only place that's been offered solid gold pisspots from Mike Rubin. There's also Yale, and Rubin's expressed a desire to be a member of the Yale Corporation. There's also Roosevelt Hospital and Sloan-Kettering Cancer Research. And there's other charities—the Heart and Lung Association, the Diabetes Foundation, the Boy Scouts, the Red Cross. You name it, and all at once Rubin wants to throw a lot of money at it. It's as though he's trying to buy instant respectability, instant prestige. He wants to be an overnight Man of Distinction, Mr. Philanthropy, Mr. Civic-Minded American. And he's also hired Walsh & Company, the big PR firm, to represent him—like he wants to be *Time* magazine's Man of the Year."

"Maybe it's just because, having made so much money, he feels it's time he gave some of it away."

"Maybe. But he's also hired two—not one, but two of the biggest downtown law firms to represent him. And all this has happened in just the last month or so. What's his big hurry? What's he scared of? To me, he's acting like a man who's trying desperately to save his skin, or to cover his ass, and I bet it all has something to do with those questionable government bonds I told you about. I discussed all this with Pete, and Pete completely agrees with me."

"Oh, Johnny," Sally says in a tone of some annoyance, "but this is all gossip, all speculation. It's all what you think, and what

Pete thinks, and what Pete's girlfriend says. You're just passing along a lot of second- and thirdhand information, and I don't think—"

"I just don't like to see you being used in some scheme of Michael Rubin's," Johnny says.

"But considering your sources—some small-time stockbroker and some little secretary—"

"I think you may be being used as a kind of pawn in some very large and complicated situation. Pete thinks so."

"Oh, to hell with Pete! I don't even know this Pete. Why should I give a damn what this Pete thinks?"

"Maybe you're not a very important pawn. Maybe you're just a very minor pawn. I still don't like it."

"Well, thanks for the information, Johnny."

"And if you're going to pursue this relationship with Jesse Rubin, I want you to do so with your eyes wide open. I don't want to see my baby sister suckered into some position that could, at the very least, turn out to be embarrassing. Or even dangerous. These guys who work for Rubin play hardball. I don't want to see my baby sister hurt."

"Sure. Well, thanks. And please stop referring to me as your baby sister. I'm twenty-five years old, and I think I ought to know what I'm doing."

There is a pause and then, with a note of reproach in his voice, he says, "It's only because I love you, Sally."

"Sure. Same here, Johnny. Now I've got to run to a meeting." She hangs up the phone without saying goodbye, immediately sorry she was so brusque with him. She spreads her hands across her desktop, staring hard at its polished surface, wishing that there really was a meeting she had to run to.

* * *

One of Clarissa's father's favorite homilies, one that his congregation asked him to repeat at least once a year from the pulpit of the little church in Riverdale where he preached for nearly thirty years, was called "The Different Kinds of Love." Though she had listened to the sermon many times, she can't remember all the different kinds of love her father described—he had a long list. She remembers some of them, and she remembers how the talk began: "The human species was not designed to love just one person, or one object, for all time, and to the exclusion of all others."

There was romantic love, for one, the love between two lovers, which might be quite different from married love, between husbands and wives. There was parental love, the love of parents for their children, and motherly love could be quite different from fatherly love. Then there was love of children for their parents, which could express itself in so many different ways. There was neighborly love, and the love of friends. There was the love of animals, and of nature, trees, flowers in a garden, clouds, and clear skies, all different. There was love of beautiful objects, love of art, love of music, love of books and learning. There was love for things that could only be imagined, never really experienced. There was love of country, love of one's home, and love of life itself. The list went on and on and on, through love of food, love of games and sports. There was puppy love, adolescent love, mature love. And she would always remember her father's closing words: "But the only love that encompasses all these different kinds of love, that generates all these different kinds of love, that gathers all loves into its arms in one loving embrace and is where all loves begin and end, is God's love which spans the universe. Let us pray."

Over the years, she has often thought of the words of her father's text, thinking that this explained why it was possible to love two men at once, though each in a different way. Because of course it was possible.

She is thinking these thoughts now, when she hears the doorbell ring and Rose's footsteps in the front hall going to answer it and admit her visitor. She starts down the stairs. "Hello, Linda," Clarissa says. "I see you got my note. I'm glad you could come."

Linda Van Degan takes her hand and performs a small curtsy. The little curtsy strikes an odd note. Someone, Linda's grandmother perhaps, must have instructed her in that, told her that this was the proper show of respect when paying a call on an older person. The curtsy contrasts oddly with Linda's outfit, which, though the day is warm, is layered as if for winter. The collars of at least four shirts are displayed under the V-neck of a sleeveless sweater, and all this clothing makes her bosom appear heavier than one might expect for a girl her age. And her lower body is covered with a pair of blue denim bell-bottoms cut so wide and long that their hems sweep the floor and cover her feet, which are no doubt encased in sneakers of some sort. She has cut her blond hair shorter than it was at their last meeting, and Clarissa realizes that Linda's hair is fine but rather wispy, and that Linda has tried to compensate for this by blow-drying it into a kind of frizz.

"I invited you to tea," Clarissa says, "but of course you can have anything you want. Would you like something cold to drink instead?"

"Do you have a 7-Up?"

Rose turns toward the kitchen, muttering, "Miss Van Degan will have a 7-Up."

"Let's sit in the library, dear. It's cozy. And I have a plate of Rose's famous brownies, fresh out of the oven." Clarissa leads the way.

The Castle is a kind of prison, and Linda Van Degan is now her prisoner there. She has checked Linda's classroom schedule, and she has nowhere to go between now and suppertime. This will not be like catching her between chemistry lab and French class. Linda seems to have sensed her imprisonment, too, for her look now is one of apprehension, a frightened, trapped look.

"Sit down, dear," Clarissa says once they are in the library. She offers her the plate of brownies. "Won't you have one of these?"

"Thank you, Mrs. Spotswood." She picks up a brownie and the small linen napkin that is offered with it. She places the napkin and the brownie, uneaten, on the table beside her chair. Rose appears with their drinks on a tray. Clarissa accepts her cup of tea, and Linda her 7-Up in a tall glass with ice. "Please close the door on your way out, Rose," Clarissa says, and Rose throws her another dark look.

"Well, where to begin, Linda?" she says when they are alone again. "You've obviously figured out that I've invited you here for some special reason. It's true. I think you and I need to talk, and we need to talk like two mature women. Please forget that I'm your headmaster's wife and that you're a Crittenden student, Linda."

The girl's look shifts. She is having trouble making eye contact with Clarissa. "Okay," she says at last.

"I'll get right to the point. There's been quite a bit of unpleasant talk around the campus that there's been a lot of sexual promiscuity involving some of the girls in Colby Hall and some of the boys. For some reason, your name keeps coming up. Is there any truth in any of these rumors, Linda?"

Linda squirms uneasily in her chair. "No. Maybe. I don't know."

"Well, which is it? No, or maybe?"

"I don't know!"

"It's a funny thing about a girl who's promiscuous," Clarissa says, moving about the room with her teacup in her hand as she talks. "My father told me this when I was about your age, and I explained it to my own daughter when she entered her teens. If a girl is promiscuous at your age, that reputation will follow her for the rest of her life. With a boy, it's different. For some reason, a boy is expected to be promiscuous. It's considered a 'guy thing,' as they say. The boy is always forgiven for it, but never the girl. For instance, when I was at Smith, there was a girl in Parsons Annex, my dorm, named Amanda Street. She was openly promiscuous, flaunted it, bragged about it. Today, Amanda Street is married, with three grown children, but whenever her name comes up among the men and women who knew her then, the women giggle and the men wink at one another. Her old reputation will never go away. I often wonder what her children must have felt about their mother when they heard the stories, as I'm sure they must have at some point. I don't want you to have that kind of reputation, Linda."

Linda says nothing, but she studies her hands folded in the billows of her bell-bottoms.

"It's the same way with drunkenness. A drunken man is just ridiculous, a joke. But a drunken woman is tragic. All the feminist rhetoric in the world won't change the way the two sexes are perceived in those matters. Men get forgiven. Women don't."

Linda still says nothing.

Clarissa sits down opposite her. "So tell me what's been going on at Colby Hall. Tell me more about the Colby Club. I want you to be honest with me, Linda, because you're special to us here."

Linda looks quickly up at her. "Yeah?" she says. "Special? Why? Because my parents are rich?"

"Well, there's that," Clarissa says. "Your family has been very generous to the school. And you're the fourth member of your family to come here—or is it the fifth?"

"Fourth."

"That's what I thought. But special in other ways, too. I took out your folder from the Records Office. You've been in boarding schools since you were eight years old. That's longer than most girls. That's kind of unusual, don't you think?"

"It's because my parents don't want me at home!"

"Well, that's too bad. But it makes you special, doesn't it? Or maybe you're not so special. You've had trouble at some of your other schools, haven't you?"

Once again there is no reply, and Linda stares down at her folded hands.

"Lots of kids that age get into trouble at school. There's nothing so special about that."

Still no response.

"But I think you want to stay at Crittenden, don't you? You don't want to be kicked out of another school."

Linda shrugs.

"You do want to stay, don't you? And graduate with your friends?"

"I guess."

"I think you do. But what if I were to call your father and say that you were in some serious trouble here? What would he say?"

The girl looks up at her. "He'd say, 'Get stuffed!' You can't kick me out of this school. Daddy's a trustee."

"That's true," Clarissa says. "But I think that would depend on how serious the trouble was."

Suddenly the girl giggles. "One time Daddy threw one of my stepmoms out of the apartment because she wouldn't do something he wanted her to do. That was, like—wow!"

"You see, your father has a temper. There's a letter from him in your file. He says that if you can't make it here at Crittenden, he'll send you to live with your mother in California."

"I wouldn't go! I hate my mother, and she hates me. She wouldn't let me live with her. All she cares about is clothes." Then she adds, almost proudly, "My mother was voted one of the ten best-dressed women in the United States. Did you know that?"

"Yes, I believe I did read that."

"She's very beautiful, you know."

"Your father also mentioned that he's considered having you made a ward of the state. That's a pretty serious threat, Linda."

"Oh, he's always saying that. He wouldn't do it. Tweetums wouldn't let him."

"Tweetums?"

"My new stepmom. She likes me. She's nice to me. She's, like, you know, a real cool mom to me, not like the others."

Clarissa has forgotten that the new Mrs. Truxton Van Degan, whose real name is Bertha, is always called Tweetums. "Well, I'm glad to hear that," she says. "But if you don't care what your father would say if you were in trouble, what about Tweetums? What would she say? You obviously care about her feelings." Once again, the response is a sullen silence.

"So, Linda, I really think you need this school more than you're willing to believe. You see, these years, these boarding school years, are the years in which a young person's character is formed. That's our job, the school's job, to try to see to it that young men and women develop into people of strong moral character. That's what all of us here—myself, my husband, your teachers—are trying to do, besides give you the best college preparatory education possible. That's our goal—to develop character. By the time you get to college, it will be too late. You'll be on your own, and no one will care whether your character is fine or flawed. That's why I care so much about you, Linda. I want this school to send you off to college as a young woman of fine character."

"I'm not sure I want to go to college."

Clarissa decides to ignore this and sits forward in her chair. "Now tell me something," she says. "Level with me, Linda. I want the truth. About two weeks ago, did you give birth to a baby in your room?"

"No!" she cries. "It wasn't mine!"

"Whose was it, then?"

"I don't—I won't—I promised not to tell, Mrs. Spotswood! I swore I wouldn't tell."

"A friend of yours, then?"

"Yes, but—"

"I respect your promise not to tell. But it was born in your room, wasn't it? This is very serious, Linda. We're talking about a human life."

"It was dead! It didn't move. It didn't breathe. I—we—we were so scared, Mrs. Spotswood!" Suddenly there is genuine panic in her eyes. "You're not going to tell Tweetums about this, are you?"

"I haven't mentioned telling anyone, Linda. But I want you to tell me exactly what happened."

"After it—happened—I, we, we were both so scared, and I—I mean she—we decided to wrap it in a blanket and hide it in the closet. And then—" Now there are tears in her eyes, and her left hand flies to her mouth, and Clarissa notices that the fingernails of both hands are painted a metallic green. Linda, seeing that Clarissa has noticed her nails, hides both hands quickly again in the folds of her bell-bottoms, and Clarissa feels a swift wave of pity for this girl, whether she is telling the truth or not; she is really only a child, not yet seventeen.

"And then?" Clarissa says quietly. "Then what happened?"

"And then I—I mean we—we couldn't decide what to do, and so we thought we'd wait a day or so until, you know, she was feeling better. But then I came back from classes—and everything was gone!"

"Yes?"

"And then I was—I mean we—were both really scared, Mrs. Spotswood. We thought, you know, that maybe the school had found it, and we'd be—But then, there's this really creepy maid who cleans the rooms and changes the beds. I mean, she's a real twit, with this gross birthmark on her face—"

"Her name is Pauline Scanlon."

"I don't know her name, but after a couple of days went by, and nothing happened, I decided—I mean, I and my girlfriend decided—that this maid had thrown everything into the garbage. I mean this maid is such a cretin and all. You know?"

"Well, that, more or less, is what happened," Clarissa says.

"And nobody knows about it?"

"Well, I know about it, and you know about it, and this girlfriend of yours knows about it, and Pauline Scanlon knows about it, and my housekeeper knows about it." Clarissa counts them off on her fingers. "That's five people by my count. Five—so far. Let's try to keep it at that figure. If any more people find out about it—well, it could be a very serious matter, Linda, for the police."

"You won't tell anybody else, Mrs. Spotswood?"

"I said, let's try to keep it at that figure. Five of us."

Linda sighs. "Thank you, Mrs. Spotswood."

"Do you have any idea—or rather, does your girlfriend have any idea—of who the baby's father might be?"

She shakes her head. "No."

The air in the room has become very close, and Clarissa has noticed an odor—faintly sour, yet oddly familiar—and suddenly Clarissa wonders whether the girl might still be lactating, and whether this might account for the layers of shirts under the sleeveless sweater. She dismisses this thought, and the smell, as her imagination. Still, she rises and goes to a window and raises the sash to let in an afternoon breeze. "Thank you, Mrs. Spotswood," the girl says again.

"You can thank me by doing what I'm going to ask you to do," she says.

"What's that?"

"Obviously, we can't have something like this happen again. You wouldn't want something like this to happen again, would you, Linda?"

She lowers her eyes and shakes her head.

"Then you can help prevent it from happening again—to some other girl or even to you. I want you to make up a little list of all the girls, and all the boys, too, whom you know to be sexually—precocious, or the word I use, 'promiscuous'—at this school." Linda looks up, alarmed, and Clarissa holds up her hand. "Wait," she says, "I'm not asking you to betray or rat on your friends and schoolmates. I promise you I won't tell another living soul that this list came from you. I also promise you that no one is going to be punished or expelled from school or even reprimanded for being on that list. It will be completely confidential. But what I'd like to do is pass that list on to the school counselor—"

"The shrink?"

"To Dr. Arnstein, yes. All I'm going to suggest is that she keep a particular eye on those students and decide whether some of them might need counseling. Dr. Arnstein is a very sympathetic woman."

"She's okay."

"And very perceptive, and also very discreet. You see, I think one reason young people are promiscuous at your age is because they crave attention and love. Perhaps because, like yourself, they don't get enough love at home. Will you do this for me, Linda?"

She seems to consider this. "You mean list *every*body? Everybody at Crittenden who has sex? That would be the whole school, Mrs. Spotswood!"

"Now, Linda, I'm sure you're exaggerating. The whole school isn't being promiscuous."

"Well, practically. Practically everybody here has had some sort of sex. I mean, get real, Mrs. Spotswood. Wise up!"

"I'm not talking about sex per se, Linda. I'm talking about promiscuous sex. That means haphazard sex. Random sex. Indiscriminate, repeated, unprotected, unsafe sex. I'm sure you see the difference."

"Well, I guess so."

"That's the kind that can be so dangerous, as you and—and your friend—have found out. If you think about it that way, your list will be rather short. I don't want you to rely on hearsay or gossip. Just list the names of the people you have good reason to believe have been behaving in a sexually reckless manner. You can put your own name on this list if you'd like. That's up to you to decide. And I'm not conducting a witch hunt. In fact, I'm not even going to look at your list. I'm just going to give it to Dr. Arnstein and suggest that some of these kids might need a little extra attention. It's just to try to prevent another tragedy. Will you do that for me, Linda? It would help the whole school, and might even help you, too."

"List everybody?"

"Just the ones you're reasonably sure are in danger of getting into the same kind of trouble that you and your friend found yourselves in. I think you know the ones I'm talking about."

"Girls—and boys, too?"

"Yes."

"And if I won't do it, I suppose you'll tell Tweetums."

"I didn't say that."

"But I suppose you would, wouldn't you? I bet you would. You want me to write down all the names?" Her look is calculating now.

"Yes, please."

The girl's eyes narrow. "Spot, too?"

"What?"

"You want Spotty's name, too?"

"What are you talking about? You mean my husband?"

The girl's look is defiant now. "He's done it to me, too! And to other girls!"

"Done what to you?"

"Fucked me!"

Clarissa steps toward her, and only an extraordinary force of willpower, summoned up from somewhere, stops her from doing the most awful thing in the world a headmaster's wife could ever do, which is to strike a student. With another effort of sheer will, she lowers her arm. "Liar!" she says. "You've told me nothing but lies since you walked in this door. You're the one who had the baby. You're a lying, evil little girl. Evil. Liar. Now get out of this house!"

Linda Van Degan leaps from her chair and rushes to the door, almost tripping on the hems of her bell-bottoms as she goes. At the door, she turns back to Clarissa and shrieks, "It's true! Wise up! *Spotty's fucked me, too!*" Then she is gone.

Still shaking, Clarissa picks up the uneaten brownie with her thumb and forefinger and drops it in the wastebasket.

That evening, when her husband buzzes her on the intercom to advise her that he is home, and ready for his martini, she picks up the phone and says, "Oh, darling, do you mind if I don't come down for dinner tonight? I just have the most awful headache—one of the worst I've ever had. . . . No, I don't need a doctor. Do you mind? I think I may be running a slight fever, but it's just a damn spring cold. I've taken a couple of Tylenol. . . . All I really need is to lie down and get some rest, I just feel so rotten. . . . Do you mind having dinner alone? No, I don't want a tray sent up. I'm sorry . . . forgive me, darling. . . ."

In the old days, back in the 1890s when Eliza Crittenden established her school with a gift of cash and land, it was believed that a school in a tiny village in the remote Berkshire foothills provided the best of all possible environments for boys of moneyed families to spend those turbulent, adolescent years. There were no interstate highways then, no radios, hardly any telephones, of course no television sets, and these privileged youths were as far from the venal temptations of the big city (which their newly wealthy parents, rich with Civil War money, knew so well) as it was possible to be. No paved roads led to Crittenden. Life was rigorous and outdoorsy. Winters were long and snowy. A healthy program of sports was essential—soccer, football, tennis, hockey on frozen Lake Kinishawah, followed by cold showers—and was designed to keep levels of testosterone and other raging hormones under strict control. Little time was left for any boy to indulge in unhealthy, more natural pastimes. The twice-a-year school dances, to which young ladies from nearby girls' schools were invited, were fastidiously chaperoned.

Diet was hearty, well balanced, and Spartan, though the boys warned one another not to put gravy on their mashed potatoes, since the gravy, it was said, was liberally laced with potassium nitrate—saltpeter—in the kitchen. Education, with a heavy emphasis on the Classics, was designed to lift boys' minds and instincts to loftier planes. Daily chapel services, twice on Sundays—morning devotions and evening vespers—repeatedly reminded these boys of their duties and obligations to that Higher Power from whom all blessings, including their own privileged circumstances, flowed.

All this was intended to turn the sons of America's more fortunate families into upright, responsible young men of sturdy moral fiber—clean-limbed, clean-thinking, well-spoken, well-mannered, and well-groomed—gentlemen imbued with a sense of leadership and sportsmanship and rectitude, and no small amount of *noblesse oblige.*

Moniti Meliora Sequamur became the school's motto: "Having been shown the higher way, let us follow it."

But Clarissa often wonders, had the Crittenden School ever really achieved any of these high ideals or aims? Ever?

TEN

"I don't think your brother liked me much," Jesse says. They are seated at Le Cirque, in one of the corner tables, finishing dinner.

"Well, Johnny's a very opinionated guy," Sally replies. "He's also very stubborn. He's like Daddy in that respect. Things are either his way, or no way. He could make a lot of money if he were willing to take on big projects—like a school, or a church, or a hospital or an office building. But he'd rather design someone's little cottage in the Adirondacks, and so that's what he does."

"So maybe that's it. Maybe I struck him as too—well, too *corporate*. There I was in my business suit and tie, and there he was in a polo shirt and jeans."

"That's Johnny. He wouldn't dress up to impress anybody. He'd walk into this restaurant dressed the same way and argue with the maître d' when they asked him to leave. He's one of those New Yorkers who gets lost anywhere north of Fourteenth Street."

"I'm sorry he and I didn't hit it off better."

"Well, I wouldn't get any gray hairs about it," she says.

They sip their wine, and he studies her face intently. "There's something on your mind," he says as last. "I can tell."

164

"Why? What makes you think that?"

"You've been awfully quiet tonight," he says. "You seem—well, a little distant and preoccupied. Is something worrying you? What is it?"

She hesitates and looks down at her plate. "I guess I'm not a very good actress," she says with a faint smile.

"What's wrong, Sally?"

"You might as well know," she says. "It was something Johnny told me on the phone. He said he'd found out it was no accident you were seated across the aisle from me on the plane to San Francisco."

"Who told him that?"

"Some friend of a friend of his who works for your company. He didn't tell me the woman's name."

"Because it's absolutely true," he says.

"He said you were on that flight on orders from your father."

"Quite true."

"You might have told me, Jess."

"I was going to. Honest. As soon as we got to know each other a little better."

"But why? That's what I don't understand."

He spreads his hands. "Honestly, I don't know either," he says. "My father doesn't always explain his business motives to me. In fact, he hardly ever does. All he said to me was, 'I want the Spotswood girl on our team.' Those were his words. He didn't tell me why."

"I don't understand it. He doesn't have to buy up a hotel chain to give business to my agency. And our agency can't help him buy a hotel chain."

"Maybe he thinks your agency is the best there is."

"Very flattering. But hardly true. We're very small-time. Nine people, including two secretaries."

"I just don't know, Sally. Sometimes my dad's motives are awfully hard to figure out. All I know is he wants you on our team. Does that bother you?"

"And having his son seduce me is just a swell way to do it, isn't it?"

"Is that the way you see it—that I seduced *you*? I thought it was more . . . more of a mutual thing, Sally."

She lowers her eyes. "Yes. I guess that wasn't a fair thing to say," she says.

"Then . . . are things still all right between us, Sally?"

"Well, it's just a rather funny feeling, Jess. It sort of erodes my trust and confidence in you a little bit, I guess, knowing that when you asked me to dinner at Chez Panisse, where we both seemed to have such a nice time, that you were simply obeying your father's orders."

"He didn't order me to fall in love with you," he says.

From Clarissa Spotswood's Journal:

Of course, I can't believe that girl's story. I couldn't believe it and go on living with Hobe. She lied, just the way she obviously lied about the baby. I knew she was lying from the beginning. I could tell how frightened she was. She would have looked me in the eye if she were telling the truth, but she didn't. And so certainly she isn't going to give me any list, or if she does, it will be nothing but a list of lies. Probably I was foolish to ask for that, but I thought it might offer her a way out, a way to save her own skin. How could I have been so naive?

The answer to that one probably goes back to being Daddy's Little Girl. I was brought up to believe that, as a clergyman's daughter, I was something special. All three of us were special people, Mother, Daddy, and I. We were a special breed. Other people lived in houses, but we lived in a rectory, the only one in the neighborhood. Other people had more money, but we had something even better than that because Daddy worked for the Higher Power, a power so high that mere money could never buy it. Neither moth nor rust could corrupt us. God was on our side, always. God was Daddy. When I tried to picture the face of God in my mind, all I could see was Daddy's face. If Daddy was holy, then we were his holy family. As a girl, I learned to use this to my advantage, of course.

He used to call me Sunny. At first, I thought it was Sonny, with an *o*, and I once told him that he called me that because he wished I'd been a son, not a daughter. But no, he said, it was Sunny, short for Sunshine, because I was the sunshine of his life.

Once I discovered that all I had to be was Little Miss Merry Sunshine, I found out I could get away with all sorts of mischief. All I had to be was sweet. Sweet was my pose, my mask. I would be worse than sweet. I would be angelic. With my angelic mask on, I could get away with all sorts of fibs—not major fibs, but fibs, nonetheless. "What did you do on your date?" "We went to see 'The Sound of Music.'" (We sat in my date's car and necked and petted, petted to climax, as it was called, though it was his climax, not mine.) "The boy didn't have anything to drink, did he?" "Oh, no, he doesn't drink." (But he got so drunk that he threw up all over the front seat.)

I got in the habit of being angelic and giving angelic answers to their questions.

When I was about to go off to college, I was afraid I wouldn't be popular. In those days, "popular" was something all my friends wanted to be more than anything else. I was afraid my clothes wouldn't be as pretty, or as nice, as the clothes of some of the other girls whose families had more money. My father said, "The best way to be popular, Sunny, is to be a good listener. Don't say too much, but always listen carefully to what other people say. Pretend to be listening, even if you're not, and people will think you're the most interesting person they've ever met. People like nothing better than talking about themselves—particularly boys—so let them. Boys are mostly interested in girls who are interested in them. Listen to them, be attentive, ask questions, don't offer too many opinions, and they'll keep coming back for more. Remember, the meek shall inherit the earth."

When Hobe was courting me and asking me to marry him, I asked him what he loved about me. He thought about this for a minute, and then he said, "It's because you're so sweet and good-natured."

I didn't say to him: "But it's all a facade, a conditioned response, a defense mechanism, a survival technique, something I've spent half my life learning how to be, practicing to be. It has nothing to do with what I really am."

There's a tiger caged inside me, Hobe.

And so, I'm forcing myself not to believe what that girl said. I can't believe it, because if I did I think I'd . . .

———

Clarissa's telephone rings on her private line, and she puts down her pen and thrusts the pages of her journal into the desk drawer, closing it and locking it with the key. She picks up the phone. "Clarissa?" his familiar voice says. "Can you get away from school for a few hours? I've got to see you. There's something I've got to show you. It's important."

"Where are you now, Michael?"

"I'm at the Marine Terminal at LaGuardia. I'm in my plane.
If you can, meet me at the Torrington airport in forty-five
minutes, I'll probably be there before you are."

"The Torrington airport? Why?"

"Then we'll fly back to New York. We'll have a bite of lunch
on the plane. There's something that you've got to see."

"But . . ." She hesitates. "I'll have to take the school station
wagon. It has the school's name painted on the side. Won't it
look—peculiar, if someone should see the school's wagon
parked at the Torrington airport? Someone might—"

"Don't worry. I'll have Pablo, my steward, park it inside the
hangar where no one will see it. We're only going to be gone two
or three hours."

"Will I be back by dinnertime—by six o'clock, when Hobe—?"

"Easy. *No problema.* Can you do it?"

"Well, I'm just wearing slacks, and a blouse. Will I—"

"Wear whatever you've got on. I'm in jeans myself. Nobody's
going to see us. We're not going anyplace fancy. Or, rather, we
are going someplace pretty fancy, but it's no place where we
need to be fancy."

"What is it, Michael?"

"You'll see," he says. "Will you come?"

"Well, okay," she says, and then, suddenly excited, "Yes!"

"Good. The plane'll be parked outside Hangar B. There's only
the two, A and B. They're clearly marked." She hears him turn to
his pilot and say, "Okay, Jim—off to Torrington!"

In front of her mirror, Clarissa quickly runs a brush through
her hair and applies fresh lipstick. She grabs her keys and purse.

Downstairs, she finds Rose in the kitchen. "That fishmonger
you told me about in Canaan," she says. "I'm going to drive over
there to check him out—just to be sure they're really fresh, you
know. The softshell crabs."

Rose looks glum. "I told you he has them flown in every day fresh," she says.

"But we can't be too careful, can we?" Clarissa says airily. "Not with softshell crabs. We don't want to see them wiggling. Then I've got a few other errands to do. I'll be back by dinnertime."

"What sort of errands?"

"Just errands."

"No lunch? I fixed chicken salad."

"I'll stop for a sandwich somewhere. Bye-bye!" And she is off.

Clarissa spots Michael's corporate 727 on the tarmac even before she sees the sign pointing toward Hangar B. Never a man for excessive modesty, the jet is slim and sleek and painted a royal blue with crimson tailfins and the legend RUBIN & COMPANY painted along the fuselage in white letters easily four feet tall. As her car approaches, Pablo, his Honduran steward, comes scrambling down the steps in a white mess jacket with blue-and-gold epaulets. He trots to her car, holds the door open for her as she steps out. She hands him the keys and notices that the gold buttons of his jacket are monogrammed "R."

Michael, all smiles, is waiting for her at the top of the stairs as she hurries up. He takes her in his arms. "Wait till you see what I've got to show you," he says. "I want today to be a day you'll never forget."

There follows a quick tour of the plane. The main salon is done all in white, with thick white carpeting, white leather walls, long white sofas, deep armchairs, and low-slung coffee tables, all covered in white leather. A white telephone sits beside each chair. Just forward of this room is the dining and conference room, with a large round table, eight armchairs in red leather, and more telephones. Next is the galley, glittery in white Formica, and then, just aft of the flight deck, is Michael's office, all done in blue leather—big desk and swivel chair—and still more phones. Michael takes her onto the flight deck and introduces her to his pilot, Jim Heinz, and the copilot. To the aft of the aircraft are two large bedrooms, each with king-size beds, walk-in closets, and each with its own full bathroom, with marble showers, gold fixtures, and bidets. There are even phones in the bathrooms. "Cute little bird, isn't she?" he says.

"Cute! Has little old Torrington ever seen anything like this?"

He laughs. "Quite a few folks came out from the Operations building to look at us when we taxied in," he says.

Clarissa settles in one of the white sofas, and Pablo appears with wine and glasses on a silver tray. "Champagne, madam?"

"Of course! Why not?"

"Dom Perignon, 1976." He fills her glass, then Michael's, and they touch glasses.

She hears the jet engines throb to life, and the captain's voice comes on the loudspeaker. "We've been cleared for taxi and takeoff, Mr. Rubin," he says. "Will you and your guest please check the security of your seat belts?" Across the forward wall of the main cabin a huge television screen descends, revealing the view from the flight deck as they move toward the runway.

At the Marine Air Terminal in New York, Michael's car and driver are waiting for them as they step off the plane. They step into the car, and the car turns toward Manhattan. Michael takes her hand in his. "I just hope you're going to like this," he says.

"I'm a little tiddly from the champagne," she says. "So I'm sure I'll like it—whatever it is."

"You'd better—I bought it for you."

"For me?"

From the Triborough Bridge, the car turns downtown on FDR Drive and exits at Seventy-Ninth Street, heading west. At Park Avenue, the car turns north and pulls up in front of a large brownstone house on the northeast corner of the avenue. "Here we are," Michael says. He leads the way up the wide stone steps to the grilled front door and unlocks a triple set of locks with three keys, and they step into a huge circular front hallway paved with black-and-white marble squares. A curving staircase leads to the floors above, and the foyer is dominated by a large crystal chandelier. "Baccarat," he says, flipping on a switch. "But let's start from the bottom, down this little flight of stairs." He flips on more switches and once more leads the way, talking as he goes.

"This is the kitchen. Look at the size of that range. Hotel size. And the size of these ovens—also full hotel size. One for baking, one for roasting, and one for warming. This is one of the last private houses on Park Avenue. Will you look at those sinks? All copper. Look at these refrigerators . . . and this is a walk-in freezer. Look—three dishwashers! This is the butler's pantry; look at the size of the dumbwaiter! Take out the shelves, and two people could ride up and down in it. This is the servants' dining room, servants' loo. In here's the larder, and this little room is the telephone center. Feds would have a hard time bugging my lines with all those circuits, wouldn't they? In here was a cook's bedroom, another loo. Poor cook gets no windows. But now here comes one of my favorite rooms. They call this the garden room." He opens a door, and they are in a long room, with French doors at the end opening out into a formal garden. In the walled and trellised garden, Clarissa sees two flowering cherry trees, garden benches, and against one wall, a lion's head fountain spews water into a lavabo, which, in turn, cascades into a larger pool below.

"They used this room as sort of a party room—look, there's the bar, and a kind of mini-kitchen. But will you look at the wall space? I'm going to hang some of my stuff down here." He moves around the room, pointing at the empty walls that are covered with pale green watered silk. "Look, I'll put a Degas there and a Cézanne there, then maybe a couple more Cézannes, then a Rousseau . . . Gauguin, Picasso's 'Boy Leading a Horse,' which is pretty big, right there in the center. Then what I bought from the Paley estate, a Bourdelle sculpture in the corner there; and then, over there, side by side, my two Manets, maybe? What do you think?"

She is breathless. "You might think of separating the Manets," she says.

"Yes. Of course, I'll have to install a lot of track lighting in here. Now let's go upstairs. We'll take the elevator . . ."

They step out of the elevator on the level they entered.

"This is called the reception floor. You've seen the entrance foyer; this is called the ladies' cloakroom. And over here is the gentlemen's cloakroom, and this is the gentlemen's *smoking* room—ever hear of such a thing? Men came down here after dinner for brandy and cigars. I haven't figured out what the hell to do with these rooms yet. . . . And here, this big room was called the sherry room. Guests came in here for cocktails before going up the grand staircase to dinner. Haven't figured out what the hell to do with this room either. Maybe more of my stuff— maybe sculpture . . . Rodin, Renoir, Bourdelle—some of the bigger pieces. What do you think? The light's good."

"Michael, tell me about this trouble you're in."

"House was built in 1910. Family named Cooper, whoever the hell they were. Cooper-Hewitt Museum? The outside walls are two feet thick. Trains go by under Park Avenue, and you don't hear or feel a thing. Let's go on up."

They step into the elevator again. "Did you hear me?" she says.

"This was called the parlor floor. This is the formal dining room. You can seat twenty-four people at that table. I'm buying a lot of the furniture, including that table and chairs. Chairs are signed Chippendale. And this is the family dining room, or the children's dining room . . . a service pantry here, where the dumbwaiter comes out, and, look, a wine cellar that'll hold a thousand bottles. And here, a walk-in safe that was for the silver, and here's the double parlor; you can turn it into two rooms with these pocket doors . . . two fireplaces in each room . . . and here, in the back end, is the library—shelf space for at least two thousand volumes—another fireplace. Shall we continue up?"

"This trouble with the feds. Can you tell me what it is?"

"Going up to the fourth. . . . This was called the master bedroom floor. In the front, the husband's bedroom, all walnut paneling, very masculine—it's called fluted walnut. Husband's dressing room, husband's bath—take a look at that shower, will you? It sprays out at you from about twenty directions! Husband's study. Wife's bedroom—she's all Louis Quatorze. Wife's dressing room and bath—but she doesn't get a shower. Only a tub. And look at that—do you know what that's called?"

"A sitz bath." He is obviously not going to answer her questions.

"Right. You sit in it. Wife's sitting room, and a little writing room . . . and then, down here, four more bedrooms, with baths—for guests, I guess. And here, at the back of the house, is what they called the morning room, I guess because it faces east and overlooks the garden—and look, a balcony!"

They continue upward. "Fifth floor. This was called the children's floor. Look—four more big bedrooms, with fireplaces yet, and their own baths. And this big room was the children's nursery—and look what the kids got—their own puppet theater! I don't know what to do with this room, either—maybe hang more of my stuff. And this was the nurse's room, and her bath-room—and will you look at this, Clarissa? Another children's dining room, and another kitchen! I guess for when the family didn't want the kids around—they made them eat up here!"

They enter the elevator again.

"Now we're on the top—sixth floor. Nothing up here but more servants' rooms—fourteen little cells, and one little bathroom for the whole lot of them to share. I don't know what to do with this whole floor. I sure as hell don't need that many servants. I thought maybe I could knock out all these walls and put in a squash court, but I'd have to raise the roof. Then I thought maybe a lap pool, but the engineers tell me the interior walls aren't strong enough to support the weight. I thought of a bowling alley, but the building's ten feet too short, and I'd have to add on to the back of the house. And that would cast too much shade on the garden, which doesn't get much sun as it is. I thought of turning this whole floor into a gym, which is a real possibility, or a media center—with a screening room for films. Or I may just turn the whole space into another gallery and hang the rest of my stuff in it—some of the more contemporary things, the Pollocks, the Frankenthalers, the Rothkos, the Motherwells. In fact, that's probably what I'll end up doing. Anyway"—he stops for breath—"what do you think of it, Clarissa?"

"Think?" And why are there tears all at once in her eyes? "I think—I think it's just beautiful, Michael. I think it's . . . just . . . just the most beautiful house I've ever seen."

"The place needs a lot of work. I'm not crazy about the decor—the French chateau style. I'd like to redo a lot of that, get a really top designer to help me with some ideas. I'd keep the chandeliers, of course, and the dining room's perfectly fine as is. But I think it could be a nice place to live, don't you?"

"Nice? It could be gorgeous."

"I'm tired of living in leased apartments and hotel suites, where you can't really trust the staff, even at the Pierre. And I'd like to have my art hung where I can look at it and enjoy it, and not have it all stashed away in storage vaults and warehouses all over town. And it's something I've never really had before, you know, a house of my own."

"Yes. And I wish we could talk a bit more about you. . . ."

"And here's the beauty part, Clarissa. The place was a steal! It's been on the market for seven years, and there just aren't that many people nowadays who're in the market for a house like this. Did I tell you that this is one of the last private residences on Park Avenue? Yeah, I think I did. It was declared a Landmark back in '86, so it can't be torn down. The facade can't be changed, so it's a tough house to divide up into apartments. The Russian Consulate was interested in buying it, but at the last minute the Russkies backed out. So now it's mine! All mine!"

"I think it's wonderful, Michael."

They stand in the long and narrow corridor that runs the length of the top floor of the house, with its rabbity warren of little servants' rooms and storage closets running off on either side—a laundry room, an ironing room, a linen room, a room for storing and hanging curtains—and there is a faint smell of dust and disuse in the area, and suddenly there is a feeling of awkwardness and tension between them. "This house only needs one thing," he says at last.

"What's that?"

"You. Living in it. With me."

"Oh, Michael . . ."

"I mean it. I bought it for you. And me. For us. You think everything I do, everything I buy, is just to boost my own ego, don't you? I think you've always thought that. Most people think that. But it's not true. Ever since I met you, almost everything I've done, I've done with you in mind. What would Clarissa think? What would Clarissa say? I've tried to get you out of my mind, but nothing's worked. I've tried marriages, more than once. I've tried to think of women as nothing but sex objects, just something to fuck when I felt horny, but none of that worked, either. None of it was you. It always came back to you. It always came back to the girl I met years ago at the Old Forge Inn and spent a week making love to, and since that time—nothing, nothing has mattered as much to me as that girl I met in the lobby and acted so obnoxious to that day, just to make you notice me, remember me. I've been called a megalomaniac, and a workaholic, and a pushy Jew on an ego trip, and worse things than that, but whatever I've done has been filled with thoughts of you, and everything else has been— like dust in the mouth, as empty and meaningless as . . . as this attic hallway. Do you hear what I'm saying? I'm saying I love you, Clarissa. I'm asking you to leave him and marry me."

"Oh, Michael, do you think—?"

"Yes, I think you could do it. I know you could do it! All you need to do is take that first big giant step. If there's any secret to my success, it's been my willingness to take the big risk, the big gamble, to have the nerve to take that one giant step. After that, all the little baby steps will follow one by one. Take the giant step, my love. I'll help you make the leap. I'll help you jump across the big mud puddle."

"But—"

"Back at the Old Forge Inn—our afternoons together—you said you loved me then. Did you mean it?"

"Oh, yes. Yes, of course."

"Do you still love me?"

"Yes . . . yes. And yet, in some ways, I don't really know you."

"There—you see? We're halfway across the puddle already. I don't think you ever loved him, did you?"

"Oh, yes. Yes, I did."

"No. You never loved him. Tell the truth."

"No, don't make me say that, Michael. Please, because I did love him—once."

"But no more. And never the way you love me."

"No, not the same way."

"There! We're two-thirds the way across the puddle now."

"But, you see, I have certain duties, responsibilities—"

"To whom? To what? Not to him. Not to your kids, who're grown and on their own."

"Well, to the school, and—"

"To the school? What has the fucking school ever done for you? For years, you've made sacrifices for that school. How many years?"

"Twenty-five."

"Twenty-five years. Almost a third of a lifetime of being a martyr to that fucking school! And what has that gotten you? Fucking zip!" He is almost shouting now. "No home of your own! A loveless marriage! No life of your own! No bouquets, no thank-you notes. All for a bunch of snot-nosed little rich kids who couldn't care less whether you're dead or alive!"

"Sometimes, there are small rewards—sometimes."

"Let me show you a different kind of life, Clarissa. Here in this house. Let's spend whatever years we both have left together. Let me show you some big rewards. Hobe will get his arts center. And I'll—"

She laughs softly. "And you'll get me. A trade-off. A deal. Always a deal. Oh, I do love you, Michael, my wonderful rascal!"

"I did not say that! I did not mean that! What I was going to say was that Hobe has always cared more about his fucking school than he ever cared about *you*."

She laughs again. "That," she says, "I'm sorry to say is probably true."

"There! You see! You're three-quarters of the way across the puddle now. Leave the bastard—leave him to his fucking beloved school!"

Clarissa starts to speak, but he quickly places his fingertips across her lips. "Take the giant step," he says.

On the green hilltop above Lake Kinishawah, in one of the music practice rooms in the Main Building, the school choir is rehearsing.

O, God, our help in ages past,
Our hope for years to come,
Our shelter from the stormy blast,
And our eternal—

"Stop!" says Mr. Singer, the aptly named choirmaster, tapping his pointer on the piano case. "Altos! I'm not hearing you, altos. Where are my altos?" He looks around the group. Someone is missing. It's Linda Van Degan. "Where is Miss Van Degan?" Mr. Singer is a tutor of the old school, who prefers to address his pupils as Miss and Mister, rather than by their first names.

"She's got the curse," one of the sopranos volunteers. There are husky snickers among the tenors and basses.

"All right," says Mr. Singer, tapping on the piano case again. "Let's start from the top again. And sing out, altos!" He gives his fingers a professional shake and place them on the keyboard.

O, God, our help in ages past . . .

And just a few hundred feet down the hall, Mlle Anne-Marie Chabot, French, all levels, has just been ushered into the headmaster's office.

He half rises from his desk. "Ah, Anne-Marie," he says, extending his hand. "Thank you for coming by. Please sit down."

"*Bonjour*, Hobie," she says and takes a seat in one of the pair of armchairs, crossing her jean-clad legs. "*Comment va?*"

"*Tres bien*," he says. "Now, Anne-Marie, I'm going to get straight to the point. As you know, I try not to get involved in the personal lives of any of the members of my faculty. But the fact is that there has been a certain amount of talk—indeed a great deal of talk—around this campus that you are engaged in a love affair with Mrs. Schlachter's husband. This talk has reached my ears from several sources. I'm going to ask you outright, Anne-Marie. Is there any truth in this?"

She sits forward in her chair. "*Mais non!*" she says. "*Ce n'est pas vrai!* Adelaide Schlachter is one of my dearest friends!"

"That may be the case," he says. "But that does not rule out the fact that people are saying that you and her husband are having an affair. You have been seen on numerous occasions entering the Schlachters' house on campus and spending considerable time there before departing. And all this during times when Adelaide has been in the Science Building, teaching her classes."

"I can explain! *J'ai une explication!*"

"Please do," he says.

"*Je pense*—in my opinion, Winston Schlachter is America's greatest living unpublished poet. He has had trouble finding a publisher for his oeuvre in America. I believe this is because, here in America, Winston Schlachter is ahead of his time. The strait-laced American reading public is not yet ready to accept his work, which is, as we say in French, *un peu erotigue*. Mr. Schlachter completely agrees with me, but both of us feel he should not try to—for a man of his talent, he would be very wrong to—write down just to cater to more prudish American tastes. On the other hand, we in France are a bit more liberal, a bit more sophisticated about such matters. Therefore, I've taken it upon myself, out of my deep friendship for Adelaide as much as anything else, to translate Winston's poems into French. This is an enormously difficult job, Hobie, translation—particularly poetry, where one must always search for *le mot juste*. It is very time-consuming. But I have been spending as much of my spare time as I can afford to spend—what time I have left over from my teaching duties, which of course come first—working on this project with Monsieur Win, as I call him. When we finish, I am hoping, through my connections with the French literary and academic worlds, to find him a publisher in Paris. That is my ultimate goal!"

"Well, it's a very worthy one, I must say," he says. "But I have a suggestion for you, Anne-Marie. Instead of meeting and working at Mr. Schlachter's house, which is right on Faculty Row, where people's comings and goings are noticed and commented upon, why don't you choose a more public place to do your work? The school library, for instance, or a classroom that's not in use. Or a corner of the school dining room, which is always quiet between mealtimes."

She frowns. "That would be *un peu*—a little bit inconvenient. All his manuscripts, all his files, are in his house."

"Or Adelaide Schlachter's office in the Science Building, since you say you do most of your work while she is in class."

"There would be distractions, interruptions, the telephone—"

"But what I'm saying to you, Anne-Marie, is that this talk about you and Win Schlachter must stop. I cannot have it at my school. It is very demoralizing, both to faculty life and student life on this campus. Gossip here travels fast enough as it is. This talk must stop, and the only way to stop it is to stop these meetings at Mr. Schlachter's house."

Still pouting, she says nothing.

"You are a very attractive woman, Anne-Marie."

She tilts her head in a Gallic manner and lifts the fingers of her right hand in a Gallic gesture of dismissal. "*Merci, Monsieur*," she says.

"You are a good deal more attractive than Adelaide Schlachter." She flutters her Gallic eyelashes. "*Merci, encore merci.*"

"You are also young. You can understand why these meetings of yours with Mr. Schlachter have created talk. You're just out of university, so you're only a few years older than most of your students. That's good. The students relate well to you, particularly the girls, and that's also good. You're young, you're beautiful—you can become a role model for these girls. But I want you to be a good role model, Anne-Marie."

Suddenly she is angry. "Why me?" she says. "Men! Why is it that you men always think that the woman is to blame for everything? It is only the American men who think like this! Why don't you have this talk with Win Schlachter?"

"Because," he says carefully, "you are a member of my faculty, and Win Schlachter is not."

"If you want to talk about sex on this campus, why don't you find out about what went on at Colby Hall two weeks ago? Gang rape!"

"I have looked very carefully into all those allegations," he says. "I have investigated that situation thoroughly. Those allegations were without basis in fact, totally without foundation. There was absolutely nothing to those stories. It was nothing but a lurid rumor—the kind of silly, adolescent rumor that circulates around every school campus at the end of the spring term. And I'd appreciate your not repeating it."

"Hah!"

"I repeat. You are a member of my faculty in good standing, Anne-Marie. So is Adelaide Schlachter. I want to keep it that way. I would hate to lose either one of you. On the other hand, Adelaide has been with the school for a good many years longer than you have, my dear. Have I said enough?"

She lowers her eyelids. "*Peut-être*," she says. In the distance, the school choir can be faintly heard singing, "Jesus, Lover of My Soul."

"I just can't imagine what you see in Win Schlachter," he says. She looks up at him again.

It is nearly dark when Clarissa pulls her car into the circle in front of the Castle, yanks out the keys, and runs up the gravel walk and up the front steps. Rose meets her in the front hall. "I'm late!" she says. "Is he—"

Rose shakes her head. Her look is solemn. "The girl—the Van Degan girl—is dead," she says.

ELEVEN

Clarissa puts her keys and purse on the lowboy in the front hall. "Come into the library, Rose," she says.

In the library, she pours a short inch of gin into a glass and drops an ice cube in it. "Now, sit down," she says. "Tell me what happened."

"Well, they're calling it a suicide, Mrs. S," Rose says. "But if you ask me, in my *candy* opinion, we've got reasons to suspect foul play."

"How did she do it?"

"Poison."

"Oh dear. How awful. Now start from the beginning."

"They found her this afternoon, about three o'clock. One of her girlfriends, the Smith girl, that Cecily Smith, found her in her room and got hysterical. Rigmo had already set in, you see, so she was stiff as a board. That's why they think it happened, the poisoning, last night."

"And all day long, nobody—"

"Well, it seems last night she told her girlfriends at Colby that her monthlies were coming on. It seems she has real bad monthlies, and she had a note from her doctor at home to give her three days *off* from classes when they come on. So, when she didn't show up for classes this morning, nobody did a thing. Her door was closed, and the girls in Colby just thought she was in there resting from the monthly troubles. Then, after classes were over, the Smith girl came over to her room to give her the homework assignments. Her door was locked, but the Smith girl had another key. That's how she found her and got hysterical. You should have heard the screaming! It was all over campus in five minutes, the news of it."

"Did the police come?"

"An ambulance. But thank heavens no sirens. Mr. S saw to that. Of course, it was too late for an ambulance. The rigor had already set in, you see."

Clarissa sips her drink. "What makes you think there was foul play?" she says.

"There was no note. Don't suicides always leave a note?"

"Not always, no."

"Well, I'm no Albert Steinway genius, but I can put two and two together. They say it was chemicals, Mrs. S, chemicals. She was poisoned by chemicals."

"Well, that could mean—"

"Now stop and think who in this school might want to see that girl dead, Mrs. S." *Besides myself,* Clarissa thinks. "Who?" she says.

"Mrs. Schlachter, that's who!"

Clarissa almost laughs. "Adelaide Schlachter? Sweet little Adelaide Schlachter in her smocks and granny glasses?"

"It's always the one you'd least suspect. She's head of the Chemistry Department, isn't she? Who else could get their hands on chemicals?"

"I hardly think they keep deadly poisons in the Chemistry Department, Rose."

"But she's the one who could get her hands on chemicals easiest. And Mr. Schlachter is one of the men they're saying was—you know, fiddling with that girl. That's what they're all saying over in Buhl Hall."

"I thought that was supposed to be Miss Chabot."

"Her, too. They say that old goat was fiddling with them both. They say he likes 'em young. At first, I thought it could have been the Chabot woman who did it. But then I decided it had to be Mrs. Schlachter."

"Mrs. Schlachter has been with the school longer than I have, Rose. There's never been any—"

"Here's the way I figure it," Rose says. "Maybe Mrs. Schlachter knew her husband was fiddling with the Chabot woman, and maybe she didn't mind too much. After all, her and the Chabot woman seem pretty friendly. But when she found out he was *also* fiddling with one of her own students, that was too much for her. That was the string that broke the camel's neck. She flew into a rage—a blind, jealous rage, a murderous rage! She got her chemicals together and snuck over to the girl's room who was already sick from her monthlies. She said, 'Here—drink this! It will ease your pain.' That's the way it always happens in my mysteries, and then, having done it, she sneaks away—"

"But you said the door was locked from the inside."

"Those locks are a joke! The students all have more keys made and give them to their friends, whoever they want to come in their rooms. Old Man Schlachter would have had a key. The missus could have found it in his pocket when she sent his pants to the dry cleaner, and that would have been her clue."

"Well, it's an interesting theory, Rose," she says. "But I wouldn't spread it around campus, if I were you."

"That's what they'll find out happened when they have the trial. You wait and—"

"Let's wait until Mr. Spotswood gets home, and we find out more of the facts."

Rose starts to leave. "He tried to phone you when it happened," she says. "But of course, you weren't here, and I had no idea where you were."

"No."

Rose gives her a narrow look. "Did you go to the fish market in Canaan?" she asks her.

"Yes."

"And were the crabs fresh?"

"Yes, nice and fresh."

"I called the fish market to see if you'd been in. They said you hadn't."

"I didn't identify myself. I just popped in to see if the crabs looked fresh. It was the last thing on my list of errands."

"I said to the man at the market, I said, 'If a thin, well-dressed lady in slacks and a yellow blouse comes in asking about fresh crabs, tell her to call home immediately. It's an emergency.' I gave him the number. Nobody ever called."

"I didn't ask about the crabs. I just took a quick look at them and left. I'm sure nobody even noticed me."

"Funny, he usually keeps them in the back room. You have to ask to look at them."

"They were right out on the counter."

Rose hesitates. "Well, buzz me if you need anything, Mrs. S," she says. She turns on her heel and leaves.

Clarissa quickly presses her fingertips against her temples. Then she rises, goes to the drinks cart, and pours herself another drink.

It is nearly eight thirty before she hears Hobe come in the front door. She has sent Rose home, and told her that, for dinner, they will just have the chicken salad that Rose had fixed for her lunch; they would serve themselves. Listening to his footsteps as he comes down the front hall, she thinks they sound heavy and old, and when he appears in the library doorway, his face is gray and haggard.

Clarissa jumps to her feet. "Poor darling," she says. "Rose told me what happened. Was it just awful? Sit down. I've got your drink ready."

He looks at her and, though he is not swaying, he seems stooped, and she guesses that he has had one or two drinks himself. "I see you've already started the cocktail hour," he says.

"I had no idea when you might get home," she says. He has never liked the idea of her drinking alone.

"I'll have to drink fast to catch up with you. You've forgotten to close the curtains."

She moves around the room, closing the drapes. He goes on, "Students could see you in here. Drinking alone."

She ignores this. "Sit down, darling. What a dreadful day you must have had!"

He lowers himself into his chair and sits there for a moment with his head in his hands. "Little bitch picked a fine time to do this to me, didn't she?" he says at last.

"Oh, don't say that, Hobe."

"Trustees coming. Commencement. Yeah, she really picked a swell time to pull this caper on me! Ungrateful little bitch!"

"Why . . . why ungrateful, Hobe?"

"I was the only school that would take her in!" he says, his voice rising. "Nobody else wanted her, because of her record! But Van Degan's on the board! They've given millions to the school! I got stuck with her. I had to take her!"

She sits quietly in the chair opposite him. "Now tell me," she says. "Tell me exactly what happened, Hobe."

He runs his hand through his hair and, with the other, reaches for his glass. "Well, I guess you know pretty much everything," he says. "What more can I say?"

"Rose said—chemicals?"

"'Lethal overdose of medicinal chemicals'—that's what the medical examiner's report says. 'Probably self-administered.' There were some diet pills she'd been taking—appetite suppressants. Also, a bunch of different painkillers prescribed for menstrual cramps. The bottles were on her nightstand. All empty."

"There'll be an autopsy, of course." Briefly, Clarissa wonders, *Would an autopsy reveal that the girl had recently given birth to a child?*

"No. The family doesn't want one. She was taken to Hartford, to a crematorium." He looks at his watch. "By now, it'll be all over. Her father is sending his chauffeur up from New York in the morning to collect the ashes."

"A chauffeur!"

"That's what the family wants. No funeral—nothing. And thank God, there'll be no publicity. I think I've managed to take care of that."

"You talked with her father, then."

"Briefly, yes. Got him out of a meeting. He sounded more annoyed with me than anything else. I interrupted his goddamn meeting!"

"And her mother?"

"Her mother's cruising on somebody's yacht somewhere in the Seychelles Islands, in the Indian Ocean. They're still trying to reach her by radiophone."

"But I doubt her mother will want to cut short her cruise just because her only child is dead! What about her stepmother—Tweetums?"

"I had a long talk with Tweetums. Her reaction was a little strange. She said she'd expected something like this to happen, sooner or later. She said, 'Linda was always an accident waiting to happen.' But she was the only one who thanked me for making all the arrangements. At least she had the decency to do that." He takes a long swallow of his drink. "Christ, what a day I've had! This has been the worst day of my life."

"Poor Hobe!"

"I tried to call you when I learned about it," he says. "But Rose said you were out. Where were you?"

"Oh, doing errands, and—"

"Rose said something about a fish market. Did you spend the whole afternoon at a fish market? That doesn't sound like you, Cissie."

"Well, I was sort of researching—you know, for the various ingredients we'll need for the trustees' dinner. Rose and I have been planning the menu, and I wanted to be sure . . ." Her voice trails off, and when he says nothing, just looks at her questioningly, she continues. "To be sure that all the ingredients we're going to need will be available at the local markets. We've got a nice menu planned."

"I see," he says.

"I didn't actually spend any money," she says.

"And by the way, speaking of that, I was looking in our checkbook this morning, and I came across an entry—two hundred forty-seven dollars and thirteen cents to Pauline Scanlon. What was that all about?"

"Pauline Scanlon is one of the maids."

"I know who Pauline Scanlon is. But why would you be giving her money?"

"It seems she came up short on her linen count a week or so ago. Miss Stimpson docked her pay by that amount. I guess, I-I guess I just felt sorry for the poor girl. Miss Stimpson is such a damned stickler—"

"Miss Stimpson is an excellent employee. I've never had any reason to find fault with her. Miss Stimpson runs a tight ship."

"Too tight, if you ask me!"

"But don't you see, Cissie? There you go again—meddling in school affairs. School affairs that are none of your business. By reimbursing Pauline Scanlon for school property that she's lost, you're just encouraging her to be more careless than she already is. What Pauline needed was to be *disciplined*, and that's what Miss Stimpson was trying to apply—a little discipline. What's going to happen the next time Pauline loses something and is made to pay for it? She'll come whining to you asking for reimbursement, that's what! I can't have that sort of thing go on."

"The poor girl isn't very bright, and—"

"Of course, she isn't. If she had any brains, she wouldn't be a maid."

"And she supports a mother in a nursing home."

"That has nothing to do with it! She's got to learn to take care of school property. I run a school, but I also run a business. Certain basic business principles have to be adhered to. Actually, we've had a lot of trouble with this Pauline woman. She's always losing things—cleaning supplies, mops, dust rags. The other day, she couldn't remember where she left her vacuum cleaner. Miss Stimpson has seriously been thinking of letting her go."

"Oh, Hobe. Aren't you being a little harsh?"

"I try not to interfere with the decisions of my department heads. An employee who keeps losing and misplacing company property is not cost-efficient. And what Miss Stimpson decides to do should be no concern of yours. You must stop interfering, undermining the way this school conducts its affairs. I've warned you about this before."

"Now wait a minute!" she says sharply. "Just wait a minute. I'm getting a little sick of your warnings. I brought a little money into this marriage when I married you—not a lot, maybe, but some. And I get an income from my father's estate—not a huge one, but a little. And if I choose to spend a small amount of money to help a poor woman out of a jam—if I choose to indulge in an act of personal Christian charity—I'm going to do so!"

"In defiance of school policy?"

"To hell with school policy! What I did was personal. It had nothing to do with school policy!"

"Keep your voice down, Clarissa. Rose—"

"I sent Rose home an hour ago. There's no one in this house but you and me."

"Sometimes I think you and I are on different wavelengths, Clarissa."

"Yes! Yes we are. Totally different wavelengths. That's the nicest thing you've said to me all evening. I'm thinking of leaving you, Hobe."

He slumps in his chair. "There you go again," he says. "Whenever there's a crisis, you threaten to walk out on me."

"This time I mean it. I'm just about ready to . . . to take the giant step. Why didn't you tell me why Alexandra Lemosney wants me at the trustees' meeting?"

He stares at her.

"Because you wanted me to *suffer*, that's why. You wanted me to think the trustees were going to censure me for what I said to that reporter—to remind me to keep my nose out of school affairs and school policy. In fact, as you damn well know, she loved what I said in that interview! Loved it. Loved me!"

He is silent for a moment, and then, lowering his eyes, he says, "You're right. I'm sorry, Cissie. I should have told you. I made a mistake."

"A deliberately cruel mistake."

"Will you forgive me, Cissie?" He holds out his empty glass. "Let's have another drink," he says.

"Yes!" she says. She jumps to her feet, goes to the drinks cart, and splashes more gin in the shaker. "Yes, I feel like getting drunk tonight. Let's both get drunk! This is an occasion for celebration! The great Hobart Spotswood has just admitted he made a mistake—a mistake of deliberate cruelty. The great Hobart Spotswood has just asked his wife to forgive him! This is an unprecedented—unprecedented!—event in the long history of our crossed-wavelength marriage! Bells should ring! Trumpets should sound! Perhaps I should make you get down on your knees and kiss my feet, kiss the hem of my garment—kiss my ass!—and *beg* for forgiveness. Yes, get down on your hands and knees—yes, I feel like getting blind, stinking, falling-down drunk tonight." She hands him his glass, overfull, and some of the liquid spills across the fingers of her shaking hand. For some reason, she begins to laugh. "Oh, oh, oh this is all too funny!" she says, reaching in the pocket of her slacks for a hanky.

"I'm sorry," he says again. "Forget about Pauline Scanlon. It doesn't matter. It's over and done with. If you have one flaw, Cissie, it's that you're too good-natured, too softhearted—"

She is still laughing. "Dots-a me," she says. "Dots-a me!"

"I've called for an assembly of the entire school tomorrow morning—eight o'clock, in the auditorium. All students, all faculty, all staff. After all, the whole school knows what happened today. I've got to make some sort of statement. They'll expect it of me. Will you come, too, Cissie? Come and sit in the front row? It would mean a lot to me."

She stifles a final giggle with her handkerchief. "What do you plan to say?" she says.

"I'm not quite sure yet. I've been working on it, thinking about it. It should be something short and fairly simple.

Something about life's mysteries, that none of us really know what may be going on in the mind or heart of another individual, what secret pain and suffering another person may be trying to endure, that some of us are able to endure these private sufferings better than others and live with them. That it's always a shock to realize that in our midst, in this small community, there was living a troubled young girl, outwardly so normal, whose secret troubles finally seemed so insurmountable, so insoluble, that she took her own life before any of us suspected that she needed our help. And now, it's tragically too late. Something like that. Then, I thought, a short prayer. Or maybe I'll just ask everyone for a minute of silent prayer for Linda."

All at once she is sober again. "But that's not true," she says. "All the signs were there."

"What do you mean?"

"We knew she was troubled. You knew it. So did I."

"Nonsense. I knew nothing of the sort."

"Hobe, all those stories about goings-on at Colby Hall. Linda Van Degan's name kept coming up in every one of them."

"I looked into those stories. There wasn't a shred of truth to any of them."

"Oh, but you're wrong, Hobe, you're wrong. There was a lot more than a shred of truth to those stories."

"What makes you think so? On what evidence do you base your—"

"I had the Van Degan girl over here for tea Thursday afternoon."

"*What?*"

"I had her here for tea. Well, actually it wasn't tea. She had a 7-Up."

"You're not supposed to invite a student to the headmaster's house for tea!"

"Why not? Is there some sort of school rule against it?"

"You're supposed to have the four class teas! That's all! The headmaster's wife has an annual tea for each of the four classes. That's the tradition. But that's the extent of it. But an individual student is supposed to come to me if he or she has a problem—didn't you know that?"

"If I broke a rule I didn't know was a rule, I'm sorry. I didn't know I couldn't invite anybody I wanted to this house."

"But this was a student! A student isn't just anybody, Clarissa. This was a student whose parents are paying twenty-four thousand dollars a year to attend my school."

"Well, anyway, I invited her, and she came. I thought that if a girl like Linda, who's never had any sort of real mother, wouldn't open up to a man, she might open up to a woman who's close to her mother's age—if she had a problem."

"There you go again—meddling in school affairs, interfering, undermining my authority."

"Your goddamn authority didn't seem to help you get anywhere near the truth about what was going on in Colby Hall—and elsewhere on the campus! Did it? Did it!? Maybe I was foolish, but I thought perhaps I could help you get to the bottom of things!"

He looks away from her. "Well, what did she say? How did she seem?"

"You mean did she seem depressed? Despondent? Suicidal? On the contrary. She was arrogant, defiant—even insolent to me."

"She obviously realized that you were overstepping your—"

"No. She as much as admitted that she'd had boys in her room for sex. She justified this on the basis that everybody else in the school was doing it."

"And what did you say?"

"I said that I very much doubted that *every*one else in the school was doing what she was doing—having casual sex, right and left, all over the place!"

"And what else did she say?"

"I reminded her that if a girl her age gets a bad reputation, that reputation can stick with her for the rest of her life."

"Did that upset her?" His tone is suddenly urgent.

"No. I don't even think she heard what I was saying."

"Are you sure, absolutely sure, that something you said to her didn't upset her enough to cause her to—"

"To commit suicide? Is that what you're implying, Hobe?"

"Well . . . girls that age are so impressionable."

"You're suggesting that I caused her to kill herself? Sorry, Hobe, but I'm not going to blame myself for that! In fact—"

"What else did you talk about?"

"Do you really want to know?"

"Of course."

"Well, since we're in a truth-telling mood, let me ask *you* a question. Did you have sex with her, Hobe? Tell me the truth."

He half rises from his chair. "What? What did you say?"

"I think you heard me. I asked you if you had sex with her."

"What an outrageous thing to ask me! How dare you!"

"Because that's what she said. She said 'Spotty fucked me. And other girls, too.'"

"Shut up!" He lunges toward her with his right fist raised and clenched, and strikes her hard across the face. She falls backward against the library table, and the lampshade, missing its crystal finial, flies off, and the lamp itself crashes to the floor. Clarissa feels her knees buckle and, as she tries to seize the table's edge for support, she feels her balance going and herself falling to the floor, and her face striking something, and the hard, sharp feel of metal piercing her flesh. There is a moment of blackness, then she touches her face and feels something warm and sticky that must be blood.

Immediately, Hobe is on his knees on the floor beside her, whispering, "I'm so sorry, oh I'm so sorry, oh god, what did I do? Oh god . . . oh god, I'm so sorry, Cissie . . . what did I do?"

Now he lifts her from the floor and scoops her into his arms, sobbing, "Oh my god . . . I didn't mean it, Cissie, I didn't mean it," over and over again. He runs, carrying her, out of the room and up the stairs, weeping. "So light . . . you're so light, light as a feather. Oh my god, I didn't mean it . . . I'm so sorry." He lays her across her bed. "Oh my god—look at your *eye*!" He dashes into her bathroom and soaks hand towels in cold water and places these across her face. "Oh god, we need a doctor, Cissie. Let me take you to the emergency room . . . let me call nine one one. Oh god!"

"I'll say I fell on the stairs."

"Let me call Doctor Jethro!"

"No! No doctors! No hospitals. I'll say I fell on the stairs."

"But your eye . . . your eye . . ."

"I'll be all right. I'll say I fell on the stairs."

"Ice pack—" She hears him run down the stairs again, then back up, and feels him place the rubber ice pack across the side of her face. He throws his body across hers, now sobbing uncontrollably. "Oh my god . . . I didn't mean it . . . so many things today. Oh, I'm so sorry, so sorry."

"I'll say I fell on the stairs," she says again. "I'll be all right. Just leave me alone now, Hobe. Please, just leave me alone."

He did sleep with her. I know he did. Of course, he did. He might just as well have placed an ad in Macy's corner window announcing that he did. Or hired a plane to spell it out in skywriting over Yankee Stadium. He did, and in a way I'm glad he hit me because that was as good as his admission that he did, and because now he knows that I know he did. Was it his baby, the one I—? It could have been, sure, it could have been, but now we'll never know. It hurts, I hurt, but I won't look in the mirror—not yet. I'm afraid to look in the mirror. I can't even see to look in the mirror.

But no doctors, and no hospitals. It's not because I'm afraid of the questions they would ask me in a hospital, I can handle that. I'm a much better liar than he is, and I know what to say. But I also know what doctors and hospitals can do to you. I found that out the hard way, and after that I promised myself, never again, never again. No thank you, kind sir. He did that to me, too, of course. Let it be done, told them to do it. One of the worst things in the world that can happen to a woman, he let it be done to me. I asked him, "Why, why didn't you wait till I was out of the anesthetic and let me be consulted because it was my body, after all, why didn't you let them ask me what I wanted done with it?" He said, "I did what I did because I wanted to save your life. They discovered the tumors while you were in labor, and I asked them, is this a good time to do this? And they said, 'There is never a good time to do radical surgery, but this is as good a time as any, while we have her here, and it will have to be done sooner or later, and the sooner the better because, in the lactation period following the baby's birth, the cells could spread, metastasize.' And so, I told them to go ahead and do it if it would save your life. During the surgery, you needed a transfusion. I gave you some blood." "Thank you," I said.

But for a long time afterward I wondered if it was his way of punishing me, or even God's. Postpartum depression, they call it. Or guilt. Crime and punishment.

It was such a long labor, with Sally. Later, I was told that I was in labor for more than twenty-two hours. But because of the morphine that was dripping into my arm, or whatever it was, I wasn't aware of much time passing, or even of much pain, or aware of much of anything at all. Now and then faces appeared over me, speaking words whose meanings floated off as soon as they were spoken. I do remember someone saying, "This isn't going well. We're thinking of taking the baby by C-section. We're facing a breech delivery." I just nodded, "Okay, okay, whatever you do is okay with me." Some of it was almost funny. Someone said, "Do you often wear bikini-type swimsuits? There will be a scar." I tried to make a joke. I said, "Oh, yes, as the wife of a headmaster of the Crittenden School for Boys, I often walk around the campus in a bikini, an itty-bitty teeny-weeny yellow polka-dot bikini." At least I think that's what I said. I'm not really sure I really said it. They said, "Were you planning to nurse the baby? Sometimes, after surgery, no milk comes. So, if you were hoping to nurse the baby, don't count on it, Clarissa." I said, "Okay, whatever, *que sera.*" That's the wonderful thing about feeling so sick—nothing matters. You stop feeling, you stop caring. That's why I'll never be afraid of dying. It's not so bad. You don't feel a thing. There's nothing to it.

It's out of your hands. Other faces hover over you, other hands probe your anatomy, touching, pinching, squeezing. "Doctor, will you please come take a look at this?" And this? And this? Needles inject or extract fluids, it doesn't matter which. "This won't hurt, just a little prick. There, that didn't hurt, now did it?" Uh-huh. Sometimes Hobe's face would float in among the other faces, then float away, and then the room would be empty. Then a new face. "We're going to shave you now." Shave and a haircut, two bits! Ha ha. Someone else said, smiling, "The wonderful thing about cesarean babies is that they're beauti-fully formed because they don't have to be squeezed out. Their heads are perfectly formed." I said, "That's nice." That's really all I remember, whispers.

All I knew was that if the baby was a girl, she was going to be named Sarah and be called Sally, because there had been other Sarah Spotswoods in the family in the past, one of them a famous suffragette who worked with Susan B. Anthony, and then of course there was Sarah in Genesis who gave birth to Abraham's son at the age of ninety and became the mother of all Jews. And then, when I was finally coming to, finally drifting out of the ether or whatever it was they gave me, and was only half awake, they came into the room with something in their arms, and said, "Look, you've given birth to a beautiful baby girl," and I took her in my arms and squeezed and counted her fingers and her toes and held her to my breasts, to feed her or not to feed her, whatever, *que sera sera*, and that's when I discovered that my left one was gone. I screamed. They snatched the baby away from me. I had to be restrained.

Later, at a party at James Falls, I ran into the doctor who did the surgeries, asked him, "Was it essential that it all had to be done at once, the cesarean and the mastectomy?" He frowned. "Not essential, no, but that became one of our options. The mastectomy was going to have to be performed at some point soon, and so we decided it was worth the risk to combine the two procedures." I asked him, "Which came first, the chicken or the egg?" Then I said, "No, don't tell me, I don't want to know." He said, "And of course there was the insurance consideration." Insurance? "The health policy the school provides for the headmaster and his family doesn't offer maternity benefits. I guess they figured the Crittenden headmaster's wife isn't expected to have babies, ha ha. So, we decided that if we combined the procedures, and performed them both at the same time, we could lump the claims together."

"That's an unfortunate metaphor, Doctor," I said. "Huh?"

Oh, well, never mind, that was all a long time ago. We can't turn back the clock.

No use crying over spilt milk. An apt metaphor, that one . . .

Daddy was hardly a Bible-thumping, fire-and-brimstone sort of preacher. High Church Episcopal? But would he have said that all that was divine retribution for my having broken the sixth commandment? And that this latest is nothing more than God's penalty for having sinned again? An eye for an eye, a tit for a tit? Hard to say, isn't it, what Daddy would have said, but please, Daddy, don't say that to me tonight.

Oh, look, it's morning already. Even with only one eye working, I can see that. There's a yellow finch at the feeder. Good morning, Merry Sunshine, and how are you today? Not so good, Daddy, not so good, there have been better days. Good morning, Merry Sunshine, will you come out and play? Oh, no thank you, Daddy, I think I won't today. It's a song. I'm writing a song. Look—two yellow finches now. They're coming back, they say, to this part of New England. So are bluebirds. They've discovered other places to build their nests besides in the rotting fence posts of old farms, since the old farms and the old fence posts in their fields have become harder for the birds to find. When I was a girl, in Riverdale, we had a whip-poor-will. Yes, even in Riverdale, which was really the West Bronx, though nobody liked to call it that, Riverdale-on-Hudson sounded better, we had a whip-poor-will. I used to hear him on summer nights. I can still hear him. Whip-poor-will! On a tree by a river a little tomtit sang, Willow, titwillow, titwillow. And I said to him, Dickybird, why do you sit singing willow, titwillow, titwillow? Is it weakness of intellect, birdie? I cried. Or a rather sharp pain in your little inside? With a shake of his poor little head he replied, Oh, willow. . . . "No, Rose, I don't want anything right now! I just want to sleep a little longer."

* * *

While the headmaster's wife sleeps, the first fire erupts. A rather modest affair, the fire is said to have started from a carelessly disposed cigarette. Seniors were permitted to smoke with parental permission, but only in designated smoking rooms. Yet the fire starts in a metal garbage can in the basement of Colby Hall, downstairs from the smoking rooms. Smoldering, it does not produce much flame but emits a substantial amount of smoke and blackens the forty-year-old pine wainscot outside a classroom. Approximately thirty minutes after it starts, apparently around at nine p.m., a young woman, a junior, exits the basement showers, still wrapped in a towel, notices the emerging flames, and bravely grabs a nearby water-pressure fire extinguisher to put out the flames.

After composing herself, the heroine student, Yvonne Cortlandt, immediately contacts her dorm's prefect and reports the incident. Yvonne's dorm prefect's report goes up the chain of command to the head prefect, the dean of students, and eventually arrives at the headmaster. At eleven p.m., Hobe is awakened from a troubled slumber and informed. As a matter of policy, the student fire brigade is also consulted, although there is little they can do, as the crisis has passed.

The second fire is discovered within twenty-four hours after the first and causes more damage and smoke. This time, the flames lick up the walls of an unoccupied classroom, again in the basement, but now in Buhl Hall. Although equipped with water-based extinguishers on all the floors, no buildings on campus are yet provided with smoke detectors, and the smoke from this fire rises unimpeded to sleeping juniors on the floors above. Although it's past nine p.m. and lights out, several students are awake studying, smell the smoke, and quickly sound the alarm, evacuating the entire dormitory within moments of the fire's detection. Minutes later, the entirety of the well-rehearsed student fire brigade is on hand to quell the flames, now reaching to the second floor. The local fire department is alerted but is miles away and by the time the first truck arrives, the fire brigade has doused the flames and averted the total immolation of the dorm. Damage to the east wing of the dorm is extensive, primarily from smoke, and the student residents are temporarily relocated to other dorms, doubling up single rooms as necessary.

Now comes the headmaster and the necessity of dealing with another potential scandal and crisis. Two fires in two days? Both with suspicious beginnings? The headmaster assembles his faculty at eleven p.m. and begins a rudimentary investigation, hoping that the two fires are only a coincidence and are unrelated.

He receives his unwanted answer at two a.m. the following day. At this late hour, one of the kitchen staff is leaving the dining hall after prepping breakfast when he sees a faint glow from the corner of the Barn. The Barn, with its century-old, hand-hewn columns and beams and completely wood exterior, offers a chance for conflagration on a biblical scale. Without any form of collective communication, the worker quickly seizes the ship's bell and commences ringing wildly. Only after some members of the faculty appear do he and others run into the Barn, grabbing some extinguishers on the way, and vainly try to extinguish what is quickly becoming a large fire. As if on cue, the student fire brigade is on the scene within minutes, connecting hoses to hydrants and pouring water onto the flames. By 2:30, after the efforts of the brigade, the fire is out, with considerable damage to the exterior of the facility and smoke and water damage inside.

Hobe is on-site immediately, along with Dean of Students John Bauer, and with darkened brows both come to the same conclusion: arson.

As prefects and faculty convene at three a.m., Hobe addresses the assembled group.

"There is little doubt in my mind and that of the dean that the fires of the last forty-eight hours have been intentionally set and set in such a way as to cause damage and harm to the Crittenden community," Hobart says, with all the authority of the headmaster.

"I've contacted the county fire marshal and the state police. Both have agreed to place personnel on campus at our disposal along with a pumper fire truck and two firefighters. The latter will be used to support our fire brigade.

"I'm going to cancel classes and institute a buddy system. No student is permitted to leave his room without his designated 'buddy.' In addition, I'll be asking for student volunteers, in pairs, to provide twenty-four-hour patrols of the campus and outbuildings until we can resolve this crisis.

"I'm calling upon the kitchen staff to provide a continuous buffet of food and beverages for the student patrols and faculty as needed.

"Please pass the word that we'll have an assembly in the chapel tomorrow at ten a.m. That's it for now. Let's find out what's going on and stop it."

Within hours of Hobe's instructions, rumors begin circulating about the arsonist, and students begin carrying makeshift weapons like pocketknives, hammers, or clubs. For now, however, such weapons will do no good.

The next morning at ten, the entire student body is convened in the Ballard Chapel as Hobe delivers a report to the assembly.

"As we know, our school and our community has been subject

to intentionally set fires in the past days," he starts. "We now know the fires were probably set to cause injuries. This will not stand, and we will catch the perpetrator and have Crittenden safe again.

"Effective immediately, we are suspending all classes and instituting twenty-four-hour, two-man student patrols, schedules to be maintained by each dorm's prefect."

He continued, "We don't know who this monster is, or whether he is a member of our community. So if, in the process of walking your patrols, you encounter a stranger possibly committing this crime, do not engage or confront! Contact the state police officer in the main Quad immediately and return to your dorm. Above all, be safe and attentive!"

With that, Hobe's plans go into effect: increased vigilance, on-site police and professional firefighters and equipment, student patrols and the convening of an investigative body. Despite his passioned admonitions, however, he's forgotten one of his most personally important instructions, as demonstrated by his earlier castigation of Clarissa: don't talk to the press.

Alexa Woodin of the *Litchfield Times* has greater ambitions for her journalistic career than to remain the women's page feature editor, and this morning is monitoring her police scanner for juicy news. There's been chatter over the past few days about goings-on at the Crittenden School, yet when she tried to reach Clarissa for information, her calls were unanswered. Alexa has good instincts and tries another number.

At eleven a.m., shortly after Hobe's speech at the school assembly, the pay phone on the first floor of Buhl Hall is ringing. Of all the seniors in the dorm, a student who, generously, could be called the class's least academically inclined (he will graduate at the bottom) is happening by and picks up the phone.

"Hello?" says David Dunbar, who, despite his low intelligence, comes from wealthy stock.

"Hi, this is Alexa, a reporter for the *Litchfield Times*. Who's this?" asks Alexa in her most alluring voice.

"Um . . . Hi. I'm David. I'm a senior here at Crittenden. I just came out of the smoking room."

"Hi, David. How are you? Are you enjoying Crittenden?" Alexa asks, smoothing the conversation and welcoming David in.

"Uh, yeah, I guess. Some of the courses are hard, but I like to play football and I've made some friends. I came in as a junior, so I've only—"

She cuts him off, "That's great, David! Say, I've been hearing some rumors in town about a fire or something going on over at your school. Do you know anything about that?"

"Oh, yeah!" says David, excited to think he's being interviewed by a real, live reporter! "There's all kinds of stuff going on, not just one fire, but five or six!" he says, embellishing. "I just came out of assembly where the headmaster, a police chief or something, and the fire chief were all talking about it. What a mess!"

With that, the cat was out of the bag.

The afternoon edition of the *Litchfield Times* would run the headline, "Crittenden School Scourged by Fires." The next morning, the *New York Times* would also run the head, "Elite Connecticut Prep School Scourged by Fires," albeit accompanied by only a few short paragraphs buried on page seven of the Metro section.

Hobe is distraught and realizes his mistake. By the late afternoon, reports are coming back that a TV news van has parked out on the main road after being denied entrance to the campus and access road, as it *is* private property.

* * *

Despite Hobe's preparations, a fourth fire does erupt in the late night of the fourth day, this time at the zoo. The discovery is made by a pair of students completing their patrol shift, and they rush to inform authorities. (Later, the pair would recall a shadowy figure running into the nearby woods, but the observation could not be confirmed.) As students and professionals race to face the fire, the school (for the first time since it was installed in the 1950s) engages the air-raid siren, abruptly awakening other students, and faculty alike; no one will go to sleep from now on, for fear that the Klaxon will sound and they would find their residences engulfed by flames and smoke.

Although the school zoo sits on a pond and near the stream, its relative remoteness to the campus makes it a difficult and dark place to patrol, let alone extinguish a fire. The ornithology building, a ramshackle conglomeration of wood and tin assembled over the years, erupts in flames visible from (too late it seems) the headmaster's house. The building is all but consumed and the fire spreading to adjacent buildings when the fire brigade arrives, struggling with their ancient carts across the bridge and connecting hoses to hydrants. In the process, one student firefighter is injured when he falls crossing the bridge, breaking his wrist. The fire truck and professional firefighters also arrive with all hands and commit to containment.

After the flames are extinguished and a modicum of calm encompasses the school, a full-fledged state investigation gets underway, supervised by the headmaster, fire marshal, state police, and a smattering of faculty members who can contribute, including Dean Bauer who, by virtue of his master's degree in psychology, may be able to offer insight into the arsonist's motives.

The first summoned to the investigative body are the historically troublesome such as Bradley Prescott, a sophomore, who now sits before a tribunal in the witness chair at nine p.m. on the fourth night of the fires. Bradley was reported out of sight of his "buddy" for a brief period while, he alleges, he was on late-night patrol at a time corresponding with the zoo fire. Pressed for details, Bradley provides them and is excused, pending future notice to appear.

Back in his dorm, Bradley confronts his "buddy," Henry Terraza, for outing him in the buddy-system timeline.

"What the fuck, Henry?" yells Bradley. "What did you tell the dean about me?"

Henry sheepishly replies, "We're supposed to report to the prefect about any time we can't find our buddy. I wasn't sure when you were coming back, so I told him, and he told Bauer. That's all."

"You knew I was going on patrol, you stupid ass. Now you've got them thinking I'm a suspect. I was questioned by Spots, the dean, and the cops!"

"Sorry, man . . ." says Henry.

Others appear, yet the investigation stalls in the fifth day, which comes and goes without incident. The fire marshal has determined that an accelerant was used in each incident, confirming the arsonist's modus operandi, yet law enforcement appears no closer to finding a suspect.

The young man sits quietly on his bed, fingering a Bic lighter calmly and dreaming of his next fire. He has a private room, as do all seniors, and the small cans of lighter fluid are carefully hidden in his sock drawer. So far faculty has not begun inspections of students' rooms. Even if they were to start, he would immediately find out and remove the accelerants, matches, and Bic lighter well before an inspection. He laughs to himself. Hell, he would probably be recruited to help with the inspection. For now, however, he reflects back on the fires set so far. He never wants anyone hurt, least of all his classmates, and is mildly upset by the student who broke his wrist; collateral damage. He recalls the first fire he set four years ago in New York.

Then, as now, he didn't really want anyone hurt. It was in a brownstone on the Upper West Side of Manhattan, only a few blocks from his family's spacious Riverside Drive home. He'd scoped the brownstone for weeks prior and figured a fire set during day would have a quick NYFD response and, since everyone went off to work in the morning, the building would be empty; that is, nobody gets hurt. How was he to know about the elderly man asleep on the top floor? How was he to know that the man would succumb to smoke inhalation and die? That wasn't his fault. The NYFD should have arrived sooner, and the guy shouldn't have been home. Oh, well; collateral damage.

The entry hall of the brownstone had a stack of eight-foot two by fours being used for some renovation on the third floor, excellent tinder. Nobody noticed the thirteen-year-old boy as he followed one of the lumber deliverymen into the normally locked entrance and confidently climbed stairs to the second floor, where he waited. His instincts were right; everyone was at work. Nobody noticed him. When the delivery was complete, the boy simply went back down, ignited the lumber stack, and, again with confidence, exited and crossed West End Avenue toward a church to wait and observe. He had time. He was not due to enroll at his prep school for another week.

As distant sirens sounded, the windows in the brownstone burst out and black smoke poured forth. The main facade, being stone, merely blackened from the flames. He'd watched (along with lots of other looky-loos) from the steps of the church until the ambulance and police ushered them back. After a time, while occasionally looking back over his shoulder at the brave firefighters, he walked calmly home to begin packing for school.

Back in the present, however, the boy is planning his next fire at Crittenden and hoping that no one will be injured, collateral damage. Indeed, he'll make a special effort this time to avoid casualties. He places the lighter and small can of accelerant in his front pocket and leaves his room above the dining hall, stopping briefly at the twenty-four-hour buffet to grab a hamburger and Coke. As he crosses the small quad he encounters two "buddies" returning from their patrol as the juniors officiously hold up their hands and say, "Halt!" with blustering bravado, since they recognize the boy and his senior stature. "Who goes there?"

Snickering, one of the juniors asks, "What's the password!?"

The boy responds, "How about, 'Go Fuck Yourself,'" and continues on.

With grandiosity, the two lower classmen bow dramatically and say, "Correct! You, sir, may pass!"

After the senior boy is out of earshot, the two patrollers laugh to themselves.

It's dark now, and the boy encounters other students who simply nod or wave, exhausted and inattentive, knowing that the young man who passes by them could not be responsible for what was about to take place. For the fifth time.

Nerves continue to be strained when, late that night, the rear entrance to Colby explodes in flames. Now seemingly commonplace, the air-raid Klaxon wails anew. Few are awakened; students and faculty alike are already awake and have not slept for over forty-eight hours.

Smoke pours from the dormitory roof as the girl students race out fire exits onto the Quad, where most are already dressed. They've slept (when sleep came) in their clothes to be ready for a quick escape or to be ready for twenty-four-hour patrols.

The professional firefighters with their pumper are close by this time and begin a thorough dousing of the flames, which now penetrate the roof and threaten an adjacent wing of the two-story building. Many students are coughing and at least one is on the ground receiving oxygen from a firefighter.

Not to be outdone, the school fire brigade arrives, having placed most of their hand-pulled carts in strategic locations in anticipation of just such an event as is now unfolding.

Dean Bauer runs from his housing on the first floor of Buhl into the melee and begins to organize and count members of the student body, ensuring most of the women and girls are out of Colby and safe. Out of the corner of his eye he watches the student fire brigade quickly relocate hoses from nearby hydrants to supplant the numerous hoses already dousing the building. Despite their efforts, the fire continues to rage. As the other students assemble in the main Quad, Dean Bauer spies a silhouette running haphazardly while simultaneously trying in vain to move full fire hoses. The figure, clearly a student, is in an apparent panic and trips over a hose near Bauer, falling face-first into the ground. Bauer runs to the boy, helping him up.

"Son, calm down!" the dean says to the facedown young man.

The boy turns his face up to the dean, his eyes wild and manic. "I have to get to the fire! I have to get to it!" he screams above the cacophony of sirens, hoses, and alarms.

In the soft light of dormitories and the reflected light from the flames, he recognizes the boy and lets him go. As the boy now runs to help his fire brigade team, the dean says remorsefully to himself, "Broadbent."

_____

From Clarissa Spotswood's Journal:

This was the most trying time. First with the tragic death of Linda Van Degan and now with the fires. I don't know how much more poor Hobe can take.

After the newspaper reports, Hobe went on damage control, meeting with faculty and staff to determine the best way to handle the media frenzy in the final days after the young man was caught. Finally, it was determined simply to close down the frenzy and not issue any comments to the press, hoping the entire event would simply go away; it did.

As it turned out, the young man who started the fires, Avery Broadbent, was discovered by our own dean of students, Mr. Bauer, who, I understand, has an advanced degree in psychology. It was this training that led him to discover poor Avery's internal demons and resulted in Avery's complete confession.

Avery had an identical twin brother who attended nearby Millbrook and was a stellar student and outstanding athlete there. As so often happens with twins (and siblings in general) the competition between the two was intense, and at an early age Avery felt inadequate. Growing up in New York City, Avery saw the heroism of the NYFD and aspired to one day join them, save property and lives and be a hero himself. As such a young man, his ambitions surpassed his age.

When Avery joined Crittenden, his assigned role in community service was in the Post Office, a job he didn't want but put up with until he could get his chosen assignment on the fire brigade, which he joined his junior year. Upon becoming a senior, he naturally assumed the role of captain of the fire brigade and found his true calling. Yet naturally occurring fires eluded him. His solution: set the fires himself and be the first on scene to save property and lives and become the hero he was always destined to become.

After Dean Bauer determined his guilt that night, Avery was quicky apprehended and arrested by state police already on the campus. Nearby, some students were convening, perhaps returning from their patrols, and began gathering around the flashing lights. They witnessed poor Avery Broadbent III, handcuffed and forlorn, placed in the back of a patrol car.

Hobe later recounted to me that one student, sophomore Bradley Prescott, turned to Hobe and asked, "Mr. Spotswood, what's going on? Who is that?"

He turned to the young man accompanied by his buddy, both of whom were carrying hammers as it was late at night now, and said, "Avery Broadbent."

Uncomprehending, Bradley said, "Broadbent? But he's the senior in charge of the fire brigade. What has he got to do with it?" As they looked on toward the arrest taking place, Hobe told me later that he heard one ask the other, rhetorically: "Broadbent. . . . What would we have done if we saw him while on patrol?"

In the end, Crittenden chose not to press charges against Avery Broadbent III, and he was assigned to the Hudson Valley Psychiatric Center in nearby Wingdale, New York, where he spent two years getting better, I believe.

Initially the investigators and Hobe thought Avery had some culpability in the death of Linda Van Degan, but this was not borne out by the evidence or the investigation. He barely knew the girl and had no connection to the Colby Club.

As a sad postscript to that difficult period, the school chose to add Avery Broadbent's name to the list of graduates that year.

TWELVE

He turns to her on the bed and touches her shoulder. "You asleep?" he asks her.

"No, just thinking."

"Thinking about what?"

"About us, Jess. You and me."

"Me too. You've forgiven me for being my father's puppet?"

"Ah, tell me what you're thinking about you and me."

"You feel like talking? Seriously?"

"Yes."

He reaches across her and turns on one of the bedside lamps. Then he pushes himself on his elbows against a pillow. "I'm thinking I'd like to marry you," he says.

"Yes, I've had that thought too."

"How does it strike you?"

She pulls the sheet across her shoulders and cuddles against him. "It strikes me as a very nice idea," she says.

"But I'm worried about my dad."

"What? That he won't approve of me?"

"No, not that."

"When do I get to meet the great man?"

"Oh, you'll meet him soon enough. And I'm sure he'll like you. That's not what I'm worried about."

"Then what is it?"

"Just the way he's been acting lately. He hasn't been himself. My dad's always been a tough man for me to figure out, but in the last couple of months it's been even tougher. There's a certain—I don't quite know how to describe it, but there's a certain almost *manic* quality about his actions lately, a kind of desperation. Crazy things—I mean like insisting that I get a seat on the plane across the aisle from you when you flew to San Francisco. What was the point of that? I've never been able to figure that one out—why he wanted us to meet, and in that particular way. What was that supposed to accomplish? Certainly not what it actually *did* accomplish—or was it? Anyway, I'm worried that he's in some kind of serious trouble."

"Financial trouble, you mean?"

"What else could it be? But at the same time, he's spending more money than ever—buying things he couldn't possibly need. He's spending money like there's no tomorrow. He just bought a huge house on Park Avenue for fifteen million. It was a bargain, he says—the land alone is worth that much. But it's a landmark house, so it can't be torn down to put up a new tower—not without a big legal hassle, anyway, that would cost him more than the house itself. The house is bigger than any man would want to live in, but that's what he says he's going to do. And now he's looking at another big house in the Hamptons. He's also buying himself—"

"Honors?" she suggests.

"Yes! How'd you guess that? Trusteeships. Honorary degrees. Things like that. He used to say that his goal was to be elected to the board of the Metropolitan Museum, but I think he's given up on that one. That's the biggest honor in the city, and I think

Dad realizes he'll never be in that league. But in the meantime, Dad is offering five million to this organization, ten million to the next, twenty million to somebody else—"

"Maybe he wants to immortalize himself."

"Yes, but why now? Why all at once? What's the big rush?"

"But if he's spending so much money, how can he be in any sort of financial trouble?"

"I don't know. Dad's always been very secretive, but lately he's become even more so. He won't talk to me. He spends all day in his office behind a closed door, talking on the phone, shooting off faxes and emails. I asked his personal secretary, Molly, what's going on in there, but she just shrugged. She doesn't know. He has his private telephone number changed two, three, or four times a week. Who's he hiding from? He used to brag that the biggest banks in town were begging him to let them lend him money. The whole mood of the office has changed. There are rumors all over the place—that the IRS is after him for something, that the SEC is investigating us. People used to speak to me in the halls. Now, when they see me coming, they look the other way, like they're embarrassed for me. People used to walk down the halls. Now they sort of scuttle, like they're scared of something. I've heard that some of our people have started updating their résumés. Some people are taking longer lunch hours than usual, and it's not to get their hair done or to go to the dentist. Just yesterday one of our top account executives quit to go over to Bear Stearns. Some vague excuse about better opportunities for advancement. When the guy announced his resignation, Dad flew into a rage, which was never like him. Accused the guy of being a rat deserting a sinking ship. Does that sound good to you?"

"No," she says softly, "it doesn't. It doesn't sound good at all."

"He said it so loud that half the people on the floor heard it.

What do you suppose people thought when they heard about that? We've got three hundred and fifty people working for us. A sinking ship? But mostly it's his expression that worries me. He smiles at everybody, but there's a new look in his eye—a kind of glitter that doesn't quite go with the smile. It's a look of desperation. A look of cold fear."

"Perhaps you ought to—"

"Confront him? I tried to, just this morning. I caught him coming out of his office, and I just stepped in front of him, grabbed him by the arm. I said, 'Dad, level with me. Something's wrong. Tell me what it is.' He just pushed me aside, and said, 'Are you going to turn out to be another one of the rats?' Then he walked away—whistling!"

"Oh, dear. Whistling in the dark."

"Yeah. Which brings me to ask you what I've got to ask you. If worse should come to worst, Sally—"

"Yes?"

"Would you still—"

"Would I still marry you if your father lost all his money? Yes."

"But would you still want to marry me if my father ended up having to go to jail?"

"What are you doing here?" Clarissa asks Hobe. "Why aren't you at your office?" He stands at her bedroom door, carrying a tray in his hands.

"It's Thursday, Rose's day off. I thought I'd stay home and look after you."

"That really wasn't necessary," she says weakly. "I can take care of myself perfectly well. Really, I can."

He steps into the room and places the breakfast tray across her knees.

"I've fixed you a nice lunch," he says. "An avocado and grape-fruit salad, sliced chicken breast, a couple of Rose's brownies. Iced tea." She stares at the tray in front of her. "I'll bet you didn't know I was such a good cook," he says.

He sits down on the edge of the bed beside her. "Does the dressing need to be changed?" he asks her.

"No. I changed it myself a little while ago."

"How does the eye look?"

"Not very pretty, I'm afraid."

"And the vision?"

"Still pretty blurry. But it seems to be getting better."

"I wish you'd let me call a doctor. Even let Jethro have a look—"

"No, no. I'll be fine."

He reaches out and touches her forehead with his fingertips. She flinches slightly at his touch, but he appears not to notice this. He rests his fingers there a moment. "I think you're still running a little fever," he says.

"I've taken a couple of Tylenol. That will take care of that."

"Any pain?"

"Some. But not as bad as yesterday. I'll be fine, Hobe."

He removes his hand. "Oh, God. God, I'm so sorry, Cissie. I don't know what got into me. I'd been under a lot of stress, Cissie, you know that. And when you said the things you said, I just—well, I just lost it. I lost my cool, as the kids say."

The expression, already an anachronism as far as she is concerned, sounds particularly peculiar coming from him. "Is that what the kids say? Well, perhaps."

"Will you ever forgive me, my darling?"

"It isn't a question of forgiveness, is it? It's done, it happened, it's over. For better or for worse, life goes on."

"You certainly don't believe what that girl said, do you?"

She turns her head away from him. "I just don't know what

to believe," she says. "The girl was nothing but a troublemaker. She's been a troublemaker all her life. Her stepmother, Tweetums Van Degan, said that to me. She said she felt sorry for Linda and tried to help her. But she said the girl seemed bent on—those were the exact words she used, *bent* on—bent on causing trouble for herself and for others, all her life. That's all she was trying to do—to cause trouble for us, and for the school. She'd steal, she'd lie—anything to cause trouble. You know there've been some thefts reported in Colby Hall. I wouldn't be surprised if it turned out that Linda Van Degan was behind all that. At every school she's attended, Linda Van Degan has caused trouble."

She sighs. "Well, somewhere—in Shakespeare, I think—there's a line: 'But that was long ago, and in another part of the forest, and, besides, the wench is dead.' Let's not talk about her anymore, Hobe."

"But I'm afraid it isn't all quite over yet," he says.

"What do you mean?"

"Well, besides dealing with the fires these last days, I had a call from Tom Finney, the county prosecutor, this morning. Somehow he got wind of what happened with Linda. He's talking about holding a grand jury inquiry into Linda Van Degan's death."

"Tom Finney? Is he any relation to Rose?"

"Probably some sort of cousin. The town of James Falls is full of Finneys—all leftovers from the Great Irish Invasion of the 1840s. The joke is that James Falls ought to be renamed Finneytown. Shanty Irish, the whole lot."

"What did you say to Mr. Finney?"

"I was polite. I was courteous. I addressed him as 'Mr. Prosecutor.' But I didn't convey any information. I referred him to Linda's parents but said I was sorry I couldn't provide him with addresses or telephone numbers. School policy. I did remind him that both parents live out of state. I know what this Finney character is after."

"Which is?"

"He comes up for reelection in November. He's looking for a big case that will get him a lot of publicity. He figures he's landed the big one. You know—old New York family, lots of money, fashionable New England boarding school, it's got all the elements. I wouldn't be surprised if the guy has an eye on the governor's mansion somewhere down the line."

She closes her one good eye. "Rose," she whispers.

"Rose? What about her?"

"Nothing. Just thinking aloud about people named Finney."

"Anyway, I think I know how to handle him."

"How?" she says. "How?"

"I called Truck Van Degan just to alert him about this, to tell him that he might get a call from this character. The Van Degans don't want any publicity about this, either. I suggested that a small contribution to Mr. Finney's reelection campaign might be in order. In this backwoods county, it wouldn't take much to call Finney off the scent. Just a few thousand. Truck Van Degan got my point."

"I see," she says. "Bribery. That's what you accused Michael Rubin of trying to do."

He looks briefly flustered. "No, it's not bribery," he says. "It's just—well, it's just politics. It's the way things are handled politically in this state."

"A payoff. Bribery. It sounds like the same thing to me, Hobe."

"A campaign contribution isn't bribery!"

She turns away from him again, resting her head back against the pillows. "I'm a little tired," she says. "I'd like to rest now. I need to build up my strength for the trustees' meeting next week. And that will be—"

"The trustees will start arriving late next week. The dinner will be Friday night. I've gone over the menu with Rose. The meeting starts Saturday morning at ten."

"Yes, and I need to be up and on my toes by then."

"Listen," he says quickly, "there is no reason why you have to attend that meeting, or even be at the dinner, for that matter. Absolutely no reason. I'll make your excuses for you. I'll mention your—your little fall on the stair—and extend your regrets. I'll take care of the whole thing. I won't have you worrying about that."

"But you don't understand! I'm not worrying. I'm looking forward to it. And I promised Alexandra Lemosney—"

"I'll take care of her."

"No, no. I'll be there."

He starts to rise. "But you haven't touched your lunch, my darling!"

She waves her hand toward the tray. "I'll get to it. Just leave it here. I just want to rest now, Hobe. Please."

"There's just one more thing, my darling."

"What is that?"

"If my idea of a contribution to Tom Finney's campaign doesn't work—and if there should be some sort of an inquiry into the Van Degan girl's death—not that I think for a moment that there actually will be—but if there should be, and if somehow your name got dragged into it, even peripherally, and if you were subpoenaed to testify—since, after all, you were one of the last people who talked to her when she was alive—what I mean is, you wouldn't repeat that thing you claim she said about me. Would you?"

"It's not a claim. It's what she said."

"But you wouldn't repeat that, would you? Not in a court-room. Of course, you wouldn't. It's a silly question, my darling, isn't it? I know you wouldn't. I know you pretty well."

"You're asking me to lie under oath?"

"No! Not lie. And certainly not under oath, darling. But if the question did come up—not that it would of course—but if it did, you would certainly be discreet enough to omit that part of your conversation with the girl, wouldn't you? You wouldn't incriminate—"

"Incriminate you?"

"Well, that was pretty rough language that little trouble-maker used. And I can't imagine—simply cannot imagine—a lady like you, the headmaster's wife, a clergyman's daughter, a lovely, well-bred lady like you using language like that in a courtroom."

"No, I suppose a lady wouldn't use language like that, not a real lady."

"Then it's a promise?"

"I haven't promised anything, Hobe."

"But in the highly—highly—unlikely circumstance that you were asked about that conversation with the girl, you certainly wouldn't repeat the—the absolutely absurd and outrageous accusation she made about me. Would you, darling?"

She says nothing.

"You wouldn't, would you? Because that would absolutely destroy—"

"You?"

"Because it's too absurd, too outrageous. Nobody would believe it anyway. So tell me you wouldn't mention that. That's all I'm asking you, darling. Just promise me that."

"Well," she says at last, "since, as you say, the circumstances are highly unlikely that I'd be asked such a question, all I can say is that I'd have to think about it."

"Good girl. I knew I could count on you." He bends over her quickly and kisses her forehead. "I love you, Cissie," he says.

"I love you more than the earth, sun, moon, and stars. I'd be nothing without you, Cissie."

She shrinks back against the pillow. "Let me rest now," she says. "Please."

When he has gone, she stares down at the untouched meal on the breakfast tray on her lap. Then she lifts the tray and places it at the foot of her bed. She puts her bare feet over the side of the bed and rises, a little unsteadily, in her nightie and goes to the window, parts the sheer curtains, and looks out. Outside, the manicured lawns and paths and hedges of the campus are deserted. The students are still in their afternoon classes, and the scene is one of unbroken calm now after the turmoil of the last week. But a breeze has sprung up, causing the new leaves of the sugar maples to shiver and reveal their silvery undersides. The air smells of rain, and in the west a few dark clouds are beginning to gather in churning bundles. One of the first thunderstorms of summer appears to be on its way.

Later that day, Simon Jethro, MD, hooks his thumbs in the armholes of his vest and, with his unlighted pipe clenched between his teeth, says, "Well, Hobe, from the symptoms you describe—the headaches, the fatigue, the loss of appetite, the dizzy spells, and now this latest fall on the stairs, I can only guess at a diagnosis without examining her."

"What would that guess be, Si?"

"There are several, but they're just guesses. Let's start with a worst-case scenario. An embolism might be indicated, affecting an area of the brain. That could be life-threatening. Also, since she had a serious bout with cancer many years ago, there's always the possibility that those nasty little cells have come back and have started multiplying again—again, in the brain. But I don't want to alarm you, Hobe. This is just guesswork. I'd have to have a look at her. A series of tests would have to be performed. We'd need to check her into a hospital, and then—"

"This she absolutely refuses to do. She simply will not see a doctor. How would I get her to go? Bind and gag her?"

He unhooks his thumbs and spreads his hands. "Then there's nothing I can tell you, Hobe," he says. "I know Clarissa. I know how stubborn and strong-willed she can be—stubborn as McGregor's mule. But look, you shouldn't even be talking to me. I'm just an old country GP. I can swab a sore throat, treat a case of pinkeye, or even the occasional case of mononucleosis. But it's been forty years since I've even yanked a pair of tonsils. She should see a specialist—a neurologist, or an oncologist perhaps. If you want, I could recommend someone—"

"No use, no use."

"How is the damaged eye?"

"I haven't had a look at it since her accident. She keeps it bandaged. She says her vision is still blurred in that one eye."

"Damn! She should see a specialist for that, too. She could lose the eye, for God's sake. You can tell Clarissa that I say she's not only being stubborn—but she's also a damned fool!"

"I've tried, I've tried. I've said all those things."

"Well, I wouldn't recommend your binding and gagging solution, but I confess I can't think of anything else. What about your children?"

"Johnny's spoken to her, Sally's spoken to her. Nothing works."

"Stubborn as McGregor's *prize* mule."

Hobe sits forward in his chair. "Maybe there's one thing you could do, Si," he says. "Since her fall, and the head and eye injuries, she's complained of a certain amount of pain. Is there something you could prescribe—?"

"Not without examining her first."

"Something for pain? Something that would be a little stronger than the damn Tylenol she's been taking?"

"No, Hobe, not without looking at her first." He looks at him squarely. "I cannot prescribe medication for a patient I haven't seen. You shouldn't even ask me to do that, because that I simply cannot do."

THIRTEEN

From Clarissa Spotswood's Journal:

Peace and quiet this afternoon. They are letting me alone. The trustees arrive in just one week's time, and I intend to be ready for them. This challenge—ha!—is doing wonders for my health, and the fever was down this morning to 99.1 degrees, almost normal, and I am almost thinking clearly again, with fewer of those stormy dreams and waking up drenched with sweat. I understand now why battered wives seldom leave their batterers. It is not fear of poverty or homelessness or loneliness, and it has nothing to do with fear of being battered again. It is, quite simply, fear of the unknown. It is why the Jews of czarist Russia always offered up blessings for their czar in their synagogues, prayers for his good health and long life. They knew what *this* czar was capable of. It was the next czar that they were worried about. The next one was the fearful question mark.

It's not that I haven't been offered comfortable—opulent, in fact!—new digs to go to. The average woman would probably leap at the opportunity I've been offered, and yet, not thinking of myself as the average woman, I'm still hesitant, still a little timid, fear of the unknown. "X" called me again this morning, as he's been calling me nearly every day, though I've begged him not to, and each time his tone is more urgent, more insistent. But I said to him: "Look, I took a nasty little tumble on the stairs the other night, and the left side of my face hit the newel post. I still look like hell, and there's still a lot of swelling and discoloration around my left eye, which is still pretty bloodshot. But I'm keeping cold compresses on the eye, and each day'll think it looks a little better. When the time comes, there's a lot I can do with makeup, and maybe sunglasses, and I really want to make it through the trustees' dinner and their meeting the next day. I just feel I owe that much to the school. After all, the school has provided me with board and lodging for twenty-five years, and for that I think I ought to owe it something. And besides, they've asked me to join them at their meeting, and I promised them I'd be there, and I don't want to break my promise. So, please, just let me get through this, and don't telephone me again until that's over, and once that's over I'll make my decision, okay? Fair enough? I promise you that, dear heart. Primrose promise."

"Say it again," he said.

"Say what again?"

"Dear heart."

"Dear heart. There. I've said it again.

"And besides," I said, "I think I can present your idea of a gift to the school much better, and with more enthusiasm, to the trustees than Hobe can. I'm just sure I can do that because Hobe, as you know, can be a little stuffy. And I think I can also persuade the trustees to accept the terms you've attached to your gift. Just give me a chance to give that a try, my darling, and I think you'll be pleased with the results. That way, we'll both get what we want. Fair enough?" I think he liked that argument.

But he keeps pushing me, pushing me to say more than I want to say to him, and that only adds to my hesitancy, my uncertainty, my unwillingness to make, as he puts it, a "full commitment" to him. He wants me to tell him that he's the only man I ever loved, and that I never loved Hobe, not even for a minute But that's going too far, that's asking too much of me because it simply isn't true. I did love Hobe. I loved him very much. I was almost absurdly, ill-makingly in love with him when I married him, and for a long time after that. I wouldn't have married him if I hadn't been in love with him, and "X" has got to understand that, accept that. And it is *not* fair (underline three times) for him to ask me to deny that! There was that summer Hobe and I spent at Blue Goose Lake, for instance.

Do you remember that, Hobe? Do you?

Do you remember our little cabin on Blue Goose Lake? It was Daddy's wedding present to us, our wedding trip. But it wasn't exactly a honeymoon because we were married in October, and you had a full school year of teaching ahead of you, so we couldn't take our wedding trip until the following July. But you said postponed honeymoons are always better, and you were right. You said that most honeymoons are spent with the newlyweds wondering why they were insane enough to think that marriage was such a good idea to begin with, with the young couple staring at each other blankly over a room-service breakfast on the terrace of some resort hotel. Remember *Private Lives*? Better to plunge right into work and the everyday job of being married, which is difficult enough as it is, and save the honeymoon holiday for further down the road.

Our cabin at Blue Goose Lake had no roads leading to it. The village was eight miles down the lake. Twice a week Reggie, our native guide, arrived in his outboard with our groceries and supplies, and the mail, if there happened to be any. We could hear his putt-putt coming from miles away and would go down to the dock to meet him and help him unload. Our only transport was the canoe. The cabin had no telephone, no electricity. We lighted it with kerosene lamps and candles. I cooked on an old woodburning stove, and luckily there was a woodpile because you turned out to be not very good at chopping wood. Water came from a well and had to be pumped up by hand, though one day walking in the piney woods we discovered a natural spring, where the water was even sweeter, and we carried that water home in pails. If you didn't count the hand pump, there was no plumbing. We took our baths naked in the icy waters of the lake. If we wanted to chill a bottle of wine for dinner, a nest of rocks along the lakeshore was our cooler. Down a path behind the cabin was the two-holer outhouse. Previous summer renters had tacked little messages, some of them slightly off-color, to the walls of the outhouse, and I remember one of them: "It's a short walk to this privy / a short way to go / But to come here at midnight—it's the longest walk I know!" Do you remember that? Do you remember the sounds of the loons howling over the lake at sunset?

A fat porcupine lived under our foundation. He (she?) seemed to have no family and lived there alone. We gave him a wide berth, but he was very considerate of us. His thick, waxy quills made a distinct clicking sound as he waddled out of his den each evening to warn us that he was in the vicinity. Naturally we named him Porky, and by the end of the summer he was almost tame. He would almost, but not quite, come close enough to me to eat a banana out of my hand when I offered it to him.

We fished from the canoe. Do you remember the day in the canoe when we saw a mother moose swimming across the lake with her calf paddling a few feet behind her? Then, around a tiny spit of land, we saw a whole herd of moose making its way across the lake, the big bulls in the lead, the cows following, each with her calf in tow. They swam right past our canoe without appearing to notice us, and without making so much as a ripple in the water.

You were out after lake trout and bass and, perhaps, a land-locked salmon. Reggie said there were landlocked salmon in the lake, though we never caught one. And do you remember the day I caught the eel? It was my luck to catch an eel. It was such a heavy load on my rod and line as I began to reel it in that I thought I must have hooked into an old tire. But when I got it to the surface, it was this huge freshwater eel, nearly four feet long. It took the two of us to get the hook out of the creature's mouth, and when we did it thrashed and flung itself about so much on the floor of the canoe, trying to leap back into the water, that I was afraid it was going to capsize us. I wanted to throw it back, but you had decided that we were going to have eel chowder for dinner, and we started paddling for home.

But still the eel kept flopping dangerously about the bottom of the canoe, its mouth gasping for air, its little eyes looking accusingly and belligerently at me. It would not die, and so finally you stuffed it into the picnic basket that had contained our lunch and clamped down the lid. But all the way home the picnic basket lurched and jumped as the captive tried to fight its way out.

At home, you beheaded it with a hunting knife, but that did not stop the animal's writhing contortions. You nailed it to a tree to clean it, but even after it had been skinned and boned and gutted its body continued to flail about against the tree trunk. While I heated the woodstove, you cut the eel into bite-size pieces, but when I placed the pieces in a hot skillet with butter to sauté them, the pieces of eel kept jumping about the pan. I added potatoes, onion, corn, sliced carrots, and heavy cream to the pan, and let the whole thing simmer for more than an hour. But even after the vegetables had cooked, and we ladled the chowder into our bowls, we could see the squares of flesh in our soup were still quivering, still jerking reflexively from some unconquerable life force.

Naturally we couldn't eat it. It had fought too hard and was still fighting. We set our bowls aside, and I think both of us had tears in our eyes. Do you remember that?

How could I say that you and I didn't love each other then? And there were other times as well. Two months later I discovered I was pregnant with Johnny.

It is hard to write this with only one good eye, and I can hardly read my own handwriting. But I ask myself: Is it possible to believe that those two people in the cabin at Blue Goose Lake are the same two people who are living in this big house today, the house they call the Castle? Yes, I am afraid it is quite possible.

———

"Dad! What a nice surprise! I didn't know you were coming down to New York."

"Well, I had a Development Committee meeting at the Yale Club, and we ended early, so I thought I'd come downtown and see where it is you're living."

"This is it," his son says. "Not very fancy, but it suits me. If we'd known you were coming, we'd have tidied up the place a bit. Dad, this is my roommate, Peter Stites."

Peter switches off the television set and stands up. "Nice to meet you, Mr. Spotswood," he says, shaking his hand.

His son lifts an empty pizza box from the sofa and places it on top of the television set. "Sit down, Dad. Can I fix you a drink?"

"No, thanks. I'm going to be driving back to Connecticut this afternoon."

"I'm going to have a beer," his son says. He goes to a small refrigerator in the corner of the room, opens it, and takes out a can of beer and flips it open with his thumb. "Pete?"

"No, thanks," Peter says. "I've got some errands to do, so I'll leave you guys alone to have a visit."

"Pick up a bag of kitty litter," John says. "And jelly. We're out of jelly. We've got a serious jelly crisis."

"So," his father says, looking around the room when they are alone, "you have a cat."

"Yep. Another Missy. This is Missy the Fourth. She hides under my bed when company comes. You may see her looking around. A Siamese . . ."

"So," his father says again, "this is where you live, Johnny."

"This is it!" He laughs nervously. "I know what you're thinking. You're thinking, 'What . . . a . . . dump!' The old Bette Davis line."

"No, I wasn't thinking that at all, Johnny. I mean it's—well, it's rather cozy. Very . . . homey."

"Be it ever so humble." He gestures to the refrigerator. "We don't have a full kitchen, so we eat mostly carryout."

"Three of you fellows live here?"

"It was three until last week. Dave Barker left us to get married. Right now, it's just Pete and me, but we're looking for a third to—you know, help with the rent. You won't believe what rents are like in New York these days, Dad."

"What sort of rent are you paying?"

"Thirteen fifty."

"Thirteen hundred and fifty dollars a month—for this?"

"Yep. And we consider ourselves lucky."

"Well!"

"Yep."

There is a short silence between them. Then his father sits forward in the sofa, facing his son who straddles a kitchen chair, his beer can cupped in his right hand. "I've wanted to talk to you, son," he says. "It's about your mother."

"Oh? What about her?"

"She had a fall last week. On the stairs. Her head hit the banister, and she's got a really ugly gash just above her left eye. There's a lot of swelling, a lot of inflammation. I'm worried about infection. I want her to see a doctor, but she absolutely refuses. She won't even let Si Jethro take a look at the eye, and I thought maybe you—"

"How did she happen to fall?"

"I-I didn't actually see it happen, but she'd had quite a lot to drink, and—"

"Mom? I didn't know Mom had a drinking problem, Dad."

"I'm afraid she does. She sneaks drinks when I'm not around. When I found her there, on the stairs, I carried her up to her room and I was astonished at how light and frail she's become. She hasn't been eating properly, and that's what alcoholics do, you know. When they drink, they ignore their diet. I'm really worried about her, Johnny." Hobe takes a deep breath. "Then, on top of that, we had a student who started setting fires on campus the same night your mother fell. So I've been occupied with that . . . oh, don't worry; that's all resolved now. Right now, I want to stay focused on your mother."

He whistles softly. "Golly, Dad," he says, "you've been dealing with a lot. As far as Mom is concerned, the last time you and I talked you told me she was perfectly fine. Though I mentioned how thin she was."

"That was a while back. And, actually, it was that very conversation of ours that alerted me. After that, I started watching her more closely."

"So what do you want me to do, Dad?"

"Speak to her. See if you can persuade her to see a doctor. See if she doesn't need some sort of medication. She'll listen to you when she won't listen to me. You know she thinks the sun rises and sets on you, Johnny."

"Well, sure, Dad. I'll speak to her."

"Will you? And can you do that soon? Go up to the school as soon as you can, and speak to her? You see, the trustees are meeting next week, and they want her at the meeting. And I don't want her—"

"Mom? At the trustees' meeting? Isn't that a bit—?"

"Unusual? I'll say it is! It's highly unorthodox. It's unheard of. It's outrageous!"

"But why would they want the headmaster's wife at their meeting?"

"Your mother gave an interview to a reporter from the local newspaper a couple of weeks ago. In it, she said a number of unfortunate—in my opinion quite unwise—things about the school and its policies. She may have been drunk when she gave the interview. But anyway, somehow Alexandra Lemosney down in Texas got hold of the item. Now she wants your mother to attend the meeting to 'air her views' on the school, as she puts it. Alexandra Lemosney is a bit of a nut, of course—really quite crazy. But she is the president of the board, so I more or less have to comply with her wishes. But I don't want your mother appearing at that meeting looking the way she does."

"You don't want her there because of how she looks?"

"It's not just that, Johnny. You don't understand. Your mother has had absolutely no experience with these meetings. I've been going to them for twenty-five years. They can get pretty rough. They can turn into regular cat-and-dog fights, Johnny. People hurl insults at one another, call each other names. They shout and scream at one another. It's insane, but it's a fact. Your mother just isn't up to that sort of thing at this point, son. I don't want to have your poor mother subjected to some of the verbal abuse that can go on at these meetings. It wouldn't be fair to her."

"You're sure you're not afraid of something she might say, Pop? You mentioned airing her views."

"Absolutely not! That's just Alexandra Lemosney talking. She's a complete crackpot. All she cares about is keeping things stirred up."

"Well," his son says, "tomorrow's Saturday. What if I hop in my car and drive up to see her?"

"Good," his father says. "That'd be great. See if you can talk some sense into her, get her to see a doctor. She needs medication."

"I'll do what I can."

"I tried to call your sister, but apparently she's out of town. If you talk to Sally before I do, see if you can have her talk to your mother, too. But I think she'll listen to you more than anybody else."

"Sure, but old Sally's all tied up with this guy she's been going with—this guy she's thinking of marrying."

His father frowns. "What? Who's she thinking of marrying? This is the first I've heard of any marriage plans."

"His name's Jesse Rubin. She seems to have fallen head over heels."

"What? Jesse Rubin? Michael Rubin's son?"

"Yep."

"Why would she want to get involved with someone like that?"

"I dunno either. I wasn't much impressed with the guy. He struck me as a big talker. But, like I say, she's fallen for him. So, what can I say?"

"Jesse Rubin went to Crittenden. I remember him well. Nebbishy little kid. He was a terrible athlete, but those people always are."

"Well, he's not a nebbishy little kid anymore. He's six foot three and damned good looking."

"In four years on the soccer team, he never made a single goal! It must be his money."

"No, I don't think so, Dad. From the way she talks, this is the real thing."

"Oh, for heaven's sake," his father says. "Maybe you can talk some sense into her, too. The *Rubins*. Why would she want to get our family involved with people like that?"

"You mean because they're Jewish?"

"Now don't try to imply that I'm prejudiced, Johnny. I most certainly am not. Don't forget, I was the first Crittenden head-master to get rid of the quota on Jewish students. I was the first headmaster to take in a Black. I was the first to admit Orientals and Latinos, and the first to take in women. When it comes to racial and religious tolerance, my record is well known. I have nothing at all against the Jewish people. But, I must say, no Spotswood has ever actually married a Jew."

"Would that be such a catastrophe, Dad?"

"These interfaith marriages almost never work out, but that's not the point. There's more to it than that. Let me ask you some-thing, Johnny. Have you ever studied that portrait of the old general that hangs in the library at home?"

"I know the portrait you mean, but I've never really studied it, no."

"You should. I have. Often. I find it means a great deal, and says a great deal, to me. He is, of course, your seven-times great-grandfather. When you come up to the school tomorrow, study it. Study the eyes, study the nose. You have the same nose, Johnny, that same long, thin, straight nose. I have it too, and the eyes. There's American *history* in that portrait, Johnny—long, proud pages of American history, going back to before the Revolution. In that portrait are represented some of the greatest of the great American families, and some prodigious historic achievements. When you come up tomorrow, I'll get out the Spotswood family tree, which is also in the library, and let you take a look at that. You will see all the great names there. You are related to the Browns and Hoppins of Rhode Island, to the Chews and Ingersolls and Morrises of Philadelphia, as well as to the New York Morrises and the Pelis of Pelham. You will see how, through marriage, you are related to the Livingstons of the Hudson River Valley, which also makes you related to John Jay, the first United States Supreme Court Chief Justice. On the distaff side, the Spotswoods are also related to the Schuylers, the Van Rensselaers, the Roosevelts, and even the Astors, though we're not particularly proud of them. You are related to the Lowells and Gardners of Boston, and you will note that there have been three presidents of Harvard in the family. You will see how, through marriage again, we can now connect our family to four United States presidents, the two Adamses, and the two Harrisons. We are also related to both the Lees and the Randolphs of Virginia, though the Randolphs never amounted to much after the second generation. A Randolph married a Hobart, where my name comes from, but the Hobarts weren't anybody—Civil War money. You are also related to such old New York families as the Stuyvesants and the Gracies and the Fishes and Beekmans and Lispenards and de Lanceys and Canfields. And here's an interesting thing. Collaterally, Spotswoods can claim descent from both Aaron Burr and Alexander Hamilton. And you mustn't be embarrassed by the Burr connection. History has misjudged Aaron Burr, in my opinion. How many families can claim descent from both the duelists? You are related to nearly every American family that made this country what it is today—in government, business, and education. Surely all that fine old blood that courses in your veins should give you and your sister something to be proud of, a family tradition to uphold and carry on. But now your sister wants to mingle that blood with—someone named Rubin?"

His son smiles. "It's all very interesting, Dad," he says. "But somehow I don't think it's going to cut much ice with Sally."

His father is still frowning. "Well, if genealogy doesn't mean anything to her, maybe genetics will. Michael Rubin's father was a druggist in Kew Gardens. His grandfather was an illiterate immigrant from the Kraków ghetto named Shmuel Rubinsky. I can see I'm going to have to have a long, hard, serious talk with your sister."

At the white-painted Litchfield County Courthouse, the young county prosecutor ushers his visitor into his office. "Sit down, Rose," he says. "Now, before we get started, despite having the same last name, you and I are not really related, are we?"

"I think you're my second cousin once removed," she says. "I think your grandmother was my great-aunt Alice."

"Alice was my grandmother's sister. Anyway, it's not very close, and Finney is a pretty common name in these parts. We're not closely enough related for it to matter. And, in fact, you and I have never met before—correct?"

"No, sir."

"Is that correct?"

"Yes, sir, is what I meant."

"No one could call us friends, or even acquaintances."

"No, sir."

"That's a very important point to establish, right at the beginning. That we are only very distantly related, and that we are in no way friends, or even acquaintances. Is that clear? Will you remember that, Rose?"

"Yes, sir."

"Good. Now let's get down to business," he says.

"Have you heard anything more from the county prosecutor's office?" Clarissa asks Hobe when he appears at her bedroom door Friday evening after his return from New York.

He sets down the tray beside her bed. "No, but that Truxton Van Degan is an ass. A complete horse's ass. He was at our Development Committee meeting in New York this morning, and I took him aside afterward and explained the situation to him. He offers a thousand dollars as a campaign contribution. We may be small-town up here, but we're not that small-town. A measly thousand dollars isn't going to stop that guy from dragging his daughter's name, and the Van Degans' good name, and the school's name, through the mud. I told him to make it fifty thousand and be ready to negotiate up from there. Son of a bitch acted as though fifty thousand would wipe out the Van Degan family fortune. Fifty thousand is chicken feed to a man like Truxton Van Degan, and I told the son of a bitch so!" There is a silence.

"Hobe, I'm wondering whether you and I should offer some kind of contribution too," she says, after a moment.

"You and me? Why? I don't have that kind of money."

"I have a little capital. From Daddy's estate."

"Why should we get involved? This is Van Degan's problem, not ours."

"But aren't we all more or less in this together—the Van Degans, and you and me?"

"No!"

"But we could be, couldn't we?"

"No, we could not be—you fool!"

She turns her head away from him, against the pillow. "Are you going to hit me again?" she whispers. "Please don't."

"Of course I'm not going to hit you!" He sits down on a corner of her bed. "For God's sake, Cissie," he says, "can't you ever forgive me for that? Can't you understand—can't you appreciate—the kind of stress I've been under?" His tone is gentler now. "Please try," he says. "Please try to understand."

She says nothing.

"Meanwhile," he says, "my secretary left this clipping on my desk while I was gone. It's from the *Wall Street Journal*. I thought it might interest you." He removes the clipping from the breast pocket of his jacket and hands it to her.

She takes it and peers at it for a moment, then hands it back to him. "I still can't read very well with one eye," she says. "You read it to me."

"Very well." He adjusts his glasses to his nose and reads. "The headline says, 'More Woes for Manhattan Financier.' 'In addition to claims of both unreported and underreported income by the IRS, the New York financier Michael J. Rubin faces new fiscal woes, the *Journal* has learned today. Several of the nation's banks are now claiming that for the past two years Rubin has been engaged in a pattern of borrowing money to purchase equities, and then adding these equities to his corporate portfolio, thus inflating the portfolio's value, and then using the inflated value to borrow additional funds. This was being done, the banks claim, while Rubin was also failing to report prior indebtedness on the required disclosure forms. This sort of high-wire leveraging—borrowing money against borrowed funds—can work successfully for the investor in a rising stock market. But in the market's recent sharp fall, investors such as Mr. Rubin can find themselves in a serious bind, as banks demand additional collateral for their loans. In Mr. Rubin's case, the situation is complicated by the fact that many of Rubin & Company's larger loans are so-called syndicated loans, shared by several different banks. And failure to disclose prior indebtedness, as the banks allege, can constitute fraud. And it would further appear that Rubin's troubles do not end there. Recently, the Rubin firm has been dealing heavily in US obligations, namely Treasury bills. Now the government alleges that some $500 million of these T-bills appear to have been counterfeit. If these allegations are proven correct, and the company has been found to have been possessing, passing, and dealing in counterfeit T-bills, a conspiracy charge could be leveled against Rubin's firm, which could result in a heavy fine or prison sentence, or both, for Mr. Rubin. Reached for comment at his office today, Mr. Rubin's response was characteristically glib and nonchalant. "If any of that is true, and I'm not saying it is, maybe I just trusted the wrong guys," he told the *Journal*.'"

He puts down the clipping. "Well," he says, "what do you think of that?"

"It's all allegations," she says. "Claims of this, claims of that. Michael has the best lawyers in the country working for him. I'm sure it will all sort itself out."

"But is this the kind of man from whom I'd want my school to accept a major gift? Even more important, is this the kind of man whose son we'd want married to our daughter?"

"*What?* What are you saying?"

"It seems that Sally and Jesse Rubin are planning to get married. That's what I'm saying."

She pulls herself up on her elbows. "Oh, no," she says. "Oh, no—we can't let that happen, Hobe!"

"For once, I agree with you completely."

She reaches for the telephone. "I've got to get in touch with her," she says. "We've got to stop this."

"Calm down," he says. "There's no big rush."

"Oh, but there is! I've got to—"

"Right now, Sally happens to be in Melbourne. From there she flies to Singapore, and then Bombay and Tokyo. She's not due back in New York for twelve more days. We'll both have a serious talk with her then. I'm glad you're backing me up on this one, Cissie. We simply can't have Sally marrying someone like that."

"Mom?" John says, stepping into her darkened bedroom on Saturday morning. "Mom—are you awake?"

She turns and sees him and her hand flies to her face. "Johnny! What are you doing here? No—don't come in! My bandage has fallen off! Let me—"

He walks slowly toward her bed, and she buries her face in the pillows. "*Don't* look at me now! Please let me—"

He switches on the beside lamp.

"No!"

He reaches down and takes her chin in his hand and slowly turns her toward him. "Oh my god," he says softly. "There's an infection there."

"Just a little pus—"

He presses his hand against her forehead. "You're feverish, too."

"It'll go away. I'm—"

Quickly he wraps the sheet around her body and lifts her from the bed.

"What are you *doing*?"

"I'm taking you to the emergency room right now."

"No, no—please. Not that." She pounds her fists weakly against his neck and shoulder blades. "Put me down," she sobs. "Please put me down, Johnny. Please don't do this to me. I'm going to be fine. Please put me down!"

"I'm sorry, Mother," he says a little grimly, "but the situation is now completely out of your hands."

He carries her out of the bedroom and down the stairs, out the front door to his car. "Will you try to get hold of Sally for me?" she asks him.

"I will," he says. "Primrose promise."

PART TWO

SUMMER BREAK

FOURTEEN

The scene is the Litchfield County Courthouse, the grand jury room. The twenty-three grand jurors, all white, most of them in their middle to late sixties, many of them retirees and nearly all of them representatives of families who have been prominent in the county for many years, sit at a long table, each with a yellow legal pad and pencil and each with a water glass and small carafe of ice water. A bailiff in uniform guards the closed doors, and a court stenographer—the only Black person in the room—sits poised at her machine on its tripod. The witnesses who have been subpoenaed for today's session sit on benches at the rear of the room. There are no spectators, since these sessions are closed to the public. The day is warm, but the building is not air-conditioned, and the windows are closed. An overhead ceiling fan creates a slight breeze, but still several of the jurors and witnesses can be seen dabbing at their foreheads with handkerchiefs.

The young prosecutor, Tom Finney, slim and dapper in a blue pin-striped suit and yellow tie, rises from his desk and addresses the panel. "Ladies and gentlemen of the grand jury," he says, "we are here today to examine the circumstances of the death of Linda Van Degan, a minor, to determine the cause of that death and to decide whether a felony has been committed, or whether there is probable cause for prosecution. Ladies and gentlemen, I would like to call my first witness, Miss Pauline Scanlon."

Pauline Scanlon rises from the back of the room and takes a seat in the witness box. She is visibly very nervous.

"Please state your name," Tom Finney says.

"Pauline Mary Scanlon."

"Please speak a little louder, Miss Scanlon, so the stenographer can hear your responses."

"Pauline! Pauline Mary Scanlon!"

"And your occupation?"

"Busser at the Dairy Queen out on Route Forty-Four."

"And prior to that?"

"I was on the housekeeping staff at the Crittenden School."

"Would you please describe your duties in that capacity, Miss Scanlon?"

"Duties?"

"What did you do in that job?"

"Oh. Hoovered the corridors in the dorms every day. Checked the soaps in the shower rooms. Mopped the floors. Cleaned the commodes."

"Nothing in the students' rooms?"

"Oh, yes. Changed the sheets and pillowcases in their rooms. Once a week. Mondays. And vacuumed in there, too, if it seemed to need it."

"And one of the dorms you cleaned was Colby Hall, correct?"

"Yes, Your Honor."

"That is a girls' dormitory, correct?"

"Yes, Your Honor."

"You don't need to call me Your Honor, Miss Scanlon. I am not a judge. And was one of the rooms that you cleaned in Colby Hall assigned to Linda Van Degan, a student in her junior year at Crittenden?"

"I believe they was all juniors in that building, yes."

"And did one of those rooms belong to Linda Van Degan?"

"I'm not sure, sir."

"What? You're not sure?"

"I never paid no attention to their names, sir."

"Well, let me put it to you this way. Was one of the rooms you cleaned number two eleven?"

"Oh, yes, sir. Two eleven was one of my regular rooms. That's where it happened. That's where I found it. It was in two eleven."

"Excuse me." He turns to the panel of jurors and hands them a sheet of paper from his desk. "Ladies and gentlemen," he says, "this is a page from the Crittenden School Directory. You will see that room two eleven, Colby Hall, was assigned to the aforementioned student, Linda S. Van Degan. I request that this page be marked Exhibit 'A.'" The jurors nod in agreement.

He turns back to the witness. "Now, Miss Scanlon, would you please tell us what you found in room two eleven of Colby Hall on the morning of Monday, May the third?"

"I'm not sure."

"What do you mean you're not sure, Miss Scanlon?"

"I'm not sure that was the date. I'm not too good on dates, sir."

He looks briefly annoyed. "Well," he says, "let the record state that May the third was a Monday. And if it was a Monday, you would have been cleaning room two eleven, correct?"

"Yes, Your Honor."

"Then tell us, please, Miss Scanlon, what you found in room two eleven when you went into that room to clean it and change the linen that Monday morning."

"Nothing! The sheets was gone! The blanket was gone! The bedspread was gone! That bed was stripped bare! It was like she'd left the school and taken all the bedclothes with her! But that room was on my checklist as due for a linen change."

"And what did you do then?"

"I didn't know what to do! I could have just made that bed up, with everything fresh, but we're supposed to turn in all the soiled linen for the linen count. We're not supposed to do this, but I thought I'd just take a look in the closet, and—"

"What do you mean you're not supposed to do this?"

"Look in their closets. That's strictly against the rules. Only Security is supposed to do that, but that's what I did, and that's where I found it."

"What did you find, Miss Scanlon?"

"Everything! The sheets, the pillow, the pillowcase, the blanket, the spread—all stuffed in the back of the closet, and everything covered with blood!"

"Fresh blood or dried blood, Miss Scanlon?"

"Dried blood."

"You know what dried blood looks like?"

"Of course! We find dried-up blood on the girls' sheets all the time!" There is a low murmur of talk among the jurors.

"But this was somehow different."

"You bet it was! It was all over everything. It was almost like somebody had bled to death in that bed. It was terrible, Your Honor. You wouldn't believe it. I still have bad dreams, nightmares from it. My cousin Bernice, whose husband is a lawyer, says I ought to sue the school for the mental of it, what it did to me."

"I see," he says. "Now tell us what else you saw."

"Well, I pulled out the sheets and pillowcases, and then—then there was the blanket, all like all rolled up, and I started to unroll it, and then—and then—" Suddenly she sobs. "And then I saw there was more blood, and there was a *baby* in it!"

She is sobbing uncontrollably now.

"Please try to get yourself under control, Miss Scanlon," the prosecutor says. From a box on his desk, he extracts a handful of Kleenex and hands it to her. She blows her nose noisily.

"Oh, it was awful," she says.

"You say you found an infant wrapped in the blanket."

"I didn't see all of it—just a little hand, and a little foot."

"In your opinion, was the infant dead or alive?"

"It looked dead. It was covered with blood, but it was blue, and, you know, seemed stiff. It didn't move."

He pauses. "Let the record state that the infant was dead only in Miss Scanlon's opinion. She is not a licensed medical examiner, nor did she thoroughly examine the baby." He turns to the witness again. "Were you able to determine the infant's sex?" he asks her.

"The sex of it? No, sir."

"And then what did you do when you made this—this shocking discovery, Miss Scanlon?"

"Do? What I did was scream bloody murder. But there was no one else in the building to hear me."

"And then what did you do?"

"I was so scared, Your Honor, I just stuffed everything into one of my heavy-duty garbage bags that was on my cart."

"Including the infant wrapped in the blanket?"

"Everything. Including that."

"It didn't occur to you to notify the head of Housekeeping, or to summon the campus police?"

"I was scared, Your Honor. I was scared they'd think I had something to do with it."

"So would it be safe to say that you were so distraught after your discovery—"

"Distraught?"

"So upset by what you found, by what appeared to be an infant homicide, that you weren't thinking clearly? Would that be safe to say?"

"Yes," she says. "I just stuffed everything into one of my heavy-duty trash bags. Brown, with a ziplock top."

"And what did you do with the bag and its contents?"

"I took everything home, to my room in Buhl Hall, where I was living then, and hid it in my closet there."

He turns to the jurors. "Buhl Hall is the residence hall for unmarried members of Crittenden's grounds and housekeeping staffs," he says. Then, to his witness again, he says, "Did you tell anyone about your experience?"

"Not for a few days, no."

"And then, whom did you tell?" He places an elegant emphasis on the word *whom*.

"I told Rose."

"Rose? Rose who?"

"I don't know her last name."

He turns to the jury again. "She is referring to Rose Finney— no relation of mine, by the way—who is the housekeeper at the school headmaster's residence. Miss Scanlon, why did you choose to tell Rose?"

"She was always nice to me, which most of the others weren't. And she worked for the headmaster, and so I thought she'd know wh-what to do."

"And what did Rose say to you?"

"She told me that the girl in two eleven was a very important student, that her family was millionaires, that a building was named after her and all. She said she'd take the matter up with Mrs. Spotswood."

"Did you tell Rose that there was a—presumably—dead infant in the garbage bag?"

"Not at first, no. A couple of days later I told her that. I don't remember exactly when."

"And what did Rose do when you first told her about the bag? And told you she'd speak with Mrs. Spotswood about it?"

"She came back later that day and said she'd spoken with Mrs. Spotswood, and that she herself would take the bag to Mrs. Spotswood, and Mrs. Spotswood would get rid of it for me."

"Get rid of it? How?"

"She didn't say, sir. I was so relieved to get that thing out of my room, I didn't ask."

"I see," he says. He pauses, steepling his fingers. "Now, Miss Scanlon, can you tell us a bit about how this whole episode affected you—personally?"

"Yes! She docked my pay! Miss Stimpson docked my pay for being short on my linen count that week!"

"Miss Stimpson, being Geraldine Stimpson, the head of housekeeping at the Crittenden School."

"That's her!"

"Your wages were docked in what amount, Miss Scanlon?"

"Two hundred and forty-seven dollars and thirteen cents, that's how much! Almost two weeks' pay!"

"You were not reimbursed?"

"Yes, I was, thank God!"

"By whom?"

"Mrs. Spotswood."

"Mrs. Spotswood? Why, I wonder?"

"I don't know."

"Have you ever met Mrs. Spotswood?"

"No."

Turning to the jury, he says, "Ladies and gentlemen, I offer you here for your inspection, a photocopy of a personal check drawn on the Scoville Bank, dated May eleventh, payable to Pauline Scanlon in the amount of two hundred and forty-seven dollars and thirteen cents, signed by Clarissa Spotswood. I request that be marked 'Exhibit B.'" He turns to the witness again. "Doesn't it strike you as curious that, after offering to dispose of evidence that might have pointed to a serious crime, Mrs. Spotswood also reimbursed you, a woman she'd never met, for the cost of the bedding that concealed that evidence? Were you instructed to keep quiet about all this, Miss Scanlon?"

"Rose told me Mrs. Spotswood said I wasn't to breathe a word to anybody about any of it."

"Curious," he says. "Very curious. Two hundred and forty-seven dollars was, in effect, your hush money. I have no further questions."

A woman juror from the panel raises her hand. "I have a question for the witness," she says. "Miss Scanlon, why was your employment at the school terminated?"

"Terminated?"

"Why are you no longer working for the school?"

"They fired me, that's why!"

"For any reason?"

"For being short on my linen count. For looking into their closets. Students' closets."

"But no one knew about looking into closets except Rose, and, presumably, Mrs. Spotswood."

"No," she sniffles.

"It's just that 'hush money' seems an odd term to me, Mr. Finney. One wouldn't ordinarily pay an employee a small sum as hush money, and then turn around and fire her, would one?"

He bows to the woman politely. "I think you will see why I use that term as I develop my case, ma'am," he says. "You may step down, Miss Scanlon."

She leaves the witness stand still sniffling in her Kleenexes.

"And now I'd like to call my next witness, Miss Chabot. . . . Your name, please?"

"Anne-Marie de Lucy de la Coudert Chabot."

"Please spell that for the stenographer. . . . And your occupation?"

"Instructor in French language and literature at the Crittenden School. All levels."

"And will you tell us please, Miss Chabot, where you happened to be on Friday morning, May the seventh, at approximately eleven o'clock?"

"I was taking a shortcut across the lawn in front of the head-master's house, on my way from my ten o'clock French Two class to my apartment on what is called Faculty Row. It is a route we faculty members often take."

"And what did you see as you took that shortcut?"

"I saw Mrs. Spotswood loading a large brown plastic garbage bag into the back of her station wagon. Mrs. Spotswood is a small woman, a little on the frail side, and the bag seemed heavy for her."

"Did you exchange words with Mrs. Spotswood?"

"I remember I said something to the effect that it seemed a pity that the headmaster's wife had to carry out her own garbage."

"And what was her reaction to that comment, Miss Chabot?"

"*Eh bien*, she became a bit, as we say in Paris, *de haut en bas*."

"Please restrict your responses to English, Miss Chabot. May we have a translation, please?"

"Well, I believe you would say snippy. Snooty. High-hatty to me."

"Did she seem nervous? Anxious? Distraught?"

"*Oui—yes! Très distrait, très anxieuse—*very anxious and distraught and guilty-seeming."

"Guilty? As though you had caught her in the act of doing something that she did not want to be caught doing?"

"Yes! *Oui—exactement!*"

"Thank you, Miss Chabot. You may step down. And now my next witness—" He looks around the room. "Is George Waterson here?"

"Right here, Tommy-boy!" a man in the back row calls out, raising his hand. He strides toward the witness box, pausing to clasp Tom Finney's hand. "Good to see you, Tommy!" he says.

"Will you state your occupation, Mr. Waterson?"

"Hells bells, do we have to be so formal, Tommy?" he says as he settles his large frame into the chair. He turns to the panel of jurors. "I've known this young whippersnapper since he was knee-high to a grasshopper," he says. "Since he was yea high." He lowers the palm of his hand to within a foot from the floor to demonstrate.

Looking slightly ruffled, Finney says to the jurors, "My family and Mr. Waterson's family have known each other for many years. But that fact won't color your testimony here today, will it—George?"

"Hell, no! And in fact, while I'm up here in front of all you fine folks of Litchfield County, I'd just like to say that I'm damn proud of what this young man here, Tommy Finney, has done for the citizenry of our fair county. You've done a hell of a fine job as county prosecutor, Tommy. And as long as I have this opportunity to speak to you all, I'd like to make a prediction for you. One day, in the not-too-distant future, all of us here are going to see this fine fellow as president of these United States of America. Yessir, from up here in the sugar maple hills of little old Litchfield, you all are going to see this young man living at sixteen hundred Pennsylvania Avenue in Washington, DC. You've got my vote in November, Tommy!"

There is a sprinkle of applause. Tom Finney, visibly blushing, continues. "Thank you," he murmurs. "Now, George, will you please tell the jury your occupation?"

"Sure. Foreman at the power plant for the Crittenden School. Seventeen years at the job, and never missed a day of work."

"That power plant contains an incinerator, does it not?"

He chuckles. "Well, now, Tommy, that's kind of a tricky question you're asking me. It does contain an incinerator, but an incinerator requires a smokestack, and a power plant also requires a smokestack, and that smokestack provides me with the biggest headache of my job. You see, some of the good folks of James Falls think that smokestack constitutes what they consider an eyesore. They feel it spoils their views. The school's tried planting pine trees around it, and that's helped some, but you can still see the dang thing from some of the hilltops, and people complain. Others say that a smokestack is part of New England heritage because a hundred years ago this part of the state was mined for iron ore, and smokestacks were all over the place. They say smokestacks are *tra-di-tion-al* and should remain a part of the landscape. It's created what we in the school business call a town versus gown problem, which is to say that a lot of James Falls folks like the school being here, but at the same time they don't like it, and of course a lot of that has to do with the kids from the school going into the town and performing the occasional little schoolboy prank—you know, your ordinary sort of teenage mischief, and that's created—"

"Tell us a little more about the incinerator, George."

"It's a powerful mother. Two thousand degrees Fahrenheit, gas generated. It'll turn a Coke can into dust, that's how powerful she is."

"At what hour of the day do you customarily operate this incinerator—to dispose of the trash delivered there by the school's sanitation trucks?"

He chuckles again. "That's the tricky part of your question, Tommy," he says. "You see, the folks in town that hate that smokestack, they hate even more to see smoke coming out of it. They call themselves *en-vi-ron-men-talists*. They say my plant's polluting the only air they have to breathe. They say my plant's giving them all cancer. Several years ago, I hit on a solution; I only burn at night. That way, they can't see the smoke, and so they don't even know it's there. That's why I like winters here the best. I can get my job done earlier."

"Now I want you think back, George," he says. "On the morning of May seventh, at approximately eleven thirty, did you receive any complaints about smoke?"

"Did I! My phone started ringing off the wall! 'We see smoke! Black smoke! It's blowing our way! We can't breathe!' That sort of thing."

"Now tell the grand jury, George, what happened at the plant just prior to the time those calls started coming in."

"That's the funny part. Mrs. Spotswood—you know, the head-master's wife—she drove up to the plant in her station wagon. I saw her coming half a mile away, and I thought to myself: What does she want? Turned out she had a big brown plastic bag of garbage for the incinerator."

"Was this sort of visit from her customary?"

"Hell, no! In all the years I've been with the school, I've never seen her come to the plant before. Didn't know she knew the way."

"Her visit struck you as—unusual?"

"Hell, yes. But she said she had some trash that the truck had failed to pick up and needed to be incinerated."

"Did she say what was in the bag?"

"No."

"Did you ask her?"

258

"No."

"Did you notice anything unusual about the bag?"

"Well, it smelled kind of bad. But garbage often does."

"And what did you do next?"

"Tossed it into the incinerator for her."

"And then what happened?"

"Well, that was funny, too. She said, 'How do you turn this thing on? Is it this red button?' And then she pushed the button. And it turned on."

"Do you think that action of hers was deliberate or accidental?"

"Well, it looked pretty deliberate to me."

"In other words, it appeared as though whatever it was she wanted incinerated, she wanted incinerated right away."

"Well, that thought did pass through my mind," he says.

"And that caused the smoke. And you began to get the telephone calls. Did you tell the callers that Mrs. Spotswood pushed the button?"

"No, I just said, 'Sorry, we had a little accident here. It'll be over in a minute.'"

Finney pauses. "Now, tell me, George. I want you to search back in your memory and tell me—was there anything in Mrs. Spotswood's demeanor, in her behavior that morning, that struck you as unusual or different?"

He thinks about this. "Well, now you mention it, she did seem a little squirrelly," he says.

"Squirrelly?"

"Edgy, jumpy, jittery. Like she was on edge about something."

"Nervous?"

"Yes."

"Acting as though she might be trying to hide something?"

"Now that you mention it, yes."

Finney turns to the jurors. "I have no further questions for the witness," he says. "Now I suggest that we take a forty-five-minute break for lunch, and reconvene here"—he glances at his watch—"at shall we say one o'clock? I have only four more witnesses to call. We should be finished here this afternoon."

"And now," the prosecutor says when they have returned from their lunch recess, "I would like to call my first witness this afternoon, Miss Cecily Smith. . . . Miss Smith, your occupation, please."

"Student at the Crittenden School."

"You, I believe, were Linda Van Degan's best friend?"

"Huh? No way."

"No?"

"She didn't have any best friend. She was too weird. We called her Linda Van Cretin."

"You're implying that Miss Van Degan was not a particularly good student," he says.

"She was the dumbest girl in the class."

"But she was, I believe, a member of a little club you girls had in Colby Hall—the Colby Club." The girl merely shrugs.

"So she must have had some friends."

"We took her in because she was rich, mostly. She gave us stuff."

"Stuff?"

"Yeah."

"What sort of stuff? Drugs?"

"Yeah. Reefer, mostly. Sometimes a little meth, when she could get it."

"Miss Smith, please describe the activities of the Colby Club."

"There weren't any, like, real activities. We just, like, hung out together. It was just a club-type club, you know?"

"Was sex involved?"

She giggles. "Not really."

"What do you mean 'not really'?"

"Well, there was just the initiation part, I mean."

"What was the initiation part, Miss Smith?"

"Well, to get into the club, for the initiation, you had to—am I allowed to use the word 'blow job'?"

"Yes, Miss Smith."

"To get in, you had to give one of the senior boys a blow job." She giggles again. "That was all."

"I see. Now, Miss Smith, would you describe Linda Van Degan as a promiscuous young woman?"

"No more than a lot of the girls."

"No more than you yourself?"

"Do I have to answer that?"

"No. I'm not interested in your sex life. I'm interested in Linda Van Degan. Your room was just down the hall from hers, wasn't it?" He checks his notes. "In room two seventeen, correct?"

"Yeah."

"Did Linda Van Degan entertain boys in her room?"

"Yeah."

"For sex?"

"I guess so. I mean, I didn't actually *see* any of that."

"Did she also entertain male members of the faculty in her room?"

"Yeah, sometimes. I mean, I saw Mr. Schlachter go in there a couple of times. But he's not really faculty. His wife is. She told me he was helping her with an English essay she was trying to write."

"Did she also entertain male members of the school's administrative staff in her room?"

"Yeah."

"Including the headmaster, Mr. Spotswood?"

Another giggle. "Yeah—well, she said so. But she lied a lot, you know?"

"Miss Smith, I think you have just described a promiscuous young woman. Now, tell me, did you or any of your friends suspect that Linda Van Degan was pregnant?"

"Well, we knew she was fat!"

"But did you suspect she might be pregnant?"

"Well, some of us kind of hinted at that. But we didn't know for sure. She never said anything."

"Miss Smith, do you know of any reason why Linda Van Degan would have taken her own life?"

"No, unless it was because the rest of us were thinking of kicking her out of the club."

"Would that have sufficiently upset her to take her own life?"

"I don't think so. She was sort of losing interest in the club, it seemed to me."

"Is that why you were thinking of kicking her out?"

"Yeah, and because a bunch of us were really mad at her."

"Why?"

"Because she'd started sucking up to Mrs. Spotswood—really sucking up to her, you know? We were afraid she was going to tell Mrs. Spotswood about the club, and about the BJs and all, you know? That really made us mad, you know? She was having all these secret meetings with Mrs. Spotswood."

"I see. Now, Miss Smith, you were the one who discovered Linda Van Degan's body, were you not?"

"Yeah."

"Tell us about that."

"She said she had the curse that morning. She had a written excuse from home to cut classes when she got the curse. I was bringing her her homework assignments that afternoon, and I knocked on her door. There was no answer, so I tried the door, and it was locked. So I opened it with my own key."

"You had a key to Linda's room?"

"Yeah. A lot of us had keys made for each other's rooms."

"Did boys have keys made for girls' rooms?"

"Yeah."

"And I presume, male faculty members also had keys, and male members of the administrative staff."

She shrugs. "Yeah, I guess so."

"And what did you see when you unlocked the door?"

"She was lying there on her bed—"

"Fully clothed?"

"Yeah, but with this clear plastic thing over her head, one of those clear plastic bags they send your clothes home in from the dry cleaner."

There are excited whispers among the members of the jury and several of them scribble hasty notes on their legal pads.

"And what did you do, Miss Smith?"

"Do? I burst out laughing!"

"Laughing?"

"She looked so funny; you know? I thought she was trying to pull some funny trick. I mean she was always doing weird things like that—to get attention, you know? And I heard that sometimes people use those cleaner bags when they're having sex, and I thought that was what she was trying to do, you know, and that maybe she was trying to have sex with herself—am I allowed to use the word 'masturbate'?"

"Yes."

"She used to do that. She had this vibrator thing. Anyway, that's what I thought at first. Then I saw her bathrobe cord was tied around her neck." More scribbling from the jury.

"Tied loosely or tightly?"

"Loosely, but kind of tightly too. I untied the knot and took the dry cleaner's bag off her head, and then I saw she wasn't breathing, and that kind of grossed me out. I went back out to the hall phone and called the campus cops."

"What did you do with the dry-cleaning bag?"

"Threw it in her wastebasket, I think."

"And the bathrobe cord?"

"Hung it back on the hook in her closet."

"Miss Smith, are you aware that in performing those acts you were tampering with vital evidence in what may turn out to be a case of murder?"

She shrugs again. "I didn't know that," she says.

"Miss Smith, did you notice any empty pill bottles on the nightstand beside Miss Van Degan's bed?"

"No."

"Miss Smith, are you aware that the death certificate prepared by the physician who first examined her lists the cause of death as 'lethal overdose of medicinal chemicals'?"

"Yeah, I think I heard that."

"But you saw no sign of any medicine lying about?"

"No."

"None?"

"None."

"No further questions," he says. "You may step down. Now, as my next witness, I would like to call to the stand Doctor Simon Jethro. . . . Doctor Jethro, please state your occupation."

"Resident physician at the Crittenden School."

"And your age?"

"Seventy-four."

"Doctor Jethro, are you a state-licensed medical examiner?"

"No, sir, I am not."

"Your special field?"

"General practice."

"Doctor Jethro, on the death certificate you signed for Linda Van Degan, under Cause of Death, you wrote, 'lethal overdose of medicine chemicals, probably self-administered.' Am I correct?"

"No. I wrote 'Apparent lethal overdose.' The operative word here is 'apparent,' because that was the way it appeared to me."

"And on what did you base that opinion, Doctor?"

"On the fact that there were several—six, to be exact—empty bottles of prescription medications on the nightstand beside the girl's bed."

"Were these medications that you had prescribed?"

"No, none of them were. I never prescribed any sort of medication for Miss Van Degan."

"Who prescribed them then?"

"Various physicians in New York City. One name I recognized was from a psychiatrist."

"Can you briefly describe these medications for us, Doctor?"

"Yes. Appetite suppressants, so-called mood elevators, painkillers, and sleeping pills."

"And these drugs, taken in combination and sufficient quantity, would be enough to cause death?"

"Yes. Absolutely."

"Doctor, did you notice any signs of bruises or lacerations around the victim's throat or neck?"

"I did not."

"Did you examine the contents of the victim's stomach?"

"I did not."

"Doctor, is it also possible that the victim died from suffocation or strangulation, either self-induced or applied by some other, outside force?"

"Well, yes, I suppose it's possible. But from the evidence—"

"Doctor, why did you not order the victim's body examined by a state-licensed medical examiner for autopsy as to the cause of death?"

"Because her family, who were contacted immediately by the headmaster, did not wish to have this done. In cases like this, we always adhere strictly to the family's wishes."

"Doctor Jethro, the headmaster, Mr. Spotswood, and his wife are personal friends of yours, are they not?"

"I like to think that the Spotswoods are friends of mine and my wife's, yes."

"Then let me ask you one final question, Doctor," he says. Raising his arm and pointing his finger at Dr. Jethro, he says in a rising voice, "Isn't it true that you would do anything—absolutely anything in your power—to protect the reputations of Mr. and Mrs. Spotswood and their school? That you would stop at nothing—absolutely nothing—to save the Spotswoods and the Crittenden School from public disgrace, mortification, humiliation, and a sordid scandal?"

Dr. Jethro sits forward in his chair. "I object to the way you've phrased that question, Mr. Prosecutor," he says testily. "Let me just answer it by saying that I would do nothing for anybody that ran counter to my professional ethics as a physician."

Finney waves his hand in a gesture of dismissal. "Thank you, Doctor. You may step down now and return to your important work."

He turns and faces the jury. "Ladies and gentlemen," he says, "I am about to call my next-to-last witness. I would like to ask you to listen very carefully to what this witness has to say because the body of my case will rest, in large part, on her testimony." He turns back to the room. "Will Miss Rose Finney please take the stand?"

Rose rises and strides purposefully toward the witness box, carrying a large pocketbook. She is dressed, perhaps somewhat inappropriately for an occasion as solemn as a grand jury session, in a large floral print, moderately low-cut to display an inch or so of cleavage, and with a wide Bertha collar, but it is one of her best frocks.

"Miss Finney, will you please state your occupation?"

"I am a member of the housekeeping staff of the Crittenden School, with a special assignment as head housekeeper at the school headmaster's house."

"Miss Finney, before we get started, I think we should make it clear to the grand jury that, though we have the same last name, you and I are not related to each other in any way we know of. Is that correct?"

"That's correct."

"And we're not friends or even acquaintances, for that matter. Correct?"

"I think I may have seen you at Mass at Saint Barnabas's," she says.

He smiles. "I don't think so, Ms. Finney. I do not worship at Saint Barnabas's. The point I want to make is—the fact that we share a surname will not shade your testimony, will it?"

"It won't."

"Good. Now, Miss Finney, will you please describe your duties at the headmaster's house?"

"Plan and prepare menus and meals. Supervise cleaning people. Supervise laundress. Supervise gardeners."

"In other words, you're pretty much in charge of everything, Miss Finney."

"Yes."

"How long have you held this job, Miss Finney?"

"Since nineteen and fifty-four."

"Pretty impressive. Would you say you have a finger on the pulse of the Spotswoods' household, Miss Finney?"

"Absolutely."

"Would you describe it as a happy household?"

"Absolutely not!"

"Why not?"

"They yell and scream at each other all the time. They fight like cats and dogs. He calls her stupid, and she calls him a hypocrite, and they call each other worse things than that—things I wouldn't dare repeat in front of decent ladies and gentlemen. Sometimes I can't get my housework done for all their drunken fighting."

"Drinking is a problem for the Spotswoods, then?"

"Oh, yes. The minute he gets home, those two can't wait to get out the bottle, but they always keep the curtain closed so no one can see them at their drinking. And sometimes she drinks all alone."

"Would you call the Spotswoods alcoholics?"

"Absolutely. So're most of the faculty. Drink like fishes."

"Now let's go back a little, Miss Finney. Let's go back to the day Pauline gave you the garbage bag with the soiled bedclothes in it, and you gave the bag to Mrs. Spotswood to take to the incinerator."

"The incinerator was her idea!"

"Did you know that there was a dead baby in that bag?"

"No! Pauline told me about that later."

"Did Mrs. Spotswood know there was a baby in the bag?"

"I'm sure she did."

"What makes you think so? This is important, Miss Finney."

"Because of two things. First, because of how upset she got when I told her what Pauline told me about the baby. She said to me, 'You'd better keep your damned trap shut about this.' Those were her exact words. Then she wrote out the check for me to give Pauline. And second, because of what I heard her say to that girl."

"The Van Degan girl, that is?"

"Yes!"

"The Van Degan girl paid a call on Mrs. Spotswood?"

"Mrs. Spotswood sent for her."

"Was this customary—for the headmaster's wife to summon students for a private visit?"

"No. Never happened before in my living memory."

"And what did you overhear during that visit?"

"I heard Mrs. Spotswood yelling at the girl. She yelled, 'Evil little girl! Liar!' She's a fine one to talk about liar. She lies all the time herself."

"About what, for instance?"

"Tells me she spent all afternoon at the fish market, when I found out for a fact that she'd never been near the fish market."

"And, during Miss Van Degan's visit, what did you overhear Miss Van Degan saying?"

"She used the eff word. I won't repeat it, but I think you know which word I mean. I heard her say, 'Spotty'—that's what the kids call the headmaster—'Spotty effed me.' That's when I heard Mrs. Spotswood scream, 'You're the one who had the baby!' Oh, she was so mad, I honestly thought she was going to kill that girl! Right there, on the spot."

He pauses, then repeats the words slowly for emphasis, "You thought Mrs. Spotswood was going to kill the girl."

"That's how mad she was, Mr. Finney."

"Miss Finney, do you think it's possible that Mr. Spotswood was the father of that girl's baby?"

"Of course, I think it's possible. I also think it's possible that Mrs. Spotswood killed the girl in a jealous rage. Or that

Mr. Spotswood killed the girl to hush her up, because Mrs. Spotswood wanted the girl to name names of all the people who had—had been tampering with her. Or maybe they were both in on it together, to protect the reputation of the school. But we'll never know, will we, since Mrs. Spotswood destroyed all the evidence."

"I think," he says carefully, "that we may know, once we hear from our next witness. No further questions, Miss Finney."

She starts to step down, but one of the female jurors— a different woman from the one who questioned Pauline Scanlon—raises her hand and says, "I have a question for your witness, Mr. Prosecutor."

"Certainly, ma'am."

"Miss Finney," she says, "you seem to harbor a certain animus against the Spotswoods, particularly Mrs. Spotswood. Why is that?"

"Animus? What's that?"

"Animosity. Hard feelings. Resentment. Dislike. Working for them, as you have been, all these years, that must have made your job very difficult for you."

"I didn't always not like those two," Rose says. "But then, in light of what happened, I changed my mind. I used to think they were both okay. But then when she did what she did, she showed me her true colors."

"What exactly did she do?"

"She threatened to fire me, that's what! When I started my own private investigation of this murder, and of all the other shady things that's been going on at the school, she threatened to fire me for it. That would have been an illegal firing. Because I don't work for her. I work for the Crittenden School. The only person who can legally fire Rose Finney is the head of the Housekeeping Department, and that person's name, for the record, is Geraldine K. Stimpson! When Mrs. Spotswood tried to pull that illegal firing on me, to get me to stop my personal investigation of these crimes—well, that's when I decided that she is a woman who's no better than she should be, and that's my candy opinion of them both. I also have reason to believe that Mrs. Spotswood has been cheating on her husband—in the marital sense, if you receive my meaning, though I don't have actual proof of that. She gets phone calls on her private line, for one thing, that doesn't have an extension in the kitchen so you can listen in. She makes calls on that line, too. For another thing, there's that fish market story—right after one of those calls came in! In my opinion, they're both cheats and liars!"

"Thank you, Miss Finney."

"And now," Tom Finney says, "I'd like to call my final witness to the stand, ladies and gentlemen—Mrs. Clarissa Spotswood. . . . Mrs. Spotswood, do you solemnly swear to tell the truth, the whole truth, and nothing but the truth, so help you God?"

But, in fact, none of the preceding actually happened. Clarissa spent three days and three nights in St. Vincent's Hospital, slipping in and out of consciousness after undergoing delicate surgery. In dreams, her thoughts were disordered, disconnected from any reality. As she lay there in her hospital gown, the doctors and nurses and orderlies and other hospital staff came and went, more nurses than doctors, checking her vital signs with their machines, her blood pressure and temperature, sticking her with needles ("This won't hurt, honey"), extracting and injecting fluids ("This will help you sleep, honey. . . . Wake up, honey, it's time to check your vitals. Do you need to move your bowels? To urinate? We can catheterize you, if you'd like"), and offering her inedible meals on her tray table at hours when she never felt like eating anything.

But at other times, fully awake and fully conscious and in full possession of her faculties, sitting bolt upright in her bed, she would run this scenario over and over in her mind, imagining the scene that could easily transpire in the grand jury room of the Litchfield County Courthouse, Prosecutor Thomas Finney presiding. As she ran it through her mind, there were variations to this scene, of course, but it always came out something like the foregoing, and she always stopped herself at the point where she was called upon to testify, asked to place her left hand on the Holy Bible and raise her right hand and swear to tell the truth, the whole truth, and nothing but the truth, so help her God. Her father was her God.

She also had thoughts like this one: One afternoon, going through her husband's dresser drawers, she found an unfamiliar-looking key under a stack of his shirts—the way she had found the key to the center drawer of the lowboy in the front hall, found it tucked in a ring cushion, but this key told a different story. She picked up the key, and turned it over, and there was a number etched on it: "211." But that didn't happen either. That was just her imagination running wild again.

As it happened, events that summer took an altogether different turn.

FIFTEEN

On the night before Clarissa's discharge from St. Vincent's, by sheer coincidence, the students of Crittenden staged a School Scream. Screams had been performed in the past, though not in recent years, and just which boy or girl had come up with the idea for this one was never officially determined, but obviously one individual must have initially proposed it, and the concept spread quickly by word of mouth throughout the student body. It was a notion of youthful imaginations in the late spring, when the end of the academic year is at last within sight.

The Scream was organized with all the secrecy and care of a military operation. Timepieces were synchronized throughout the school, and the plan was simply this: At the precise stroke of midnight on that Monday night, every bedroom window in every dormitory on the campus would be flung open, and all four-hundred twenty students at the Crittenden School would lean out their windows and scream at the top of their lungs for exactly one full minute. Then the windows would quietly close, and that would be the end of it.

The Scream echoed out across the quiet hillsides, and across the dark waters of Lake Kinishawah. Birds rose crying from their nesting places in the trees, and all over the town and campus dogs began to bark. On the campus and in the village, faculty and townsfolk were roused from their innocent or drunken dreams. Older householders, who remembered Screams from years past, immediately recognized the prank for what it was and merely rolled over grumpily in their beds, cursed the school, and tried to sleep again. But a number of newer residents, alarmed by the unearthly sound, dialed 911, and the police department dispatched two cruisers to investigate the source of it. The wail of their sirens added to the night's disorder, though of course they were unable to come up with anything.

Crittenden's headmaster, Hobart Spotswood, was also awakened by the Scream, but, though annoyed, wisely decided there was nothing he could do about it. It would be patently impossible, after all, to impose any sort of punishment or disciplinary action on his entire school, a situation that the students themselves had clearly anticipated. The next morning, however, at a school assembly, he delivered a stern lecture on the importance of being considerate to others and the Golden Rule. He then required all the students to line up and place their signatures on a letter of apology for the disturbance, which he had drafted, addressed to the townspeople of James Falls. The letter was published in the local newspaper later that week.

Then he drove off in the station wagon to collect his wife at the hospital, not in the best of moods.

"Cissie," he is saying to her as they make their way home in the car, "the trustees' dinner is just three nights away. Please don't feel you need to bother attending that. After what you've been through, you need all the rest you can get. Everyone will certainly understand, and I can manage the evening by myself. Rose and I have worked out the menu and the seating plan, so there's no reason for you to—"

"No," she says. "I'm fine. My name is on the invitation. I'll be there."

"But the meeting the next morning. That's just too much for you to take on at this point. I'm going to insist, for your own sake, that you beg out of that one. I'm not going to let you put yourself through that. I'll offer your excuse."

"Nonsense," she says. "I said I'd be there. And I'll be there. And that's final." They say nothing to each other for the rest of the drive home.

And now the day has arrived. The trustees came on Thursday afternoon and Friday morning from all parts of the country, at least two of them in helicopters, landing on the soccer fields. Most have established themselves in rooms at the Old Forge Inn booked by the school. Missing from the Friday night gathering are only Truxton and Tweetums Van Degan; as Mrs. Van Degan explained in her e-mail message to Hobe, "My husband feels it would be too painful for him to revisit the scene of his only child's death so soon after it occurred. I hope you understand."

("Son of a bitch just doesn't want to confront me about the Tom Finney problem," Hobe muttered when he received this.)

Now everyone has gathered outdoors on the L-shaped verandah of the Castle for cocktails, and Rose and a helper are passing hors d'oeuvres, including her famous bite-size hamburgers. Clarissa circulates among her guests, kissing, shaking hands.

"Clarissa, dear," Alexandra Lemosney whispers to her, "whatever happened to your eye?"

"I took a little tumble on the stairs," she says easily. "But don't you think my eyepatch makes me look distinguished? Remember those old ads—the Man in the Hathaway Shirt? Doesn't the eyepatch make me look a little bit like the Man in the

Hathaway Shirt—distinguished, sexy, and mysterious? I do. I've even got them in different colors. And, when everything heals, the doctor says that I'll probably have up to twenty percent of my original vision in that eye. And a nice little contact lens."

"You were lucky," Alexandra says.

Clarissa moves inside the house to check the place cards against her dinner seating plan. At these functions, guests have been known to rearrange the place cards, which is always a nuisance, but everything seems in order. She plucks a wilted-looking daisy out of one of the centerpieces. Rose has started setting out the cups of iced watercress soup for the first course. Clarissa glances at the menu card in front of her own place setting. "What happened to the soft-shelled crabs?" she asks Rose. Her left hand has begun to tremble.

"We were in luck," Rose says. "At the last minute, Mr. S remembered that Mr. Lemosney is allergic to seafood. So we're having a crown roast of lamb with mushroom stuffing."

"Which we served them two years ago," Clarissa says.

Rose merely sniffs. "You can start bringing them in to the table now," she says. "Whenever you're ready."

The next morning, the trustees, minus their spouses, assemble at ten o'clock in the conference room next door to the head-master's office in the main building. Alexandra Lemosney, as president of the board, quickly takes charge of the proceedings.

"Good morning," she says. "Ladies and gentlemen, members of the Board of Trustees of the Crittenden School, I'm partic-ularly happy to welcome to our meeting this morning Mrs. Clarissa Spotswood, who will have a few words to say to us later on. Meanwhile, Clarissa, we all want to thank you for the deli-cious dinner you and Mr. Spotswood hosted at the headmaster's house last night. We all had a wonderful time! Clarissa . . ."

There is a polite round of applause, and calls of "Hear, hear."

"Now, as our first matter of business, I know we were all shocked and saddened to learn of the tragic death of Linda Van Degan here at the school. Linda Van Degan, under what pressures all of us can merely guess at, took her own life, and I would like to ask the board's secretary, Mr. Passmore, to draw up a letter of condolence to Mr. and Mrs. Van Degan, for all of our signatures, expressing our sadness and sympathy in the loss of their beloved daughter. Hunter, will you take care of that?"

"I will," he says. "I'll have that letter ready for us to sign before we all leave the campus tomorrow morning."

"Thank you, Hunter. Understandably, Truck Van Degan was not able to join us for this meeting today. And on the same subject, I'd also like to thank the headmaster for his adroit handling of the Van Degan girl's suicide, which must have been a very stressful time for him. When terrible events such as this happen at a school such as Crittenden, the result can often be unpleasant publicity. But, thanks to Hobe's handling of the situation, there was none. Thank you, Hobe."

Hobe dismisses her thanks with a wave of his hand.

"And now," Alexandra says, "I'd like to turn the meeting over to our gracious and charming headmaster's wife, who has been a stalwart and caring member of the Crittenden community for twenty-five years, the headmaster's strong right arm and an all-around great gal, Clarissa Spotswood, who has a few words to say to us. Clarissa?"

Clarissa stands, a little uncertainly at first, steadying herself briefly with her fingertips pressed against the top of the big table, and Hobe sits forward attentively in his chair. "Thank you, Alexandra," she begins. "I don't think I deserve such high praise. I've only tried to do what I believed was best for the school, and to assist my husband's stewardship of it. That's been my primary mission. But I admit I'm honored to be asked to join all of you today in this room, where I've never sat before, and where I know I have no official place. Nevertheless, before I get to the subject I think you've all come to hear me talk about, I do have a happy announcement to make. A friend of the school, one of our alumni, has offered the school a major gift to create a Center for the—"

"Excuse me, Clarissa," Hobe says, "but I was planning to make this announcement to the trustees. It is in my capacity as—"

There is a chorus of hushing sounds around the table. "Shhh . . . shhh . . . Let her finish, Hobe . . . Your wife has the floor . . ."

"To create a Center for the Arts at Crittenden," she continues. "This alumnus is offering the school the sum of twenty million dollars."

"No, Clarissa," Hobe says, "you've got the figure wrong. It's only ten million."

"No," she says firmly. "I've spoken to the prospective donor recently, and he has promised to double his original gift offer. The figure is twenty million dollars, Hobe."

Now the chorus about the table is of oohs and ahs: "Wow! Twenty mil . . . How about that?"

"This, I believe, constitutes the largest individual gift the school has ever been offered in its history. Furthermore, the potential donor has assured me, personally, that he will add to this sum if necessary to create the magnificent arts center he has in mind. This will be something the likes of which no other secondary school in America has ever been able to boast of. And on top of all that, this man has a major collection of nineteenth- and twentieth-century paintings and sculpture. So that the rooms of his center that are devoted to the plastic arts will not open empty, he has offered to donate certain pieces from his collection. He hopes this will inspire other art collectors to follow suit. He also offers to place other items from his collection on loan to the school from time to time, on a rotating basis."

"But the condition, Clarissa!" her husband says. "You haven't told them the conditions of this gift."

"Yes, there is a condition," she says. "Before handing over this magnificent gift, the donor would like to be invited to join the school's board of trustees."

"Outrageous," Hobe mutters. "Unheard of."

"Well," Alexandra Lemosney says, "that doesn't seem so outrageous to me. Considering the amount of money involved, that seems a small favor to ask in return. Besides, we can always use more rich members on the board, can't we?" There is light laughter at this, and Hobart Spotswood clears his throat portentously.

"I'd like to remind the board that gifts like this one are a double-edged sword," he says. "Aimed, as they are, at one particular discipline—the arts, in this case—all they do is inspire interdepartmental jealousy and friction among the faculty. This faculty envy and dissension can provide a school administration with enormous headaches. Such jealousies can make a school unrunnable! Sure, all the faculty in the music and art department will walk around campus with their chests puffed up, saying, 'Look what *we* got!' But what about other departments—science, history, languages, and literature? These department heads will be left with their noses severely out of joint. Their attitudes will be, 'Why can't *our* disciplines share in some of this munificence? Why are *we* being shortchanged?' This sort of thing can create an intolerable situation. A large part of my job is to keep my faculty happy and working as a well-oiled team. A gift such as this will have a profoundly deleterious effect on faculty morale.

We could have widespread faculty defections. The school could suffer enormously. Therefore, I recommend—"

"Hobe, will you please stop interrupting your wife!" Alexandra says in a tone of some annoyance. "Clarissa, can you tell us—we're all positively salivating to know—the name of this fella? Is it—Santa Claus?"

"Michael J. Rubin of New York City."

"Wonderful!"

And suddenly Clarissa seems to sag as she stands, her hands gripping the table's edge, her head and shoulders falling forward. Immediately, the two gentlemen on either side of her rise and seize her elbows to steady her.

"Clarissa—dear, are you all right?"

Hobe also rises. "Ladies and gentlemen," he says, "my wife has very recently undergone extremely delicate surgery. She is still on medication. She should not have come here this morning. Come, Clarissa, I'm taking you home."

She immediately stands up straight again. "No," she says, "I'm perfectly fine. And there are one or two other things I did want to talk about, since you've asked me here—"

"Please go on, Clarissa," Alexandra says. Hobe and the other two gentlemen resume their seats, but Hobe continues to stare fixedly at his wife.

"Several weeks ago, a woman reporter from the *Litchfield Times* came to the school to interview me," she begins. "The occasion was the coming conclusion of my husband's twenty-fifth year as headmaster of Crittenden, and what this reporter said she wanted was what I guess is called 'the woman's angle.' I believe Alexandra has supplied all of you with copies of the newspaper story that resulted."

The others all nod.

"I tried to be candid and honest in my responses to the

woman's questions, and I feel that I was reasonably well quoted. Some of you may feel I was *too* candid and honest in some of my comments about the school. I know my husband did." She smiles at him. "In fact, my husband was more than a little annoyed with me for expressing my feelings as frankly and openly as I did. But they were my feelings, nonetheless.

"Let me begin by saying that when Crittenden decided to become coeducational in 1979, we all knew we faced enormous problems. It seems to me that we've succeeded in facing and solving many of those problems, but not all of them. Let me also say that this school has handled these problems no better and no worse than other coeducational secondary boarding schools across the country. We've looked to other schools for guidance, and they've looked to us, and my feeling is that right now we're all of us pretty much in the same boat.

"Of course, I'm not talking about what goes on in our classrooms. I think statistics show that in terms of preparing students for college Crittenden can hold its head up among the best of them. But it's in the area of what goes on outside the classroom that I think schools like ours still have problems. For instance, I mentioned to the *Times* reporter the abandonment of any strict dress code. The result has been a generally sloppy appearance of the kids as they walk about the campus, and I'm not sure whether the kids themselves are happy about this. They dress competitively—who can wear the floppiest bell-bottoms, who can show off the most outrageous pair of sneakers. Are they really pleased with the way they look? I don't know. The point is that we haven't really asked them.

"The craze for body-piercing and tattoos shows no sign of ending. Crittenden has ruled against piercing any part of the body except the earlobes, and visible tattoos are another no-no. The result hasn't just been multiple ear piercings—a dozen earrings on a girl's ear is no longer much of a surprise. But students are also secretly having parts of their bodies pierced that can't be seen—their tongues, navels, nipples, even their penises. The same with tattoos. Why are they doing this? Just because it's a challenge to break the rules. I think that if the school made it a rule that every boy and girl at Crittenden *must* wear a nose ring, the students would stage a mass protest—don't you? Of course, I'm only talking about cosmetic matters, but cosmetic matters are important to boys and girls this age.

"The reporter asked me about drugs and sex, and I told her that we did have problems here. I think we must all admit that drugs and sex are intimately connected with each other. Young people do drugs to have sex, and they have sex when they do drugs. Drugs and sex go hand in hand. In the recent, sad death of Linda Van Degan, sex and drugs were both involved, unfortunately."

"You have no proof of that!" Hobe says.

"Please, Hobe," Alexandra Lemosney says a little sharply. "Please don't interrupt. We're all fascinated by what Clarissa's saying—at least I am."

"Sex and drugs were both involved," she says again. "Every year, the list of rules involving the use of drugs and sexual relations between boys and girls gets a little longer at schools like ours, and the rules are being systematically flouted. And sex-education classes aren't the answer, or lectures on the dangers of drug abuse. Just the other day, new rules were drawn up outlining the times of day, and the length of time, a boy can be allowed to visit a girl in her room, and vice versa. Believe me, those rules will be flouted as well. Those rules won't work.

"At the same time, we've got to remember that this generation of kids at Crittenden is the most sexually sophisticated in history. They're bombarded with sex in movies, television, magazines, and in their daily newspapers, and if they want more information about sex they can call it up on websites. There is absolutely nothing they don't know about sex, and, at this age, almost nothing they wouldn't like to try. The same is true with drugs.

"I'm not saying that all Crittenden students are promiscuous and drug-crazed. I think if you asked Crittenden students why they're here, they'd tell you, honestly, that they're here to get a fine education that will help them get into the college of their choice. I think hardly any of them would say they're here to do drugs or to have unlimited sex. Most would agree that unlimited drugs and sex can get a person into trouble. I don't think any Crittenden girl would say that she wants to be a mother at sixteen, or that she is eagerly looking forward to her next abortion. And yet, we have to send at least one poor girl home every year for just such reasons. What are we doing wrong?

"We do a lot of talking here about role models. Parents are supposed to provide role models for their children, but most parents are not particularly good role models for their sons and daughters. I can't honestly say that my husband and I have been good role models for my own two children. Here at Crittenden, the teachers and the administration are supposed to offer themselves as role models for children away from home. And at schools like Crittenden, where many of the children come from moneyed homes, the role models they have at home are worse than those of children from impoverished backgrounds. In my opinion, the only role models children have are other children. Perhaps that should be part of our job here—helping young people choose the role models from among their peers, role models who will make life easier and happier for all concerned.

"No school, and no society, can exist without rules and restrictions, we know that, and the children also know that. I'm not advocating anarchy, but I'm suggesting that the children be given a greater part in the rule-making process. Let them help decide what is right or wrong, which kind of behavior is constructive, and which is destructive. It's not just a matter of asking them, 'What would traffic in Manhattan be like if there were no traffic lights?' An act that is right or wrongful can be decided by asking an even simpler question: 'What would the world be like if everyone did that?'

"Children—young people—even adults—love attention. I think we need to pay more attention to the students, listen to their thoughts and their opinions. After all, we who work for Crittenden are in a service business. We're here to help the children, not to supervise them or discipline them or punish them when they make mistakes. We're here to serve them, to help them help themselves and help one another. Let's stop thinking of ourselves as *guides* or *models*. Let's think of ourselves as helpers in their search.

"Meanwhile, some of Crittenden's rules on what is accept-able, sexually or otherwise, remind me of regulations in a well-landscaped penitentiary. A few nights ago, though I wasn't here to hear it, the students staged a midnight scream. We talked about that at dinner last night. Many people dismissed it as just another silly teenage prank. But somehow I was uncomfortably reminded of prisoners all banging their tin cups on the iron bars of their cells.

"We may never have a perfect school, and we certainly won't achieve one overnight. But I believe if we listen more atten-tively to the children and hearken to what they feel will be best for them and best for their school, we'll end up with a school community that is more considerate, better behaved, better mannered, and maybe even better looking and better groomed and better dressed than it is right now. A community where coeducation will really work, and where Linda Van Degan's senseless death would not have occurred.

"Listen to the children! Listen to the children! That's really all I have to say." She sits down, touching her brow with the tip of her index finger of her right hand.

There is a short silence. Then the applause begins, quietly at first, then growing louder, around the big table. It seems to go on and on.

SIXTEEN

"Sally, dear," her mother says, "I'm really so glad you came up. You and I really need to talk, and it's just not the sort of talk we can have on the telephone." Clarissa picks up her keys from the sideboard. "Let's go for lunch at the Old Forge. I'm a little bit tired of Rose's cooking, and I'd like to get out of the house for a while. Besides," she says with a grin, "I want to show you how good I'm getting at driving with one eye."

As they walk down the gravel walk together toward the car, she whispers, "I'm also getting more than a little tired of having Rose eavesdrop on every conversation that takes place in that house!"

At the Inn, the dining room hostess says, "Would you like your usual table in the far corner, Mrs. Spotswood?"

"Yes, please, if it's free."

"It is." She leads them to the table. After seating them, the hostess asks, "Would either of you care for a cocktail before lunch?"

"I'll have a glass of Chablis," Sally says.

"Iced tea for me," her mother says. "I'm not quite ready for one-eyed driving *and* drinking."

When they are alone again, Sally reaches out and covers her

mother's hand with her own. "Mother, I just want to tell you how much I admire you. You've been so brave through all this."

"Brave? Nonsense. It's just a case of *que sera sera.*"

"A good sport, then."

"What else can one try to be? I hate doctors, and I hate hospitals. I'm just glad it's over."

"I didn't know about any of this until Johnny called me when I got back from overseas."

"Let's not talk about me. How was your trip?"

"Successful, I think. Oberoi Hotels. I think I've landed the account."

"Good. Congratulations."

"Ten million in billings."

"Wonderful!"

Their drinks arrive. "Are you ladies ready to order yet?"

"No, we're in no rush," Clarissa says, and when they are alone again she says, "Now tell me—what's this about you and Jesse Rubin?"

"How did you find out about that? Johnny must have told you."

"Johnny told his father, and his father told me. Is it true?"

"Oh, Mother, we're both so happy! We didn't want to make anything official until—"

"Oh, Sally—no. This can't happen."

"What do you *mean* it can't happen? It is happening!"

"Are you having an affair with him?"

"Well, since you put it to me that way—yes. And we want to get married."

"No, no, Sally, you can't. You simply *cannot.*"

Sally's eyes flash. "What do you mean I can't? I certainly can, and I certainly intend to!"

"No, no. You don't understand."

"Is it because of the things they've been saying about his father in the financial press—is that it? None of that's been proven, and none of it has anything to do with Jess. Jess is a wonderful man, Mother!"

"I'm sure he is, but it has nothing to do with any of that."

"Is it because he's Jewish? I'm sure that doesn't sit very well with Daddy. I can just hear him on *that* subject. The glorious Spotswood name, all those distinguished ancestors, our illustrious family tree—tracing us back to 1620 to the ancestor he found in the parish records of the village in Sussex who's listed as 'Goodman Spotswood,' indicating that even *then* the Spotswoods were people of substance, the next thing to nobility! I've listened to that shit all my life, Mother!"

"It has nothing to do with that, Sally."

"God forbid that a Spotswood would ever sully the family name by marrying a Jew!"

"No, no—"

"I'm surprised at you, Mother. I can hear Daddy talking like that. But I thought you were more intelligent!"

"Sally, please. Have you heard what I'm saying? It has nothing to do with any of that. It's that—"

"What is it, then? I mean, it would be nice if Jess and I had your and Daddy's blessing, but if we can't—to hell with it!"

Clarissa pauses, stirring her iced tea with her spoon, and looks away briefly. "You see, I didn't even know you knew Jess Rubin. If I had, I would have—but—well, there's something I need to explain to you, Sally. Years ago, I had an affair."

Sally, taking a sip of her wine, nearly chokes on it, and grabs for the napkin in her lap. "You?" she gasps. "You had an *affair*? You mean before you married Daddy?"

"No. After. During my marriage, I guess you'd say."

She laughs out loud. "You? Oh, Mother—well, I always knew

you were human, but not *that* human. I thought you were Miss Goody Two-shoes!"

"No, I wasn't. Not always, I'm afraid. Are you shocked at me?"

"I think it's . . . wonderful! Was it that for you? Wonderful?"

"It began right here, at the Old Forge Inn." Clarissa glances up at the ceiling. "Right upstairs, in room one oh three. Funny, but I've never forgotten his room number. It was with a young man who'd come back to Crittenden for his class reunion."

She claps her hands. "And was it—you know, all gorgeous and fun and passionate and wildly sexy?"

"Oh, yes. It was all those things. And it got me pregnant."

Sally is not laughing anymore. She glances at her mother. "Mother, if this is a cautionary tale about the perils of having an affair, please don't bother. I assure you every precaution is being taken."

She covers her daughter's hand with hers. "I'm sure of that, dear," she says. "There are so many things available to a woman now that weren't around in my day. But that's not why I'm telling you this story."

"Then, what happened? What did you do?"

"Do? Well, at first, I panicked. I knew the baby couldn't possibly be Hobe's, and so I panicked. You see, a woman knows very quickly when she's pregnant—or at least I did. I didn't have to wait to miss my period—that just confirms what a woman's begun to suspect after the first week or so. She begins to feel the little changes as those hormones begin to kick in. The nipples start to swell and become tender to the touch—those things begin to happen very fast, and I remembered them from having Johnny. There was no question in my mind about what had happened to me, and the question became—"

"But how could you be so sure the baby wasn't Daddy's?"

"It had been so long since Hobe and I had any sort of sex that I was sure he'd know the baby couldn't possibly be his. And he'd ask me—"

"What did you *do*?"

"In my panic, my first thought was an abortion. The Supreme Court decision on *Roe versus Wade* had been handed down the year before, and so I could have gotten an abortion perfectly safely and legally and, with luck, without him finding out about it. You see, the only thing on his mind at the time was this job at Crittenden, so I thought I could sneak away and have it done without him noticing anything. That was Plan A, an abortion."

"You mean you didn't do that?"

"No. It's not just that I've always hated doctors and hospitals. It was because—well, I don't care what the pro-choice people say. I've never known any woman who was happy to have her child aborted, and I just couldn't bring myself to do that. I decided to move on to Plan B."

"Which was?"

"Before I told him I was pregnant, I had to figure out a way to get him to assume that the baby was his. I decided I had to seduce my husband, and I had to do it very quickly. That was Plan B. It probably sounds a little crazy, but then I *was* a little crazy. Looking back, I call it my Victoria's Secret or my Frederick's of Hollywood solution. I bought a very sexy French nightie, with naughty little cut-outs in it and everything, and I put it on and paraded up and down in front of him, begging him to make love to me. But it didn't work. Nothing seemed to work. He was always too tired, with too much on his mind about the school job, to pay any attention to me. And so that's when I decided I was going to have to tell him the Big Lie."

"What was that, Mother?"

"I was going to wait for as long as I could, until the fourth or fifth month, until I really began to show, before telling him. And then, when he said the dreaded words—'It can't be mine. Whose is it?'—I was going to say, 'But, darling, of course it is! Don't you remember that night last spring, when you were so worried about the headmaster's job, and I reached out for you under the covers and discovered you had an erection, and I snuggled against you, and then pressed my body on top of yours, and we made love? Don't you remember? You were half asleep, of course, but you seemed to wake up at the end because you kissed me and put your arms around me? Don't you remember that? I certainly do! That must have been when it happened, darling—the night I found myself being the active partner.' But then, almost in my fourth month, when I finally told him, the funny thing was that he never said the dreaded words or asked the dreaded question. I never had to tell him the Big Lie."

"Mother—how very strange!"

"Yes, strange. But lucky for me. I've thought about it often over the years. I can think of only three explanations. One, he'd been so preoccupied with getting this job that he couldn't remember whether he'd had sex with me or not. Or, two, that he became so obsessed about the politics of my pregnancy that how the pregnancy happened was the last thing on his mind. He immediately started worrying about how the pregnancy of the new headmaster's wife would *look* to the school, and to the trustees who'd just appointed him. Would it look as though he'd concealed some important fact from the trustees during all the interviews? 'Why didn't you tell me sooner?' was all he kept asking me, and all I could say was, 'I wanted to be sure.' And he made me promise to keep the whole thing secret until the very last minute. He was sure there would be repercussions, but of course there weren't." She smiles a little ruefully and spreads her hands. "And there's the third explanation for it."

"What is that?"

"That our sex life meant so little to him at that point that he hardly noticed whether we had sex or not—never noticed from one day to the next, or from one month to the next."

"Oh, Mother—that's so sad!"

"Sad, perhaps. But also lucky for me, don't you think? I was never asked to explain a thing. The real explanation of Hobe is probably a combination of all of the above. I'll never know."

"It's so hard to believe—that any man—"

"But Hobe was never just any man, Sally."

"But then—what happened to the baby?"

"Sally, haven't you guessed? . . . The baby was you."

Her eyes grow very wide. "Then who was my real father?"

"Michael Rubin."

Her eyes squeeze tightly shut again, and her hand flies to her mouth. "Oh my god," she whispers. Tears appear from her clenched eyelids. "Oh my god. Then Jesse is my—"

"Your half brother. You see, that's why I had to tell you this."

"I've got to tell Jesse!"

Her mother hesitates a moment. "Well, of course that's up to you," she says. "But from my personal standpoint, I'd rather you didn't. It could just complicate life for me. And for Jesse's father, too, I suppose."

"His father doesn't know?"

"No, I've never told him. And, besides, I shouldn't think you'd want Jesse to feel—"

"To feel the way I feel now? No, I guess I wouldn't."

"How do you feel, Sally? I mean right now."

She dabs at her face with her napkin. "Numb. Just numb, and a little sick to my stomach. As though I'd just like to crawl off into a little hole, and bury myself, and die. Oh god," she says again. "What a mess I've gotten myself in! I can't drag Jess into it."

"It was my mess that got you into your mess," Clarissa says.

"Have you ladies had a chance to look at our menu?" their waitress says. "Let me tell you about our special. Today's special is a Chilean sea bass, which our chef prepares chargrilled with—"

"Oh god," Sally says, "I don't give a damn what I have to eat. Do you have something like—like a chef's salad?"

"Yes, indeed. One chef's salad. And for you, ma'am?"

"I'll have the same," Clarissa says.

"Very good! Two chef's salads."

When they are alone again, Sally says, "Does Johnny know about this?"

"No. You're the only person I've ever told. I never thought I'd really need to. But now, under the circumstances—I'm sorry, Sally."

There is a long silence, and then Sally says, "Now tell me what happened to your eye, Mother. Let's change the subject!"

"Oh, it was such a stupid accident. Hobe and I were on our way upstairs to bed, and I slipped on a stair and my head hit the newel post."

Her daughter gives her a long look. "I don't believe you, Mother," she says.

"What do you mean?"

"Daddy—but I've got to start calling him something else now, don't I, now that I know he's not my father? He told Johnny that he was in another part of the house when it happened, and that he found you lying on the stairs."

"Well, perhaps that's the way it was. I don't remember it too clearly—"

"And that staircase has no newel post. It's one clear sweep of railing from top to bottom. Johnny and I used to slide down it when we were kids. I grew up in that house, remember? I know it like the back of my hand."

"The banister is what I meant to say."

"Johnny says the right side of your face was badly bruised, and the left eye was—gouged."

"I guess I fell flat on my face, as they say!"

"Injuring both sides of your face at the same time? Were you drunk, Mother?"

"I'd had a few drinks, yes. But I don't think I was what you'd call drunk."

"Hobe told Johnny you were drunk. He told Johnny you've become an alcoholic."

"He told Johnny that? Well—"

"I think he hit you, Mother."

"What?"

"He hit you, didn't he?"

Clarissa toys with her napkin. "Very well. I'll tell you exactly what happened," she says. "Hobe and I were in the library, and we were having—words. There's a lamp in the library that's missing its finial—just a bare screw sticking up where the finial should be. I said something to Hobe that angered him, and he gave me a little shove. I lost my balance and fell against that lamp with the screw sticking up—"

"I think he gave you more than a little shove. I think he belted you one across the face. Correct?"

Clarissa lowers her eyes. "Yes, he struck me," she says quietly. "But—"

"But what?"

"But what I'd said to him gave him every reason to lose his temper. So, you see, it was really my—"

"Don't you dare say it was your fault, Mother! It was not your fault. Don't turn yourself into what they call an 'enabler.' Don't try to take the blame for the criminal thing he did by saying you made him do it!"

"All right," she says. "But do me just one favor. Don't tell Johnny about any of this. There's nothing to be gained by turning Johnny against his father. Promise you won't tell Johnny."

"Okay," she says.

"Primrose promise, as we used to say. That means a promise that you'll never break."

"Okay, primrose promise. Now, next question: What did you say to Hobe that upset him so? That seemed to make him lose his famous self-control? This is our afternoon for nothing but the truth."

"I am not going to tell you that," her mother snaps. "I am not on a witness stand! We were arguing about a personal matter that has nothing to do with you, and, frankly, is none of your business. Suffice to say I said something that was unladylike—and cruel."

"Not as unladylike and cruel as making you half blind!"

"Words can hurt, too."

Their salads are placed in front of them. "Would you ladies care for some fresh-ground pepper?" their waitress asks them. She wields a gigantic pepper mill nearly half as tall as she is.

Both nod, and the waitress performs her pepper-mill routine with great flourish and leaves.

"I'm not sure I can eat this," Sally says, looking down at her plate.

"Let's try," Clarissa says and picks up her fork.

There is a little silence, and Sally toys with her food. Then she says, "Did you love Jess's father very much, Mother?"

"Oh, yes. In many ways I still do."

"You mean—"

"Yes. Our affair has gone on, off and on, over the years—between his various marriages! He still says he loves me. He's still asking me, all over again, to leave Hobe and marry him. But—"

"Well, why don't you, Mother? Surely Hobe's given you every reason in the world to do that now."

"I've thought about it. Particularly in the last few weeks, I've thought about it a lot. But I told him I wanted to get through the school year—through the trustees' dinner, and their meeting, and the school graduation—and then I told Michael I'd make a decision."

"And have you decided?"

"I don't think it would be the right thing to do."

"For Hobe, you mean?"

"No, for me. And for the school."

"But Michael Rubin's been the love of your life, Mother!"

"No, not really. One of them, of course. But to call Michael the love of my life is putting it a little strongly. Oh, I loved him very much, and still do. And he was a wonderful lover, and still is. But he was always a lover who wasn't, if you know what I mean. I don't even know what I mean, but there was always a part of him that was missing, a part of him that should have been there, where I was, but wasn't. It's hard to explain, because I never really knew what that missing piece of the puzzle was. All I knew was that it wasn't there. Am I making any sense to you?"

"Was there ever one great love in your life, Mother?"

"Oh, yes. It was Hobe. There's no question about that. It was always Hobe. And, in a funny way, I know he loves me. One of the things I love about him is that he'd never believe it was possible for me to be unfaithful to him. Of course, it hasn't been a particularly happy marriage—I'm sure you and Johnny have both noticed that, over the years. But it's possible for two people to love each other, and still not be able to live very happily together. And the reverse is also true."

"I wish I could believe that."

"It's possible," Clarissa says. "You'll see."

Suddenly Sally laughs. "Oh, in some ways it's funny, isn't it? I mean, think of it—Hobart Spotswood, who would die a thousand deaths at the thought of a Spotswood marrying a Jew. What would he say if he knew there already was a Jewish Spotswood?—and it's me?" Her eyes darken again, and the laugh dissolves into a small sob. "Oh, but why am I laughing, Mother? Mother, what am I going to do?"

"I'm sure you'll do the sensible thing," she says. "You're a sensible girl, and you'll do the sensible thing. My father had a favorite saying: 'Always be up for it.'"

"What did he mean by that? Up for what?"

"Up for the hand life deals you. He wasn't a gambler, but he used to say, 'Play the cards you're dealt. Play them the best you can.' That's what I've always tried to do." She searches for her daughter's eyes, but they remain withdrawn. "I know Hobe was shocked by what he did to me. He's really not a bad person, you know."

"But do you know something?" Sally says. "I think he always knew he wasn't my real father. I think he knew but was afraid to ask. He didn't want to know the truth. I've seen him do that so many times—faced with a problem, he'll deny there is one, hoping that by ignoring it the problem will go away. The old ostrich approach to danger."

Her mother hesitates. "Well, of course you may be right," she says at last.

"I think that explains his attitude toward me when I was growing up. I always felt that he looked at me as someone who was in the way, a potential embarrassment, a potential danger to him."

"But think what would have happened if the truth had come out. The wife of the brand-new headmaster of the Crittenden

School is pregnant with another man's child! That would have been the end of everything—his career, our marriage, everything. We would all have led very different lives, Sally, if I had told the truth."

"Oh, yes, I'm sure."

"And think of the school. What would have happened to the school? Being headmaster of a school like this is a miserable job. It's a wretched job. Not too many men would even want the job, much less be willing to be the success at it that he's been. And whatever you may say about him, he's been a magnificent headmaster. Magnificent. Against all odds, Sally. *Against* all odds. Love him, Sally. Love him for that."

"In the end, the school is everything, isn't it?"

"Oh, yes. Everything."

Just a few miles away, across the lake, under a red-and-white-striped tent set up in the main quadrangle of the Crittenden School campus, Hobart Spotswood is just now coming to the conclusion of his commencement address to the graduating class, a ceremony from which the headmaster's wife traditionally excuses herself. This is an emotional moment, both public and intensely intimate, this final confrontation between the headmaster and the boys and girls he has tried to guide and inspire for four long years, his little flock. On the four front rows of folding chairs, the graduates themselves sit politely and attentively facing him. Their white diplomas, tied in rolls with red ribbon, which the headmaster has just bestowed upon them, rest in their laps. Their parents and other relatives occupy the rows of chairs just behind them, some of them dabbing at their eyelids with white hankies. The boys, in their best dark suits, white shirts, and red-and-white-striped school neckties, look very manly. Their feet are planted firmly on the ground, their knees apart. And the girls, in their best party dresses, look serious, well-scrubbed, and even radiant, with their bouncy, freshly done young hair. The girls' feet are crossed at the ankle, knees together, just so. The headmaster may be the master of ceremonies of this event, but the graduates clearly know that they are the stars.

Nevertheless, from the podium the headmaster cuts a striking figure. Tall and lean and at the same weight as when he rowed in the Harvard crew, his posture is erect, and his belly is firm. His bearing is still athletic, virile. It has often been noted that schoolmasters never seem to age the way other men do. The reward, or punishment if you will, for working with the young is a kind of perpetual youthfulness, and certainly, standing there, addressing his students, with his full head of pewter-colored hair, his long, thin Spotswood nose and firm jawline, Hobe looks much younger than his sixty years. Of Hobe it has been said that one reason for his tenure as Crittenden's headmaster has been that he so perfectly looks the part.

"And now," he is saying in his strong, rich baritone, "you are all about to leave the cloistered, protective, even insulated world of Crittenden, to venture forth into the more challenging world of colleges and universities, which you have spent your years here in preparation for. There, you will be on your own. And then, upon completion of that next phase of your education, you will face the even greater challenge of assuming your country's social, business, civic, moral, and even artistic leadership."

There is a pause and then, speaking without notes, he continues, "It is difficult for me to believe that this is the twenty-fifth graduating class of Crittenden that I've addressed, but it's true. And as I look back over my twenty-five years as headmaster of this school, I'm not so much proud of what I've accomplished here as I am proud of what Crittenden alumni and alumnae have accomplished in the world. Since I came here twenty-five years ago, Crittenden has produced one United States Supreme Court Justice; five United States senators, two of them women; four mayors of major American cities, one of them a woman; six Pulitzer Prize–winning journalists, half of them women; two college presidents, one of them a woman; the conductor of the Cleveland Symphony orchestra; a major motion picture producer; one of the country's leading epidemiologists, plus many other physicians, attorneys, architects, and engineers. I could go on and on. These are the people of whom I'm proud, and I expect you to join their ranks.

"And what have I learned from all this? In the Old Testament, the Lord asks Isaiah to seek out a watchman to tell him what he sees. Isaiah asks, 'Watchman, what of the night?' And the watchman replies, 'The morning cometh, and also the night.' As your headmaster, I've learned that, though night may come there is always a morning, and I see you students here as an ever-returning morning. I also see you as my watchmen who will tell me what is coming. I have learned from you as much or more than you have learned at this school, and I am continuing to learn—from you. Young people have been *my* teachers. My wife, Clarissa, put it rather eloquently the other morning at a meeting of the school's board of trustees. She said, 'Listen to the children.' You have taught me to listen to young people. What you have to say will tell us what of the night and the morning that follows. In what your voices tell us from now on will be the answer to the riddle of the future."

There is a long pause, and he lifts his handsome head. "And now, will you all please rise, and we will sing 'O, Crittenden.'"

The well-dressed audience rises, and the organist strikes the stirring opening chorus of the old hymn. *Dum-dum-de-dum-de-dum-dum . . .*

"*O, Crittenden triumphant, O-ver land and sea . . .*"

In Clarissa's study, the telephone rings on her private line, and she answers it. "Well," he says, "the Ides of March are here."

"What?"

"You said you wanted to get through the trustees' dinner and their meeting—"

"Which went very well, you'll be pleased to hear. They're thrilled with your gift offer, and the trusteeship looks good for you, too, though I don't think they've had a formal vote yet."

"And then you said you needed to get through graduation. Then you said you'd make your move."

"The commencement services ended barely half an hour ago! Hobe hasn't even come home from his office yet!"

"Well, you know what they call me—Mr. Fifteen Minutes. Are you ready to go?"

"Oh, Michael, please," she says. "Don't keep pushing me, *pushing* me, leaning on me like this! Just stop!"

There is a silence, and then he says, "I don't think you're ever going to leave him, are you? Be honest with me. You'll never leave him, will you?"

SEVENTEEN

"How did Mom seem to you?" he asks her. They are sitting in their favorite watering hole, the Union Square Cafe.

"Oh, a little bit weak and tired, perhaps," Sally says. "That's understandable. But her spirits and morale seemed very high, and I thought that was pretty remarkable. You've got to say this about Mother. She has guts."

He nods. "Sal," he says, "when I was with her in the hospital, they gave me some very bad news. From some routine blood tests."

She looks at him quickly. "Tell me," she says. "Tell me."

"It's lymphatic cancer. They found it when they were working in the lymph nodes. Everywhere. There's really nothing they can do."

"I see," she says quietly. "How long do they think—?"

"Not too long. Months, perhaps. Maybe a year. Maybe less than that. If it had been diagnosed earlier—those headaches—then perhaps—but now—"

"Will she be in much pain, Johnny?"

"They can medicate for that."

"Does Mother know?"

"They asked me whether they should tell her, and I said no.

And I didn't tell her. Somehow, I just couldn't bring myself to deliver her death sentence."

"Does Spotty know?"

"I didn't tell him because—"

"Because you didn't want him to use that knowledge to torture her."

He gives her a startled look. "Torture? Well, not exactly. But you know how Dad is."

"Yes. Indeed, I do know. I know very well."

"Since when did you start calling him Spotty?"

"That's what all the kids at school call him. It's just you and I who know how sick she is, except—"

"Except the doctors."

"Yes, but I meant I think Mother also knows."

"Do you? What makes you think that?"

"I just suspect it. I suspect she knows. Something about the way she talked when I went up to see her."

"What did she talk about?"

"Oh, about when she was younger. About the past. About mistakes she might have made. About her father. About things that happened to her before I was born. Reminiscing sort of things. Yes, I'm sure she knows. And I think she's preparing—organizing things in her mind—finishing unfinished things—getting ready—"

"Which is good, I suppose. Is it?"

"I think so," she says. "I mean, what else—Oh, Johnny," she says suddenly, "you know what I think you and I should do? I've got a vacation coming, and you can take a week or two off this summer, can't you? I think we should both take some time off, and we could go up to the school and stay with them for a week or two. Wouldn't that be good? We could spend some real quality time with Mother—keep her spirits up? You know how summers are always the worst time for them up there. With no school to run, rattling around in that big house together, just the two of them, getting into each other's hair, getting under each other's feet, bumping into each other, making each other crazy, with no one else in the house but that dreadful old Rose Finney—can we do it, Johnny?"

"Well, I can think of better ways to spend a vacation than at my parents' house," he says.

"Oh, but think of all the things we could do with Mother. There's the music at Tanglewood, there's the theater at Williamstown. There're new art galleries, antique shops—Spotty never did any of those things with her. But we could."

"We should include Dad on some of these junkets, shouldn't we?"

"Yes, but mostly we should do things for her. She's the one who needs our attention and our love right now."

"But, in terms of the two of them, maybe you and I could act as sort of a—"

"A buffer zone between them? Well, perhaps. But the main thing would be to show her how much we love her. After all, this may be our last chance, Johnny. Will you do it? Look at your calendar, and I'll look at mine, and we'll set aside two weeks this summer just to go up to the Castle and be nice to Mother. Just to give her the best time we possibly can."

"Two weeks? Can you tear yourself away from your new lover for that long?"

"Oh," she says with a wave of her hand, "that's over."

He gives her a startled look. "It *is*?"

"Yep. Over and done with."

"What happened, Sal?"

"Nothing happened. I just decided he's not the man for me. And don't go thinking that *you* had anything to do with it. I know you didn't like him much, but this was my own decision."

"How did he take it? I got the impression he was crazy about you."

"I don't know how he's going to take it. I haven't told him yet."

"I see," he says.

"I'm seeing him tonight, and I'm going to tell him then."

"Well," he says. "Well, well. That's all I can say—well, well, well."

"Yep. That's all there is to say."

"Same old Sally. Never complain, never explain."

"Yep. My philosophy of life."

He gives her a narrow look. "And so, in a sense, this idea for a trip up to see Mom and Dad is sort of a substitute for the nice summer holiday you might have spent with your about-to-be ex-boyfriend. You want to go to James Falls to forget Mr. Jesse Rubin."

She frowns. "Well, maybe that's part of it."

"A big part. Right?"

"No! I really think Mother needs us now. I think we can help her a lot. I think when a person is sick, a lot depends on a person's mental attitude. I think that's even been medically proven. With the right mental attitude, all sorts of strange and wonderful things can happen. There was something on *Sixty Minutes*—a boy with AIDS, and his doctors had told him he was going to die, but he just decided that he wasn't going to be sick and wasn't going to die. His T-cell count suddenly went up. The virus is now virtually undetectable! He's healthy again, gaining weight! That sort of thing can *happen*, Johnny! You and I can't just sit back and *let* Mother die. Who knows? With the right mental attitude, she might cure herself. I really believe it's possible, and that you and I could help."

He looks dubious. "I dunno," he says. "The doctors—"

"What do the doctors know? Doctors are always making mistakes. Those doctors for the boy with AIDS. They're just shaking their heads. They can't understand it. They don't understand the human will. Our mother's not the kind of woman who's going to die unless she wants to. You and I can give her something to live for. That's something she'll never get from old Spotty—you know that!"

"You're being awfully hard on Dad," he says.

"You know what I'm talking about."

"So," he says, folding his napkin, "we're going up to Connecticut to be nice to our parents, and be charming and fun and upbeat, and turn into a nice, normal, happy little family all over again."

"Well, let's not ask for the moon, Johnny. Let's just ask for a reprieve for Mother."

The Truxton Van Degans' apartment at 2 East Eighty-Sixth Street is in one of those grand old New York luxury buildings put up in the Hoover era when the nation was assured that it had attained a permanent plateau of prosperity, and when not to be very rich was almost a personal embarrassment. One simply didn't know anyone who wasn't. Most of the apartments in the building are floor-through with their own private elevator entrances opening into long, wide central foyers from which the other major rooms branch out. Nearly all the apartments, particularly those on the upper floors, have spectacular views of Central Park and of the Metropolitan Museum, just across Fifth Avenue, and the Van Degan apartment is one of these, decorated and furnished in no particular style or period, but with the expensive good taste that is customarily associated with well-aged, serious wealth. Across the top of the concert grand piano in the living room where Clarissa sits are arrayed many photographs in silver frames of various Van Degans of various generations—Van Degans in yachting caps at the wheels of schooners; Van Degans in plus fours holding golfing trophies; Van Degans in hunting pinks jumping fences astride their thoroughbreds and holding the reins of racehorses in the Winner's Circle; Van Degans in beach attire at Rio, with Christ of the Andes on the mountaintop beyond; hatted and gloved Van Degan women chatting with the Queen and Prince Philip at Ascot; Van Degan men in officers' uniforms of branches of the US military; Van Degans and their friends and relatives all in poses showing them enjoying being rich together. But nowhere in this collection of photographs, Clarissa notices, does there appear to be a photograph of Linda.

Truxton Van Degan steps quickly into the room and extends his hand.

"Clarissa," he says with a little bow, "how good of you to come." He is a small, compact man of roughly Clarissa's age, dressed in a dark business suit, but who, with his brisk and authoritative manner, manages to convey the impression of a man of greater girth and stature. He is clearly a man accustomed to giving orders. "Sit there," he says, pointing. "I usually sit here. Would you like a drink?"

"No thank you," she says, seating herself in the designated chair. "We missed you at the trustees' dinner, Truck."

"Well, I read the minutes of the meeting," he says. "Sounds like it was pretty damned successful, what? Twenty million, what? That Rubin character is smart. Wouldn't want him as my enemy. Wouldn't want him in my house, either, for that matter—what? Ha ha!" His laugh is a sharp, mirthless staccato. "He's something of a scamp, you know, but the school can't say no to that kind of money, can it? What? The fellow pisses money and he'll probably die in the poorhouse if he doesn't land in Fort Leavenworth first. But as long as he pisses some of his money our way, I say grab it. Give the pisser what he wants, I say. For that kind of money, I'd kiss his arse in Macy's window—ha ha! Now, what can I do for you, Clarissa?" He glances at his watch.

"First, I wanted to offer you my personal condolences," she says. "It was so sad about Linda."

"Oh, yes. Poor Linda. Well, Linda was all her mother's fault, you see. All my first wife's fault. Child needs discipline, what? She got none of it from Peg. Peg let her do whatever she wanted to and gave her all the money she wanted to do it with. No way to raise a child. And I'm a busy man. I couldn't be a father and a mother, too. Besides, while Linda was growing up I was down in Washington trying to help Ronnie Reagan run this country—ha ha! Anyway, Tweetums and I thought a school like Crittenden might help. Crittenden helped make a man of me! But it was too late. The harm'd been done." He lifts his cuff and peeks at his watch again. "Now, what else can I do for you, Clarissa?"

She sits forward in her chair. "I think my husband mentioned to you a little problem we're having up in Litchfield County," she says. "There's a young county prosecutor named Thomas Finney who's talking of mounting an investigation into the cause of Linda's death."

"Oh, yes. Hobe mentioned something of the sort. But what's to investigate? Perfectly cut-and-dried suicide, wasn't it? That's what the doctor said. She took a bunch of pills."

"But," she says carefully, "some people at the school and in the town have been hinting that foul play may have been involved. There's been talk that Linda may have been pregnant, and that she may, in fact, have given birth to a baby at the school, a baby that died, and that the school is trying to keep all this hushed up."

"A baby, eh? Well, I can't say that surprises me. Her mother again. Peg went off on a trip to Ireland while I was in Washington, supposedly to buy horses. Gone almost a year and came back five months pregnant. Tried to claim the baby was mine. Ha ha! I can count, what? That was the end of Peg."

"Somehow, this county prosecutor has gotten wind of these rumors. He sees a chance to build a case that, even if he ends up not proving anything, will get him lots of publicity—even national publicity. This man Finney is young, handsome, with lots of what they call personal charisma. He's also terribly ambitious. Some people say he even has his eye on the White House."

"Democrat or Republican?"

"Oh, Republican," she says quickly, though she is really not sure of this. "He wouldn't get anywhere as a Democrat in Litchfield County."

"I've worked pretty closely with a couple of Republican presidents," he says.

"I *know* you have!"

"But how's he gonna get publicity out of Linda?"

"Truck, the Van Degan name is well known, nationally known. Your name is well known. The Van Degan name is closely associated with the Crittenden School. Many Van Degans have gone to Crittenden, including you, and you are one of the school's trustees—possibly its best-known and most important trustee. Your great-grandfather, Jared Truxton, was a member of the school's very first graduating class."

"Damn right. That's old Jared over there"—he gestures toward the piano—"when he played quarterback for Yale. Good-looking devil, what?"

"And we have Van Degan Hall, which your family gave. The names Crittenden and Van Degan are practically inseparable, and—"

"Ho ho!" he says suddenly, jumping from his chair. "Look who's here! It's Tweetums!"

Tweetums Van Degan enters the room. "Saks was a madhouse," she says. "I thought this country was headed toward a recession, but you wouldn't know it from the crowds at Saks. I couldn't get a soul to wait on me, and all I was looking for was a pair of slippers for Uncle Archie's birthday."

How would you picture a woman whose nickname is Tweetums? Someone soft and round and cute and baby-faced and cuddly, an ex-chorine? This is not the Tweetums, whom Clarissa has never met before, whom she sees now for the first time. Tweetums is tall, an inch or two taller than her husband, and pencil-slender, dressed in slim-cut black pants that emphasize her long legs, a white silk blouse, a short black jacket, and black pumps. Her blond hair is pulled away from her face and intricately knotted in a bright, green-printed Hermès scarf, the only touch of color in her outfit. Years from now, Tweetums will be the sort of woman who will be able to wear a great deal of jewelry, but for now she knows better. She wears only a wide gold wedding band. She is not techni-cally beautiful. Her cheekbones are a little too high, her fore-head is a little too narrow, her mouth is a little too wide, and her dark eyes are set a little too far apart. But she is easily the most striking-looking woman Clarissa has ever seen. She is probably only in her middle to late twenties, and she wears no visible makeup. But she is almost ferociously self-conscious, defiantly daring the world to deny that she is a valuable pres-ence in it.

No, this Tweetums is no Kewpie doll. She could not even be described as a trophy wife; if anything, it is she who has bagged the trophy. She moves with catlike grace across the room with just a hint of Chanel's Allure wafting in her wake and kisses her husband on both cheeks. "Darling," she whispers in a smoky voice.

It is astonishing the way Truxton Van Degan's personality is transformed by her arrival. He is suddenly all smiles and bumbling obsequies and little attentions, squeezing her hand and stroking her wrist as she reaches up to remove an invisible speck of lint from the lapel of his suit jacket, while, on tiptoe, he pursues his lips as though expecting a more intimate kiss, which is not forthcoming from his wife. "This is Clarissa Spotswood, Babycakes," he says. "The Crittenden headmaster's wife."

"So nice to meet you," Tweetums says, turning to Clarissa with a bright smile, and taking her hand in a warm, firm grip. "But you two are having an important business meeting. I'll leave you alone."

"Oh, no, please stay," Clarissa says.

"Yes, stay, lovey," he says. "There's a little problem up at the school of ours, and maybe you can give us some advice."

Tweetums Van Degan slides her slender frame into a chair and crosses her long legs at the knee. With one hand she smooths the back of her hair and, with the other, reaches for a cigarette from a silver box, all seemingly in the same motion.

"Oh, I wish my Babycakes wouldn't smoke!" he says in an almost plaintive tone, but she ignores this.

"What's the problem?" she asks, lighting her cigarette from a heavy silver table lighter, and exhaling smoke in a long, thin stream.

"Some little pip-squeak DA up in Connecticut seems to think he can make some political hay out of Linda's death," he says. "Seems there's talk she may have been pregnant—by some boy at the school, I suppose."

"Oh, dear," Tweetums says.

"Actually, it's the Litchfield County prosecutor," Clarissa says. "He's talking about launching an investigation."

"You know, I wondered about that when she came home for Easter," Tweetums says. "I even asked her if she might be pregnant, but she just laughed at me."

"Naturally, my first concern is for the school," Clarissa says. "Even though nothing can be proven, an investigation like that could give the school a terrible black eye."

"Well," Tweetums says, "it certainly has all the elements, doesn't it? Old New York family. Money. Sex. Snobby New England prep school. I can imagine what the *New York Times* would do with the story—say nothing of the supermarket tabloids."

"And I'm also thinking about Linda's reputation," Clarissa says. "We ought to try to protect her memory."

"What does her reputation matter now?" he says. "She's dead."

"But what about your own reputation, Truckie?" his wife says. "After all, she was your daughter. Or my reputation. She was my stepdaughter, and I was supposed to have some sort of influence on her, wasn't I? Especially when her real mother showed no interest in her."

"Do you know that Tweetums and I have had no word from Peg since her daughter died?" he says. "Not a single word. Can you believe that? Some kind of mother, what?"

"Don't be too hard on Peggy," his wife says. "She may be just too devastated—"

"Ha! Devastated? You don't know Peg!"

"This young prosecutor is running for reelection in November," Clarissa says. "We think he may be looking for a case like this to give his campaign a lot of free publicity."

"So," Tweetums says, stubbing out her cigarette in a crystal ashtray, "he's going to have to be stopped."

"My husband thought perhaps a contribution to his campaign fund," Clarissa says.

"Now, wait!" Truxton Van Degan says, and he begins pacing back and forth across the room, his hands clasped behind his back. "Now just stop and think about this. This sort of thing could boomerang. It could backfire badly and hurt us even more. Suppose this pip-squeak DA is the kind of fellow who wants to prove to the world, and to the voters, that he's absolutely incorruptible? That he cannot be paid off! If I go to him with money, he could start screaming, 'Payoff! Bribery of a public official!' He could grab even bigger headlines that way. In addition to his sex scandal, he'd have the fact that Van Degan offered him hush money to cover the whole thing up! Where would that leave us? Up shit creek without a paddle, what?"

"I thought of that, too," Clarissa says. "There is that definite risk. Also, I think there's a legal limit to how much an individual can contribute to a politician's campaign fund. Whatever you might be able to offer him might not seem enough of a trade-off for dropping a potentially big case."

"Then we've got to think of something else," Tweetums says, reaching for another cigarette. "What about hiring a detective to dig up something about his own sex life? There's usually something, you know—particularly with a politician."

Truxton Van Degan keeps shaking his head. "Blackmail. Too dangerous."

"I had one thought," Clarissa says. "I've noticed, over the years, that a number of Van Degan family gifts to the school have come from something called the Knickerbocker Foundation."

Tweetums snaps her fingers. "That's it!" she says.

"Tell me something about the Knickerbocker Foundation."

"Family foundation. Both Tweetums and I are on the board."

"And its aims are deliciously vague," Tweetums says. "To improve American health, education, agriculture, and government—something like that."

"This Mr. Finney is from a poor family," Clarissa says. "His father is a laborer for the State Highway Department. A grant from a foundation would not be a political campaign contribution—"

"It would be for *him*. To spend however he wants. No strings," Tweetums says. "Hard for a poor boy to refuse."

"Now wait a minute," her husband says. "I'm not sure I want my money to go to some pip-squeak, hayseed politician in Connecticut!"

"But it's not your money, Truckie," his wife says. "It's the foundation's money, and there's quite a lot of it to give away."

"I still don't like it. It could still be dangerous. It could still backfire."

She stubs out her second cigarette. "But I'd like to try it, Truckie," she says with a grin. "Let me try it. I can sort of see myself, sitting in Mr. Finney's gray little office, wearing something—loose. I'll be sitting there with my checkbook open, ready to write out a blank check, and I'll say—" She sits forward in her chair, striking a dramatic pose. "I'll say, 'Mr. Finney, your dedication to the good government and welfare of this county, and of this state, have not gone unnoticed by the Knickerbocker Foundation. And therefore, we're offering you this special grant, without restrictions, to encourage and reward and underwrite your further good work in the community.' But then, just before I reach for my pen to sign the check and hand it over to him, I'll say, 'And of course the Knickerbocker Foundation also strives to improve the quality and climate of American education, and we naturally assume that we have your assurance that, in accepting this grant, your office will not pursue or engage in any activity that might discredit or dishonor or cast in an unfavorable light one of our foundation's other major beneficiaries, the Crittenden School. We'd consider that sort of thing a conflict of interest, of course.'" She looks around at them. "What do you think of that little speech?"

"You wouldn't mention Linda's name at all," Clarissa says.

"Absolutely not. But I think he'll know what I'm talking about, don't you?"

"How much?" Truxton Van Degan asks. "How much are you going to offer him?"

"Clarissa—what do you think?"

"Knowing his circumstances, I think he'd be very happy with fifty thousand dollars," Clarissa says.

"Actually, that would constitute one of our smaller grants," she says.

"Well, it's an idea," her husband says. "It might work."

"It's Clarissa's idea," she says. "Do I have your permission to try it, Truckie?"

He sighs. "Well, of course you can try it, lovey," he says. "But I'm still not sure I like it."

"Wait and see," she says. "After all, here's a man who's being offered a sum of money—money he won't have to report to anybody. Not to his campaign manager, not to the public, not even to his wife if he doesn't want to. It'll be strictly between him and the IRS. Is there any man in the world strong enough to resist that?"

He chuckles. He reaches down and puts his hands on her shoulders, gently massaging them. "Or strong enough to resist you, honeybunch?"

She laughs her throaty laugh. "Well, I do think I'd be better at persuading him than you would, Truckie." She reaches for another cigarette and gives Clarissa a broad wink. "If this doesn't work, darling, I promise you I'll quit smoking," she says. "Clarissa, you're my witness to that promise."

"But I don't understand!" he says, slamming the fist of his right hand into the palm of his left. "I just don't understand what's happened. How can you say it's over—just like that?" They are sitting in the living room of Sally's apartment on East Sixty-Seventh Street.

"I just don't think we're right for each other, Jess. It's that simple."

"But what made you change your mind? It must have been something. Is it because of what they've been writing about my father in the papers?"

"No, no, Jess."

"They're saying he could go to jail. Well, let me tell you something. He'll never go to jail. My father will never go to jail. If necessary, if things get that bad, he'll leave the country. He told me that. He said, 'If things get too bad, I'll just leave the country till this whole damn thing blows over.'"

"I'm glad," she says. "I certainly don't want to see your father go to jail."

"Is it because you're afraid he's going to lose all his money? Is that it?"

"No, no . . ."

"Because he's not, you know! He'll always have plenty of money. He's got money stashed all over the world—in Switzerland, in South America, in Israel—"

"I never cared about your father's money, Jess."

"Is it because I'm Jewish?"

She shakes her head. "Please, don't be absurd," she says.

"I'll bet that's it! Don't forget your old man was my prep school headmaster! I know what he's like. I can just hear him. 'A Spotswood can't marry a Jew!'"

"I've never even mentioned you to my father, Jess."

"Then what is it?"

"Oh, a lot of things. My mother is ill. She's sicker than we all thought. But it's not just that. Mostly, it's just a feeling—that you and I are wrong for each other. Just—wrong. To marry someone, everything should seem exactly right. But it doesn't seem right. I'm sorry."

He puts his head in his hands. "I—just—don't—understand," he almost sobs. "Everything seemed so perfect. But now . . ."

"Look," she says, sitting forward in her chair, "I'm very fond of you, Jess. I really am. I always will be. I think you're a wonderful man. Couldn't we be . . . just friends?"

He jumps to his feet. "No!" he says. "I will not accept that! That's not good enough! That's not acceptable to me."

"Can't two people who were once lovers remain good friends?"

"No! I can't do that."

"Then I'm very sorry, Jess. Because in some ways I'll always love you very much. I won't be able to help that, will I?"

"Then what will you do?"

"Just go on alone, I guess. As I've pretty much always done."

"There's not someone else, is there?"

"No, no. There's no one else. Maybe there never will be. But in the meantime, I'll miss you very much."

"I don't understand you!" He is very angry now. "I don't think I've ever understood you!"

"Maybe that's why we're wrong for each other, Jess. Maybe that's why we'd better just say—goodbye."

He stands over her where she sits in the sofa, and there are tears in his eyes. Her own eyes withdraw from his.

"Goodbye! I just hope your heart breaks the way you've broken mine!"

"I think it already has," she says.

Jesse turns on his heel and strides across the room to the door, opens it and closes it with a slam.

"Goodbye," she whispers to the empty room. Then she leans sideways and buries her face in the rough kiss of the sofa cushions.

"Doesn't it strike you as strange?" Clarissa is saying to her husband. "They both want to come and spend part of the summer with us here at the Castle. *Both* of them—Johnny and Sally. They haven't done that sort of thing in years. It just strikes me as very peculiar. They don't give me any particular reason. It's almost as though they thought I was going to die!" She laughs.

"Cousin Tommy?" Rose Finney whispers into the kitchen telephone. "I think I've got some more dirt on the Spotswoods!"

"What is it, Rose?"

"She hurt her eye. Said she fell on the stairs, but I don't believe it. She's had to have an operation to save the eye, and now she wears a patch on it. I think he hit her."

"What makes you think that?"

"The first few days after it happened, he took her meals to her on a tray. Wouldn't hardly let me near her. Why would he do that? Guilty conscience, of course!"

"Rose," he says in a tone of some annoyance, "I wish you wouldn't bother me with this sort of speculation."

"I thought I was your star witness, Tommy!"

"Please," he says, "please let me conduct this investigation in my own way. These telephone calls from you aren't very helpful. I promise to call you if I need anything else from you. Okay? Bye, now."

EIGHTEEN

This is one of the pleasant little hiatuses that break the long and rather tedious and idle weeks of summer on the Crittenden campus: a new face. In this case it belongs to a young man named Alan Herrick, and a very nice face it is indeed: clean-shaven, pink cheeked, sandy haired, eager, with intelligent-looking hazel eyes. Mr. Herrick is just twenty-two, fresh out of Harvard with a Phi Beta Kappa key and a cum laude degree in contemporary literature and is a candidate to fill an opening to teach Freshman English at the school, starting in the fall. This invitation to lunch at the headmaster's house, at the end of the screening process, is an almost certain indication that he has gotten the job.

Otherwise, summers for the headmaster and his wife generally pass without incident. Only a few summer students remain on the campus, most of them doing makeup work for various courses, taught by a skeleton teaching staff under the supervision of the assistant head. Many faculty and their families have departed for the mountains or the seashore—the Cape is a favorite destination—and those who remain amuse themselves with outdoor barbecues and cocktail parties, to which the headmaster and his wife are always invited, but such invitations, by tradition, are usually declined. (There is a feeling here that the head couple and their faculty see quite enough of each other during the course of the normal academic year. Where his faculty are concerned, Hobe has a little motto: "Too much familiarity breeds content. I don't want a contented faculty. I want a faculty that's on its toes!")

"Interesting name, Spotswood," young Mr. Herrick is saying as the three of them sit at the luncheon table at the Castle. "I have a hunch that the name was originally 'Spottiswood,' with two *t*s and an *i*."

"That is correct," Hobe says. "And there was also an *e* at the end—S-P-O-T-T-I-S-W-O-O-D-E, before my three-times great-grandfather shortened it."

"And I'll also bet that when it was first shortened it was written 'Spot'swood,' with an apostrophe."

"That's true!" Clarissa says. "I've seen it written that way on a number of old family documents."

"One of the earliest uses of the apostrophe," Mr. Herrick says. "You know, the correct use of the apostrophe is one of the hardest things for a beginning English student to grasp—the difference between 'it's,' the contraction, and 'its,' the possessive. English is the only language that uses the apostrophe in this manner, and students have a heck of a time with it. But I give them a little rhyme to try to help them remember the difference—The old Manx cat will rant and wail / It's mad because it's lost its tail.'"

"How clever!" Clarissa says.

"And to show them how the contraction works, I use another one. 'If she's a cat, and he's a dog, it just makes sense that it's a log.' I've found that couplets like these provide good mnemonic aids for young students."

Clarissa nods. He is, of course, showing off a bit. But, under the circumstances, this is understandable.

"I see you're unmarried," Hobe says, changing the subject. "Are you engaged, or is there some young woman in particular, Mr. Herrick?"

"There's a girl I've been dating in Boston," he says.

Nibbling on an artichoke leaf, Clarissa smiles to herself. This is her husband's way of trying to find out whether the young man is a homosexual. He is also being given the artichoke test and is passing it beautifully. He is arranging the eaten artichoke leaves in a neat semicircle along the edge of the plate, not heaping them in an unruly pile, the way some teaching applicants have been known to do. This sort of thing is important to Hobe, and Clarissa has noticed her husband's look of approval at the way Alan Herrick observes this nicety.

"Well, Boston's not too far away," Hobe says.

"I realize that, sir," he says. "But that's not the reason why I applied to your school. It was because of Crittenden's excellent reputation."

Hobe nods. "Of course. We have a certain amount of dating here, among the male and female single members of the faculty. We can't outlaw that, but we don't really approve of it, either. We don't think it's particularly good for student morale, that sort of thing. We tend to discourage it."

"I understand, sir."

"And of course, at your age, you're only four or five years older than some of our female students. Romantic relationships between faculty and students are absolutely taboo—you do understand that."

"Oh, absolutely, sir!" the young man says.

"We did have a situation some years ago, when a young history teacher ran off to Canada with a female student and married her! That, as you can well imagine," he says with a grim little smile, "created a considerable mess for the school. We had to deal with the girl's parents, the police and immigration authorities in two countries—an unholy mess."

"I can certainly imagine it would," he says, "create a real mess."

"But the story has a happy ending," Clarissa says. "The girl's parents finally accepted the young man as her husband, and the two of them are happily married to this day!"

"But the young man was never able to secure a decent teaching post again." Hobe looks at young Mr. Herrick, to make sure that this has sunk in. "I believe he now sells life insurance." He clears his throat. "Our school community here is very small," he says. "It's not like Boston, or like Chicago, where you're from. We're almost insular here. It's like a very small town, of just a few hundred people. I hope you'll be able to adjust to that kind of close-knit, small-town atmosphere. Some people have found the smallness and closeness of the Crittenden School community claustrophobic, even stifling."

Mr. Herrick appears to hesitate, unsure whether he has been asked a question or not, or whether his reply should be something about his own emotional stability. "I've always loved this part of New England," he says at last. "When I was a kid, my family used to spend summers in southern Vermont. I expect I'll be able to fit in here very nicely."

"When you join this community, we expect a long-term commitment," Hobe says. "The job itself has strains, of course, but there are other pressures. Gossip travels fast in a school community like ours. You mentioned a lady friend in Boston. If, for instance, you were to invite her to spend the night, as you'd have a perfect right to do, I can assure you that the entire campus would know about it the following morning. I need to warn you about things like that."

"I certainly would never dream of doing a thing like that, sir," he says.

"Good. Always be discreet. Discretion is a good watchword for adjusting to life in a school like ours. You will make friendships on the campus, of course, but you will be better off if they are polite, discreet friendships. Close, intimate friendships will just cause talk. Save those for off-campus, is my advice to you."

"Well said," Clarissa says, not looking at her husband, as Rose removes the artichoke plates and serves the main course, a breast of chicken Kiev. Chicken Kiev is another test of poise. Attacked wrongly, melted butter will spurt out in all directions, including on Mr. Herrick's necktie. The toothpick in the center is the clue, and Clarissa is gratified to see that he realizes this and removes the toothpick before gently pricking the breast with the tines of his luncheon fork, allowing the butter to drizzle out slowly on his plate. Final candidates for teaching positions at Crittenden are always served this rather challenging menu, Hobe's idea.

"And this brings me to the subject of the town of James Falls," her husband continues. "What is often referred to as the problem of Town versus Gown. Up here on the hill we tend to refer to the village as 'across the lake.' It's a small village, across the lake, some twelve hundred souls including many good people, and we try to maintain good relations with the village people. We always participate in their local fundraising events—United Way, Community Chest, Red Cross, and so on. The school contributes generously to these drives. We can always remind ourselves that we are the largest single employer in the area. But still, we realize that some people in the village resent us, resent the fact that we sit up here on two hundred acres of valuable lakefront property and pay no taxes. And the students themselves, even though they and their families bring business to the town, can occasionally be obstreperous. Their teenage pranks can sometimes annoy the town. We've found it best to keep the townspeople themselves at a somewhat aloof distance, at arm's length, so to speak. Do you understand?"

"I think so, sir."

"For example, many of our faculty run up to Massachusetts to buy their liquor, where there's no tax. The townspeople resent that, and I try to discourage it, and it actually is illegal. My recommendation to you is, whenever possible, to patronize the local shops—the liquor store, the grocery store, the drugstore, and hardware store, and so on—for your personal needs. The townspeople will appreciate that, however begrudgingly. But don't try to *befriend* the townspeople. In our experience, that only makes them suspicious of your motives. Don't try to become involved, socially or otherwise, with the townspeople. That only leads to trouble. For another example, those of us who are churchgoers worship at the local churches, but we are careful to sit in the back, in the last rows of pews. Most of us vote here, but I caution my faculty not to become involved in local politics."

"At times, it can be a little like walking on eggs," Clarissa says. "Once I happened to be in New York, and I had my hair done. When I got home, the woman who normally does it noticed it immediately. 'Who's been messing with your hair?' she wanted to know. She was furious at me!"

"Once you get used to the attitude of the townspeople, it's just a matter of using good judgment and common sense," her husband says.

"And politeness, politeness, and more politeness," Clarissa says.

"Politeness—with a certain distance," Hobe notes.

"Distance, but not so much as to seem condescending," she clarifies.

"Just remember that they think of it as their town, not ours," Hobe goes on.

"I understand."

"Several years ago, we had a young female teacher—biology, an excellent teacher. She fell in love with a local lad."

"Madly in love. Head over heels in love," Clarissa says.

"I had to let her go," Hobe says. Once more, he looks across the table to young Mr. Herrick to be sure that this message has sunk in. "Well," the headmaster concludes, "I have a couple of things to clear up at my office. Why don't you and Mrs. Spotswood have coffee in the library and, when you're done, drop by my office and I'll go over a few of the details of your contract." He rises, and Alan Herrick also rises.

"Welcome aboard, Herrick!" Hobe extends his hand, and Mr. Herrick, clearly relieved that this ordeal is over, gives him a vigorous handshake.

As he and Clarissa move toward the next room, he says, "Your husband is a remarkable man, Mrs. Spotswood."

"Yes—remarkable."

"His whole life has been devoted to this school, hasn't it?"

"Oh, yes. His whole life."

"And yours, too, I can well imagine."

"Yes. My whole life." She pauses in the hallway. "Tell me something, Mr. Herrick," she says.

"Yes?"

"Where would you like to be fifteen years from now?" He looks at her.

"You really want to know?"

"Yes. Tell me."

"I'd like to be the headmaster of a school like Crittenden."

He reaches quickly for her elbow, since she suddenly seems unsteady. "Mrs. Spotswood? Are you all right? You're laughing. Did I say something funny?"

"No, no," she says, trying to suppress the unwanted laughter, which, against her will, seems about to turn to tears. "It was just such an unexpected answer to my question," she says. "It caught me quite off guard."

"It's the truth. This beautiful campus, this beautiful house."

His hand is still on her elbow, and she presses it tightly against her side, so tightly she can feel the outline of his Harvard class ring pressing against her rib cage. "You really mean that, don't you?" she says. "Oh, you poor thing. You poor, dear, sweet young thing. I wish you luck. I wish you success." They continue together toward the library, where the coffee service is laid out on a silver tray.

"I just don't get it, Pops," Jess Rubin is saying to his father. "One minute we were, like, really, really in love. We both said it was the real thing. There were no questions, no doubts. We were going to get married, Pops! I was going to take her and let her pick out a ring! It was that serious. And then, suddenly—boom!—out of the blue, when I came by her place to take her out to dinner, she said it was all over. We should just be *friends*. Can you figure it? I'm sorry, but this has really hit me, Pops. I don't know when anything has ever hit me as hard as this thing has."

It is late at night, and they are sitting in his father's big corner office, high above the deserted canyon of Wall Street, where Jesse Rubin has finally found Michael, sitting alone. Despite the hour—close to midnight, with even the building's cleaning staff gone home—muted telephones continue to ring in this computerized room. Fax machines purr steadily, delivering their messages in neat folds of paper, and email moves from softly glowing screens into printers, which stack and sort the pages with efficient clicking sounds. Lights of different colors wink and blink. Digital clocks reveal the times in other parts of the world: London, Zurich, Frankfurt, Tel Aviv, Tokyo. His father's office has always eerily reminded Jesse Rubin of a command station on some futuristic spaceship.

Jesse's father leans back in his big swivel chair and places his feet up on his deck. "I had no idea this affair with Sally had gone this far," he says.

"Well, you haven't exactly been the most accessible guy in the world these past few months," he says. "It hasn't been easy to get to talk to you, Pops. Where've you been, anyway?"

His father gestures around him. "Mostly right here," he says.

"Sleeping?"

"Here. I keep a few changes of clothes in the closet, and those sofas are quite comfortable. But I've never needed much sleep, anyway."

"What do you think happened, Pops?"

"You mean about the Spotswood girl? I have no idea."

"It was you who got me into this, you know—putting me on that plane with her. I've never understood what that was all about. What was the point of that, anyway?"

His father frowns and starts, in an almost automatic gesture, to touch the large dial at his wrist.

"And don't give me that stopwatch crap, Pops!" his son says. "I'm not here to cut a deal with you. I'm your son—remember?"

"I don't have all night to sit here and discuss your romantic problems, Jesse. Other problems are on my mind right now."

"I'm not asking for all night. I asked you a simple question, and I'd like a straight and simple answer."

"It's none of your business."

"Goddammit, it is my business! We're in business together, and any problems you're in are going to be my problems before we're through!"

"There are no problems, Jesse."

"Stop lying! You just said there were other problems, and everybody on the street knows there are. But I also think what's happened to me and Sally has something to do with you. Why did you say to me, 'I want the Spotswood girl on our team?' What's this team? And what position on the team was I supposed to play?"

"Not marry her! Those were not my instructions."

"Then what? I don't recall any further instructions."

"I just wanted you to be nice to her."

"Why?"

"To convince her that we at Rubin & Company are not bad people."

"Again, why? Does it have something to do with the gift you're offering to the Crittenden School? I think it does."

"Nonsense. I've always believed in elite private education and believe that those who received it should support it."

"You're lying again. There's more to it than that. You always said you hated that school. They called you Kikey Mikey. Is it because you always secretly wanted to be a WASP, but you never could be? But now, maybe with this gift, they'll let you join their club? Is that it?"

His father swings his feet off the desk and plants them firmly on the carpet. His face is angry now. "That is not it!" he says. "That school did not play fair with me. They cheated me out of something I richly deserved. The school screwed me."

"And so, you reward them—you thank them—by tossing them a bunch of money? That makes no sense."

"It does to me! Because in order to get that money, they're going to have to give something to me. But now, by God, they're going to notice me!"

"Ah," Jesse says. "Now we're getting closer to the truth. But there's something else, isn't there? What else is it you want, Pops? The truth!"

His father is silent for a moment. He averts his eyes. "Clarissa," he says, almost in a whisper.

"Clarissa? You mean Sally's mother?"

He nods. "I've been in love with her for years. Years and years."

"Ah," he says.

"I want to take her away from that shitty husband of hers, and away from that shitty life she leads."

"Ah," Jesse says again. "Now I'm beginning to understand. You want to take the headmaster's wife away from him. But, as a businessman, you want to play fair. You'll pay for the headmaster's wife by giving the school a bunch of money. Now *that* begins to make some sense."

"The things a man wants most in life he can always get with money. That's true in business and in life."

"But . . . you talk about love! Where does love enter that equation? You're still not being honest with me, Pops, or being honest with yourself. Admit it, Pops, with you, it's all about ego, about power, about manipulating people to bend them to your will. You use people, you buy people, to get them to give you what you want. You used Sally, because you know she's close to her mother, to lure her into your little web. You used me as the lure. But something went wrong, didn't it, Pops? Sally went up to the school to have lunch the other day—and right after that Sally told me that she and I were through. Coincidence? I don't think so. Sally's mother must have told her something at that lunch that day—something about *you*— that made her change her mind. So, your goddamned power play didn't work, did it? So how do you feel about ruining my life for me, Pops?"

Suddenly his father seems to weaken before his eyes, and he all at once seems tired and old. His jaw slackens, and his eyes dart anxiously about that garishly blinking and humming space-station of an office. For the first time in Jesse's memory, his father looks defeated. "I used to believe you knew what you were doing, Pops," he says. "But no more."

His father looks at him blankly now. "Have I failed, son?" he says. "Am I a failure?"

Jesse jumps to his feet, seizes his father by the shoulders, and presses his father's face against his chest. "Oh, Pops, Pops," he says, "I love you so. But you mustn't lie—to me, or to yourself. You don't really love Clarissa. Love isn't just getting another notch on your belt. But I do love Sally. Do you see the difference?"

His father pushes himself away from the embrace a little roughly. "Let's act like grown men," he mutters.

"What did Sally's mother tell her that made her change her mind?"

"I don't know," Michael says. He takes a deep breath and, with that, seems to be his old self again. He swivels away from Jesse in his chair. "I don't know," he says again, "but I'm sure as shit going to find out!"

NINETEEN

And the slow summer weeks have drawn on. July was exceptionally hot and dry, and the green hills turned to a dusty amber. The weatherman kept promising rain, but no rain came, and instead a summer haze hung over the valley, and Lake Kinishawah, normally a clear, sparkling blue, echoed the sky's leaden color, and its surface lay flat and still. From time to time a warm breeze would spring up from the west, ruffling the surface of the water, and there would be a distant rumble of thunder, and people would look up from watering their lawns and gardens and think that the drought had finally ended, but still no rain came.

And now it's August, and Clarissa is feeling as drained and dry as the hills and sunless sky above. It is the medication they are making her take, she is sure of that, the damn medication. "Time for your meds, Mrs. S," Rose says.

"I don't want to take the damn meds. They make me feel so groggy."

"Doctor's orders, Mrs. S. We have to take our meds." Rose stands at her bedside, making sure that all the pills have been swallowed.

"I hate these things," Clarissa says. "After I take them all I want to do is sleep."

"Doctor's orders," Rose says again. "And notice? No more headaches. No more dizzy spells."

"I'd rather have the headaches and the dizzy spells. I was used to them."

"And no more falls."

"I haven't had any falls."

Rose gives her a narrow look. "You fell on the stairs. Don't you remember?"

"Oh, that. That was nothing."

"That's why we have to take our meds."

Suddenly this house has become her prison, and Rose, armed with her holster packed with meds, has become her jailer. If she could find where Rose hides the pills, she would flush them all down the toilet, but, thanks to the pills, she hasn't had the energy to hunt for the hiding place, and so the naps have grown longer and more frequent. She hasn't even had the energy to write in her journal. From time to time, she has forced herself out of her chair or out of the sofa or out of her bed to go downstairs and into the garden to pull a few weeds, but soon that little effort exhausts her, thanks to the pills. She tries to remember the last time she really felt like herself and decides it was that day, in late June, when young Mr. Herrick came for lunch, and she has decided that when he comes back, in September, to officially take up his duties as an English instructor, Mr. Herrick will be her friend. She looks forward to that. By September, everything will be different, and she will feel better again.

But now, worst of all, the children, Johnny and Sally, have come, and they show no signs of leaving. Why are they here, why did they come, why won't they go away? She knows she should not resent her children being here, and yet she does. The meds, it must be the meds, make her want to be left alone.

The trouble is the children are always wanting her to do things with them.

"Let's go for a drive, Mother, just drive around the countryside."

"But I've already seen the countryside. I know it like the back of my hand. I'd rather rest."

"Is there anything you'd like, Mother?"

"Yes. I'd like a dry, very dry martini."

"But the doctor says you mustn't mix alcohol with the medicine you're taking." The meds again, the goddamn meds.

There are other little interruptions. "That Mr. Michael Rubin called again," Rose says. "So did Tom Finney, the county prosecutor."

"Thank you, Rose."

"Haven't you returned those calls?" Rose's look is reproachful.

"I will, I will. I just don't want to talk on the phone when I'm feeling so groggy."

"I don't know what that Mr. Rubin wants, but he keeps calling. But Mr. Finney—he's the county *prosecutor*, Mrs. S. It must be something very *important*."

"I'm sure it will wait."

"I wouldn't want to get on the wrong side of the county *prosecutor*, Mrs. S."

"If you'd stop feeding me your goddamn meds, I'd feel more like talking to people!" Clarissa snaps.

Rose gives her a disapproving look and makes a clucking sound with her tongue. "Doctor's orders," she says.

And now, in her medicated sleep, Clarissa is having a wildly erotic dream. In it, she and young Alan Herrick are making love. She is watching as his naked, athletic body arches over hers, and as he guides his beautiful, swollen, uncircumcised cock inside her with his hand, and her own body thrusts upward in response to him. She comes almost immediately, and then comes again. And then, incredibly, again, *again*!

"Mother? Are you awake?"

She opens her eyes, startled and embarrassed by the violence of the orgasm she has just experienced, or dreamt she experienced, it is hard to tell which. It is Sally in the room.

"It's so dark in this room," Sally says. "Don't you want the curtains opened a little?

"Lately, the sun has been bothering my eyes," she says, and she sees Sally wince. It is because she has spoken of eyes in the plural. "It's because of the goddamn pills you're all making me take."

"The medicine is to make you feel better, Mother."

"It doesn't! It makes me feel worse!" Dear Sally, she loves her daughter so much, and she knows Sally loves her. How can she let herself speak so crossly to her daughter?

Sally sits on the corner of her bed. "Johnny and I have tickets to Tanglewood this afternoon," she says. "They're singing 'Parsifal.' Do you feel like going?"

"Oh, no, no. You two go. I feel like resting. I know it's all I ever seem to feel like doing—thanks *to* you and the doctor and the goddamn pills!"

"I spoke to the doctor about that this morning. He wants to try a change in the prescription."

"Anything. Anything would be better than this." Clarissa closes her eyes. She would like to go back to the dream, but that particular dream will not return. Is Sally still there?

"Sally?"

"Yes, Mother?"

This last dream was so chaotic, so unfocused, it has left her disoriented. "You're still here?"

"Yes, Mother."

"I thought you were going to Tanglewood."

"This afternoon, Mother. I wish you felt well enough to go with us."

"Perhaps some other time. Sally?"

"Yes?"

"Do you remember that piece of silk you brought back for me from Thailand? With reds and purples in it?"

"Of course."

"Do you still have it?"

"Yes, I do."

"I don't know why I said I couldn't use it. I know exactly what I could use it for."

"I'll bring it back to you."

"A dress I saw in Bergdorf Goodman's window yesterday. I'm going to have a dressmaker copy that dress for me."

"Mother, you couldn't have seen it at Bergdorf's yesterday. You haven't been out of this house for weeks."

"Yesterday, or the day before. I showed it to my mother."

"Mother—"

"It was a design by Elsa Schiaparelli. Beautiful. Reds and purples, with gold and silver threads."

"Mother, Elsa Schiaparelli has been dead for years."

"No! I know it was Schiaparelli. It said so in the window. I'm going to wear it to the Yale prom."

Sally reaches out and touches her mother's forehead with her fingertips, pressing them there a moment. "I think you're running a little fever, Mother," she says.

"No more pills! Get away from me with your goddamn pills! Leave me alone!" . . .

Another day. It is so hot in this room, and she can scarcely breathe. She has got to have air. Clarissa steps out of bed and moves to the window and throws up the sash. Behind her, there is a scream, and someone seizes the collar of her nightie. "Mrs. S, what do you think you're doing? Get back into your bed! Right now! You could have fallen out that window—fallen to your death! Now get right back into that bed—you hear me?" . . .

Downstairs, Rose says, "Mr. John and Miss Sally, I think you've got to think about getting private duty nurses for your mother. I just caught her leaning halfway out a window! I'm scared she's going to hurt herself, and I just can't be held responsible if something happens. I can't take on that responsibility— that and trying to run this house as well. It's too much to ask." . . .

And another day. The doorbell rings, and John Spotswood goes to answer it. "Is Mrs. Spotswood in?" the tall, silver-haired man standing on the front steps asks him.

"Yes, but I'm afraid—"

"You must be Johnny," he says.

"That's right."

"My name is Michael Rubin," the older man says, extending his hand. "I'm an old friend of your mother's."

Johnny shakes his hand. "Yes," he says, "but I'm afraid my mother can't see anyone right now."

"Please, Johnny," the older man says. "It's terribly important."

"I'm sorry."

"Please," the older man says again. "I may be leaving the country in a few days, and I really need to talk to your mother."

"I'm sorry, but I can't ask you in, Mr. Rubin. My mother hasn't been well."

"I understand that. But it will only take a few minutes, and I promise not to upset her."

"I'm very sorry."

"Johnny—it's urgent. I must see her."

"No."

The older man starts to step forward, but Johnny blocks his path. "Mr. Rubin! I said you may not come in!"

"And I said I must!" Michael Rubin reaches for Johnny's shoulder, but Johnny strikes his hand away.

"And I say you cannot!"

"Get out of my way, Johnny. I'm coming in."

Johnny raises his arms and braces himself against the doorjambs. "You are not going to force your way into this house, Mr. Rubin!"

"I said get out of my way!" He raises both hands.

"No! You're not wanted here!" And suddenly they are both in a pushing, shoving match, and the older man, who is a few pounds heavier, forces his frame another inch or so inside the doorway. "Get out!" Johnny cries.

"I'm coming in, Johnny! You can't stop me."

"Do you want me to start yelling? There's a housekeeper in the kitchen, and my sister is also here. Do you want me to start yelling for help? If I do, the campus police will be here in thirty seconds. Shall I start yelling? Shall I?"

"Fuck off!"

"*You* fuck off, Mr. Rubin! Okay—here goes—" He opens his mouth wide.

And suddenly Rubin takes a step backward, and Johnny slams the door closed in his face, snapping the deadbolt lock and, for good measure, securing the chain. "Get out—and never come back!" he shouts through the locked door. "Never come back, you son of a bitch!"

There is a loud thud as Rubin kicks at the door with the toe of his shoe, and Johnny thinks he hears the man's voice wail, "*Claris-sa!*" Johnny leans, panting, against the door. Then he reaches for the telephone on the lowboy and punches three quick numbers. "There's a man on campus who has been trying to force his way into the headmaster's house," he says. "Please escort him off campus and see that he never comes back." . . .

Upstairs, his mother says, "I heard voices downstairs. Did we have a caller, Johnny?"

"Yes. It was that crook Michael Rubin."

"Don't call him a crook, Johnny. We don't know that."

"Forged US Treasury notes? Not just stolen—*forged*. That's what he's been dealing in. Could anything be much more crooked than that?"

"Did he have to leave?"

"Yes. He had to leave."

She puts her head back against the pillow. "Oh, I would have so loved to have seen him," she says.

And then the day comes when Sally goes looking for Hobe and finds him in his study. "She's hallucinating badly again," she says. "She seems to think she's back in Riverdale, in her father's house. I think you'd better go up."

"Oh, my darling," she says when he steps into her darkened bedroom. "I knew you'd come."

"How are you feeling, Cissie?"

"Wonderful. Just wonderful," she says. "I don't think I've ever felt more wonderful."

Hobe sits beside her on the bed. "I have good news," he says. "Guess what? Tom Finney's called his investigation off. Lack of evidence. Ha! That just means that horse's ass Truxton Van Degan finally made him an offer he couldn't refuse. But isn't that good news, Cissie?"

"Oh, yes, that's wonderful—wonderful news."

He reaches for her hand. "I love you, Cissie," he says.

"Oh, yes. Do you remember all those afternoons at the Old Forge Inn? I was thinking of those afternoons just now—I'll never forget those afternoons."

"You mean when I was here for all those interviews? It was a pretty stressful time for me, of course. But the school treated us pretty nicely."

"It was wonderful. Sometimes I think those afternoons were the happiest time of my life. Room one oh three—I'll never forget."

"As I recall, we were on the third floor," he says. "I think you may have your numbers reversed. It could have been three oh one."

"Oh, no. It was one oh three. I'll never forget that."

"And I was thinking, Cissie, of those weeks we spent at Blue Goose Lake. Those were happy times, too—remember? Our postponed honeymoon? Do you remember the day you caught the eel? The eel that wouldn't die?" He squeezes her hand. "Remember that?"

"Oh, yes . . ."

"I love you, Cissie," he says again. "You're so beautiful."

"And I love you too. Blue Goose Lake—oh, yes. At night there were so many fireflies in the air." With her free hand, she reaches out and runs her fingers through his hair. "Oh, look—look at that little spark of light. It's—yes, a firefly has just landed in your hair!"

There are tears in his eyes now. "Oh, Cissie, I know I haven't been a perfect husband. I've tried to be, but I haven't always succeeded, have I? I've made mistakes, I know. Will you ever forgive me my mistakes? But I've always needed you so much. Maybe that was one of my mistakes—needing you so much, and never admitting to myself how much I needed you, lying to myself, telling myself I could do everything myself, and even hating myself for needing you too much. I couldn't have done anything I've done without you; do you know that? I need you so much right now, maybe more than ever before. Do you know how hard that is for me to admit to you now? Do you know how hard that is? Cissie, I just don't think I can go on without you. I really don't think I can. Don't leave me, Cissie. Don't leave me now. Oh, Cissie, I love you so. Oh, Cissie, please don't die!" With a sob, he flings his body across hers on the bed.

She smiles, continuing to run her fingers through his hair. "It's not so bad," she says. "I'm up for it."

PART THREE

ONE YEAR LATER

TWENTY

And now Mr. Michael J. Rubin—"The Flamboyant Financier," as the media have been calling him—has been officially declared a fugitive from justice.

While his exact whereabouts are still unknown, some facts have become clear. On August twenty-seventh of last year, he boarded an American Airlines flight to Chicago, supposedly on a short, routine business trip. From Chicago, he purchased a first-class ticket on a flight to San Diego, where he rented an Avis car and apparently drove across the Mexican border to Tijuana. The car rental was returned to the Avis desk at the Tijuana airport, and in Tijuana he boarded an Aeroméxico flight to Mexico City. After that, his movements are less clear, though it is assumed that from Mexico City Mr. Rubin flew, under an assumed name, to Central or South America. According to at least one uncon-firmed report, Rubin was recently sighted in the bar of the Hotel Carrera in Santiago de Chile, ordering a pisco sour.

One interesting aspect of Rubin's disappearance is that on the domestic portions of his flights he had booked two seats, as though expecting to be joined by a companion. On the other hand, according to his son, Jesse Rubin, his father routinely reserved a pair of seats, side by side, for privacy reasons, whenever he flew commercially, which was seldom because the elder Rubin normally flew on Rubin & Company's corporate jet, since sold.

Meanwhile, in New York, Jesse Rubin has been doing his best to restore Rubin & Company to its former prestige and prominence from the considerable financial disarray in which his father left the investment firm. What with government-imposed fines and penalties, the firm has suffered severe losses over the past year, and close to three hundred employees have been let go. But the younger Mr. Rubin continues to insist that his father is innocent of the charges leveled against him and that, in his words, "My father was a victim of unscrupulous partners and business associates who lied and misrepresented facts about the validity and provenance of certain securities and other equities that he was given to sell. A man of honor, he trusted the wrong people. My father is not in hiding. When the real malefactors have been exposed, my father will be vindicated and will immediately return to the United States."

At the Crittenden School, life goes on much the same as always. Students come; students go. The seasons change, and so do the faces. Some succeed, others fail. They are graduated, they are censured and disciplined for misdemeanors, they are dismissed for serious transgressions, or for inability to do the work. But for the most part they complete their four years of secondary education and go on to Ivy League or Seven Sisters colleges. The school may change and shape lives (though some might argue this), but for the most part Crittenden itself does not change much. Returning alumni, going back to their old haunts, are pleased to find that the dormitory corridors still smell of a pleasant combination of Old Spice and old sneakers.

Even last spring's humiliating defeat in baseball by Millbrook has been forgiven and more or less forgotten. Everyone agrees that, without its team's star pitcher, Crittenden didn't have a chance.

There has been one interesting innovation. As a result of Clarissa Spotswood's plea at last May's trustees' meeting, it has been decided that three members of the school's Student Council should be appointed each year to serve as ex officio members of the Board of Trustees. These students are expected to represent the thoughts and feelings of the students themselves, to keep the board abreast and up-to-date with student issues and concerns. The result, it is hoped, will be increased rapport between students, the board, and the school administration, which will give students a greater sense of involvement in administrative areas.

This move on the board's part was widely hailed by the Crittenden students. The reaction from the faculty was more guarded. And whether the desired results can be achieved, or what changes in campus life, if any, this move will bring about, it is just too early to say. But, in the meantime, hopes are high.

And, at the trustees' meeting last fall, those worthy men and women voted unanimously to renew Hobart Spotswood's contract for another five full years—not just the customary three—with an appropriate increase in salary. By no coincidence (though this was not mentioned) this will bring him to his mandatory retirement age of sixty-five.

There were sentimental considerations in the trustees' voting, to be sure. The trustees not only wanted to express their deep and continued satisfaction with his stewardship of the school, but also their deeper sympathy with the headmaster over the recent loss of his beloved wife. In terms of the school's history, this unprecedented extension of Hobart Spotswood's contract will mean that, upon completion of his next term, he will have served as Crittenden's headmaster for longer than any of his predecessors. As the trustees put it in their announcement, "Hobart Spotswood has now achieved a permanent position in the pantheon of great New England boarding school headmasters, alongside such legendary figures at Frank Boyden of Deerfield and George Van Santvoord of Hotchkiss. We feel that no one is more able or qualified than Hobart Spotswood to guide the Crittenden School into the twenty-first century."

In January of this year, it was announced that an anonymous benefactor had made a gift of twenty million dollars to the school to create the Clarissa Spotswood Center for the Arts. At first, the trustees wanted this to be called the Clarissa Spotswood Memorial Arts Center, but speaking through his attorneys in New York, the donor made it very clear that he did not want the word *Memorial* attached to his gift. "The word 'Memorial' has a mournful, elegiac ring to it that our client does not wish," the lawyers wrote. "Our client does not wish Mrs. Spotswood's name to appear as a 'memory,' but rather as a living person, as she was to those who knew her." The donor of the gift was so adamant on the subject of the word *Memorial* that he threatened to withdraw his gift entirely if the word were used, and so the trustees quickly acquiesced to his preferred nomenclature.

Needless to say, there has been a great deal of speculation, on and off the campus, as to who this anonymous benefactor might be.

To design the new arts center, the benefactor proposed Mrs. Spotswood's son, the architect John Spotswood. At first, John Spotswood refused the assignment, saying that it smacked of nepotism. In the end, he agreed to take on the job, but only on the condition that he be paid no fees or commission for his work. His design for the new building is considered something of a triumph, a design that seems both handsomely contemporary and comfortably traditional, striking and yet in keeping with the redbrick Georgian style of the other campus buildings—"A twenty-first-century building that will look quite at home among its nineteenth-century neighbors," as one architecture critic put it. "With a courtly bow to a more elegant past, and a twinkle in its eye toward a confident and happy future, it is a fitting tribute to the architect's mother."

Today, the groundbreaking ceremonies for the new buildings are taking place, and it was surprising to see how many townspeople from the village of James Falls turned out for it. Clearly, Clarissa Spotswood had many admirers in the village as well as within the smaller campus community. That the entire school community turned out was no surprise. Their attendance was more or less mandatory, after all.

Johnny Spotswood and his sister, Sally, have left the ceremonies a little early and are walking back across the campus to their car. "I thought Dad's speech was pretty good," he says. "One of the best, in fact, that I've ever heard him make."

"Yes," she says. "He almost sounded as though he meant it."

"Aw, Sal," he says. "Don't talk like that."

"Why not? Considering the fact that he killed her." He stops in his tracks.

"What do you mean?"

"Maybe not literally, but metaphorically. Emotionally. Psychologically."

"What a terrible thing to say!"

"She kept a journal," she says. "I found it in a locked desk drawer. She kept it for years and years, almost to the very end, though some of the last entries are almost illegible. In the end, she started making lists—'Reasons to Love Hobe, Reasons to Hate Hobe'—things like that. But it's hard to make out what the various reasons were. I'll let you read it, if you think you

347

have the stomach for it. It was written for you and me. Read it, and you'll see what he put her through for all those years. No wonder she took a lover."

"What? A lover?"

"Oh, yes."

"Our prim and proper little mother had a lover?"

"Oh, yes. It was quite a passionate affair, apparently,"

"Who was it?"

"She never quite comes out and gives his name. But if you read between the lines, I think you'll be able to guess who it was."

He whistles softly between his teeth. "Well, I'll be damned!" he says.

A young girl is running toward them across the grass, a book-laden backpack slung across her shoulders. She wears a tank top and what appear to be a pair of army surplus camouflage fatigue pants, nowhere near her size. On her feet are army boots, their laces elaborately untied. "You're Spotty's son, aren't you?" she says.

"Yes. And this is my sister, Sally."

"I thought that's who you were. My name's Valerie Winston. My classmate was Linda Van Degan—you know, who killed herself?"

"I didn't know Linda Van Degan," he says. "But I remember my parents speaking of her, and that there was some kind of trouble. And of course, I know Van Degan Hall . . ." He nods in the direction.

"Same family. And so, when I was listening to all the speeches, back there at the groundbreaking, I thought there was something about your mother that you might like to know."

"Sure. What is it?"

"Linda Van Degan was a funny girl. She was a real weirdo,

and nobody really liked her. But her family had a lot of money and so, you know, we all put up with her. We all lived in Colby Hall, and we had something we called the Colby Club and we let her in it, even though she was really unpopular. And one day she told me she had been talking with Mrs. Spotty—you know, your mother. And she told me how much she really liked your mother. She said your mother was nicer to her than anybody in this school. She told me your mother talked to her, you know, like an adult. She hated her own mother, and she'd had a bunch of stepmothers that she didn't like much, either, though some of them were nicer to her than others. She said to me, 'But I really like Mrs. Spotty.' But it wasn't like Mrs. Spotty was like a real *mother* to her. It began to be something more than that. It began to seem like she was, you know, sort of in love with your mom—a real schoolgirl crush, you know? We all thought it was kind of weird, but that was Linda, because she was weird, you know? I think she only talked with your mom a couple of times, but she said to me, 'Mrs. Spotty has had more influence on my life than any other person I've ever known. She's my idol!' Those were her exact words. I remember those exact words."

"Well, that's very nice to hear," he says. "Thank you for sharing that with us, Valerie."

"But then, one night she comes into my room, and she's—like, you know, hysterical. She can't seem to stop crying, and she keeps saying, 'I've done the most awful thing, Valerie. I've done the worst thing I've ever done in my life. I've just told Mrs. Spotty the most terrible, awful lie. I've told her the most terrible lie, and now she'll probably never speak to me again. I told her an awful lie, and now I've lost the only friend I ever had in the world. I just want to die, Valerie.'"

"What was the lie, Valerie?" Sally asks her.

"She wouldn't say. So I go, 'Tell me what the lie was. Maybe it wasn't so awful.' And she goes, 'I can't tell you, it was so stupid, so awful.' And so I go, 'Just tell her you're sorry. Tell her you lied, and you're sorry.' And she goes, 'It's too late, it's too late.' And so I go, 'You see, that's why nobody likes you, Linda. People try to be your friend and be nice to you, and then you go and fuck up.' Pardon my language, but that's what I said to her. And she goes, 'You hate me, too.' And I go, 'Everybody hates you because once they try to be your friend, you fuck up. Get real, wise up, get a life!' And she goes, 'I just want to kill myself,' and I go, 'Well, whatever,' and that was the night she did it, killed herself."

"Well," Johnny says after a moment, "that's a very sad story, Valerie. I'm sorry you got involved."

"I just thought you'd like to hear it," the girl says. "Because that was how it happened. Someone who loved your mom so much. Well, I've got to go." Hitching her backpack across her bare shoulders, she runs off, her undone shoelaces trailing in the grass behind her.

"Well," Sally says, shaking her head, "what in the world was that all about?"

"God knows," he says. "But Mom had to put up with that kind of shit, too."

Sally's eyes follow the girl as she disappears into one of the dorms. "Whatever happened to sweater sets?" she murmurs. "When did they all start dressing like the Manson family?"

"More shit Mom had to put up with." Then he says, "But going back to what you said—that Dad helped kill Mom, psychologically, or whatever. I don't think it was him. It was this place."

"Crittenden?"

He gestures wordlessly around him—at the manicured lawns, the sculpted evergreens, the clipped-edged gravel paths. Hobart Spotswood takes great pride in the appearance of his campus, its landscaped perfection. The taxus foundation plantings must always be pruned to a certain height. The English ivy on the walls must never trail across a windowpane. The alley of London plane trees that lines the entrance drive must always be trimmed in perfect, identical conic shapes. Weeds were anathema to him, dandelions a curse. He had been known, when spotting an offending dandelion, to leap out of his car and pull up the plant by its roots with his fingers before it had a chance to go to seed. He hated certain shrubs—hydrangeas, for example. Once he had seen his grounds crew planting hydrangeas and ordered them to stop. "Hydrangeas are a New England cliché plant," he said. "The hydrangea is the Edgar A. Guest of botany." He felt the same way about peonies, phlox, pansies, and chrysanthemums. He loved deep-red geraniums in window boxes, but the blooms must be fist-sized, and yellow leaves must be snipped off. Gravel drives must be raked daily. To litter was a worse sin than sloth, greed, or lust. His campus was about order, and order was next to probity, which was next to godliness. Living in a world of horticultural exactitude and symmetry, he believed, inspired serenity and calm and rectitude in adolescent souls and minds, and, of course, gentled the stirrings in fuzzy little pelvises.

As Sally and Johnny stand there looking at Hobe's world, there is the sound of singing in the distance. The groundbreaking ceremony for the new arts center is nearly over and, from where they stand, they can hear the voices of the Glee Club as they move into the second stanza of the school song:

O, Crittenden victorious, As you charge down the field!
O, Crittenden victorious, Your teams shall never yield!
O, Crittenden victorious, Thy banner and thy shield shall glitter ever
*   glorious,*
Before all eyes unpeeled . . .

"I suppose Jesse Rubin should have been here today for this," he says. "You know, to represent—"

"I thought of that, too," Sally says. "And I invited him to come. But his answer was that his presence might threaten the anonymity of the gift."

"That's a little silly. Doesn't everyone know where the gift came from?"

"Not really. The trustees know, of course, and Spotty knows, and you and I know. But the general public has no idea. Here on campus, the rumor is that it's more Van Degan money. That rumor's being encouraged."

John scuffs the toe of his loafer in the grass. "Amazing, isn't it?" he says. "The guy's company goes almost belly-up. Hundreds of working stiffs lose their jobs. And he's still got twenty mil to toss to Crittenden."

"Jess told me that his father has personal money in banks all over the world."

"Typical. His company's broke. Lives are trashed. But that crook bastard is still rich as Croesus. Only in America."

"Please don't talk that way about him, Johnny."

"Well, they say that the beach at Viña del Mar is very noisy and smelly—even for those people who live in villas at the top of the hill. At least you and Jesse are still in touch."

There is a trace of bitterness in her laugh. "Not exactly," she says. "That response to my invitation came from his secretary. He won't come on the phone for me."

"Ah, that's too bad, Sal," he says.

"I'm still so fond of him," she says. "I want so much to keep him as a friend. But I've hurt him so badly." She reaches up and brushes a fingertip quickly across a lower eyelid.

"You'd think he could use every friend he can get right now."

"That's true, but—" All at once she brightens again. "But

don't worry. I'll think of a way to get him back and keep him as a friend. Wait and see. I'll think of some way. In fact, I'm already working on a plan to get him back. Don't underestimate your baby sister! I have a fighter's genes in me."

In the distance, there is a great chord from the school organist, Mrs. Ballantine, and then, *con fortissimo*, the final chorus of the song:

> *O, Crittenden, all conqu'ring, Long may thy banner wave!*
> *O, Crittenden, all conqu'ring, Strong and young and brave!*
> *O, Crittenden, all conqu'ring, This praise for thee we save,*
> *O, Crittenden, all conqu'ring, Our hearts thou do'st enslave!*

"It left its mark on us, too, didn't it," Johnny says as the song dies down. "On our hearts, too. This place."

He takes his sister's arm. "Let's go," he says, and they walk slowly in silence back to where he parked the car.

AFTERWORD

The Headmaster's Wife is, of course, fiction.

I uncovered the original manuscript (typed sometime around 2000) when my father's partner and I were going through my father's things shortly after his death in 2015, finding this novel back in a closet. It was apparently written around 2000 and, after I purchased the copyrights to all my father's works from his estate in 2019, I spent the ensuing years converting and editing the paper manuscript and seeking a publisher.

My father attended the prestigious Hotchkiss School in Lakeville, Connecticut, and I surmise much of what is contained in this novel comes from his fertile mind as well as his experiences in prep school.

I also was destined to attend prep school but was rejected by Hotchkiss (notwithstanding the prominent legacy), eventually being accepted by Millbrook School in Millbrook, New York, where I completed four years before attending Franklin Pierce College and New York University.

In editing this book, I've taken some liberties with the story, based on my experiences at Millbrook. Much of the campus description in chapter one was derived from my own memories of Millbrook, which classmates from the '60s and '70s will no doubt recognize. The history in that chapter, however, is entirely fictional.

The fires described in chapter eleven are based upon actual events that occurred at Millbrook over five days in November 1971. The details described closely reflect the events that fall, including the identical twin nature of the young man who lit those fires. The student, whom I will refer to here as "M," did actually trip in front of the dean of students, in this case the very real Jack Bower, and it was Mr. Bower who discerned M's psychosis. M was arrested and the school elected not to press charges. I don't know what happened to M after the arrest, yet I don't think he was committed to Harlem Valley Psychiatric.

The young Bradley Prescott who was interviewed by the investigative commission is actually me. I was briefly a suspect in connection with the fires, similarly as I describe in that scene.

The description of fellow students who confronted M and saw him being placed in a state trooper's car is also accurate, as well as I remember. Students making patrols had various "weapons" (I had a hammer) and afterward asked ourselves: What would we have done if we had encountered M actually setting a fire? We imagined a psychopathic killer six feet tall with sharp teeth and a killer's demeanor. M was a popular student and well-liked by fellow students and faculty. We imagined we would simply stare agog. And let M go. It happens so often that we cannot fathom a neighbor, friend, or acquaintance committing a crime, and we don't know what to do when such happens.

Carey G. Birmingham
Summer 2022

ACKNOWLEDGMENTS

This book would have never seen the light of day were it not for the help of Dr. Carroll Edward ("Ed") Lahniers, my father's partner for over forty years. It was Ed who found and transferred this manuscript and was instrumental in making my purchase of my father's copyrights a reality.

My thanks also goes to my editors at Open Road Media, Mara Anastas and Jacob Allgeier, for taking a flyer on publishing this story.

As always, I owe any success to the love of my wife, Lisa, and my daughter, Caitlin.

ABOUT THE AUTHOR

Stephen Birmingham (1929–2015) was an American author of more than thirty books. Born in Hartford, Connecticut, he graduated from Williams College in 1953 and taught writing at the University of Cincinnati. Birmingham's work focuses on the upper class in America. He's written about the African American elite in *Certain People* and prominent Jewish society in *Our Crowd: The Great Jewish Families of New York*, *The Grandees: The Story of America's Sephardic Elite*, and *The Rest of Us: The Rise of America's Eastern European Jews*. His work also encompasses several novels including *The Auerbach Will*, *The LeBaron Secret*, *Shades of Fortune*, and *The Rothman Scandal*, and other non-fiction titles such as *California Rich*, *The Grandes Dames*, and *Life at the Dakota: New York's Most Unusual Address*.

STEPHEN BIRMINGHAM

FROM OPEN ROAD MEDIA

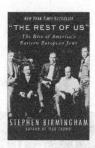

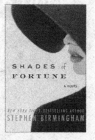

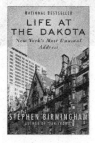

OPEN ROAD

INTEGRATED MEDIA

INTEGRATED MEDIA